No Quiet Water

Shirley Miller Kamada

Black Rose Writing | Texas

ISBN: 978-1-68513-097-8
PUBLISHED BY BLACK ROSE WRITING
www.blackrosewriting.com

Printed in the United States of America
Suggested Retail Price (SRP) $23.95

No Quiet Water is printed in Garamond Premier Pro

*As a planet-friendly publisher, Black Rose Writing does its best to eliminate unnecessary waste to reduce paper usage and energy costs, while never compromising the reading experience. As a result, the final word count vs. page count may not meet common expectations.

Cover image courtesy of National Park Service/ Manzanar National Historic Site

For Isao Kamada and Yuriko Yamamoto Kamada.
And for Jimmy.

CONTENTS

No
Quiet
Water

BAINBRIDGE ISLAND, WASHINGTON STATE, 1941

CHAPTER ONE

FUMIO

Fumio awoke to his father's muffled footsteps padding toward the cast iron stove. He listened to the familiar sounds. The opening of the door in the stove's side with its square pane of milky-clear mica. The small coal scuttle being used to add shiny, black chunks to stoke the fire. The door clanking shut, the scuttle thumping to the floor. A scrape of wood against wood told Fumio a chair had been pulled near the stove. His own chore coat would be hanging on its back.

Soon, his door opened, and his father said, "Fumio! It is time to start the day. Those chores will not do themselves!" Now that he was ten, his chores started early in the morning instead of after school. Hunching his shoulders against the cold, Fumio crawled out of bed, jumped into his work clothes, pulled on a pair of thick socks, and hurried to the kitchen where he shoved his feet into rubber barn boots and his arms into the warmed coat. He zipped to his chin, then tugged on his gloves.

Fumio followed his father as he stepped out onto the porch and switched on the yard light. To the left, sharp-edged shadows were cast by the barn, with its large implement-repair shop, and on the right, by the chicken yard's rectangular wire-mesh enclosure and the coop, inhabited by a large flock of laying hens, plus one rooster.

Flyer stood, muscles taut, ears erect, eyes fixed on Fumio, then headed straight for the chicken yard, bypassing the gate and veering toward the rear of the enclosure. Fumio and his father followed, walking behind the building and entering the dark space between the coop and a stand of trees bordering the roadway. The pre-dawn world was quiet except for their footsteps on fallen pine needles and twigs.

Moonlight reflected off the coop's white-washed planks, illuminating the earth at their feet. Flyer chuffed, his muzzle quivering.

Near the toe of Fumio's boot lay two feathers, one large, one small. Owl. He bent to study them, then straightened, peering into the darkness.

Pulling off his gloves, Fumio reached down and touched the edge of the smaller feather before picking it up. He grasped the other feather between two fingers and lifted it. His eyes aimed a question toward his father, who nodded his approval. Fumio carried the feathers to the porch and tucked them under the doormat.

• • •

In the thin light of the winter morning—late November, almost December—Fumio quickly completed his chores, fed the chickens, rinsed and refilled their waterer. He imagined the winged predator up there circling, out of sight, waiting for another chance.

At the poultry yard gate, he paused to be certain it was latched, scanned the sky one more time, then turned toward the house. He was late.

As he ate breakfast, his mother placed his lunch box on the table. "Fumio, since Zachary is coming home with you after school, do you know what kind of snack he would like?"

"I don't know of any kind of snack Zachary would *not* like, Mother." Fumio bit into a slice of toast and chewed.

His father came inside and hung his coat near the door as Fumio carried his dishes to the counter beside the sink. "Running a little late, Son?" he asked.

"Yes, sir." Fumio took his school coat from a hook near the door, and pushed his arms into it. "But I will be on time for class." He slung his bookbag over his shoulder.

From her highchair, Kimiko waved, a small spoon gripped tight in her chubby, little-girl hand. "Bye-bye, Fumio! Happy day skoooool!"

He looked back and waved. How quickly the last three years had passed, how quickly she'd gone from being snug in his mother's arms to running so fast she was hard to catch.

On the porch, Flyer sat waiting. "Ready, boy?" Fumio turned to lift the corner of the doormat. He removed the feathers and slipped them into his book bag and, Flyer following, went to the side of the house where his bicycle waited, protected from the weather, under the eaves.

• • •

At lunchtime, Fumio and Zachary sat on the school's broad steps, their usual spot for eating lunch. The concrete surface intensified the chill of the day. Fumio fastened the top button of his coat. Zachary turned up his collar.

Across the narrow road, in front of Petric's Feed and Seed, three men wearing striped overalls sat on a bench. When they waved, Fumio and Zachary waved back.

In his lunchbox, Fumio found wrapped in a small piece of newspaper, two slices of fresh homemade bread, thick with strawberry jam spread over two fried eggs, edges crisp and brown.

Zachary's sandwich had been made with leftover toast from his family's breakfast. Peanut butter and grape jelly dripped from its edges.

Fumio took an apple from his lunch box. "Hey, Zachary," he said, "I have some big feathers in my book bag. We found them this morning. Or, Flyer found them, really."

"Where did he find them?"

"Behind the chicken house."

"Behind the chicken house? Whoa! Whoa!"

"Yeah. Whoa. Father said we'll get right on it and shore up the coop."

"Need help?" Zachary bit wide into the mottled skin of a pear. Juice poured over his chin.

Fumio laughed. He took from his lunch box a threadbare handkerchief supplied by his mother to clean up spills and handed it to Zachary. "Thanks. I'll tell my father you offered. He said today he planned to look into finding materials."

Zachary wiped his chin. "Thank you. I'll get this back to you after it's washed." He dropped the cloth in his lunch box, then pulled out a cookie, broke it in two, and gave half to Fumio.

In turn, Fumio broke the cookie again, and gave part of it back to Zachary. "Your mother makes good oatmeal cookies."

Zachary smiled and stuffed the quarter-cookie into his already-full mouth.

CHAPTER TWO

Flyer

My name is Flyer. That is a good name for me, because I run fast, especially when Fumio calls me. I am a farm dog. A farm dog has a big job. He is never off duty. A farm never sleeps. And neither do I.

This farm belongs to my family, to Fumio Miyota, my best friend, his parents, Yasuo and Sachiko Miyota, and Fumio's little sister, Kimiko. And it belongs to me. Every morning, I patrol the fields. Yesterday, I smelled muskrats and saw their tracks on the edge of the pond. Muskrats dig holes in ditches and canal banks. Water could escape and ruin our strawberry beds. I must keep an eye on those muskrats.

I check our fences, too. A fence runs between our farm and the family farm of Fumio's friend Zachary Whitlock. The wire at the back of their sheep pasture has had a broken place for a long time. I guess they don't know it. The Whitlocks need a dog.

Many mornings, I find Fumio's father working on farm equipment in the shop, but today, standing in the doorway, I do not see him, so I step inside and *Yipp!*

From outside the shop, I hear, "Come, Flyer!" Mr. Miyota stands high up on a ladder leaning against the chicken house.

I go to him. *Yipp-ipp!*

He answers. "I will be down in a minute, Flyer! The owl damaged the vent cover last night. This will fix it for a while, but it will not hold up against heavy battering."

Mr. Miyota uses *pliers* to bend short pieces of wire and tie together the broken places. He is wearing gloves, but I hear, "Oww!" He jerks his hand away but gets back to work and finishes the job. Coming down the ladder, he asks, "Is there a problem with the fences, Flyer?"

Phrr-uff-uff! I answer, lift a front paw and put it down, lift my other front paw and put it down. Back and forth, back and forth. *Phrr-uff! Phrr-uff-uff!* Until Mr. Miyota comes off the ladder and follows me.

A fence post has sagged, but not fallen. We stand it straight again. Fumio's father pounds the dirt with the back of a shovel. He stomps around the post until the ground packs so hard his boot prints do not show. "An ounce of prevention is worth a pound of cure, Flyer."

He says it again later when he kicks the tires on our pickup truck. I think he means *fix small trouble before it gets big.*

"The tires sound good, Flyer," Mr. Miyota says, "but the tread shows wear, and with the rationing of tires . . ." He shakes his head. Fumio told me people want tires and sugar, but there are *shortages* because of a *war*—fighting, some place far away.

Fumio's father and I are going to Petric's Feed and Seed. I can go inside. Mr. Petric says I am *well-behaved*. He keeps a tin of treats under the counter. He calls them *dog biscuits*.

I eat *biscuits* after breakfast if Fumio's little sister Kimiko does not clean her plate. The ones at the Feed and Seed store are not like breakfast *biscuits*. But they taste good, and I like to crush them with my teeth.

When we arrive, Mr. Petric pats me on the head and gives me a dog biscuit.

"Do you buy those by the truckload?" Mr. Miyota asks.

Mr. Petric laughs and lays his hand on my back. "I don't give out many dog treats. Our pal, Flyer, is special."

I walk between the store's shelves. The smells are *interesting*. Like our farm shop: engine smells, oil and grease, *solvents* for cleaning parts, the odor of tires. Plus bins and bags filled with kibble—for dogs whose families do not have leftovers—and dried corn for chickens.

The smell of sawdust comes from a bin near a wood-framed cage. Mr. Miyota asks, "The store is selling rabbit hutches?"

"People are raising rabbits *for the table*."

Mr. Miyota says he needs to buy *wire mesh, twenty- or twenty-two-gauge,* because an owl was after our chickens last night. He tells Mr. Petric about finding the feathers.

"A predator on the hunt," Mr. Petric says. "The store has had a run on chicken wire mesh. I am sorry, Yasuo, but we sold the last roll we had in stock."

I do not know the word *predator*. But an owl is trying to get into the chicken yard, and I know that is bad. We need chicken wire! It is important!

"With the war, I have no idea when we'll get more. Tomorrow? Could be Christmas!"

"The gable vent was covered with larger-gauge fencing. We'd had no trouble, but that bird tore it up. I spliced a couple of places. We'll have to wait."

Mr. Petric nods. A bell rings, and a man with a notebook comes through the door. Mr. Petric calls, "Hello, Mr. Sherman! I will be right with you. I need to put in an order today!" He reaches below the counter, then holds out another treat for me.

Yipp-ipp? I ask, and Mr. Miyota nods. I take the biscuit, then we head for the door.

"Sorry about the shortage," Mr. Petric calls after us.

Mr. Miyota turns back. "We are all in the same boat," he says.

CHAPTER THREE

FUMIO

Pedaling the bicycle into the Miyota farmyard, Fumio slowed, and backpumped to brake. Beside the porch, feet planted on the ground, he waited for Zachary to clear the rear fender, while Flyer circled them. They had been sharing a bicycle for a week since Zachary's needed repair.

Fumio had just swung his leg over the frame when a terrible racket came from the chicken enclosure. Leaning the bicycle against the railing, he hurried toward the disturbance as Flyer dashed to the rear corner of the hen yard. "*Whroow-wrooph!*"

At the chicken yard gate two hens, claws extended, screamed and fanned their wings, feathers flying.

"What's happening?" Zachary shouted, coming up behind.

"It's war!" Fumio yelled. "The hens are defending their place in the pecking order. When they scrap like this, it's tough to stop them!"

The hens circled, lifted, and plunged. Fumio knew that if he didn't end this soon, the hens would suffer bodily damage. He turned toward the shop to look for a gunny sack when—*splashhh*—the talons of one hen came down on the rim of the chicken waterer. The container upended, its cover flew into the air, and the tray flipped, coming to rest face down in a slurry of dirty water, straw, and chicken droppings.

Fumio groaned, "Ohhh, nooooo!" and slapped the side of his head.

"*Phff-uff.*" Flyer's ears drooped.

"Well," Zachary observed, "at least the hens stopped fighting!"

"Right, but we have to clean this up. Come on, Zachary, we have work to do."

"Now?" Zachary asked. "You said your mother would be baking! We could take care of this later and go into the kitchen and help clean the mixing bowl first! Or lick the spoon! Or maybe she had too much batter!"

Coming from the shop, Mr. Miyota called out, "Glad to see you, Zachary. Hello, Fumio." He nodded. "By the sound of it, those chickens went at it tooth and nail!" He entered the chicken yard and stopped at the edge of the muddy puddle, shaking his head. "Fumio is right. Clean water must be available to the flock. Think about it." He chuckled. "Would the Lone Ranger neglect his horse and go to the kitchen for a snack?"

"No, sir, I guess not." Zachary sighed.

Mr. Miyota smiled. "Fumio knows where to find the things you need. In no time at all, you will finish and be ready to wash your hands for supper."

Beckoning to Zachary, Fumio headed to the shop and found two buckets. Into one, he dropped a bit of dish soap. At a spigot, he filled the buckets, the water in one growing sudsy. With help from Fumio, Zachary found two long-handled brushes.

Back in the chicken yard, Fumio moved the waterer's three parts to a dry corner. He dunked a brush in the bucket of soapy water and sluiced off loose dirt and debris from the metal of one part. Zachary watched for a moment, then did the same to another.

"I clean this every Saturday," Fumio said, "so I'd have to do it tomorrow, anyway." He choked up on the brush handle to scrub at stubborn crud and leaned in, eager to finish the job.

Then, a streak of white. An angry *Bwwaaawwk! Bwwaaawwk! Scrreeek!*

"Yikes!" Fumio dropped the brush and dashed toward the chicken yard gate.

"Ding-blast-it!" Zachary cried, sprinting after him.

When the boys cleared the gate, Fumio latched it and slid to the ground. His back against a post, he sat in the dirt, heaving air in and out.

"What was that?" Zachary asked, out of breath. "Something sharp hit me behind my knees!"

"The rooster!" Fumio gasped for air. "The rooster attacked us! And you said, 'Ding-blast-it!' You cussed out a rooster! I am pretty sure that would not be okay with your parents." He doubled over in laughter.

"Did I really? Oh, man." Zachary moaned. "Oh, no." His face glowed bright red.

Fumio glanced away. He knew Zachary was self-conscious about his fair skin and red hair. Not that his hair was red, really. It was, Fumio's mother had told him, what was called "strawberry blond." Still, kids at school occasionally referred to Zachary as "Red." Some had also tried out "Freckles." Those nicknames, though, never drew a reaction from Zachary.

"I can hardly believe I said that." Zachary hid his face in his hands. "I have never said anything like that before! I don't know where those words came from."

"They came from Mr. Harvey, that's where. Mr. Harvey is a good neighbor, but he sure uses some *colorful* language. My father told me I should aim to be as good a neighbor as Mr. Harvey. But I should not talk like Mr. Harvey."

Zachary's shoulders sagged. "Mr. Harvey helped my father with the truck's magneto, last week, and . . . and . . . I'm sorry."

"Hey, it's no skin off my nose." Fumio laughed. "Let's get back to work."

Fumio called Flyer, who came at a run. One bark from him and a bit of growling held the rooster at bay.

• • •

Mr. Miyota came from the shop as Fumio and Zachary, followed by Flyer, crossed the yard.

"We finished, Father!"

"Boys! Wait!" Fumio was about to hop up the steps when his father appeared at his side.

"Stop!" Mr. Miyota put out his hand.

Fumio froze, but—*thud!*—Zachary did not.

"Oof!" Fumio lurched forward as Zachary's head slammed into his back. A quick movement of his father's arm steadied them both.

"Stop!" Mr. Miyota repeated, a frown wrinkling his brow. He drew in a deep breath. "Are you two all right?"

"Yes, sir," Fumio replied.

Zachary, his face red, nodded. "Yes, sir, Mr. Miyota."

"I know you are cold and damp." He dipped his head toward Zachary. "And you are hungry. But we cannot traipse into the kitchen, making a mess. Or allow the chill inside. Step back, please."

Pushing open the door a few inches, Mr. Miyota called, "Sachiko, the boys are waiting on the steps. They are too dirty to come inside and will wash up in the pump house."

Fumio heard only the last part of his mother's response: "Might as well come in."

"But they are covered in grime!" his father responded. "And my boots are muddy, Sachiko. Would you mind bringing us soap?"

Then, in the narrow opening of the door, appeared a small figure covered in a layer of fine, white dust from the tips of her toes to the top of her head.

Fumio groaned. Kimiko. She looked up at her father and grinned.

Mr. Miyota gazed down at her. When she reached up for him, he shook his head and thrust his head and shoulders through the doorway, calling out, "What has happened?"

Heedless of his father's admonition, Fumio bolted up the steps onto the porch and ducked under his arm, slipping past Kimiko. Two steps through the doorway, he halted, wide-eyed. "Whoahhh! It looks like it snowed in here!"

Mrs. Miyota turned to face them, a broom in her hand. Near her feet rose a small mountain of white, sullied with traces of dirt. Her normally dark and shiny hair was heavily cloaked with gray. She reached a hand to brush it away from where it hung across her eyes.

Zachary poked his head through the doorway. "What is that stuff?"

Resting the broom against the sink, Fumio's mother lifted from the kitchen table a sack made of printed cotton fabric. It hung limply from her hand, empty.

Again, Mr. Miyota asked, "What happened, Sachiko? Was there a hole in the flour sack?"

"Only at the top," she replied. "I'd just opened it." She looked toward her daughter. "We had a little spill. All ten pounds of it. Kimiko wanted to help."

"Boy howdy!" Zachary blurted. "That was a bushel of help!"

Fumio snorted, then said, "Sorry, Mother." At the same time Zachary said, "Sorry, ma'am." Zachary blushed, and Fumio clamped his jaw down hard, holding in his laughter.

Mrs. Miyota began, "Well, at least now I have the fabric I need to make . . ." but stopped, glancing toward her daughter. Fumio knew his mother planned to use the flour-sack fabric, with its cheerful design of white daisies on a red background, to sew a dress for one of Kimiko's two dolls—Suzey Belle or Trixie Jean.

Mrs. Miyota made a little face and sighed. "They may as well come on in. You, too, Yasuo. The pump house will be extremely cold."

"The entire kitchen and much of the living room will have to be swept and mopped, anyway. The table, the range, the ice box, every surface must be wiped." She gestured toward the still-open door. "And the breeze from outside is spreading it even further."

CHAPTER FOUR

FLYER

The sun has gone down. Fumio and Zachary are making a *map* for school. From my blanket under the sink, I watch them working at the kitchen table. I can see into the living room, too, where Fumio's mother sits in her rocking chair, mending socks. She calls it *darning*. Toes and heels wear holes in socks. She pulls a sock over a lightbulb to make the mending easier, and as she works a needle in and out, the holes disappear.

Kimiko sits near her mother on a little rug made of scrap fabric tied together, a *rag rug*. She is playing with her dolls and singing to herself. Fumio told me that Kimiko makes up most of the songs she sings. He said she does pretty well, though, for being only three years old. She is clean and tidy now—so is our kitchen—but Mrs. Miyota says that evidence of Kimiko's *flour escapade* will turn up for weeks.

I cannot see the sofa, but I know Fumio's father is sitting there. I hear him looking through pages. He fixed a truck engine today, and he is writing the bill so the owner knows how much to pay. He usually does paperwork at the kitchen table.

Footfalls sound against gravel, and *step, step, step* up to the porch, a rapping noise at the door. I stand to let my family know. *Phfft-Phoof!* Company!

Fumio's father comes into the kitchen, goes to the door, and opens it. He says, "Good evening, neighbor!" and Mr. Whitlock comes inside.

"Hello, sir," Fumio says. He has been leaning over the map, but straightens now, with his hands held away from his sides—they are sticky with the flour that was swept from the floor and mixed with water.

"Good evening, Fumio," Mr. Whitlock replies. He looks my way. "Hello, Flyer."

Yipp!

"Father, look!" Zachary sounds happy. "We are making a map!"

"That looks like quite a project! I thought you boys were going to draw a map."

"That *was* the plan." Fumio's mother comes into the kitchen. She tells Mr. Whitlock that this *relief map* was a surprise. "The result of unforeseen circumstances," she adds.

"Well, then," Mr. Whitlock lays his hand on Zachary's head, "these boys are doing a fine job of making the best of the situation."

Zachary looks up at his father. "This gooey stuff is just right for shaping Bainbridge Island, and we're nearly done. Can we work just ten or fifteen minutes more, Father?"

"Yes, please come into the living room for a while and visit?" Mrs. Miyota leads the way.

Before he leaves the kitchen, Mr. Whitlock says, "Zachary, you have a little Bainbridge Island on your nose."

"Thank you, sir." Zachary swipes his sleeve across his face.

Talking stops in the kitchen, but the grown-ups are visiting. I go to lie near the big open doorway into the living room. Fumio glances my way; I *thump-thump* my tail.

Mr. Whitlock settles into a chair. He says hello to Kimiko, still sitting on the little rag rug, and she waves before turning back to her dolls.

Fumio says he is not sure Kimiko understands dolls are toys. I don't know about that, but I know Kimiko takes good care of the dolls.

"Doris is home," Mr. Whitlock says, "baking up a storm. Our kitchen looks like a tornado blew through it."

"A tornado?" Mrs. Miyota shakes her head. "As you see, we had a mishap in our own kitchen. A lot of flour ended up on the floor."

"Eggs, too," Mr. Miyota says.

Mr. Whitlock laughs hard. "Oh, I see," he says. "Thus, the idea of making a *relief* map."

I hear Fumio say, "Hey, Zachary! Slow down! Miss Lassiter said the map has to be neat if we want a good grade!"

Zachary mumbles something that sounds like, "Okay. There. How's that?"

"We have been fortunate," says Fumio's mother, "in the school's selection of a fifth-grade teacher. The boys seem to like her."

"Zachary repeats much of what Miss Lassiter says, word for word," Mr. Whitlock says. "He tells us she wants them to learn about their community and its place in the world. That is surely important, especially now."

"Yes," Mr. Miyota says, "especially now."

"There is trouble in the air, isn't there?" Mrs. Miyota asks.

Mr. Whitlock nods and speaks lots of words, some I know, some I don't understand. He says, "Yes, there is trouble overseas. The situation bears watching."

I know a lot about *watching*. It means, *Be on the lookout!* I know about bears, too, because a mother bear and cub wandered across our land, by the pond. Fumio showed me the tracks, and they were big. He said bears don't usually come to our island, only occasionally. I think Mr. Whitlock means: *Be on the lookout for bears.*

Mr. Whitlock says Japan's leaders are hungry for power and the military is greedy and dangerous.

I understand *hungry*. I get hungry all the time. Being hungry is not bad. But *greedy* is bad. I never take what is not mine, even if I am hungry. I go to Fumio. He will always feed me.

Mr. Whitlock runs his hand through his hair. He says more words I don't understand. "China lines up with the Allies. The US supports China's stand with an embargo, so it's hard for Japan to get petroleum, rubber, metal. That squeezes Japan's war effort pretty tight."

China is glass. It will break. I don't know *embargo*, but petroleum, rubber, and metal—Mr. Miyota has those things in his shop.

Mr. Miyota says, "It sounds as if you are reading from a textbook, Robert."

He learned all of it from a report, Mr. Whitlock tells him—not *off-fish-all*—but sent to him by friends. He says, "The news is disturbing. Our world is in turmoil."

CHAPTER FIVE

FUMIO

Fumio and Zachary moved their map to a small table near the washing machine on the enclosed porch. They returned the whisk broom to the cabinet. They cleaned the tabletop one more time. All that remained was returning the ruler, pencils, and erasers to the drawer where they belonged.

Zachary grabbed the pencil box and Fumio picked up the ruler and erasers. They walked to the living room, waiting silently in the broad doorway for a break in the adults' conversation.

His parents' expressions were serious, Fumio saw, almost grim.

"Some of that turmoil may land on our doorstep," his father said. "In newspapers, we read that Japan's battles are dishonorable, that their military may become a threat to America. Japan is a country we have never called home, for which we may have some sentiment, but no loyalty. Yet, when I go into Winslow for supplies, voices stop as I approach. I don't need to hear the words. Their silence tells me how my neighbors feel."

"Perhaps a few of your neighbors," Mr. Whitlock said, "but not *all*. Not even *most*. This is Bainbridge Island. No different than a small town. Wagging tongues often stop when *I* come around, too." He dipped his head, as if embarrassed. "Of course, that is not the same. If others believe I will not approve of their cursing or off-color joke, I can ignore that. I doubt you can take so lightly what seems to be disapproval of your heritage, or your presence in this country."

"I was born here," Mr. Miyota said. "I grew up on this very farm. Sachiko was born a few miles away, in Yama, a village that only existed because of the mill owners' outreach for laborers. Sachiko's father and my father were recruited—*invited*—to work here. And now, when our neighbors look at us, they don't see *us*. They see *Japan*. I have a legal deed for this land. We are United States citizens, not squatters, and certainly not traitors."

Mrs. Miyota leaned forward, hands clasped. "I only hope this fear will pass, next week, next month. Perhaps we will find a way to get along."

"Perhaps," Mr. Whitlock said, "but that is unlikely to happen within a week or month. Ordinary people with good hearts, fair-minded people, thrive and prosper when peace prevails. Men of greed and a need for power always create division and, too often, they profit from war."

A thump, a clatter. The pencil box had slipped from Zachary's hand, its contents now strewn across the floor.

"War!" Zachary's voice broke. "You're saying we're headed for war? With Japan?"

Fumio's breath caught. His mind filled with images he recalled from photographs kept in rice paper packets, likenesses of cousins, an uncle, his mother's parents, and her favorite aunt, whom, he saw, she strongly resembled.

"We can't have a war with Japan!" Mrs. Miyota cried. "Our family could only lose."

"All of us," said Mr. Whitlock, "all of us could only lose."

Mrs. Miyamoto's hand flew to her mouth, her gaze went to her little girl, sitting on the floor with her dolls.

Then silence fell hard upon the house and lay heavily, until, from her place on the rug, Kimiko sang,

"A-ring-a, ring-a rosies,
Pocket full-a posies,
Ashes, ashes,
We all fall down."

CHAPTER SIX

FUMIO

Gathered around the kitchen table, the Miyotas ate breakfast. Fumio scooped his scrambled eggs onto toast.

"Colder weather is coming," Mr. Miyota said. "The chickens' water could freeze. At Petric's, I'll buy black rubber water trays that hold the sun's heat. But we must be watchful."

"Yes, Father," Fumio answered.

Fumio's mother asked, "Son, last night, the conversation, did that . . .?" She frowned.

"Scare me? Not really. The war is on the other side of the earth. I am worried for our relatives in Japan. But I figure people have to eat, so the best thing I can do is help take care of this farm and keep growing what we grow."

Mrs. Miyota nodded. "Yes, Fumio, that is sensible. And, yes, people do have to eat." She smiled. "Should I get you another slice of toast?"

Fumio shook his head. "Thank you for breakfast."

Mr. Miyota pushed his chair back. "Fumio, we must finish covering the strawberry plants, but only a small amount of straw is left. Our aim is three inches of cover, so please gather needles from under the firs. It will speed the job if you take the needles directly to the field."

"Yes, Father. I'll get started right away." He felt a twinge of regret. It would go faster as a two-person job, but Zachary would be wielding a rake in his own front yard, helping to prepare the Whitlock home for their Sunday guests, members of the Friends Church who were having a meeting. And, later, a veterinarian named Dr. Valke would visit their farm to check the sheep's hooves. Zachary, of course, planned to watch, ask questions, and report back to Fumio.

CHAPTER SEVEN

FLYER

Supper is over and I watch from beneath the sink again. Outside, it is dark and cold. Inside, the lights are on and the curtains are closed. My family is doing quiet *evening* things.

Kimiko is sweeping the floor. She bumps walls and knocks things off counters with the big broom's handle, so Mrs. Miyota says she may sweep with the whiskbroom. Kimiko is happy.

On our driveway, footsteps crunch in gravel. I go to the door. *Yipp!* We have company! *Yipp-ipp!*

Rap-rap-rap!

"Bisitor, Mama, Papa!" Kimiko says, "Summuns at door!"

Fumio's father goes to the door. "Hello, Jacob! Hello, Zachary!" he says. "Please, come in!" He shakes Jacob's hand.

Jacob takes off his hat. "Mrs. Miyota."

Fumio's mother smiles. "Jacob! Your mother hoped you'd make it home today!"

Jacob is Zachary's big brother. The school he goes to is *college*, and he only comes home sometimes. Zachary told us Jacob is very busy and soon he will be a teacher.

Fumio's father says he did not hear Jacob's car. He would have turned the porch light on. Jacob holds up a flashlight. "We walked over, sir."

"I have made a pot of sencha. Please, will you have some?" Mrs. Miyota puts the teapot and cups on the table and gets milk from the refrigerator.

After moving his sketch from the table, Fumio gets another chair and brings spoons and sugar before sitting down. He is not far away. If he reaches out, I can touch him. Zachary is on the other side of the table, beside Jacob. Kimiko is still sweeping.

Fumio's mother pours tea into cups for the grown-ups and milk for Fumio and Zachary.

Jacob says he cannot stay long. He got on the road later than he planned. And he can see by the papers on the table that Mr. Miyota is busy. He says he knows it is difficult to work hard all day and make time to log it in at night.

"Father says no job is finished until the paperwork is done," Fumio puts in.

Zachary asks what kind of paperwork?

Mr. Miyota holds up the clipboard so Zachary can see it. "I keep records of supplies, costs, how long it takes to get a piece of equipment running." He flips the top page over. "And, of course, prepare the customer's bill."

Everyone sips from their cups. Fumio looks down and wipes milk from his mouth. "The veterinarian came today to check the sheep's hooves, right, Zachary?"

The veterinarian is new to the island, Zachary says. She let him watch and explained the job, so he could learn to do it himself someday.

Mrs. Miyota says there is still tea in the pot and asks if anyone wants more. Mr. Miyota and Jacob tell her no, and they thank her. Zachary asks if he may taste it. She says he may and looks toward Fumio.

"Yes, thank you," he says, "and it would be all right not to rinse the milk from the cup."

Zachary says, "It's okay with me, too, thank you."

Mrs. Miyota goes to the cabinet for the tea whisk, which is not like a whisk broom. She uses the tea whisk to stir through the pot and pours a little tea into the boys' cups.

Fumio drinks from the cup and smiles.

Zachary watches, then drinks, too. His eyes look funny when he asks, "This is tea?"

"Tea and milk," Fumio nods.

Zachary says, "It tastes different."

"Different from what?"

"Different from anything I have ever drank before. It tastes green."

"We should not waste that." Jacob reaches for his brother's cup.

Fumio dips his fingers into his teacup, then holds them down under the table. I belly-crawl closer, and *swrlllrp*, lick the tea from his fingers. The tea tastes good, like rain. *Swrlllrp*. Fumio laughs. Maybe that tickled. His grin is wide. I scoot back under the sink.

Jacob says, "Fumio, I brought something for you, and something for Kimiko, too."

He gives Kimiko her gift first. It is a long ribbon.

Fumio's mother says, "Oh, that is pretty. Blue!"

"Yes, ma'am," Jacob answers. "Extra from an apron Mother sewed. Long enough to be cut into two pieces, one for each of Kimiko's dolls."

Then Jacob says, "My roommate left college. He moved out of the dormitory and dumped things that were maybe not much good." He shows Fumio a small box. "But there was this box of colored pencils. Some are stubby. And I almost dropped this in the trash. But I found out it is a special, kneadable eraser, and only skilled artists use kneadable erasers."

"Isn't it great, Fumio?" Zachary says, "I told Jacob it is perfect for you!"

Fumio reaches out, picks up the eraser, and squishes it between his fingers. He laughs. "This is an eraser?"

Jacob nods and tells Fumio that, at the library, he can find out how to use it. Then Jacob swallows the last of Zachary's tea. He says, "I am sorry to come after dark and now we must hurry off. Zachary and I will fix his bike tonight."

"I get to help!" Zachary put in. "And, you know, I am going to keep a record of how we do it. Each step. And all the stuff we use!"

"That sounds like a good plan, Zachary." Mr. Miyota nods.

"Right! It does, little brother!" Jacob rubbed his knuckles on Zachary's head, and I know it doesn't hurt because Zachary laughs. "Well, there are big doings at the house tomorrow. Our parents will want our help."

Fumio's mother says, "Please give them our best regards."

Mr. Miyota walks with Jacob and Zachary to the door and sees them out. Then he closes the door, lowers his chin and looks at me. "So, Flyer, how did you like the tea?"

CHAPTER EIGHT

FUMIO

Fumio had been in Zachary's home during past Quaker Committee meetings. While the adults met, the boys worked on school projects or played board games on the enclosed side porch.

Today, though, Fumio and Zachary sat on a rough-barked limb of the big-leaf maple tree beside the Whitlock house. The tree stood taller than the house. Across the Whitlock's sheep pasture and over the two families' shared fence, it offered a view of the Miyota house, their farmyard, and the expanse of three large strawberry fields where, sheltered beneath mounds of straw and pine needles, the delicate plants slept. At the back of the property, the small stream-fed pond gleamed dark silver beneath a stand of Douglas firs.

If he twisted to his right, Fumio could see his family's white house and outbuildings, their pickup, farm truck, and tractor—a Cleveland Crawler—parked in a line. He surveyed the tidy garden plot subdued in winter brown and the stately old willow that grew between his father's shop and the graveled lane.

A flash of movement drew Fumio's attention. In the distance, from the branches of the giant Douglas fir trees, crows spiraled upward, then scattered to dart and pivot, complaining about a disturbance of their peace, shattering the late afternoon calm. An interloper?

Looking toward Zachary, Fumio asked, "Is today's meeting extra-important?"

"Yes. The guests from off the island belong to a committee of observers. Observers watch to see if people are being treated fairly, and they write reports—"

"Reports?" Fumio broke in. "Like at school?"

"Sort of like that. I wrote a report last night. Remember, Jacob helped me fix my bike? It got kind of late, but I wrote how we did it." From his pocket, Zachary pulled out a sheet of paper folded into a little square.

"That's your report? Can I read it?"

"Not yet." Zachary returned the paper to his pocket. "I wrote it in pencil on a sheet of tablet paper. I want to copy it neater and in ink."

"Will you show it to me, then?"

"I will. Promise." Zachary held up two fingers, like a Scout. "Anyway, observers. They share reports by mailing them to committee members or reading them in meetings, like today."

Fumio glanced over Zachary's right shoulder and asked, "Does your father write reports? Is he an observer?"

"Father does write reports. He is an observer and so is Mother." Zachary cleared his throat. He reached for his shoe and retied the laces.

"My mother says lots of people don't want to talk about their church, or how much they paid for something, or what they think of the government. Things like that. Or habits. Like, sometimes you bow." Zachary reworked the laces on his other shoe. "Did your grandfather teach you that?"

Fumio felt the bite of the tree's course bark and shifted to a new position. "Bowing is for formal greetings, or for really important people, or people who are older than me. It doesn't have to do with anyone's church. And yes, my grandfather taught me. He was more traditional than my parents are."

"You never bow to me. I'm important."

"Not that important."

"All right. But I am older, a whole month older than you."

"Forget it, Zachary. I am not bowing to you."

"Okay. But how do you know? How do you know the rules?"

"You *learn* the rules," Fumio said. "But when it comes to how and when to follow them, I decide as I go. I don't like to stand out."

Zachary nodded, appearing to be satisfied with the answer.

In the lull that followed, the sound of a vehicle's arrival. Car doors opened and closed. Conversation and laughter from the parking area at the front of the house.

"Committee members arriving late," Zachary remarked. "It's not a party, but I think Quakers enjoy these meetings. Me, I don't know that I would." He frowned. "Fumio, you remember Jacob was late leaving Pacific College to come home yesterday, right?

"Right."

"It was because he found out his roommate, his friend, is quitting college and joining the Army to fight overseas, 'because it is patriotic.' Jacob told him living the Quaker peace testimony is patriotic, too, and asked if he was certain of his choice. His friend said he thought soldiering would be an adventure. Jacob thinks his friend has no idea how real it will be."

Zachary plucked a brittle leaf, then broke bits from it and dropped them to the ground. "Do you ever think about it, Fumio? Is being a soldier an adventure?"

"No, I don't think of it like that. But what if—what if you had to fight? For your freedom or your life? What if there was no other way?"

"There is always another way. My father says there is always another way."

Fumio nodded, biting his lip. "And you would never join the Army, right, Zachary?"

"Because I'm a Quaker? There are Quakers in the military."

"There are?" Fumio felt the surprise in his stomach. "So, Jacob could—"

"Jacob could. He won't."

Fumio nodded. "And, someday, you won't either, right?"

"I don't know." Zachary sighed. "Maybe I'm not sure I want to be a Quaker. It's hard to think about it, really."

"Then don't. Don't think about it. Nobody's going to *make* you be a Quaker. And they don't let ten-year-olds join the Army, anyway."

"Hah-hah. I know that! But now there is this big decision to make someday. It's up in the air. I don't like things up in the air."

Fumio lifted an upturned palm. "Goof. You are sitting in a tree."

CHAPTER NINE

FLYER

Fumio tells me I am a special dog, *a border collie*. Fumio's grandfather, his ojiisan, said he could not understand why anyone would give up a border collie, so good at herding and so loyal. I know some words, but I don't know *herding*. I know *loyal*, though. *Loyal* means *helpful*, a dog who can be counted on.

A long time ago, a man with big rough hands that smelled like what I know now is *engine grease* pushed me into a wooden crate where the ferryboats dock. He said, "Noisy critter! I durn-sure don't need another yammerin' mouth to feed. Mangy hound, shut yer trap!" Then he kicked the side of the crate and went away.

Fumio's grandfather, Mr. Kito Miyota, was working not far away that day. He was repairing machinery at the strawberry cannery near the dock.

I tried to be quiet. But I was hungry. My stomach hurt. I was scared.

Grandfather Miyota told Fumio he heard a tiny sound, and he thought it might be a bird. *What kind of bird?* he wondered. He put down his tools and came to look. And he found *me*.

I saw a face look over the edge of the crate. I scooted far back into a corner, but I couldn't hide. Hands came toward me, hands that smelled of fuel oil. I could not help it, I started to shake. But when Grandfather Miyota picked me up and pulled me against his chest, I felt safe. He said, "What a fine young dog you are! I have a six-year-old grandson at home, and I believe he is waiting for you."

CHAPTER TEN

FUMIO

Walking back to his home from Zachary's house, Fumio saw a dark-green GMC parked in their yard, and his father talking on the porch with Mr. Harvey, a family friend and the supplier of products Mr. Miyota used in maintaining farm equipment.

Mr. Harvey wore overalls and an engineer's cap, both made of the sturdy, blue-and-white-striped fabric called ticking. When the two men shook hands, Fumio picked up his pace. "Hello, Mr. Harvey!"

"Howdy, young'un. Hey, Flyer!" Smiling broadly, the man stepped from the porch. "Just delivering a scrap of junk fencing! You got a bit of work ahead of you, Fumio. Be sure to wear gloves! Wire fencing? The stuff bites like a rooster!" Mr. Harvey slapped his thigh, laughing, then climbed into the truck and started the engine. Waving, he pulled out of the driveway.

Fumio joined his father on the front porch. "You told him."

"Yes, I told him. You know Mr. Harvey enjoys a good story. He brought news. And supplies. He called it 'junk fencing,' but it will serve our purpose. The Katos' chicken house was raided last night. They lost a couple of pullets. Still—it could have been much worse."

Fumio did not like chickens, not one little bit. But the family depended on them for eggs and meat. Neighbors bought eggs, and occasionally, a few birds were sold for stewing. So, like them or not, the chickens were farm stock and one of his responsibilities.

Flyer nudged Fumio's knee.

"Here to help, boy?"

A quick movement of the dog's muzzle—*down, up*—seemed almost a nod to Fumio, as Flyer danced and wagged.

"Good dog." Fumio patted Flyer's head.

A chilly drizzle began to fall as Fumio's father leaned the heavy wooden ladder against the exterior wall. He dumped a handful of half-inch thin-gauge nails—brads—into his shirt pocket, slipped the light-weight tack hammer under his belt, and climbed.

The vent was a diamond-shaped opening high in the gable designed to keep out predators while letting in fresh air and a measure of light for the poultry.

Mr. Miyota reached into his pocket for a brad. Coming up with two, he held one between his teeth while giving the other a few sharp raps of the hammer. Steadily, he tapped brads into place, attaching woven wire on three of the four sides.

Stepping down the rungs of the ladder, Fumio's father took the remaining brads from his pocket and poured them into his son's outstretched hand. With the brads in his pocket, Fumio grasped the hammer and began to climb. Not every blow hit its mark, but as he worked, his aim became more certain.

Minutes later, the downpour began.

"Son! Are you done there?"

"Yes, Father. Just now!"

"Come on, then! Let's finish up!"

Fumio could not resist taking another moment to scan his surroundings. He liked being up this high. *It's no wonder chickens are cantankerous,* he thought. *They are birds, and when birds cannot fly, they must become sad and angry, which adds up to cantankerous.*

He imagined himself in the cockpit of an airplane. What would that be like?

His father called again. "Fumio!"

Yipp! Fumio understood Flyer was anxious, seeing him far overhead on a wet ladder.

"Fumio!"

"Coming!"

CHAPTER ELEVEN

FLYER

The house is asleep when a scent tickles my nose. *Woof-oof! Woof-oof!*

Fumio awakens and we walk downstairs so he can let me out.

The moon comes and goes. It is dark now and from the porch, I pause to draw in scent, to give my ears range.

Crickets jitter—*creakk-kk creakk-kk creakk-kk*. The rain has stopped but leaves still drip—*plip plip plip*—a small sound. A breeze rattles a windowpane—*dh-pa dh-pa-pa dh-pa*—and brings a strong odor of fear. The chickens are afraid.

A shriek cuts through the night. I do not like that rooster. He is angry all the time, but this is different. What is going on? And what is that other noise?

Whoosh-swoosh-swoosh. Whoosh-swoosh-swoosh. The sound comes from behind our chicken yard. I know that sound. I have heard that sound before.

My family does not hear it yet. I sound the alarm, *WHOOPH-OOPH-OOPH-OOOPH—WHOOPH-OOPH-OOPH!*

Soon, Fumio and his father rush out the door. Mr. Miyota runs to the woodshed and gets an axe, ready for whatever might be found out here in the darkness.

"Flyer! Where are you, boy? Flyer?" Fumio calls.

Yipp-ipp!

"Flyer! There you are! Good dog, Flyer!" Fumio hurries to me.

The moon peeks from behind a cloud as Mrs. Miyota comes out onto the porch.

"Better go inside, Sachiko!" Fumio's father calls.

She shakes her head, *no*.

Mr. Miyota shrugs. He and Fumio head for the chicken yard. I stay by Fumio's side.

A racket comes from the chicken house.

"Fumio," his father says, "we don't know what we are going to find when we open the door of the coop. Stand back and protect your eyes. That rooster sounds upset."

"That rooster is always upset," Fumio says, "but I have never heard anything like this." He looks toward the axe. "Could a coyote be the culprit? Maybe it tunneled into the coop!" His father does not answer.

Mr. Miyota turns to me, and I know he is looking for my help. I raise my muzzle toward the scrap of moon, toward the treetops, toward the roof of the chicken coop. I *whuffle* and *whuphh*, sniffing the air. I move to face the chicken yard's side wall, and I *point*.

Fumio and his father go silent, searching the darkness. "Hear that, Son?" Mr. Miyota asks. "That sound does not come from inside the coop. Let's look in back." They walk along the wire mesh of the chicken yard. At the rear corner, they stop. They look *up*. And there, at the back of the enclosure, is the *culprit*.

"A great horned owl," Fumio whispers. "What has happened to it?" From the gable, the huge bird hangs head down, swinging from side to side.

"I believe the talons of one foot are caught in the chicken wire," Mr. Miyota answers.

The owl's beak opens, closes, opens, closes. Its cries are loud and rough. The bird must be very heavy. Its wings are as long as the axe handle! Feathers lie everywhere on the ground.

My heart beats fast, but when the owl swings to the side, I see its eyes. I think the owl is scared, too. Of being trapped, of being stared at, of not being able to hide.

The great horned owl works its beak and its *talons*. It beats its wings against the wall of the coop, and it screeches. I hear quick, low calls—*whoo-whoo-whoo*—and it makes a sound like a dog howling that raises the fur on the scruff of my neck.

Inside the chicken coop, the rooster screams and screams. He wants to scare the owl away. He does not understand that the owl is in danger.

I do. I understand. And I see trouble all around.

"A great horned owl," Fumio says again. "Father, it is huge."

"Yes, Fumio. It is also terrified." Mr. Miyota frowns. "That is a bird in trouble. But if we try to free it, we risk being badly injured. The owl's beak and its talons are sharp as knives. Yet, if we do not help it get free, it will almost certainly die, slowly and painfully. I do not want that to happen."

"It has been trying to hurt our chickens," Fumio says.

Mr. Miyamoto raises his voice to be heard. "That is the nature of an owl. It was searching for a meal. I do not want our chickens to be harmed, but I cannot lay the blame on the owl if the owl is hungry."

"Should I go get our ladder?"

"We would need our tallest—and heaviest—ladder. And, consider this, son, climbing up that ladder will bring us extremely close to the owl. Nearly nose to beak. A great horned owl is a bird of prey, a deadly hunter. Can we find another way?"

CHAPTER TWELVE

FUMIO

Fumio was surprised his father would see the owl's side of the situation, and right now, he did not know if he shared his father's opinion. But he thought he saw a solution to their problem. Working through it in his mind as he spoke, Fumio outlined his plan.

Mr. Miyota chuckled. "You have an idea there, Son!" He nodded once, twice. "First, we need to get that rooster out of the coop. He does not like us any more than he likes that owl."

"How will we do that?" Fumio frowned, thinking hard.

"I suppose we will shout at him and wave our arms to shoo him out. Then he will be in the chicken yard without overhead shelter, but I think the owl, once it is freed, will fly away fast. Later it may return, but we will keep the poultry inside the coop each evening. By Monday, I hope we can take care of the danger once and for all."

Flyer stayed steady by the chicken yard as Fumio and his father went to the shop to get what they needed to free the owl. Mr. Miyota lugged the wooden ladder and Fumio grasped a wire cutter, honed sharp.

Fumio's attention was caught by a light bobbing toward them. Enveloped in a golden glow, his mother approached, carrying a lantern. The rain had stopped, but the mist persisted. The yard was a muddy mess. Fumio hurried to her and carefully took the lantern from her hand.

Before following his father into the chicken yard, Fumio looked toward Flyer. "Stay," he said, then stepped through the gate and carefully secured it behind them.

Growling deep in his throat, Flyer remained watchful as Fumio hung the lantern on a bracket just inside the coop.

Hens, already frightened, burrowed deeper into the straw. The rooster, though, put up a fight. Fumio and his father shouted, "Go, rooster! Hey! Get out, rooster!" But the rooster thrust his wings wide and rushed at them, refusing to be displaced.

Then Flyer, from his position outside the fence, switched from a low rumble to a high wailing sound. At *that*, the rooster charged from the coop, directly at Flyer who, from behind a swath of chicken wire, sat unmoving, but for a sharp, "*Yip!*"

With the rooster out of the coop and the door closed, Fumio and his father maneuvered the ladder across the dirt floor toward the wall, directly below the gable's vent.

Near their objective, Fumio spoke, "Father, I can do it." He gestured toward the gable. "With the ladder leaning there, under the slope of the roof, you'll have no headroom. To free the owl will be easier for me. You can hold the ladder for me better than I could hold it for you." With no response from his father, and fearing he might be refused, he added, "I can do it, Father. We have a good plan."

Having talked himself out of breath, Fumio inhaled, then went silent. His father laid his hand on Fumio's shoulder. "Son, we do have a good plan. It is your plan, and seeing this through is important to you, so go ahead. But, be careful, Fumio!"

At the base of the ladder, Fumio considered the task ahead. The space would be tight. He removed his bulky coat and hung it from a perch. Clasping the wire cutters, climbing rung by rung, Fumio was thankful for the lantern's glow. At the top of the ladder, he peered through the vent's maze of woven wire and recent repairs, seeking the point where the owl was snared.

As his eyes adjusted to the low light, he saw how to proceed. To free the huge bird would require an approach very near its talons. He had to choose carefully which strand to cut first, then alternate—left, right, top, bottom. To free one massive wing while the other was still trapped might cause the owl to flail broadly, injuring himself. And Fumio.

Securing his hold on the wire cutter's grips, Fumio began making the cuts, stopping often to wait for the owl to quiet the beating of its wings.

At length, his father called, "Are you all right up there?"

"Yes! I've almost got it!" Pressing against the remnants of the ragged metal barrier, straining toward the last wire holding the owl captive, Fumio held his breath, then gasped as the owl's razor-sharp talons slashed his shirt, slicing a strip of blue-and-white fabric from his sleeve.

Panicked, the owl turned and thrashed, the ribbon of fabric twisting and tangling well above its grasping foot. At no time could Fumio reach the fabric to clip it away without endangering the owl. He would have to let it be. Cutting the final wire, he called, "Got it!"

On powerful wings, with a flash of blue and white, the great horned owl soared away.

Fumio felt the pull of flight in his arms and his shoulders. For a moment, he glimpsed what it was to be the owl, to see the Miyota and Whitlock land from above the trees.

His father called, "Fumio! What do you have to report? Are any chickens harmed?"

"No, sir," Fumio replied, peering about. "Eggs broken, here and there, probably stepped on by frightened hens." He came down the ladder.

Back on the ground, Fumio laid aside the wire cutters and removed his coat from the perch where it had hung. His father studied the coop and the poultry it sheltered. "Son, do you see any damage?"

"No—" Fumio felt a chill reach through the tear in his shirt, "except—" he stretched out his arm, "for a rip in my sleeve." He extended his arm toward his father.

"We will tell your mother about that in the morning," Mr. Miyota said, placing his hand for a moment on Fumio's head.

Fumio retrieved his coat and pushed his arms into it. The rooster was easily convinced to return to the coop. Fumio took down the lantern and secured the door. The ladder and tools were returned to the shed. Commotion past, Fumio felt glad for the quiet as he, his father, and Flyer returned to the warmth of the Miyota home.

CHAPTER THIRTEEN

FUMIO

Monday's wintery temperatures kept many students indoors during lunchtime, but those who craved fresh air bundled up and went out. Fumio mused on the weekend's events, especially the owl's attack, its entanglement, and its release. He wondered, was it the same bird that had earlier taken chickens from the Katos' chicken yard?

Across the schoolyard, Fumio spied Joey Kato sitting alone on the merry-go-round, peering into his lunch box with a horrified expression on his face.

"Joey!" he called, motioning him over.

Joey frowned, closed the lunch box, and carried it to the steps. Then he slowly reopened it and went back to staring at the contents.

"Hey, Joey, you look like there's a frog in there." Fumio laughed.

Joey shoved the metal container closer.

Fumio peered inside. "Oh. What are y'gonna do about that?"

Zachary rose slightly, craning his neck to look. "What is it?"

"Onigiri," Fumio said. Then, looking toward Joey, he asked, "With umeboshi inside?"

Joey nodded.

Zachary's brow wrinkled. "Is it something to *eat*?"

"It's a plum, with sticky rice pressed around it, wrapped in nori. Nori is dried seaweed." Fumio shook his head. "That's rough."

Zachary looked interested. "So, it's a plum! But you don't like it."

"Oh, I like it," Joey answered. "But I don't like it *here*. Not at school!" He turned to Fumio. "What do you do when this happens to you?"

"It doesn't," Fumio said. "I asked my mother not to put stuff like that in my lunch."

"You just *asked* her?"

"Yes. She said *okay*, but my lunch might be boring. I told her that was all right by me."

Joey nodded, then looked back down at his lunch and frowned again.

"I'll have it," Zachary said. "I'll trade you an oatmeal cookie."

"Really? You'd trade me a cookie?"

"Sure. I have two. You can have one, and I'll get to taste onigiri with ume . . . ume . . ."

"Umeboshi," Fumio repeated.

The trade was completed, and Joey bit into the cookie at once. He closed his eyes. "Mmmmm."

Fumio licked salt from his fingers, savoring his egg. He watched as Zachary studied the onigiri, quickly peeled away the nori, plucked out the plum, popped it whole into his mouth, and bit down.

Zachary's lips puckered, and he froze.

Laughing, Fumio spat out a smattering of hard-cooked egg yolk, bringing Joey out of his cookie-inspired trance.

Zachary covered his mouth. Around the lump of plum, he asked, "Whas-zis?"

"I told you!" Fumio sputtered, stifling a snort. "Umeboshi. You're supposed to eat it with the rice! It's in there to keep the rice from drying out and to give it extra flavor!"

"The plum makes the rice taste better," Joey put in.

"I only wanted the thing in the middle. I thought it would taste like a maraschino cherry." Zachary grimaced. "But it's salty, mostly." Then he shrugged. "Interesting."

Fumio wiped egg from his face. "Hey, Joey," he said, "Mr. Harvey told us that, over the weekend, you lost some pullets at your place."

"Yeah, something got at our chickens. Those pullets would have been laying soon, too. A bad loss, but Father says he's seen worse."

"It was an owl, Joey. A great horned owl. It hit our coop last night."

"You didn't tell me!" Zachary said.

"We got off easy, I guess, compared to your family, Joey." Fumio shook his head. "I'm sure sorry about what happened to your family's flock."

"Thanks, Fumio," Joey replied. "And Zachary, that cookie was really good. Seeing as how much you like umeboshi, next time my mother puts it in my lunch, I'll ask her to pack extra for you."

• • •

After lunch, Fumio, Zachary, and Joey returned with their classmates to their schoolroom. Miss Lassiter had completed teacher training in Oregon. This was her first year of teaching in her own classroom. Fumio liked her. She would not put up with foolishness, she had told them straight out. But learning, she had added, should be fun.

Miss Lassiter worked long hours, he knew, planning lessons, grading papers, supervising students before and after school, during recesses and lunchtimes. Zachary's older brother, Jacob, had explained that teachers were also responsible for time-consuming record-keeping, and many duties of which most students were unaware.

Fumio had noticed Miss Lassiter began every school day with her dark hair wound into a tight bun, but by the end of the day, she wore a halo of escaped curls. Though she might appear tired, she always remembered to thank students who stayed to help tidy up.

Leaving his coat in the cloakroom, Fumio went to his desk, lifted its top, and took out the drawing he had started earlier in the day: a sketch of the owl at close range, as he had seen it through the diamond-shaped openings of the woven wire.

When he heard Zachary whisper, "Fumio, let me see the picture," he turned it toward him for a moment, but quickly slipped it into his desk as his classmates settled into their places.

On the blackboard, Miss Lassiter had written, "Where in the world is Bainbridge Island?" Standing near the square, oak teacher's desk, she prompted, "Students, please take your outline maps from your desks."

The schoolroom door opened, and a woman Fumio had seen working at the post office peered into the room. "Sorry to interrupt, Miss Lassiter, but as I left to take my lunch hour, I came across a little girl needing help. Her name is Reyna, she says, and she has just moved up from California. I found her wandering near the post office. Looking for school, I assumed."

"I am not a little girl," Reyna came into view, jerking her shoulders out from under the surprised postal worker's arm. "And I was not," her gaze was defiant, "looking for school."

The helpful woman's face reddened, but Miss Lassiter smiled and spoke brightly, "Thank you very much. It is kind of you to escort our new friend to class. I've been expecting her."

The woman nodded and backed out of the doorway.

Fumio considered the class's "new friend." Reyna was tall, lanky. Her eyes were dark, her expression sullen.

Miss Lassiter went to the girl's side and spoke quietly. "I've looked forward to meeting you, Reyna, and I have a desk ready, where you can settle in. Would you like to hang up your jacket?"

"No," the girl snapped. "I don't plan to stay long."

Miss Lassiter nodded and led her toward the one vacant desk in the classroom, directly in front of Fumio's desk and at a diagonal from Zachary's.

Fumio saw that Zachary, curious as he always was about everything and everyone, was watching their new classmate's approach with interest.

Reyna's hair was her most striking feature. Shoulder-length, worn loose, no barrettes, no ribbon to tie it back. Copper-hued, it gleamed like a newly minted penny. As she moved farther into the classroom, light from the windows struck sparks in it that glowed like embers.

She stopped, glared at Zachary, and snarled, "What are *you* looking at?"

"Reyna," Miss Lassiter said, "I hope you'll give your new neighbors a chance to become your friends. Meanwhile, please be patient." She laid a copy of the island map on the girl's desk and stepped away.

Having dropped into her chair, Reyna turned the map face down and crossed her arms.

"Many of you students have lived on this island your whole life," Miss Lassiter said.

Reyna slumped down in her seat and scowled.

"I have lived here only four months," Miss Lassiter said, glancing at Reyna. "I went to the library to learn about the island!" She smiled. "Did you know that, until a little over fifty years ago, the only way to get to Bainbridge Island was by canoe or rowboat? In 1887, the Mosquito Fleet began making regular trips around the island. Today, we can cross the water on ferryboats." She gave a head tilt. "Maybe someday there will be a bridge. And did you know that, once, huge *old growth* trees covered this island?"

Students nodded.

"Many of you did!" Miss Lassiter chuckled. "What happened to those trees?"

A boy near the front of the class raised his hand, and Miss Lassiter acknowledged him with a nod. He put his hand down and said, "Loggers working for the Port Blakely Lumber Mill cut them down, and a lot of the lumber was used to build ships. My grandfather was one of those loggers!" he added. "My grandparents lived in the village of Yama."

"Good information!" Miss Lassiter responded. "Trees were cut, year after year, until there were no more trees!" She gave a tiny shrug. "At least, very few trees, and almost no massive old trees. Now, what might happen to the topsoil of an island, the soil with important *nutrients*?"

No one volunteered an answer.

"Have you ever built a sandcastle, students?" Miss Lassiter asked, and a few children nodded. "What happens when the tide comes in and waves wash over it? Or, what if rain falls on your sandcastle? What happens? Anybody?"

One hand inched upward. Miss Lassiter smiled. "What is your idea, Reyna?"

"It's not an *idea*; I've seen it. On the beach near San Diego, we built sandcastles, with moats and everything. They got washed away real easy."

She went silent for a moment. "But I was a little kid. It was just a dumb game."

"A game, perhaps," Miss Lassiter replied, "but a good example of erosion. When water washes away land, that is called *erosion*. The topsoil—and sometimes even the plants from meadows and fields—disappear into the sea. Over time, erosion does happen, but trees slow the process. What happens to wildlife when there are no trees?"

"The animals have to find another place on the island to live," a girl responded.

Their teacher nodded. "Yes, that is true. But many birds build nests in trees and find leaves and insects on the trunks to eat. If there are no good-sized trees, then what of *birds*? Can you imagine them packing up their tiny suitcases and moving off-island?"

A ripple of laughter spread through the classroom. Miss Lassiter went on, "I think we can see that cutting most of the large trees on Bainbridge Island has worked a great deal of change. I propose we can see some of that change in the sorts of wildlife we have here."

"But we still have deer!" a boy in the front row remarked. "And one or two coyotes skulk through from time to time. My dad told me."

"An owl tried to attack the chickens at Fumio's house last night!" Zachary blurted. "He saw it up close. It was a great horned owl!"

"So, Fumio," Miss Lassiter said as she attempted to tuck in a flyaway curl, "an owl threatened your chickens?"

"Yes, ma'am," Fumio answered, "but it got its talons caught in the wire that covered an air vent. My father and I had to cut the owl free."

"That owl was going wild!" Zachary put in. "Fumio, show Miss Lassiter the picture!"

"A great horned owl! Those birds are enormous! Yes, Fumio, please do show all of us."

Fumio held back a sigh as he took the drawing from his desk and handed it to his teacher, who then took a moment to look it over. He felt his chest warm, however, when she looked back at him and asked, "May I?" When he nodded, she took it to the front of the room and pinned it at the very top of the bulletin board. "Up high," she said, "where it will feel at home."

CHAPTER FOURTEEN

FUMIO

Fumio and Zachary were wheeling their bicycles toward the road after school when Fumio caught sight of his family's blue half-ton pickup truck parked in front of Petric's Feed and Seed. "Look! Father must be there, in the store!"

Zachary laughed. "Flyer is here, too, ready to drive the Chevy home!"

Flyer, panting happily, sat at attention in the driver's seat, the window partially lowered.

"*Yipp-ipp!*" he greeted the boys as they walked up.

"You've been waiting for us, haven't you, boy?" Fumio reached to ruffle Flyer's ears.

But a voice Fumio recognized as Dirk Brown's called, "Hey, Zachary! Hold on a minute!"

"Willikers," Zachary mumbled, "do we have to talk to him?"

"Wait up!" Dirk pedaled across the road slowly, his bicycle wobbling, and came to a stop near the truck. "Wanna ride bikes over to the dump? We could throw rocks at the rats, maybe."

"Yuck!" Fumio had no love for rats, but he would not throw rocks at them.

"Whatsa matter, Fuuum? Are some of those rats your cousins? I guess I heard some rats've got yellow eyes." Dirk slapped his side, making a show of loud laughter.

From the driver's seat of the Miyota truck came a warning growl. Flyer was on alert.

"Yeah, I'm talking *yellow*," Dirk jeered. "Fumio's gotta get help from his father and a smelly dog to take down a ragged old owl and save some stupid chick-chick-chickens. I could've done that all by myself. Shoot, chickens are no big deal."

"What would you know about chickens?" Zachary asked, heat in his voice.

"I know you guys *are* chickens!" Dirk flapped his arms. "*Wuakkk-wuakk-wuakk!*"

"Knock it off, Dirk!" Fumio shouted, moving to confront the boy.

Flyer shoved his head through the open window and barked.

From the path in front of the school, a voice rang out. "Hey, you there! Yeah, you! Junior thug in the checkered shirt! Your name is Dirk, isn't it? Or is it *jerk*? I'm not sure I heard it right. Anyway, are you this town's rat expert? You seem to think you know a lot about them."

Fumio turned to look over his shoulder and groaned.

Reyna made her way across the road and confronted Dirk. "I think you better apologize. That was rude."

Glowering, Dirk rounded on Reyna. "Rude! I'm rude? And what are you, huh?" He gestured toward Fumio, "I know he's a Jap." He pointed at Zachary, "And he's a yellow coward." His eyes squared on Reyna, "*You*, though, you're nothin' but a girl."

Reyna lifted her chin and stepped several inches closer.

Dirk took a step back.

Flyer growled, scrabbling to leave the cab, resumed barking, the sound of it echoing from Petric's front wall.

A man's voice thundered from the porch of the store, "That's enough!"

Reyna glared at Dirk. "Loser!" She spat on the ground in front of him and walked away.

Mr. Harvey called to her, "Miss Torres! Give my regards to your grandfather!"

Reyna quickened her pace.

Fumio stared up at the towering figure that was Mr. Harvey. "Sir, do you know her?"

"Let's say I know *of* her, son. She's moved into her grandparents' care."

"Fumio! Zachary! There you are!" Mr. Miyota came around the corner of the building. "Let's get those bikes in the truck and go! I assumed you'd want to help, Zachary. I have gloves and tack hammers for both of you!"

Turning on his heel, Dirk stalked off.

Mr. Harvey thrust his hand toward Mr. Miyota. "Hello, neighbor! How's everything going in your neck of the woods?"

"It is going well, Mr. Harvey!" Mr. Miyota grasped the man's hand. "And you?"

"Good, yes, all's good at our place! Doris sent me into town with our sugar coupon." He gestured toward his truck, parked up the street in front of The Mercantile. "We sure never used to run out of sugar. Now the stuff's as scarce as hen's teeth."

As they stowed the bicycles in the truck box, Zachary asked Fumio, "Why is Dirk so bent out of shape? He has no reason to go after us! Maybe some kids bait him, but we never do!"

"He was just saying the first mean thing that came to his mind." Fumio shook his head in exasperation. "Like he does to everybody."

Fumio saw his father and Mr. Harvey move onto Petric's broad porch. They talked, frowning, but as he and Zachary came near, the men went quiet. Zachary released a sigh so deep Fumio thought it must have started in his friend's toes. All *was not* going well, he understood. But he remembered something Grandfather Miyota had sometimes said, "Shikata ga nai." *What could be done about it?*

Fumio climbed onto the running board and into the cab. "Move over here, pal," he said as he urged Flyer nearer. "Let Father get behind the steering wheel!"

Zachary got in and, with a solid *thunk,* pulled the door closed.

Mr. Miyota and Mr. Harvey descended the steps and came to the truck. From the big front pocket of his overalls, Mr. Harvey took a small scrap of pastry wrapped in a handkerchief and reached toward Flyer. "Here you go, buddy! I was sitting by the window in the café, having myself a kruller, as they sell out of *doughnuts* by noon, when I happened to see you and Mr. Miyota pull up. I saved this for you."

"*Yipp-ipp!*" Flyer took the flaky bite, swallowed, and licked his muzzle.

Mr. Harvey said farewell, promising to give the Miyotas' best regards to Mrs. Harvey.

A young man came out with two boxes marked "Wire Staples" and loaded them into the truck box. "Thanks for your business, Mr. Miyota!" he called.

Mr. Miyota nodded and waved as the young man turned to go back inside.

"*Yipp!*"

"All right!" Mr. Miyota exclaimed. "Let's get moving! We're burning daylight!"

CHAPTER FIFTEEN

FUMIO

His early Sunday morning chores complete, Fumio came into the kitchen just as his mother opened a jar of jam preserved from the farm's strawberries. His mouth watered.

Sitting with his family at the table, he smoothed the glistening spread to the edges of a piece of toasted bread, but thinly. Fumio understood that the pantry's supply must last until harvest, in four-and-a-half months. With each small bite, he savored the berry bits and the feel of tiny seeds tickling his tongue until the last morsel was gone.

"Mo' toast and jam?" his sister asked, a smear of red at each corner of her mouth.

"Kimiko, dear," her mother answered, "we can use only a little jam now, or we will run out before April, when our strawberries ripen and I can make more."

"'Kay, Mama," Kimiko said, licking her fingers.

His father read the most recent edition of the *Bainbridge Island Review*. Today was December 7, but the paper, a weekly, was printed on December 5, 1941. As his father turned the page, a furrow of worry could be seen plowed between his eyes.

Mrs. Miyota sighed. "Kimiko," she said, "let's clear the table. Will you put the napkins in the laundry hamper, please?"

Fumio helped his mother with the dishes, then pulled on his coat and went out with Flyer to survey the fence his family shared with the Whitlocks. As he walked along, eyeing each post and strand of wire, he heard a shout.

"Fumio!" Zachary stood in his family's pasture, surrounded by sheep. "Fumio! Come over later, will you?"

• • •

The sky was clear and pale as ice. Fumio's breath fogged as he and Flyer followed the lane to Zachary's house. Catching sight of his friend sitting in the big-leaf maple, Fumio whistled two short blasts, just as Zachary, noting his approach, lifted an arm and waved.

Fumio went to the Whitlocks' front door and knocked, as he always did when visiting Zachary. Mrs. Whitlock answered. "Good morning! Won't you come in for a moment? We are having our second cup of coffee. No meetings planned for today!"

"Thank you, ma'am." He looked toward Flyer. "Stay, boy!" In the kitchen, Fumio was greeted by the scent of warm cinnamon. Mrs. Whitlock had been baking. Quiet music played from the family's tabletop radio.

"Good morning, Fumio," Mr. Whitlock said, greeting him with a single nod.

Fumio inclined his head. "Good morning, sir. Good morning, Mrs. Whitlock."

Mrs. Whitlock smiled. "Fumio, I have reason to believe that Zachary is outside, and I suspect you know where to find him. Later, would you please return a couple of canning jars to your mother for me?" She gestured toward two jars on the countertop. "I will put them in a bag."

Fumio knew the jars had held preserved berries to make blueberry cake for last week's meeting. Today, each held a brown paper packet tied with string.

"Sugar," Mrs. Whitlock explained, following his gaze. "My mother taught me to never return a borrowed container empty. Your mother used part of her sugar ration to preserve those berries." She lifted an upturned palm. "This is truly the least I can do. Please come back to the kitchen and pick them up, Fumio, before you leave for home."

"Yes, ma'am, I will." Then he headed through the front door once again and, with Flyer, walked around back toward the maple. The tree reached a window of the second story, providing easy access to Zachary's bedroom.

Pausing near the trunk of the tree, Fumio gazed upward through the broad spread of its limbs, now bare of summer's abundance of bright green leaves.

"Come on up, Fumio! Hey, Flyer!" Zachary called from a sturdy branch where he sat, kicking his legs back and forth.

Branch by branch, Fumio climbed. Once he got up to Zachary, he situated himself in a suitable spot and looked about for Flyer, who stood by the sheep pen, head angled.

Zachary, fastening his coat's top button and turning up his collar, said, "Those sheep are better dressed for this weather than I am."

Fumio grinned. It appeared that Flyer was trying to converse with Maizie. He tipped his head and chuffed. Maizie chewed, grinding her jaw without thought, or so it seemed to Fumio. *Who knows?* he mused. *Who knows what sheep think about? Food, probably. That makes Zachary and his flock a good match.* Fumio smiled to himself.

"What do you suppose Flyer is thinking about?" Zachary asked. "Do you suppose he's wishing Maizie could talk? I know I do." He shrugged. "You know, if you'd gotten here earlier, you could have listened to *The Lone Ranger* with me."

"Who'd he save this week?"

"A little kid on a runaway horse. Maybe the kid's horse saw a snake, I don't know. Anyway, it took off running." Zachary cupped his hands and beat them together in a galloping rhythm. "The little kid yelled, 'Help me! Help me!' The Lone Ranger hollered, 'Hang on!' Trumpets played. *Bah-p-p-pah!* Then more pounding hooves." Zachary's hands recreated the effect again. "The Lone Ranger caught the reins of the runaway horse. The kid was grateful. 'You saved me, Masked Man!' Then the trumpets again. *Bah-p-p-pah!*"

"And, 'The End'!" Fumio grinned. He called to Flyer, "Hey, boy!" as the dog returned from visiting the sheep pen and settled under the maple tree.

"Jacob will be home for Christmas. For a week and a half! He's finishing a couple of classes early, so he is bringing work with him. But he's coming home!"

Since his brother's roommate had joined the Army, Zachary had shared his worries concerning Jacob with Fumio. Other students from Pacific College had enlisted, he said, and he repeated something overheard from a Quaker meeting: "Things overseas are heating up."

Fumio remembered the earlier conversation between his parents. "This morning, my father read part of an article in the *Bainbridge Island Review* to my mother. It said, 'No way around it, it will be a miracle if...'" Fumio gazed out past the tree's branches.

"If what? What will be a miracle?"

"I don't know. That's where he stopped reading. '*It will be a miracle if...*'" Fumio shrugged. "I would guess a lot of people are hoping for one. A miracle, I mean." He knew the governments of the United States and Japan were *negotiating*, trying to reach an agreement that would keep the United States out of a war.

"*Grrrr-Rrrr-Rrr.*" Flyer sounded a low rumble.

From the big firs by the pond, dark birds lifted, circled, and flew away into the distance.

The sound of an engine drew Fumio's eyes to the road. Mr. Harvey's truck roared toward the Miyota farmyard, turned in at the driveway, and stopped.

Fumio saw his father come from the shop.

Mr. Harvey opened his truck door, then slid from behind the steering wheel to the ground. He beckoned, and Mr. Miyota walked over. The men talked, Mr. Harvey gesturing excitedly—something he did when telling a colorful tale—but neither man smiled.

Putting one foot on the running board of his truck, Mr. Harvey grasped the steering wheel, lifted himself up, and reached into the cab. Fumio heard the blare of a radio, a loud voice, but he could not understand the words. His father stood, arms crossed, facing the sound.

Finally, Mr. Harvey turned the radio down and backed out of the cab. He turned and, with both hands, gripped Mr. Miyota's shoulders, then stepped back.

Fumio's father unfolded his arms, and the men shook hands. Mr. Harvey climbed into his truck and drove away. Mr. Miyota walked slowly to the porch and sank to the steps, dropping his head into his hands and covering his eyes.

Fumio's stomach knotted, and his vision grayed. His ears began to ring. "Flyer!" he called. "Flyer, we have to go home! Meet me by the front door!"

"*Yipp!*"

Shifting his weight, Fumio reached for a handhold, preparing to climb down from the tree. "Zachary, I am going home. Something has disturbed my father."

"Oh! Sure! But let's go through the window, into my room, and down the stairs to the kitchen. Mother hopes you will take home the canning jars she borrowed."

Fumio willed his heart to stop racing as, grasping the tree limb, he worked his way toward the window. He must do as he was taught: remember his manners, respect his elders. He must take the jars with him, as Mrs. Whitlock had asked. When his feet touched the floor in Zachary's bedroom, Fumio forbid himself from running. As he rushed down the staircase, the sound of the Whitlocks' radio, volume raised, was easily heard, and he recognized the unmistakable tones of a news broadcast.

Mr. Whitlock stood with his head bowed, one hand atop the radio, the other clenched at his side. Mrs. Whitlock sat in a low chair, twisting a handkerchief, her eyes closed.

Fumio approached the radio where it rested on a small wooden table. The burnished case glowed, its dials gleamed, but the atmosphere buzzed with static, and the newscaster's harsh tones grated like sandpaper on Fumio's ears.

"A dark, dark day . . . in a betrayal of national honor, Japan's Imperial Navy . . . airborne evil . . . unthinkable destruction . . . the United States fleet . . . Pearl Harbor."

CHAPTER SIXTEEN

FLYER

I am waiting in front of Zachary's house when Fumio runs out and leaps down the steps.

We cross our yard to the porch of our house. Fumio's father sits with his head down, but he must have heard Fumio's footsteps—or maybe my panting—because he looks up and I can see by his face that something terrible has happened. Maybe the owl is back. I try not to pant, not to whine. I try to stay still. It is my job to help, but I don't know what to do.

Fumio stands, waiting. No one speaks until he asks, "Father, is it war? War with Japan?"

Mr. Miyota rises. "Not yet, Son, but almost certainly *soon*."

Stepping onto the porch, Fumio goes to the door and opens it for his father. Then, "Come in, Flyer."

I go into the kitchen. Fumio walks with his father into the living room. I hear quiet voices, a few words, then no more.

The door is left open. Cold air comes in. With my nose, I close the door as best I can.

The kitchen smells like dinner, but I am not hungry. I do not lie under the sink. I go to a corner where a broom stands against a wall. Behind the bristles is my rubber ball, a toy that Mr. and Mrs. Harvey gave me, Fumio said, after Grandfather Miyota rescued me. I chewed on the ball when I was a puppy. But I grew up, and now I just like to know where it is. Sometimes, Fumio and I play ball outside in our yard. Not today. I leave the ball and go to the wide doorway between the kitchen and living room and lie down where I can see my family.

Mr. and Mrs. Miyota sit on the couch. Kimiko is nearby, on the little rag rug, with her dolls. Fumio lowers himself to sit on the floor, leaning against the couch.

Mrs. Miyota's eyes are shiny. Fumio's eyes are shiny, too. I creep closer. Still, I am too far from Fumio, too far from my family, so I go into the living room, sit beside Fumio, push my head under his arm, and lean against his leg. He puts his hand on my head. The only noises are sighs and the beating of Fumio's heart.

I hear *tap-tap-tap-tap* and go back through the kitchen to the door. Through the narrow open space, I see Zachary and his parents.

"Hello, Flyer," Zachary says and slowly pushes the door open wider. His mother comes in first, carrying a basket, his father next, carrying a bag. Zachary comes inside last. He shuts the door, then pats me on the head, runs his hand along my neck. "Hey boy, rough day, huh?"

Mr. Whitlock puts the bag on the table. He looks my way and says, "Jam jars."

Jam jars? I answer, *Yipp!* Mr. Whitlock goes to the rack by the door and hangs his coat.

Zachary's mother says, "I brought cinnamon rolls," and sets the basket on the kitchen counter. She does not take off her coat.

In the living room, no one talks. Zachary's parents sit in chairs. Zachary is on the floor beside Fumio with an arm across his shoulders like I have seen him do after a baseball game. I am by Fumio's feet. Kimiko sits quietly, tying blue ribbons in her dolls' hair.

CHAPTER SEVENTEEN

FUMIO

On Monday, as he did every school day morning, Fumio stood, hand over his heart, and recited, "I pledge allegiance to the flag of the United States of America..."

Miss Lassiter directed the students to be seated. She talked with them about the attack on Pearl Harbor. She asked, did they have questions? A few students shook their heads, and no one raised a hand. The teacher began a lesson on proper versus common nouns.

Fumio looked about the classroom and saw empty seats. Joey Kato was absent.

At lunch, Zachary asked Fumio how his parents were doing.

"I guess all right." He took an apple from his lunch box and began polishing it on the leg of his pants.

"Are you worried about your family in Japan?"

Fumio didn't answer, but continued polishing the apple.

"Fumio, you are going to rub the skin right off that apple. Are you upset with me?"

"No, I'm not upset with you. I heard my father say, when he didn't know I could hear, that people in this country are angry with us because we have relatives in Japan. And Japanese people might be angry with our relatives there because they have family members here, in the United States. We are in America, so nothing bad can happen to *us*. But what about Mother's brother, Daishin? He may be in danger."

"I hadn't thought about that." Zachary studied his sandwich, blackberry jam and butter on brown bread, cut corner-to-corner. "I wish I could help."

Fumio finally bit into his apple, then wiped his mouth on his sleeve.

"Where's Joey?" Zachary asked.

"I don't know." Fumio frowned. "Maybe he'll be at school this afternoon."

After lunch, Miss Lassiter sketched a map of Japan on the blackboard. She pointed out the various small islands and talked about the terrain: hills, gullies, the uneven coastline.

Zachary raised his hand. Miss Lassiter nodded. "That means that, in some ways, Japan is like our island, doesn't it?" he asked.

A rude noise came from the back of the classroom.

Miss Lassiter lifted her chin, narrowed her eyes. "That is enough, Dirk. Zachary is correct. There are many similarities. It is a shame we have not been able to reach agreement based on our commonalities."

The classroom door opened. The visitor did not enter, but handed a note to Miss Lassiter. The door closed.

As she read the message, Miss Lassiter bit her lip, looking troubled. "Students," she said, "I am not surprised, but I am saddened it has come to this. The United States government has declared war on Japan. President Roosevelt has signed the Declaration. In light of this, we are instructed to dismiss students early today."

From somewhere behind him, Fumio heard a gasp, a sob. A boy to Fumio's left pumped his fist in the air. Fumio looked toward Zachary. With a small movement of his head, Zachary nodded. Fumio nodded in return.

• • •

When he reached home, Fumio propped his bicycle in its usual place under the eaves. Leaning against the porch rail was an unfamiliar green bicycle. A girls' bicycle. Fumio spoke to Flyer, "Stay, boy," and hurried into the kitchen.

Etsu Kato, Joey's older sister, sat at the table wearing heavy slacks, a practical shirt, and a gray cardigan as she clutched a mug of what, judging by the aroma, Fumio guessed was warm milk with honey. As he draped his coat on a hook, he saw that Etsu's coat hung nearby—a wool headscarf peeking out from one pocket, a pair of mittens nearly escaping the other.

"Hello, Etsu," he said. "My friends at school and I are wondering about Joey."

Etsu glanced up from beneath dark lashes. She quickly wiped her eyes with a napkin, lifted her chin, and nodded, once. Pushing back her chair, she said, "I should go, Mrs. Miyota."

"Don't hurry away, Etsu," Fumio's mother said. "Fumio has work to do. Kimiko is still napping. Perhaps you and I can talk a while longer."

Fumio went to his room. Something was wrong at the Kato house. Maybe Joey was hurt or sick. His mother would tell him after Etsu left. He took out his spelling list, found paper and a pencil, and began writing each word three times, as Miss Lassiter had suggested.

On the final repetition of his last spelling word, at the sound of the front door opening and closing, he went into the kitchen.

His mother's voice sounded strained. "Fumio, yesterday, men came to the Kato home. They said they were agents of the government, and they took Mr. Kato away. They gave no real reason but spoke of *suspicions*. There are some who believe people of Japanese heritage, even American citizens, would help Japan by plotting against the United States."

Fumio's chest felt tight. "But that doesn't make any sense!"

"It doesn't seem to, I know. Mr. Kato has no dealings with the shipyard or the naval base in Bremerton. He sells no produce to the Navy's radio operators' school." She shook her head.

"Mr. Kato is president of the Strawberry Growers. They all promised to do whatever it takes to grow even more food next year than last, just like the government asked."

"Unfortunately, it may be because he is president of the Growers Association that he was taken. Your father says some people may fear Mr. Kato will use his influence to help Japan."

How could this happen? Fumio felt swamped by disbelief. "Where did they take Joey's father? When will they let him come home?"

"Etsu said the agents gave her mother no information."

"Could it be—forever?" Fumio pulled out a chair and sat down.

"I am sure that won't be the case. The government must have a process, a plan, for bringing him and the others home."

"There are others?"

His mother nodded.

"How many? Who?"

"We don't know exactly. Today, we went to the Kato home to see how we can help. Your father is at a government office right now, trying to find out *something*." She sighed. "And he will talk with Mr. Whitlock to see if there might be someone, maybe a lawyer."

"But, Joey, you know he wasn't at school today?"

"I do, yes. Etsu said Joey insisted on staying home. He was afraid the agents would come back, and his mother would be alone, except for little Yushi, a toddler like our Kimiko."

An image came to Fumio of FBI agents faced down by a three-year-old covered in flour.

Fumio pushed back his chair. "Mother, is Father a person of influence?"

CHAPTER EIGHTEEN

FUMIO

School was out for the day. Fumio and Zachary wheeled their bicycles toward Petric's.

"What is it you have to buy," Fumio asked, "before lambing season starts?"

"Dr. Valke said, to prepare for birthing lambs, we should have a couple of halters and—"

"Halters? Why do you need halters? Aren't those for horses?"

Zachary leaned his bicycle against the store's railing. "Some kinds are for sheep. And I want a headlamp."

A headlamp? Fumio didn't ask.

The boys pushed through the door and went into the store. Mr. Petric was with a customer, but soon he asked, "How can I help you, boys?"

"I made a list," Zachary said, handing Mr. Petric a small piece of paper. "Dr. Valke says lambing season is here, now! These are the things I need to buy."

"Dr. Valke knows her business. I will send someone to the storage loft to bring down a choice of halters. You can look at the headlamps on aisle three, Zachary, near the lantern wicks and trouble lights." He turned to Fumio. "Hello, young man. Where is that smart dog of yours today? Did Flyer have commitments elsewhere?"

Fumio laughed. "No, sir, Mr. Petric. By now, Flyer is probably outside on the store's porch waiting for me."

"Why not bring him in? I am always glad to see Flyer."

Fumio went out the front door and scanned the porch, puzzled. A quiet "*Yipp*" came from beneath a bench that sat in the shade of the roof's overhang. Flyer's tail thumped on the wood of the porch as Fumio headed toward him.

"There you are, boy!" Fumio sat down on the bench.

Flyer came out to sit by Fumio's feet—panting, eyes bright, tail still thwacking against the boards. He lay his head on Fumio's knee. Fumio smiled, smoothing his fur, then scratching him behind the ears.

A voice came from across the alleyway. "Dang Jap kid and that scruffy mutt, taking up space the way they do."

Fumio's hand stilled; he did not turn toward the speaker.

"Put a lid on it," came a deeper voice. "The kid can probably hear you."

"Why should I care?" the first man asked.

Fumio caught a bitter whiff of tobacco smoke.

"Because they're a kid and a dog, minding their own business and not bothering you."

"I say their kind have no business here in the US of A. Won't bother me much longer, though. Gov'ment's kicked those squatters off Terminal Island." He laughed. "I say we send these here ones back to Japan where they come from."

"*Rrrr-Grrrr-Rrrr.*"

Now Fumio looked toward the men—one very tall, the other shorter and broadly built. Both wore gray shirts and pants, and steel-toed work boots.

From over his shoulder, Fumio heard Zachary's voice. "My friend was born here, his father and mother, too. They own a farm here. Where are you from?"

The tall man frowned. "Peddler's Creek, North Carolina. Why?"

"Curious, I guess. I've never heard of Peddler's Creek. When are you going back there?"

The other man shook his head. "None too soon, I'd say. I'm sorry, boys, and your canine friend. I must apologize for this fellow. He doesn't know local ways. He wasn't born here." He shrugged. "Step on that stoke, man," he growled.

The tall man's face reddened as he twisted his boot, grinding ashes into dirt. The two headed for the café.

Fumio stood, frowning, as he turned toward Zachary. "I was going to say something."

"I know you were. Let's just say it was my turn. C'mon back in. It's cold out here."

·   ·   ·

From the counter in the Feed and Seed store, Mr. Petric greeted Flyer, "There you are, friend, right where you belong, with Fumio! And Zachary, shall I put this on your family's account?"

"Yes, sir." From a stack on the counter, Zachary picked up a yellow book with the word *LEDGER* in large square letters on its cover. "There's nothing in it! Except page numbers!"

"Right! A book like that can make the difference between success and failure in any line of work. Keep track of to-do lists, finished jobs, supplies, costs of items purchased, what's been planted, and how big the harvest is—the weather, even. I know someone who has the date of his wife's birthday in his record book. He never forgets to buy her a box of bonbons. And she shares them with him." Mr. Petric smiled broadly. "You know, if you've got a heavy weight on your mind, you can write it down and forget about it for a while. Let the record bear the load."

Returning the ledger to the stack, Zachary nodded.

With a quick motion, Mr. Petric removed a price tag from the handle of a canvas bag with the store's name on it before dropping the purchases inside and extending it to Zachary. He leaned forward to give Flyer a biscuit and, reaching below the counter again, came up with a wrapped peppermint stick in each hand. "For our loyal customers."

"Fumio, I don't think we have tools for punching holes in leather. If we do, I don't know where they are."

"I know where our tools are. We can punch the holes right away."

"That'd be good. Thanks."

After stopping to let Mrs. Whitlock know where Zachary would be, they rode over to Mr. Miyota's shop.

"Fumio," his father said, "there is enough daylight left for you to go to your ojiisan's tool room and use his leather punch and a mallet, if you wish." Mr. Miyota took a key from a hook and handed it to Fumio. "Bring back the key when you finish."

"Yes, thank you, Father."

Past the house and toward the building behind it, Fumio led the way and Zachary followed, Flyer padding along.

"Zachary, you've never been inside my ojiisan's tool room, have you?"

"No, I haven't. When I was really young, I wouldn't have understood how the tools were used. And then, your grandfather became ill. Fumio, I— my family—we miss your grandfather. Here, in his shop, you have kept all his tools?"

Fumio nodded. "I come out here and sweep, sometimes." He inserted the key into the lock, slipped the hook from the hasp, and the door swung inward. "Flyer, stay!" he called, and then stepped inside the dim space. Floorboards shifted and groaned. The sun's rays beamed from the low angle of a winter afternoon. Before long, Fumio's eyes adjusted. He beckoned to Zachary. "Come on. You can see okay once you're in."

One foot inside the door, Zachary paused. "Boy, oh, boy! This is the tidiest place I have ever seen. It outdoes Mother's kitchen. In fact, this outdoes the library."

Fumio watched as Zachary studied the contents of the room: carefully arranged tools; sealed containers of paint and wood stain; neatly stacked lengths of beautiful, unique wood.

A pair of worn work gloves lay on a shelf near a window. Fumio stepped closer. *Ojiisan's gloves.* He pressed his palm against the leather, measuring his own hand span against his grandfather's.

Studying a collection of blades with unusual handles, Zachary asked, "Are these carving tools? They look really old."

Fumio nodded. "Ojiisan learned to carve when he was a boy. He brought these from Japan. The handles are shaped to be held at certain angles. And the blades, to cut different types of grooves. The box on the table in our living room—the one with a mountain scene carved on its top—Ojiisan made that for my mother."

Zachary pointed to a small notebook laying on a workbench, along with a pencil and a penknife. "He made notes and records like your father does, Fumio."

"Ojiisan wrote down everything. When the first strawberries ripened, and were harvested. The number of chickens in our flock in June and December. Which trees on the property were taken down, and when ..." He went silent. The next strawberry harvest would be the first the Miyota family had experienced without Ojiisan's presence.

After Grandfather Miyota's memorial, neighbors spoke of his great understanding of machinery and construction, and they spoke of his compassion. If he learned a neighbor's home was falling into disrepair due to hardship, he might drop by claiming great thirst, but soon he would be busy repairing broken pipes or shoring up sagging steps. People praised his work at the mill and, later, as maintenance mechanic at the strawberry cannery. They described his skill and determination in building the Miyota home, as well as the barn and outbuildings.

Fumio found the leather punch. Moving to a place near a window, he showed Zachary how to use the punch, then watched silently as Zachary made the needed holes in the halters and the strap of the headlamp. When the job was done, Zachary examined his work and smiled. Fumio put the punch away.

Outside the door, in a patch of fading sunlight, Flyer danced. Eyes up, he peered toward a troupe of cobwebs fluttering on the door frame, pine needles and a small feather caught within their clasp. "Good job, Flyer," Fumio said before getting the broom and sweeping the frame.

Taking one last look at Grandfather's shop, Fumio stepped out into full sunlight and locked the door. Flyer came close and softly bumped the side of his leg. With an easy move of his knee, Fumio bumped him back.

CHAPTER NINETEEN

FUMIO

Fumio sat, homework propped on his knees, pencil in hand, near the top of the stairway that led to the second floor of the Whitlock house. Zachary sat three steps below him. Mr. Harvey had stopped in to drop off a pie his wife made and was talking with Mrs. and Mrs. Whitlock.

"Mrs. Whitlock, ma'am," Mr. Harvey said, "could I trouble you for a mite of sugar?"

"Certainly," Zachary's mother answered. Fumio heard footsteps, the opening and closing of a cabinet door, and the clinking of spoons against cups. "Is the coffee bitter?"

"No, ma'am," Mr. Harvey answered. "It isn't bitter. But my attitude might be."

"Your attitude? What has happened?" Zachary's father asked.

"They're at it again. Men in black suits and black fedoras, driving big black autos with government plates. Got deputy sheriffs with them. The FBI—again—on official business."

Fumio shifted, ready to move elsewhere. He knew it was not his place to listen if adult matters were discussed when his presence was unknown. *Eavesdropping.*

But Zachary put his hand on Fumio's arm and whispered, "He is leaving in a minute. If he realizes we're here now, he'll just be embarrassed."

Fumio set his pencil down. The smell of coffee drifted upward. Zachary angled forward so extremely that he looked like he might tumble down the steps.

"It gets my dander up," Mr. Harvey said. "Random searches of homes. Folks who've done nothing wrong."

"So they're still looking for contraband," Mr. Whitlock said. "I was relieved that they did not disturb the Miyota farm the last time the agents raid—*umm*, the last time they made an *appearance* here. And now agents are at it again?"

"Yup," Mr. Harvey answered. "As we speak, FBI agents and sheriff's deputies are dropping in, uninvited, at various island locations. Can someone tell me, please, what's the sense of it? Cameras? What can they photograph that's not in plain sight? The Winslow Shipyard? Hundreds of people work there. You couldn't miss it if you wanted to! And maps are contraband? Maps are a dime a dozen at any gas station!"

Mrs. Whitlock sighed. "Anything with connection to Japan is suspect. I know people who burned photographs and old letters from relatives to avoid being charged with espionage. Some risked keeping items only to have them later confiscated by the FBI. Government agents stealing family history."

Zachary glanced toward Fumio. "So, that's why your family photograph albums are in our attic," he whispered.

Fumio frowned. "They are? Nobody told me that." A chill rattled his spine.

"Nobody told me, either, but I saw them when I went up to find a carton of Mother's knitting charts."

"I've read in reports," Mr. Whitlock said, "that the FBI has taken farm tools needed for clearing brush, things like axes and machetes."

"And dynamite!" Mr. Harvey's voice rose. "Men have ended up in detention camps because TNT was found on their places. It was the government that gave 'em the TNT, encouraged farmers to use it blowing up giant stumps so they could haul 'em off the land!"

Zachary's eyes widened. "TNT is dynamite!" he whispered. "That was written on a wooden box in your grandfather's toolroom! Dynamite! In your grandfather's toolroom!"

Fumio felt his mouth drop open, but words would not come. His breathing stopped.

Zachary pushed off the stairs and clattered downward.

Gasping for air, Fumio followed.

"Father! Mother!" Zachary burst out. "There is dynamite! At Fumio's! Dynamite!"

"Oh, Fumio! I didn't mean to—" Mr. Harvey stood up quickly.

"Dynamite at the Miyota house?" Mrs. Whitlock protested. "No! Certainly not!"

"Not in their house. In Grandfather Miyota's toolroom."

"How do you know this?" Zachary's father asked. "You must be mistaken."

"No, Father. I saw a wooden crate with a label that read TNT. But I—"

His father interrupted. "Maybe it is just a box. Maybe it once held dynamite, but is empty now." He paused. "Even so—" He shook his head. "When did you see this, Son?"

"When we punched holes in the straps for the sheep halters. I didn't think anything about it then, but—"

"Stop!" Mr. Whitlock raised his hand, palm out. "We don't have time! If dynamite is in there, Fumio's father could be—"

"Don't, Robert!" Mrs. Whitlock spoke quietly, but with urgency.

"Right." Mr. Whitlock cleared his throat. "If dynamite is found there, Mr. Miyota would be very displeased," he said. "Boys, get ready to go!"

"I'd better come along!" Mr. Harvey went for his coat.

"Thank you, Mr. Harvey, but that shouldn't be necessary. It's just one crate of dynamite." Mr. Whitlock's laugh sounded ragged.

"My friend," Mr. Harvey's voice had quieted, "I know you're up to the job. But someone needs to get that dynamite off the property now. And you," he jerked his head toward Zachary, "do not want it on *your* property. I know a place. I'll take care of it."

Mr. Harvey carried his cup to the sink, then headed outside.

Fumio bounded up the stairs, pausing for his pencil and homework and, in Zachary's room, grabbing his schoolbag and dropping them into it. Back in the kitchen, he and Zachary waited, their coats zipped. Fumio shifted from foot to foot.

Mr. Whitlock emerged from his study, waving a ring of keys and calling, "Found them!" Buttoning his coat, he stopped and turned to Mrs. Whitlock, a troubled expression on his face. "What if we are too late?"

"Do what you can do." She put a hand on his shoulder, "But, Robert, the agents may be there already. You need a reason to go there." She turned to the counter, pulled a clean towel from the stack and wrapped the pie. "Here, take this with you. I think the Miyota family may be in need of a rhubarb pie."

She walked to the door and held it open as Mr. Whitlock, Fumio, and Zachary went out.

"Flyer, come with me!" Fumio called.

They made their way down the lane to the Miyota home, the Whitlock truck in front, Fumio and Zachary standing in the bed, looking ahead over the roof of the cab, Flyer watching out the back. Mr. Harvey followed in his GMC.

In the Miyota farmyard, Mr. Whitlock jumped out of the truck. "Boys, come with me!" He strode toward the house. Fumio, Flyer, and Zachary leaped down and followed.

Mr. Harvey maneuvered his truck into a nose-out position, climbed down and stood at the back of its box to wait.

Mrs. Miyota came onto the porch pushing her arms into a cardigan, Kimiko trailing behind, clutching her mother's skirt. She lifted her hand in greeting toward Mr. Harvey. Fumio saw the lines of worry on her face and knew she understood something was wrong.

Mr. Whitlock stepped up to the porch. "I am sorry for the disruption, Mrs. Miyota, but where is Yasuo, please?"

"He is in the barn, working on a tractor," she answered. Then, "Fumio, has something happened? Are you all right, Son?"

"I am all right, Mother." Fumio stepped closer, lowering his voice. "I think you should keep Kimiko close by, while we," he swallowed, "while we look into something. I'll come talk to you soon, I promise."

Mr. Miyota came through the door of the barn. "Is there trouble, Robert?"

"There might be." Zachary's father plowed his fingers through his hair. "FBI agents and deputy sheriffs are combing Bainbridge Island."

"Again? Today?"

"Yes, today!" came the reply. "We have to move fast!" Mr. Whitlock turned. "Zachary, Fumio, let's get this done!"

Mr. Whitlock sprinted to the small shop behind the house and turned. "May I enter this building, please?"

"It's kept locked," Mr. Miyota answered. "Fumio, you know where the key is!"

Fumio ran to his father's shop, returned with the key, and opened the door.

Stepping inside, Mr. Whitlock asked, "Zachary, where is the crate?"

"In the corner, Father. Under the tarp."

Mr. Whitlock lifted the corner of the tarp and stepped back. "We have to get this out of here now."

"Dynamite. How?" Mr. Miyota whispered.

"You knew the government gave dynamite to landholders," Mr. Whitlock said. "In fact, there, on the crate, is the official stamp."

"Yes. I assumed my father had gotten rid of it. He often spoke of wanting one more strawberry field, but I thought I had convinced him. No more stump-blasting."

"I'm sorry," Mr. Whitlock said, "but the agents could be here at any moment."

Fumio's father sighed. "And they will not accept my explanation."

"They have jailed men, accusing them of attempted espionage, for possession of explosives such as these." Mr. Whitlock grasped a corner of the tarp.

"Wait!" Mr. Miyota's voice rang out. "Stop! Dynamite becomes unstable with age. Even though I was young, I heard the words of those who used it. They turned the dynamite every year, without fail. Lives depended on it." He stepped closer to the crate. "Look. Under the stamp, my father's writing. Dates noted in builder's crayon. Each one is about a year after the one before. Those must be the dates when my father turned the dynamite." He paused. "Yes, he turned it this past April."

"Your father was a dependable man, Yasuo."

Mr. Miyota fixed his gaze on the two boys. "Dynamite is dangerous. You must treat it as if it were a coiled snake. Do you understand?"

"And," Mr. Whitlock spoke firmly, "when you see something dangerous sitting about, you must always tell an adult. Never assume they know. Understand?"

"Yes, sir," both boys spoke at once.

"Fumio, can you please drag that axe to Mr. Harvey's truck?" Mr. Miyota asked, gesturing toward the out-sized implement, its iron head topping a wooden handle that appeared to Fumio as big as a tree trunk.

"Better give Fumio a hand, Zachary. And don't just heave it into the back and let it drop," Mr. Whitlock said. "Take it easy."

"Then you boys go sit on the porch," Mr. Miyota added.

"Yes, Father," Fumio answered. "But shall I lock the door first?"

Fumio saw his father hesitate. "No, Son. Our footprints are plain here. Rather than ask for the key, the agents might force the lock."

Moving slowly, Mr. Miyota and Mr. Whitlock carried the crate of dynamite toward the waiting truck.

Mr. Harvey climbed up into the box and helped settle the crate on the truck bed, then arranged the tarp to cover it. Back in the driver's seat, Mr. Harvey started the engine and drove out of the yard, waving as he pulled onto the lane.

Carrying the rhubarb pie, Mr. Whitlock walked with Mr. Miyota to the house.

In the kitchen, he placed the pie on the counter and turned. "Let's try to see your home as an FBI agent might see it. Your rabbit rifle is no longer on the premises." He nodded toward Mr. Miyota. "We took the axe out of

Mr. Miyota-san's shop. It's perhaps too large to be allowed as an ordinary farm tool."

From the living room came Zachary's voice. "Excuse me, do you think this might draw attention?" In the living room on the small table sat Grandfather Miyota's gift, the hinged wooden box, open to display the interior. Framed inside the lid, Fumio knew, was his mother's name calligraphed in the Japanese art of shodo.

The box held items needed to practice Asian calligraphy, wooden-handled brushes, slender dark sticks of ink, a stone to grind the ink, and narrow sheets of mulberry paper.

"Ohhh," Mrs. Miyota sighed, laying a hand over her heart. "Those are the tools my aunt used to record important events in the lives of our family in Japan, and to create poetry. My brother, Daishin, sent them to me, and Fumio's ojiisan made the box for their safekeeping." She clasped her hands. "Those are not weapons; they are not maps or coded instructions."

"The agents will not know *what* they are," Mr. Miyota said. "Sachiko, do you want to take the chance?"

She shook her head.

Mr. Miyota pulled a woolen afghan from the couch, wrapped the box, and handed it to Mr. Whitlock. "Will you please take this to your home?"

"Certainly. Zachary, please take this to the truck. Wait for me there."

As Zachary went out the door, Fumio studied the Miyota living room. The tabletop looked oddly deserted. Then, his father pulled a thick book, titled in bold Japanese characters, from the bookcase's bottom shelf and laid it on the table. It was, Fumio knew, a book of recipes sent as a gift, years ago by their relatives in Japan.

In the kitchen once more, Mr. Whitlock spoke to Mrs. Miyota. "Doris sends her regards. She asked me to bring you this pie." He gestured toward the counter.

Fumio's mother turned back a corner of the toweling, ready to express her thanks. A tiny smile blossomed on her face, before she could prevent it, when she saw the pie was already cut. A piece was missing.

"We came to that decision rather suddenly," Mr. Whitlock said, his tone apologetic.

• • •

From the porch, Flyer barked twice.

Fumio followed his father and Mr. Whitlock outside. A black automobile, shiny under a mottled coat of road dirt, came to a stop in front of the Miyota house. Its doors opened. Three men got out, brushing dust from their suit jackets, straightening their ties, adjusting the position of their dark, wide-brimmed fedoras. A low rumble began in Flyer's throat.

Mr. Whitlock reached out then and shook Mr. Miyota's hand, loudly declaring, "Sorry we cannot stay. We've got to check on the sheep. Glad you can use that extra pie. Mrs. Whitlock hates to let a pie sit. We thought—" He cleared his throat. "Looks like you have company."

From the truck, Zachary waved. Fumio returned the gesture, barely lifting his hand.

Flyer growled as the three men walked toward the porch.

One man was broad-shouldered and thick-necked. Another man was very tall. The third man, after exiting the vehicle, paused to straighten his hat. It struck Fumio that his sharp nose and chin would be interesting to sketch. The agent appeared to take in the construction of the house, the number of outbuildings, and the layout of the fields.

"No, Flyer. Forbearance," Fumio urged quietly, his fingers spread atop Flyer's head. "*Shh-shush.* Be still." He could feel the muscles, taut, in Flyer's neck, but the growling ceased.

Fumio had seen drawings of FBI agents—they were called *G-men* in comic books some of his classmates brought to school—and the men who now stood in front of his home, all in dark suits, dressed the part.

Mr. Miyota went to meet them. "What can we do for you, gentlemen?"

"Federal agents!" the stout agent replied, giving each word a great deal of weight, as though heavy stones were being dropped into shallow water. "We are here to search your house and the entire premises for contraband."

Mr. Miyota leveled his gaze. "What sort of thing might we have here that federal agents would consider contraband?"

"Cameras, short-wave radios, maps, charts, or other tools of espionage," the agent began. "Flashlights, searchlights, lanterns, weapons, ammunition, explosives . . ." As his recital dwindled, the agent raised an eyebrow.

Fumio's father stepped to the side of the door. "I see. Please, come in."

Telling Flyer to *stay*, Fumio hurried inside ahead of the men and went to stand beside his mother, where she sat in a chair near the kitchen table, holding Kimiko. They watched as the agents entered the house.

The tall man stepped through the door first, removing his hat and wiping his shoes on the mat. His face had reddened, Fumio noticed, and he kept his eyes lowered as he went through the kitchen toward the living room.

Not pausing on the mat, the sturdy man with the harsh voice was next to come through the kitchen. Fumio moved to stand in front of the sink and watched the too-small hat bounce atop the agent's head as he strode toward the room that had been Ojiisan's.

The third man entered slowly, his eyes sweeping from side to side and up to the ceiling, where glass-shaded lights hung on thick cords, then down at the floor mat and the scrupulously clean floors. He looked toward Mrs. Miyota. "Ma'am?"

Fumio edged back near his mother. She responded, "How may I help you?"

"I apologize for disturbing your home, ma'am."

Mrs. Miyota nodded.

The man carefully wiped his shoes on the mat, removed his hat, and headed for what he would soon see was Fumio's bedroom.

Fumio's father followed the third agent through the door and came into the kitchen. He lifted Kimiko and carried her to the living room behind Mrs. Miyota, who sat down on the couch. Once Mr. Miyota had placed his daughter on her mother's lap again, he and Fumio began moving from doorway to doorway, as the men searched each room of their home.

The three agents were not destructive. They often asked before pulling out drawers and opening doors, but Fumio felt certain that they would have done so, with or without permission.

When the men had nearly run the gamut of the contents of the house, the tall agent came to a stop in front of the small table in the living room and lightly touched one beautifully carved leg, "Nice piece of furniture," he said, and picked up the bulky old book Fumio's father had placed there just half an hour earlier. "Let's just have a look."

He studied the Japanese characters on the cover. "We're going to have to take this," he said and carried it out to the black automobile. The other agents followed.

With the three strangers out of the house, Fumio sat on the porch and Flyer came to sit at attention by his side. Together, they watched as the agents investigated each of the outbuildings. The loud, sturdy man entered the chicken yard and ventured through the door of the coop. A moment later, he quick-stepped out, chased by the rooster.

Fumio held in a laugh as Mr. Miyota hurried to shoo the rooster back into the enclosure and close the gate, and he had no doubt his father was chuckling.

"Whooph!"

Next, Mr. Miyota and the agents moved around to the back of the house. Fumio and Flyer waited on the porch. When he could stand the waiting—and the worry—no longer, Fumio spoke, "Come, Flyer," and went inside to stand at the window with a view of the backyard, where Mr. Miyota and the federal agents approached the old toolroom. An ache pulsed behind Fumio's eyes. But, a minute or two later, the men came out, closed the door, and walked to stand next to their car, where, it appeared, they compared notes.

Soon, the agents got back into the big black automobile. The setting sun illuminated its departure as the sound of it faded into the distance.

CHAPTER TWENTY

FUMIO

Notices were posted on Tuesday, March 24. Fumio watched from the school yard as a uniformed man nailed one to a pole. Executive Order 9066 stated that persons of Japanese heritage must leave West Coast Prohibited Zones, beginning immediately. Japanese American families on Bainbridge Island had six days to prepare.

Fumio found his mother in the kitchen, surrounded by boxes. While Kimiko watched, Mrs. Miyota wrapped drinking glasses and bowls with pages of the *Bainbridge Island Review*.

She shook her head, sighed, and reached toward him. He went to her, and for a moment, she held him tight. "Fumio, you're a fine, brave boy." She pulled away just enough to meet his eyes. "We will be all right"

"Of course we will. Mother, what can I do to help?"

"Three shirts, three pairs of pants, six sets of underwear. School shoes, work shoes, rain boots, and your winter coat. Let's see, what else?"

"My drawing paper, my pencils, erasers, and sharpener—oh, and my baseball mitt."

"Yes, Fumio. Gather those things on top of your bed and then go see what you can do for your father. We have the strawberry crop to think of, and the chickens, and . . ."

CHAPTER TWENTY-ONE

FLYER

I am waiting here for Fumio.

"Stay," he told me. "Stay, boy!"

I don't want to stay. I should be with Fumio. But this morning, I look down a slope to see him with his parents and little sister among a crowd gathered near a dock. A white ferryboat sits on the water nearby.

From so far away, looking after my family is hard work—too many people to watch all at once, too many feet and knees, too many scents. Stacks of cartons tied with twine. Babies held close, babies with runny noses, babies crying, babies hiccupping. Mothers call out children's names. People bump into each other. "Excuse me, Makiko-san." "Forgive me, Arika-san."

Trucks in a long line carry neighbors in the back where grown-ups do not usually ride. From one truck box, a woman hands a suitcase to a young girl. A man stands near, his arms around a bulky cloth sack.

I see and hear strangers everywhere. Many men wear pants and shirts all alike. Their heavy boots are laced up tall. On their heads are shiny hats like upside-down food bowls. And they carry guns, rifles with long, sharp knives.

I know about guns. They are for hunting rabbits. Fumio says never fire a gun at a person. Or a dog. People are all around and some dogs, too. Rabbits would never be here. So why do those men bring guns?

I wish we could go home to our farm, but Fumio says he has a job to do.

Fumio holds a bundle under one arm and carries a big metal suitcase in his other hand. If I stood beside him, he could lay the bundle down. I would guard it for him.

On the bundle and the case are stiff paper tags. One hangs from Fumio's shirt collar, too, like the tags on burlap bags at Petric's Feed and Seed. Fumio reaches up to pull on it. It doesn't come off. I don't know what it is, but I think he doesn't like it.

His mouth is tight. His eyes are shadowed. He looks sad. When Fumio feels sad, I do, too. If I were closer, I could lean against his side. He would reach down and pat my neck, and we would both feel happier.

I tug hard on the leash attached to my collar. Zachary holds it steady.

But, *no!* I need to go to Fumio *now!* I have a job to do, too!

Then, I remember. Fumio said, "Stay."

My job is to stay. He looks toward me. He does not call me.

His father, mother, and little sister walk toward the dock with its wide, wooden planks.

Fumio turns away from me. He walks, too. He slows, stops. Over his shoulder, he looks back. His hands and arms are full. He cannot wave. He jerks his chin upward, once. Goodbye.

Then Fumio disappears into the crowd, behind men who are strangers, carrying guns where there are no rabbits.

And the leash holds me tight.

CHAPTER TWENTY-TWO

FUMIO

Fumio, his parents, and Kimiko walked from the dock past a placard bearing the words "Restricted: Japanese Only" and boarded The Kehloken, a ferryboat that, according to his father, was chartered by the government from the Black Ball Line for this purpose.

Fumio stowed his burdens, sank onto a bench, and surrendered to the hum of the boat's engines and the lift and fall of the oil-stained waters upon which it idled. He scanned the crowd, waved at Joey, who sat between his little brother, Yushi, and his older sister, Etsu, then watched the practiced movements of the crew on the dock as they made ready to cast off.

Kimiko pressed her nose to a window, giggling. "Mama, a sea girl!" she cried, pointing, and Fumio followed the motion with his eyes. A seagull.

"She is a very pretty bird, isn't she?" Mrs. Miyota said. His mother held her purse tight against her midsection. Fumio thought of the many lists she had made as she prepared for this day, how those lists had expanded, then been rewritten, shorter. While his father made arrangements for the many possessions the family would leave behind, Fumio's mother had considered, from every angle, what little they could take with them.

The ferry's engines increased in volume and the journey began. The boat's towering wheelhouse was in its middle, and it had portals at each end that served as both entrances and exits. Capable of arriving at the dock and leaving again with no need to turn around, the ferry was always, Fumio thought, coming and going at the same time.

The Kehloken picked up speed. A child, two front teeth missing, whooped and laughed when the boat began rocking, tossed by turbulence as it crossed the wake of another vessel.

Fumio watched the ocean's rise and fall, its constant surging toward the shore. He saw the islands of Puget Sound passing by.

Reaching Seattle, the ferry nosed in at Colman Dock, as the sign read, and the Bainbridge Island neighbors were hurried—or *herded like Zachary's sheep*, as it seemed to Fumio—down a gangway. Fumio's parents had planned to stay near the Kato family, to be of help to Mrs. Kato in her husband's absence. The demands of the guards, though, kept them at a distance.

Swept along, Fumio and his family exited the ferry. Toting baskets, boxes, and bundles, they quickly paced a narrow walkway through a mass of spectators, some of whom watched from a second-story gallery and waved.

But at street level, one white-haired bystander wiped his eyes with his sleeve, and others, as if uncomfortable, shifted from foot to foot, hands in pockets. On parade: Fumio and his neighbors wearing their best clothing, forced from their homes, shock on their faces.

Fumio remembered a kind of dodgeball called The Gauntlet, taught during recess by boys who had learned it at Scout camp. It was a rowdy game, and Fumio did not care for it. One team was declared "It," while members of the other team faced each other in two rows. The "It" team ran down the middle while balls were launched at them. In such close quarters, where was the challenge? Still, the other boys had joined in, and he had not wanted to be called a scaredy-cat. The game bored him, and Fumio had felt—*trapped*.

As his family trudged toward the train station, Fumio thought that his father, who shouldered a large carton and lugged a steamer trunk as he moved along the walkway, pressed in upon by onlookers, must have felt the same way.

And his mother, weighed down by a bundle of bedclothes and kitchen linens while holding the hand of his little sister, who clutched a furoshiki knotted around the one doll and the doll clothes she could bring.

On his left shoulder, Fumio bore the weight of his duffel bag, as well as a canvas bag filled with Kimiko's bedding. In his left hand, he gripped a rattling basket packed with cookware and dishes. In his right, he grasped the leather-covered handle of their large metal suitcase. The oppression he felt, however, was not because of his burdens, rather, the gaze of men in uniforms writing in black notebooks.

On the train platform, soldiers in khaki stood at attention, rifles vertical, bayonets fixed. Fumio and his family were prodded with sharp words. "Move along. Keep going! We have a schedule, you know."

No, Fumio thought, *he did not know*. He knew nothing about a schedule or how long they would travel, no hint where they were being taken.

Once in the train car, Fumio shoved the two bags into an overhead storage compartment, slid the metal suitcase—which barely fit—under the seat, and placed the basket between his feet to hold it upright. Here, he hoped, his family would finally gain some privacy. At least, he thought, they would be in the company of neighbors. His mood lifted. But, then, the echoed stomping of heavy boots came from the entrance, and soldiers trooped into the car, their weapons banging against the metal door frame and bumping into the curved ceiling. One soldier snarled at another, "Walk on your *own* feet, will ya?"

Eventually, just two soldiers remained in the car. As the train began to move, they assumed their duties as guards and, struggling to manage their bayonets, moved from row to row, leaning across seats and closing window shades. Gloom overtook the car's interior.

When the soldiers were finally seated and the commotion had settled, Fumio heard babies crying and mothers murmuring to soothe them. He heard the rise and fall of the train's noise. And he became aware of the smell. A bitter odor and the tang of dust filled his nose and mouth.

Had the Katos been loaded into a car as down-at-the-heels as this one, Fumio wondered? For his friends' sake, he hoped not. The fabric that covered the cushioned seats and backs had split, and stuffing poked through.

Kimiko's eyes drifted closed. Fumio took off his jacket, folded it, and handed it to his mother, who tucked it beneath his sister's head. Then he leaned back, feeling himself pulled, against his will, into sleep.

OWENS VALLEY RECEPTION CENTER,
CALIFORNIA, APRIL 1, 1942

CHAPTER TWENTY-THREE

FUMIO

He had endured three days of uncomfortable, dusty travel, and Fumio longed for his mother's good food, his family's bathtub, and his bed. Now, leaving the train, he was glad to see only a few cars were parked near the depot, and no crowd awaited the train's arrival.

Photographers holding large cameras had positioned themselves at inconspicuous vantage points and, soon, Fumio became aware of the rattle of shutters working: Pop-pop! Pop-op-op!

Who were the pictures for? Would his classmates see him in the *Review*, loaded down with bags and bundles of household items? He didn't know what to feel. Embarrassed?

A sign on the depot declared "Lone Pine Railroad Station—Lone Pine, California." This was not, he knew, the final destination, "Almost there!" shouted a man standing near the folding door as he hurried them onto an old-model commercial tour bus. "Next stop, Owens Valley Reception Center. Almost there!"

Almost where? Fumio wondered, settling into another uncomfortable seat. Owens Valley? Somewhere in California. He had learned about California in fifth grade geography, but he was not prepared for the dry, brown landscape stretching from the highway to the horizon. The pictures in their textbooks were nothing like this. He had seen pictures of palm trees, beaches, and a huge sign perched high on a cliff that said, "Hollywood."

People and possessions were jostled as the bus, leaving the highway, encountered rutted roads. A field of white tents came into view, along with military transport jeeps, then rows of box-shaped buildings, long and low, with shallow roofs.

The bus slowed and came to a stop, the engine still idling. The driver opened the doors and spoke to a man in uniform who carried yet another clipboard, then closed the doors again, released the brake, and pulled forward. Gears grumbled and brakes squealed. "Owens Valley Reception Center! This is it! Everybody out!" the driver called. "Check overhead and under the seats. Don't be leaving anything on this bus, 'cause you won't be seeing *me* around here again."

With groans and a few yelps, passengers unbent their stiff, aching limbs, dislodged themselves, and scrambled for their baggage.

Fumio's feet tingled as he reached for his duffel bag and the bedding-filled canvas bag, then pulled the big metal suitcase from under the seat. Mrs. Miyota, a bundle of household linens tucked under an arm, grasped the large basket in one hand, and took Kimiko's hand in her other.

When a break occurred in the line of passengers, Fumio's father stepped into the aisle, descended the steps first and turned to lift little Kimiko from her mother's arms. Then he went to retrieve the large carton and steamer trunk from the belly of the bus.

The door of the old bus was hinged in the middle and folded back upon itself. Fumio stood with his shoulder against it, straining to grasp Kimiko's bag as well as his own load. He could not see his feet and hoped he might, by luck, find that first step down. He held his breath—left, right, left—exhaling noisily when, at last, he sensed solid earth, then saw in the dirt, a mosaic of footprints from those who had descended the steps before him.

He lifted his eyes and flinched. The sun shone from a cloudless sky. His vision adjusting, he saw in the distance a jagged line of massive stone peaks, their flanks softened by ragged tufts of plant life. Sagebrush. All cowboy movies featured sagebrush. And here it was, for real.

In front of the mountains, bare stone shapes—rounded like boulders, but big as ships—clustered in random groupings. Shading his eyes with his hand, Fumio tilted his head back.

"The Alabama Hills," came a gravelly voice. The bus driver had climbed from behind the steering wheel. He motioned with his head. "And over there's the Sierra Nevada. Don't you know where you are, boy? Tom Mix, Gene Autry, Roy Rogers—all the great cowboys—they make movies here."

Fumio could only stare at the man, open-mouthed.

"Yeah, Lee Powell, too. He'd be The Lone Ranger to you. I sat next to him at a lunch counter last week. The man's an American hero. You'll never meet him." He mounted the bus steps, then turned back. "But it is what it is." He nodded toward the Assembly Center's entrance and the knots of people milling about, waiting to be processed. "Sorry, kid."

• • •

Four hours later, the Miyotas still waited, along with other families grouped randomly in front of a wooden building bearing a sign that read "Owens Valley Reception Center Registration Office." Military guards carrying rifles with bayonets stood on either side of the office door. Soldiers working in pairs beckoned forward one family at a time for a search of their possessions.

Beyond the registration office stood rows of rectangular buildings, walls and roofs covered in tar paper tacked down with narrow strips of unpainted wood. Hundreds more were under construction. Carpenters swarmed the area.

Shifting from one foot to the other and always holding on to his sister—her hand, sleeve, even the back of her collar—Fumio waited. Occasionally, he nudged forward the trunk, his duffel, and Kimiko's canvas bag as families inched along.

Kimiko cradled Trixie Jean in her arms, using one small hand to shade the doll's eyes.

After studying her daughter's reddening face, Mrs. Miyota pulled a wide-brimmed hat from Kimiko's bag and secured it on the little girl's head.

Near the Registration Office, Fumio saw a group of three people being processed for entrance by two uniformed men. One soldier stood guard, a bayoneted rifle upright at his side, as the other soldier, who, by the roundness of his face appeared younger, checked each person's tag, matching numbers to the information he had on a form. He went through their bags and boxes, also tagged, searching, Mr. Miyota said, for what was considered contraband.

The younger soldier often stopped writing and peered about as if looking for someone until the other soldier called him back to his task. Nevertheless, in time, the family of three received their block and barracks numbers and were waved on.

The Miyotas gathered their possessions, ready to move forward. Just then, a plume of dust signaled an approaching vehicle. Its engine sputtered as it was shut down. A man, his shirt emblazoned with, as Fumio had learned in the past few days, sergeant's stripes, climbed from behind the wheel and moved toward the two soldiers flanking the office door. They saluted, he returned the gesture, then stepped to the side of the younger soldier and spoke quietly.

"You can't mean that!" the young soldier burst out. "He was s'posed to've taken over this post a *long while* back! It's hotter'n *blazes* out here. I wanna *talk* to that piker!"

"Would you prefer he showed up here and puked on your boots, Private?" the sergeant retorted. "Or are you going to stay here and do your duty?"

"Nah," came the sullen reply. "I mean, *No, sir*! I mean, *Yes, sir,* Sergeant!" He saluted again. The sergeant turned and walked backed to the vehicle.

The older soldier muttered, shaking his head.

"Can it, Dub!" the young private snapped, scorching the older man with a look of fury before turning to the Miyotas, taking their registration papers, and checking the numbers against the tags they wore. He started going through the steamer trunk, and after directing Mr. Miyota to loosen the knots of the twine holding it closed, the large carton.

Next, he searched the bundle of bed linens and towels, casually dropping two pillowcases in the dirt, then snatching them up and tossing them back in the bundle.

Kimiko managed the small canvas bag as best a three-year-old could. The private noted the doll she held close. "Got yourself a baby doll, huh? So, what name's she go by?"

"Her name is Trixie Jean," Kimiko replied quietly.

"That don't sound like a Jap name," he said.

Fumio pulled his sister closer. Mrs. Miyota took Trixie Jean from Kimiko's arms and gently tucked the doll into the basket. The soldier gave little attention to the canvas bag's few, neatly folded articles of bedding.

Finally, the private addressed Fumio's duffel bag, reaching inside, and pulling out a dozen or so sheets of Fumio's drawing paper. "Whoops," he intoned, opening his hand and releasing them into the unceasing wind, watching as they skittered about.

Fumio caught one sheet in the air, stepped on the edge of another and picked it up. His mother reached forward, took them from him, and slipped them into her purse while Fumio, once more, took Kimiko's hand.

Wearing an unpleasant smile, the soldier pulled from the duffel a clean white handkerchief in which Fumio had wrapped three TrueLine writing pencils. Two were nearly new, one was merely a stub with a worn-down pink eraser. In the small bundle, also, were Fumio's much-prized drawing pencil and the kneadable eraser Jacob had given him. The young private loosened a corner of the handkerchief and the stubby yellow pencil fell back into the duffel. Then, smirking, he flicked his wrist and snapped the handkerchief *hard*.

As Fumio watched, the newest of the TrueLines, his drawing pencil, and the eraser hit the ground, bounced, and ricocheted out of sight.

"Stop tha—!" his father began but snuffed the demand. These were pencils, after all. Fumio understood this was not the time, nor was there sufficient reason, for conflict.

The soldier plunged his hand into the duffel again and rummaged through its contents. He held up a schoolbook, Fumio's fifth-grade arithmetic text, then shoved it back, deep into the bag.

At the bottom of the duffel, the soldier's fingers must have closed on the soft disarray of Suzey Belle's hair. His fist jerked upward, and he yowled. The doll whipped into the air and one little shoe flew off.

Kimiko cried out at the sight of Suzey Belle. When the shoe struck the ground not far from the young soldier's feet, the three-year-old burst free of Fumio's hold, her hands outstretched.

At the charge of the tiny tot, the soldier spat, "Stay back!" Kimiko surged onward, but Fumio lunged for her, caught the hem of her dress, and drew her near.

His mother rushed forward and pulled both her children into her encircling arms. Fumio's father stepped up beside her, reached down, and lifted the sobbing Kimiko.

Maybe it was unusual for a ten-year-old boy to carry a doll in his duffel bag, but his sister had been sad to leave one of her beloved dolls behind and the remedy was simple. He retrieved the second doll, buried his baseball mitt in the carton bound for the Whitlock attic, and tucked the doll into his bag where his mitt had been.

Fumio's eyes shifted to the ground. He caught sight of one of his pencils and took a half-step toward it.

"That's far enough," the private snarled. "This *is* your bag, boy?"

All that Fumio had been taught by his parents and grandfather came to mind. *Do not boldly meet the eyes of your elders. Do not speak except to answer a question or obey a command.* Fumio nodded, his gaze landing slightly to the side of the man's face.

"Look at me, kid!" the soldier barked. "Do you expect me to believe a boy your age would bring a doll to this rodeo?" He turned to the other soldier. "That don't seem right, does it, Dub? What do you think about that?"

"I don't know, Stanley. I guess I had a doll when I was—" He bit off the words, shrugged again.

"You don't say." The private laughed. "A doll, huh? Well, okay, maybe you did. But in this *particular* situation, I gotta believe there is *contraband* hidden inside this doll." He pinned Fumio with a look. "What is it, kid? A camera? A short-wave radio? Some other kind of spy gear? Spill it!"

Fumio shook his head.

"Not gonna own up to it, huh?" The soldier lifted the doll to his own eye level and announced, "Well, I know how to find out!" Pulling a large knife from its sheath, he turned to watch Fumio while drawing back his arm, then slowly advancing the blade directly toward Suzey Belle.

Fumio's ears began to ring. His field of vision blurred. Actions slowed. He'd known this feeling before—submerged in the community pool on a dare to see how long he could hold his breath, and again on the day the bombs fell on Pearl Harbor.

"Forbearance, Fumio," his mother had murmured after the dark-suited agents took away the cookbook her great-aunt had given her. *Confiscated*, they'd called it.

"Forbearance!" his father had urged when they found that the fragile catch on his grandfather's ancient footlocker had been broken by an FBI agent during the search of the Miyota property.

But now, Fumio cast aside the manner of a child toward an elder, even though this one wore a uniform and held a big, sharp knife. He was tired, the ride had been long, and this was too much. "No!" he shouted. "No! Don't you hurt my little sister's doll!" And, again, "No!"

A voice rang out. A woman's voice demanded, "Stop that! Stand down, soldier!"

Kimiko's eyes flooded with tears as she reached out for Suzey Belle. Fumio, his parents, the soldiers, the doll, all were frozen in place at the entrance to Owens Valley Reception Center.

The woman with the commanding voice was well-dressed in a dark blue suit, several small brass pins gleaming from her lapel. She wore gloves and a hat. She carried a black bag with an insignia, the same insignia, Fumio saw, that she wore on the lapel of her jacket.

The soldiers snapped to attention and saluted. "Captain!"

Private Dub lowered his arm. Private Stanley swabbed his brow with his sleeve.

"Private," the Captain's stern gaze targeted the younger soldier, "you will sheath that knife properly and hand over that doll. As of now, it is in my custody. You will return to your assigned duties."

The young soldier moved to give the doll to the woman, but she pointed to the small shoe on the ground. He picked it up and held it out, too, still met by the woman's disapproving gaze. He dipped his head, slipped the tiny shoe on the doll's foot and, using both hands, extended the doll to the woman once more.

The Captain seized Suzey Belle from the soldier's hand, flipped open the clasp on the black case and dropped the doll inside. *Click.*

Turning, she spoke quietly to Mrs. Miyota. "I am sorry. Protocol must be observed." Looking toward Fumio, she straightened the lapel where the gleaming insignia was fastened, then she walked purposefully toward the cluster of white-painted buildings beyond the gate.

CHAPTER TWENTY-FOUR

FLYER

Zachary comes from caring for the sheep and sits down on a bench by the door. He pulls off his boots and asks, "What are you thinking about, Flyer?"

I should answer, *Yipp*, or thump my tail. But, no.

"Flyer, you haven't touched your food. I got that new metal bowl for you Mr. Petric recommended. Don't you like it?" Zachary sounds sad. I don't want him to be sad. But more than that, I don't want to eat.

My real home is just across the field. But my real family is not there. I lay all day on the Whitlock porch and watch Zachary and his parents—and now, Jacob—come and go.

Mrs. Whitlock stands just inside the screen door. She says, "It is hard to see Flyer so unhappy, isn't it? Pacing the length of the porch or walking in big circles . . ."

Zachary asks, "Mother, what can I do?"

"Love him," she answers. "Let him know you love him."

"It's not me he wants," Zachary says. "If he doesn't start eating, he could starve."

"He is a good dog," she says, "a smart dog. He will figure it out."

I hear the words. But I do not feel the meaning. Some days, people are hard to understand. Today it is too much work.

CHAPTER TWENTY-FIVE

FUMIO

Thursday morning, after a long wait in the mess hall line for a bowl of watery oatmeal cereal, Fumio crossed the expanse between his apartment and that of Joey Kato's family. A gust of wind picked up debris and blew sand into his eyes, stinging his face and spreading grit over his clothing. He tugged down the cuffed sleeves and flipped up the collar of his light jacket, questioning his decision to leave his bulky winter coat in the Whitlock attic.

But it's April! Spring! Fumio thought. *How could I guess we'd end up some place where you can see your breath on an April morning?*

Soon, coming from a door in another of the fourteen barracks in Block 3, Fumio saw Joey walking his way, each of his footsteps triggering a burst of fine sand.

Surrounded as Fumio was by what fit his definition of shacks, an image of their chicken house at home sprang to his mind. Given a choice, he figured he would just as soon bunk with the Miyota hens. *That chicken coop was built solid,* he thought, *and it was kept respectable with a fresh coat of whitewash every two or three years.* He sighed. When he and Joey came close, Fumio jerked his thumb left, and the boys pivoted.

"What's the plan?" Joey asked.

"We're going to the laundry room," Fumio replied.

"The laundry room? Why?"

"Because my mother asked where I'd be, and I told her you and I were going to play marbles on the concrete floor in the laundry room, out of the wind."

"Okay. My mother didn't ask. I think she was glad to get me out of—she calls it *the tar paper shanty*. And it is. I could lose a shoe through the gaps in that floor in fifty-dozen places."

"Well, if your mother does ask, and you tell her, you're probably going to be in trouble. Are you up for that?"

"Yes, I am. I'd rather be in trouble than *bored*."

"So," Fumio pointed to a tar-paper-covered building, longer and broader than the barracks, "we'll play marbles in the laundry room for a minute or two. Then, I'm going to get that doll back. Ever since Kimiko saw that it's here, at Manzanar, she's been asking about it."

"Jeepers! How did the doll get in your duffel bag in the first place?"

"Maybe I should have let well enough alone—the doll packed away in the Whitlocks' attic. But it looked awfully sad laying in that carton with the other left-behinds."

"Kinda like Flyer, huh? Left-behinds."

"No, Joey." Fumio scowled. "Flyer is not a left-behind. Flyer is bunking with Zachary for a while, that's all." His pace quickened. "Let's get a move on! We have a job to do."

"Sorry!" Joey called, scrambling to catch up. "I didn't mean—I just—"

"Forget it." Fumio pressed his lips together. "I guess I'm worried about that doll. I hoped we'd have it back by now. I thought that lady might sneak it to us when no one was looking."

"When no one's looking? When would that be?"

Fumio shrugged. All around them, people walked quickly, some carrying containers for water—which was only available from one of the center's spigots—many waited near administration offices, some, wearing layers of coats, sat on steps leading up to yet one more black barracks building.

Walking through the door of the laundry room, Joey gave a low whistle. "Are those washboards, like the pioneers used?"

"Yes, they are!" shot back a woman bent over a wash tub. She was up to her elbows in water with no visible suds.

For ten minutes, the boys played marbles. Then they headed outside toward the medical clinic in what Fumio's father had said was its temporary location.

Once outside, Joey spoke, "Boy, that was quite a showdown, yesterday, you and that Army guy."

"Yeah, my mother wasn't too happy about it."

Joey lowered his voice, jamming his hands into his pocket. "*My* mother cried last night. I guess she thought, with us being on top of those crackly bags of straw, we wouldn't hear her. Maybe she was crying because the apartment only has one light bulb, no running water, no toilet. But I think she cried because she's afraid for Father."

Fumio studied the dust coating his shoes and the cuffs of his pants before asking, "Do you think your father is all right?"

Joey kicked at a rock; it went flying. "*Dun-no*. We haven't heard from him. He probably doesn't even know where we are." Silence. Then, "Anyway, *your parents*—how'd that go?"

Fumio thought for a moment. "I guess I'm lucky. They weren't angry at me. We talked about what happened. Mother said the design on the lady's pin and on her black bag showed she was a nurse, someone with authority. A supervisor, my father said. I figure she's the boss of the nurses. Mother told Kimiko that Suzey Belle was in good hands. The lady wouldn't hurt her, even though it looked like she wasn't going to give the doll back."

"Tough break for Kimiko. That super-nurse lady should've done better by her."

"We'll make it right when we get Kimiko's doll."

"What if the lady won't give it to us? She could have given it to Kimiko as soon as she took it away from the soldier. But she didn't."

"Yup, she could have. And, nope, she didn't. But I hope she wants to give it to me today, because I intend to—" The words froze in his throat. Fumio had been about to say *I intend to take it home*. It hit him like a punch in the stomach. Home? Not here. He would never call this place home.

Near the medical clinic, a few vehicles were parked. A handful of people came and went.

"Will you break in?" Joey asked. "Did you bring a crowbar or something?"

"Geez, Joey, do you *see* a crowbar?" Palms up, Fumio threw his arms wide.

"Well, how are ya gonna do it?"

"All legal-like. I'm just going to walk through the door and—there! That guy who was standing by the backdoor smoking went in and, see? The door's still partly open. Someone around here doesn't know how to hang a door." He took a deep breath. "Let's go."

The boys slipped into the building and along a deserted hallway until they saw four boxes ready for unpacking. One was marked "Margaret Stone, Supervisor of Nurses." The boxes were stacked beside a door. The door stood open. It seemed an invitation. Fumio led the way.

Inside the office building, the glare of midmorning sun highlighted dust motes, errant cobwebs, and a few twigs. Even here, debris blew in.

Fumio walked toward a wall with a bank of floor-to-ceiling shelves, and Joey followed. Next to it, boxes rested randomly on a table, on a desk. Fumio was drawn to the desk.

"Fumio!" The whisper startled him. He drew back and turned toward Joey.

"Are ya sure you wanna steal that doll?"

Fumio leveled a look at his friend. "It's not stealing. It's my *sister's* doll. Anyway, we haven't found it, yet."

"But you will, won't you?" came a woman's voice.

Joey jumped, bumping into the wall of shelves behind him, and knocking a book to the floor. Grimacing, he bent to pick it up, then returned it to the shelf.

Fumio turned and saw in the doorway a familiar figure wearing a dark, tailored suit and a cap. He lowered his eyes out of respect, as he was accustomed to doing, took a deep breath and said, "Ma'am, that's why I'm here. I've come for my sister's doll."

"I thought you might. But I was expecting you to go to the front desk and ask to see me. Or if you came right to my office, that you would at the very least knock." She reached for a switch and turned on the overhead light.

"For one thing, ma'am, I don't know your name. And for another, why did you take the doll in the first place?"

"I was saving her life."

"So why didn't you give it back?"

"*For one thing*, young man, *rules*." She removed her gloves and laid them on the desk. "That young soldier was showing off, yes. But if he suspected something was hidden inside the doll, it was his job to investigate. True, he went about it the wrong way. Fortunately, I outrank him. *And for another thing—*"

A man's voice interrupted. "Margaret, do you—oh! You have guests!" A tall blond man entered then frowned. "What's going on here?"

"Major," the woman greeted him, smiling, "may I introduce—"

She stopped, turned toward Fumio. "And *that* is the other thing, young man. I do not know *your* name, either." She lifted her hand to her collar. "But I had hoped you would notice my lapel pin and find a way to contact me."

The major asked, "How did these boys get in here?"

"The back door was open," the woman put in, briskly. "In fact, none of the doors in this building can be closed properly."

"That's because they were hung wrong." Fumio surprised himself.

"Fumio's father could fix that for you," Joey said. "Fumio's father can fix anything."

"Is that so, young man? Your father can fix anything?"

Fumio nodded. "Yes, ma'am. Pretty much anything."

"My, my, that is interesting." She turned again to the tall man. "You and I spoke of a bit of trouble during the registration process yesterday." She gestured toward Fumio. "The doll in danger of being rent asunder belongs to this young man." Then she turned back to Fumio. "What did you say was your name?"

"Fumio, ma'am. Fumio Miyota. And it's not my doll. It belongs to my sister."

"Fumio, then. And who is this?"

Over the course of the conversation, Joey had edged himself far back into the corner of the office, but now, he stepped forward. "Joey, ma'am. I'm Joey Kato."

"Miyota. Kato. Yes, I will remember your names. Mine is Captain Margaret Stone. I am the Nurse Supervisor of Owens Valley Reception Center. The Army oversees this facility. We are obligated to follow military protocol. I must tell you, young Fumio, I am not confident the soldier yesterday was incorrect. It is unusual for a boy your age to have a doll. You say it belongs to your sister, but that does not mean you did not hide something inside it. I would regret the necessity of damaging the doll."

"I suppose you want to X-ray it," put in the Major, a trace of laughter in his voice. "However, we cannot entertain this foolishness. You boys will just have to—"

"Wait a minute, Major. There is another way. But believe me, young Mr. Miyota, I did not want to do this in front of your little sister."

Captain Stone removed her cap, pulling free a hatpin. Tipped with a dark-blue glass bead, its brass shaft was nearly six inches long. She laid the cap on the desk, opened the desk's top left drawer, and from it took Kimiko's doll.

"What is this doll's name, young man?"

"Suzey Belle." Fumio's face grew warm.

The captain's laugh was surprisingly musical. "Ah, Suzey Belle!" she addressed the doll. "My apologies, dear." She looked toward the major and announced, "You will be my witness," before she ran the hat pin straight through the doll.

Fumio gasped. Joey squeaked.

"I imagine you boys have experienced a few too many needle jabs in the past several days, am I right?" The expression on Captain Stone's face was thoughtful, her movements careful, as she pierced the soft cloth body of the doll, over and over, from its head to its toes.

Finally, she pronounced, "No bomb, then," and held the doll out to Fumio.

He reached out, but she pulled back, exclaiming, "Oh, wait!"

She walked to a shelf, picked up a small carton, dumped its contents out onto her desk, and put Suzey Belle inside.

The captain replaced the cap on her head and, using the pin, secured it once more. "I will walk with you to the back door, gentlemen." She nodded to the major. "I shall return shortly."

When the boys stepped out into the glare of sunlight, Fumio lifted his right hand to shield his eyes. With his left, he clasped the box to his side. "Thank you, ma'am—Captain Stone, ma'am. Thank you, very much," he said, his gaze settling on the gleaming pins on her lapel.

"You are welcome," she said, a smile tugging at the corners of her mouth. She turned from the door, then looked back. "And, boys, next time, *come to the front desk.*"

• • •

Fumio climbed the steps to their barracks quarters with feelings of both relief and reluctance. He was relieved to bring the doll home. Suzey Belle would be safe with Trixie Jean and Kimiko, who would no longer fret about her doll alone in a dark attic.

He had gone to the office of the nursing supervisor without telling his parents, though, supposing they would say no—certain of it, actually—and he would face their disapproval on that score.

It was as he expected: laughing, hugging from Kimiko, widened eyes, a look of surprise from his mother, a lifted brow followed by a frown from his father.

"How did you come by that, Son?" his father asked.

As Fumio answered, he watched his father's expression, attempting to assess the sort of punishment he would receive.

Finally, he asked, "Father, what else could I do?"

"I cannot say, Fumio, but now the people in charge know your name, your face. I wish it were not so, but I think they are waiting for us to make trouble. It would be better if you—and Joey, too—were not so recently on their minds."

The conversation with his father and the details of the day stark in his mind, Fumio began a letter. His pencil slipped and the lead broke, so he went for his duffel bag. After the incident with the disagreeable guard, Fumio had dropped a pencil into the bag's outer pocket. He slid his hand inside and, ah-hah! There it was! But his hand brushed against something unexpected.

He slipped his hand back into the narrow space and withdrew one of Flyer's most-treasured possessions, a rubber ball given to him by the Harveys when he was a pup. Sometimes, Flyer would be seen toting it in his mouth. Occasionally, Fumio and Flyer had played "toss and fetch" in the yard. Clutching the ball, Fumio sank to the floor, his back against the wall.

His mother turned from cleaning the window, tucked a towel into her pocket, and came to his side. Arranging her skirt carefully, she sat down. Fumio dropped his head to his knees. His mother laid her hand on his back and the two sat on the rough plank floor until his breath calmed.

She handed Fumio the towel to dry his tears, used her hand to wipe her own, then got up and, after checking on Kimiko, who was napping, returned to cleaning the window.

Fumio inhaled a ragged breath, took the pencil from his pocket, and wrote.

April 3, 1942
Owens Valley Reception Center
Independence, California

Dear Zachary,

Father is working on what Mother calls our "apartment" to make it better. "Shoring up the barracks," he says. These buildings were rushed. The lumber wasn't dry. The boards are shrinking. There are gaps in the walls and floors. Wind blows in around doors and windows. Dirt comes in, too.

Father says, "Do not concern yourself, I will fix it." But how? He can't go to Petric's for supplies. I guess he'll figure it out.

Father has a job rehanging doors in the medical building. He's real glad about that. We are all okay, except for being stuck in a <u>reception center</u>.

Thank you for doing my chores.

Please read this letter to Flyer and show him the picture I made. Tell him I will be here for—

Fumio stopped writing. For how long? No one seemed to know. He shrugged, then finished the sentence:

Tell him I will be here <u>for the duration</u>.

Your pal, like always,

Fumio

CHAPTER TWENTY-SIX

FLYER

Zachary was happy when he read words from a paper that came from Fumio. But they did not sound like Fumio's words.

Fumio talks about chickens, which he does not like. And he talks about school, which he does like—except for one mean boy, Dirk. Fumio talks about his bicycle and about an owl that tried to steal our chickens and peanut butter sandwiches in his lunch box. And staying inside when it snows—even though it does not snow very often. And growing strawberries. None of those things were in the letter.

Fumio talks about our trucks and our tractor, a Cleveland Crawler.

One morning, when I was still a pup and Fumio was too young to go to school, we got to go along with his father and grandfather to the Eagledale Dock to meet the ferryboat.

That day was important to my family, so I remember. Grandfather Miyota brought his *good hat* to Fumio's mother and asked her to please brush the brim and smooth the band. When Grandfather Miyota put on the hat, he said, "Thank you, Sachiko-san. It is *not every day* a tractor comes to Bainbridge Island on the ferry."

Fumio's grandfather had seen "Tractor for Sale" on a flyer at Petric's Feed and Seed. A *flyer* is a sheet of paper with a message on it. Flyers can be put on *bulletin boards* in stores and the post office or handed out to people.

News on a flyer travels far and wide. And *fast*. That is why it is called a *flyer*. Not a Flyer like me. But I go fast, too.

The flyer said, "Send a letter, if interested," and gave an address.

It was an unusual tractor, and the price was right, Grandfather Miyota said. He wrote a letter. The tractor's owner wrote him back.

The "Tractor for Sale" would come to our island on a ferryboat. If Grandfather Miyota and Fumio's father liked the look of it, they would buy it.

Buying a tractor makes good sense, Grandfather Miyota told us. With a tractor, one man could do heavy work that by hand takes several people. We would not need many hired workers at harvest time. If we owned a tractor, we would not need draft horses.

"Horses," Grandfather said, "have to be fed whether or not they are working."

"While a tractor," Fumio's father said, "just sits there and rusts." He laughed. "I think you have decided to buy this tractor."

"What kind of tractor is it, Ojiisan?" Fumio asked.

"This tractor is called a Cleveland Crawler."

"Crawler? Like a caterpillar?"

"That is a good comparison," his father said. "This tractor has tracks instead of wheels. It can travel over soil without packing it down. It seldom gets stuck in damp earth or mud."

At the ferry dock, I sat up on the seat, in the middle, and put my paws on the dashboard to look out. We watched for the ferry, bringing a truck carrying a tractor.

Grandfather Miyota and Fumio's father turned little cranks to roll down the windows. A breeze blew in. I smelled old wood and diesel oil. I heard sea gulls squawking overhead, bothersome, like chickens. The water smelled like oil and wet feathers, fish and creosote.

A man in overalls climbed out of his truck and walked toward us. "Hello, neighbors!" It was Mr. Harvey!

Reaching his left hand out the window, Grandfather Miyota greeted him like *farmers* do: pointing up, then down, but with two fingers instead of one.

Fumio's father nodded once and lifted his hand.

Grandfather Miyota got out of the truck, left the door open, and put one foot up on the running board.

"Fumio, it's good to see you!" Mr. Harvey reached through the open driver side door to shake hands with Fumio. But Fumio was just five years old. His father took Fumio's hand, and they shook Mr. Harvey's hand together.

"Good morning, sir." Fumio said, and he giggled.

Mr. Harvey looked right at me and I wagged my tail. "Flyer!" he said, "I didn't see you, there! Why aren't you behind the steering wheel?"

He always asks me why I am not behind the steering wheel.

"I reckon you fellows are here on business this morning," Mr. Harvey said. "That Crawler you're interested in, that's my cousin who's got it for sale. Ed Driscoll's his name, but everyone calls him *Driz*.

"Driz grows sugar beets, these days. Most farmers in his part of the country do. That calls for different equipment. Not much interest in the tractor, there."

Mr. Harvey reached up and took hold of his suspenders. "Here on the island, farmers are switching from draft horses and mules to power equipment. I told him there'd be a market for that tractor on the island. He's had a few inquiries. I told Driz he should talk to you, first."

I heard the ferryboat's horn, long blasts of sound. We spotted Mr. Driscoll's truck right away. It was at the front of the boat and was much bigger than our truck, bigger even than Mr. Harvey's truck. When it pulled off the ferryboat, people on the dock stared.

We got out, and Fumio's father took him by the hand. I stayed close by as we walked toward the truck.

"Fumio," his father said, pointing, "that truck is built to carry heavy loads. See, at the back, that truck has two wheels on each side. *Dual* wheels."

Mr. Driscoll parked the truck. I know, now, it is called a *flatbed* truck.

People gathered around, talking about the machine it carried.

A woman asked, "What on earth is that?"

I heard a boy ask, "Is that an Army tank?"

"Nah, kid, it's a tractor!" a man answered.

"Well, it's the same color as an Army tank!" the boy said.

"It *is* the same color," I heard a woman say.

I saw a man with shiny shoes, something hung from a strap around his neck.

Mr. Miyota said quietly, "Father, that man is one of the owners of Bainbridge Island's newspaper. He brought a camera." The man held the *camera* up to his eyes. I heard a tiny *click*, and the man walked away, off the dock.

"This tractor is for smaller acreages farmed for a high crop yield," Mr. Driscoll told a man who asked about it. "It features a Hercules gas engine!"

A sound came from the crowd, "*Ohhh!*"

Touching the brim of his hat, Grandfather Miyota said hello to Mr. Driscoll. Mr. Driscoll climbed up into the truck box to stand beside the tractor. Grandfather Miyota pulled himself up, then turned and reached down for Fumio. Once Fumio was in his grandfather's arms, Mr. Miyota climbed up, set Fumio down, and took his hand, again.

I waited below, watching, while Grandfather Miyota walked around the tractor. Fumio's father tilted his head and squinted. Fumio squinted, too. Mr. Miyota tapped a steel track with his foot. Fumio did, too.

On the dock again, the men shook hands. A woman in the truck rolled down the window. Mr. Driscoll introduced her as Mrs. Driscoll. She waved. "Friends and customers know me as Verna Fay!" she called. Mr. Driscoll got behind the steering wheel and started the engine.

Grandfather Miyota led the way. Mr. Harvey was next. Mr. and Mrs. Driscoll followed and delivered the *Cleveland Crawler* to our farm!

Mr. Driscoll turned off the truck's engine and climbed from the cab holding a small book that he handed to Fumio. It was important, he said. *An operator's manual.*

From the porch of our house, Mrs. Miyota called to Fumio. He went to her and handed her the little book.

But I stayed near the barn. I did not want to miss anything.

Mr. Driscoll unfastened the heavy chains that held the tracks tight to the truck bed. Then Mr. Harvey got the ramps out of the bed while Mr.

Driscoll jiggled a knob and turned the key. *The tractor started!* The engine was loud!

Very slowly, Mr. Driscoll drove the tractor off the truck bed, down the ramps, and to the center of our farmyard. He stopped the engine and climbed down.

Grandfather Miyota gave Mr. Driscoll a small piece of paper. The men shook hands.

Everyone said goodbye, and Mr. Harvey and Mr. and Mrs. Driscoll drove away.

We stood in our farmyard in a circle around the Cleveland Crawler. Grandfather Miyota put his hand on the tractor's hood. "It is dusty," he said.

Fumio's father took out his handkerchief and ran it across the hood. He shook the handkerchief. "Idaho dust."

I walked close. It *smelled* like dust. It smelled like oil, too, and things used for cleaning up engines. The dirt on the tractor's tracks smelled sweet! I sniffed twice to be sure. *Whooph!* My nose tickled. *Idaho dirt is interesting*!

Grandfather Miyota patted the tractor's side panel. "This tractor is sturdy. Do you see the company's motto under the name?" He pointed. "Built To Endure."

Many times, I have heard Fumio ask when he can drive the Crawler, and he has been told, "Not yet. You are not old enough."

One Christmas, though, Grandfather Miyota carved a little Cleveland Crawler from wood and gave it to Fumio as a gift. The toy tractor even had a tiny farmer that could be fit into the driver's seat.

Fumio used the little Crawler to push down *big* pretend trees and build *high* pretend bridges. He used it to make *long* pretend roads and dig *deep* pretend ponds. One day he decided to bring it indoors, for safekeeping.

Now, the little toy tractor sits on a shelf in our living room next to a clipping of the newspaper article and a photograph of Grandfather Miyota standing beside the Cleveland Crawler.

CHAPTER TWENTY-SEVEN

FUMIO

Fumio sat on his cot, leaning against his pillow, thinking about the letter he would write to Zachary. He had promised to stay in touch. And he wanted to know how things were going at home on Bainbridge Island.

He wondered about the crops—the strawberry harvest must be winding down—and how the Whitlocks were getting along with the chickens. Most of all, he wanted to hear about Flyer. Fumio's brow furrowed, then he began to write in his tablet, his thoughts in motion with the pencil lead.

June 4, 1942
Manzanar Relocation Center
Independence, California

Dear Zachary,

You see our address is different. We haven't moved. The US Army is in charge of this place now, and the name has changed. "Reception Center" meant a place for us to wait. "Relocation Center" means—I guess it means the same thing.

For you, school has been out for a while. I bet you miss it, right? Ha-ha! You must be always busy. Besides your sheep, you have our chickens to look after. And you have probably finished the harvest and are putting our strawberries to bed.

The pencil went still. *Our* chickens. *Our* strawberries. Were they? Fumio had not been at the Miyota kitchen table with his father and Mr. Whitlock when the deal was struck. Who did the chickens belong to, now that the Miyotas were not caring for them? Who owned the strawberries harvested from their fields when the Miyotas were not there to truck them to the cannery?

He had heard talk around camp. Many families had lost almost everything over the past few months. They had lost ownership of their farm animals, selling them for pennies on the dollar. They had walked away from plants heavy with big Marshall strawberries, leaving them for someone else to harvest, collect, and then, in more than a few cases, keep all the profit.

Fumio hoped for better for his family. After all, the Whitlocks were their friends.

Using part of his pencil's fast-dwindling eraser, he changed the letter to read *the* chickens and *the* strawberries.

The Miyotas had left their fields carefully tended, their farm buildings consistently maintained. But Mr. Whitlock had no experience in caring for a crop or construction skills for repairing the effects of time and weather.

The whole Whitlock family was working overtime. Jacob was helping on the Miyota farm as well as preparing to step into the role of headmaster at the junior high school in late August. Zachary cared for the Whitlock sheep. He was doing Fumio's chores. And he was looking out for Flyer.

I guess you don't have much time for marbles, baseball, or riding your bike. If I were home, I would be busy, too. It's strange. Now that I have time to goof off, I don't much want to.

He gazed across the cramped room. Lunch on the steps of his school on Bainbridge Island, games of marbles during recess, that life seemed a distant memory.

Boots sounded on the barracks steps. The clatter of tools in a tool belt announced Mr. Miyota's arrival as the door opened. "Sachiko," he asked, "will you need Fumio to help carry laundry today?"

"Not today, no. Tomorrow we will strip the beds and wash the linens, heavy work. I would like his help, then, for myself and some of the older women, too."

"Good, then." Mr. Miyota remained near the door. "Son, I need you this morning. Bring whatever you are writing, there. This is a two-man job. But there will be some down time."

"Yes, Father." Fumio tore the letter and a second sheet from his tablet then folded the pages in quarters to fit easily in his pocket with his pencil.

Fumio and his father walked across the dry, bare dirt of the compound. Whatever dew moistened the earth during cool desert nights evaporated quickly with the sun's rising.

"Today, Son," Mr. Miyota began, "I will re-hang doors of apartments in which people *live*. We might be in their way. A second set of hands can make the work go faster. We will pick up supplies, first."

"Yes, sir."

At the lumber warehouse, Mr. Miyota picked up trim for the door frames. From a tool supply room, he chose an extra hammer, a hack saw, a sanding block, and, last of all, a wood plane. He handed the tools to Fumio.

"Be very careful with the wood plane. If damaged, it would be almost impossible to repair. We would be billed for its cost."

"Even it was an accident?"

"Even then."

Fumio adjusted his grip on the plane.

The door of the first apartment they approached hung crookedly from its hinges, out of square with its frame. Mr. Miyota knocked.

The gentleman who answered said, "This June weather is warm. We do not mind having the door open while you work."

"Especially since, with the door hanging straight," his wife said, "I will no longer need to sweep an inch-high ridge of dust from inside the sill, morning and evening."

Mr. Miyota explained each step of the process to Fumio. When the job was done, the residents insisted that Mr. Miyota and Fumio accept a glass of water—not cold, the gentleman apologized, but freshly drawn from the spigot that morning.

Walking with his father toward the next apartment, Fumio saw a truck full of workers bumping over uneven ground just past the outermost row of barracks. The vehicle slowed and a broad-chested man wearing a bright orange shirt signaled to the driver about where to pull up. Before the men, most carrying hard hats and wearing leather tool belts, could get their feet on the ground, the broad-chested man began shouting orders.

One man, who was tall, thin, and, Fumio thought, younger than the others, was called by the orange-shirted man to follow him to the truck's cab. The young fellow wore a faded, red shirt. His gait was slightly uneven, but brisk. He was handed a hard hat and put it on.

So, Fumio thought, sighing, *this is the site of one of the guard towers going up*. Four, for now. *The Manzanar Free Press* reported that, eventually, at least four more would be built.

• • •

Door by door, Fumio's work with his father progressed. At the last apartment before the corner of the barracks, Mr. Miyota paused to observe. "Fumio, this door has taken the brunt of the heat from the morning sun. I must replace part of the frame, but I do not have the wood for that with me. I will go back to see what is available. Why not find somewhere to sit and write?"

"Yes, Father," Fumio agreed.

"But Fumio, we must not inconvenience the residents by sitting on their steps." He gestured, "I am afraid you will have to sit on the ground."

"Yes, sir, I understand." Fumio found a place to sit, leaning against the southeast exterior wall where there were no doorways or windows. For a few moments, he studied the job site, the massive bulk of beams, the gleaming metal of tools, the scurrying swarm of workers. He took his paper and pencil from his pocket.

While Father goes for extra supplies, I am watching men build a guard tower. A few trucks with "Charlie Summers, Contractor, Lone Pine, California" painted on their doors are parked around. There are big stacks of lumber.

While people wait in line for meals, and mail, and papers for permission to do stuff, they talk about the guard towers. A lot of them are angry. There were no guard towers in April, none in May. Why build them now? We are surrounded by desert.

At least we have drinking water here. It is so hot and dry in the sagebrush around us, jack rabbits try to sneak in*! Rattlesnakes live there, too. So, if the soldiers in the towers are supposed to keep us safe, I hope they guard against* rattlesnakes*.*

I don't think they need guard towers. Nobody's snuck out of here and run off. Not for keeps, anyway.

Don't tell anyone, but since the barbed wire is only at the front and partway down both sides of this place, and the ground is real uneven at the back, you can crouch down low and maybe not be seen. So, some guys slip out and head for the creek. And they go fishing!

I asked my father if we could do that. He said, "No!" Some of those men have been caught and thrown into jail. I thought the fish must taste pretty good for them to risk that, but Father says it is not about the fish.

So, I dropped the idea. But, if I caught a fish, I could bring it home to share. Maybe we could build a little fire. Mother could cook the fish and we could eat it, just us, together.

He turned the paper over and began to sketch the details of the structure: the guard tower, in its contrast to the towering Sierra Nevada in the background.

Fumio heard a shout.

"Hey, kid!"

He looked up.

The young man in the faded red shirt shouted again. "Workin' hard or hardly workin'?" The other workers laughed.

The crew boss, snarled, "Shuddup, Hoppy! No fraternizing!"

A scowl flashed across the worker's face. He bent to his task, making no reply.

Fumio considered finding some other place to wait for his father, but he was sure he sat even farther from the boundary than the required ten feet. His presence was within the rules.

The sun was hot. The builders' faces were red. The crew boss heckled them, "Get moving, will ya? Are your legs painted on? You, there! You are *this close* to losing your job!"

Fumio's father had told him the men were dependent on these jobs. "Their families have to eat," he had said. Still, Fumio wished they were building something other than a guard tower. Like, maybe, a school. They would need one come September.

He picked up his pencil and sketched the lines and angles of the lower section of the guard tower taking shape before him. He heard a woman's voice.

"Fumio!"

He turned.

"There you are!"

Then a sudden blast of wind, heavy with sand, surged around the corner of the barracks. Fiercely rotating, it erupted through the open spaces in the footings. Carrying pebbles, twigs, and three-point burrs, it roared along the exterior wall. A tumbleweed danced in its wake.

A metallic clatter sounded from the direction of the tower site. Random curses rang out. "Dad-blamed whirlwinds!" And, "Hang onto your hard hats, men! It's a billy duster!"

The wind buffeted Fumio's body like a big cat playing with prey. His pencil slipped to the ground, bounced on its scrap of pink eraser and disappeared into the mad swirl. The sheet of paper—his letter to Zachary, the sketch of the guard tower—was pulled from his grasp. He leaped to his feet, grabbing for it. But his hat blew off, so he scrambled forward, running after it.

The woman shouted, "Fumio, stop! Stop!"

He slammed headlong into something solid.

A man howled, *Ay-yy-oww*, and shouted, "Oh! My toe! My toe!"

The windstorm was over in a couple of minutes, very long minutes, during which Fumio feared he might suffocate. The gritty dirt had made its way down his collar and up his sleeves and into his shoes and socks. His nose and ears were filled with it. His eyes stung as if they had been worked over with sandpaper.

Brushing his wrist across his face, he became aware of a thin figure in a faded red shirt and a dozen other men, all nearby. A pair of hands clamped onto Fumio's shoulders. His attempts to wrench himself from his captor's grip were futile. Instead, he heard, "Give it up, Jap! You ain't goin' nowhere but the brig or, maybe, back to the Emperor."

Fumio pulled away hard and twisted around far enough to see a thick arm and shoulder swathed in bright orange, and then, the face of the man who held him.

"Just look what you done, kid!" the man snarled. Then, "Hey, Hoppy! Open yer eyes and look't who attacked you!" The older man snickered. "It's a Baby Jap!"

"Attacked me?" the man called Hoppy responded. "No one attacked me!"

"I saw it, Hoppy!" another man put in. "That little kid stumbled into you. And you shrieked like a banshee!"

"Blame it on the billy duster!" Hoppy sputtered. "The twister startled me, and," he pointed to his boots, "I dropped my hammer on my toe!"

Boisterous laughter broke out. One of the men picked up Fumio's hat, slapped it against his knee, removing some of the dust, and handed it to him.

The orange-shirted man snatched the paper from Fumio and eyed the carefully rendered image of the guard tower with the Sierra Nevada in the background. He turned it so it faced the crew. "We all know it is against the law for prison—*errr*—for residents to make pictures of this place. This here might as well be a set of builder's plans for them towers, and it's as good as a map, to boot!" He pointed. "This kid's communicatin' with the enemy. He is a spy!"

Then, to the edge of the loose knot of men, marched Captain Margaret Stone. Covered in the same fine dirt as the others, her blue uniform now appeared to be gray. Her cap, with its upturned brim, also veiled in gray, sat crookedly on her head. But she stood perfectly straight and addressed the crew boss with a level stare. "What is the meaning of this? The person you are restraining is a ten-year-old boy!"

The man all but spat. "Ma'am, the boy crossed the boundary line. You see where he stands. And there is this." He held out the sketch. "He plans to give this to the enemy!"

Captain Stone stepped forward, took the paper, inspected it. She glanced toward Fumio. "Fumio, are you all right?"

Fumio blew dirt from his mouth, wiped his lips. "Yes, ma'am. I am."

Captain Stone addressed the crew boss. "You have laid hands on a person with whom you are forbidden to have interaction. A dozen men whom *you* supervise are loitering here. Upon whom," she glowered at the man, "will the blame be placed?"

The older man turned back to his crew. "What're ya lookin' at? Get back to work!"

"Nothing more will be said of this," Captain Stone commanded the crew boss as she slipped Fumio's sketch into her bag. "And I mean *nothing*."

She nodded to Fumio and they began walking back across the invisible boundary, now indelible in Fumio's mind. "I need to talk to your father."

Fumio's heart fell to his stomach. "He will be disappointed in me."

"Why? What did you do wrong?"

"Well . . ." Fumio risked a glance upward, "nothing, really."

"Exactly. You did nothing wrong. But that *was* a bit of a dustup, wasn't it?"

Fumio hesitated. "Ma'am, was the man who yelled a lot Mr. Summers?"

Captain Stone frowned. "Oh! It is on the truck doors. No, Mr. Summers has the general contract. He is unlikely to visit the job site. The ill-mannered man you're referring to is a crew boss. But as I said, I need to speak with your father. About doors, Fumio. We must be able to lock the medicine cabinets, and we cannot lock them if we cannot close them."

"He went for more lumber. I would have been left for just a few minutes, but then . . ."

Now Mr. Miyota was in view. "Fumio! I have looked for you. I have been worried! Captain Stone, ma'am, it is good to see you again," he said, removing his cap.

"Likewise, Mr. Miyota. I was looking for Fumio, too. As you see, I found him."

"Excuse me, ma'am, but I must know, is my son in trouble?"

"No, Mr. Miyota." Major Stone smiled. "Not at all. I asked Fumio to help me locate you. Cabinet doors in the drug dispensary must be reworked. We hoped you might look at the job."

Mr. Miyota nodded. "Yes, Captain Stone. Will tomorrow be acceptable? I would like to take my son home, now."

"Of course, Mr. Miyota. Tomorrow will be fine."

CHAPTER TWENTY-EIGHT

FUMIO

For as long as Fumio could remember, Monday had been laundry day in the Miyota household. However, for more than two-hundred Bainbridge Islanders to do their washing in Block 3's long, narrow laundry room on the same day was, as Fumio's mother put it, a disaster. By early June, his mother and others had declared *Tuesday* to be their laundry day.

On Laundry Tuesdays, Etsu, Joey's older sister, looked after their younger brother, Yushi, as well as Kimiko and a few other toddlers, in the Kato quarters, keeping them safe and out from underfoot. Fumio and Joey were responsible for hauling loads to and from the laundry room, which was at times tricky business. Corners of the concrete-floored laundry and ironing rooms served as havens for the younger set of marbles players. For that reason, the floors became minefields as Fumio and Joey came through, peering around their burdens. An errant step on a cat's eye or a shooter could send them sprawling.

Today, Fumio's job was more taxing than usual, because his mother was doing the washing of a neighboring family, too. After his third heavily loaded trek, he was glad when his mother told him he was not needed for the next hour. He and Joey walked out onto the rutted dirt, planning to head to the Miyota quarters.

"Hey, hold up, there!"

The boys turned to see Joey's cousin Sam, with his oil-slick hair, self-satisfied smirk, and practiced almost-a-teenager swagger coming their way.

"Joey! Hey, bub!" Sam called.

Joey ran over to meet his cousin, exchanged a few words with him, then returned to Fumio's side. "We're gonna go work on the clubhouse," he said. "I guess I'll take off."

Fumio, head tilted in confusion, made no reply.

"You know," Joey murmured, "I told you some guys were making a cave under a barracks in Block 2." Joey glanced at Sam, then looked back at Fumio. "Umm, wanna come?"

Fumio shook his head. "See you later, Joey. I'll be back here in an hour."

Joey gave Fumio a quick jerk of his chin. "See ya, bub!" He hurried to join his cousin.

"Workin' hard, or hardly workin'?" Partly hidden behind a large metal tank, a lanky carpenter balanced himself on a ladder propped against the laundry building's back wall. "I see you're doin' laundry!"

Fumio, recognizing Hoppy's faded red shirt and easy grin, answered, "Carrying laundry. It's heavy. My mother needs my help." Shielding his eyes from the sun with both hands, he paused for a moment. "Why are you working here? I thought I saw the other guys still over there," he moved one hand from his eyes and pointed, "building guard towers."

"They are. I'm not. I got fired from that job."

"Oh! I'm—I'm sorry about that."

"It's okay. I like this job better. I'm puttin' in these oil tanks so's the laundry rooms will have hot water. Besides, it wasn't your fault. I'm pretty sure the crew boss was lookin' for a reason to get rid of me. Just as soon's you and that Navy person—boy, she sure must be important if she can tell a crew boss what's what! Anyway, soon as you were out of sight, he hollered, 'Hoppy, give me that hard hat, grab your gear, and get out. Tell payroll you're done!'"

Fumio studied the toes of his shoes for a moment. "Why do they call you 'Hoppy'?"

"They don't, not anymore. Now the men call me 'Dusty.'" He grinned. "They stuck me with 'Hoppy' 'cause they thought I was Hopi. But I'm not.

I'm Paiute. They don't know the difference. This is Paiute land. You're all invaders."

"Not me! I don't want to be here. My family has a farm on Bainbridge Island. That's where I want to be."

"You came from an island? Sunshine, sandy beaches, and palm trees? I guess you fished. Bet you miss that place!"

"We get a lot of rain. We've got some beaches, but no palm trees. We didn't fish. We farmed. Strawberries, mostly. And, yeah, I miss that place."

"Farming is hard work, long hours. Isn't this easier?"

"I don't care about easy." Fumio frowned. "This place is crowded. I can't go anywhere without being elbow-to-elbow with other people."

"But you can't go home."

"No. I can't go home."

Hoppy-now-Dusty pursed his lips, rubbed his chin. "You know, there's a couple of old farmsteads here, still inside the boundaries, but near the edge, far off the highway. Might be a place to spend some time away from the barracks, the crowd."

"Where? How far?"

"One's about a fifteen-minute walk. You could take your pal."

"You mean Joey. He has other friends these days. But what's there? What will I see?"

"Cottonwood trees. What's left of the old well—the stem but not the pump handle. Part of the barn, half of the hayloft, anyway. You break your leg don't go blaming me." He snorted a quiet laugh. "Truth is, the most interesting thing you'd see is right on the ground. You don't need to go climbing. It's a bird called the poor will."

"Whippoorwill, I've heard of that bird."

"No, not the *whip*-poorwill. This bird is just *poor*. Poor will. It lives on the ground, doesn't even build a nest, just settles in among the rocks, lays its eggs there, too."

"Because it can't fly. Like chickens."

"It can fly. Not like an eagle, but it can fly."

"Then why stay on the ground, on the dirt?" Fumio asked.

"Because that's where it nests, in the rocks. The poor will, come winter, goes into a deep sleep, almost hibernates like a bear, instead of flyin' south. This is the poor will's home."

Fumio frowned. "So, are there any birds there that *can* fly?"

The carpenter grinned. "Owls. Screech owls. Great horned owls."

"Great horned owls! I saw one, once, up close. I heard its call, too. I'd sure like to see a great horned owl again."

"Maybe you will. But leave that up to the owl. Don't you go calling it. You could get it killed. You call it, it comes. Some wily, four-legged predator comes, too. And then it's dinner. No. You go to that farm, you're just a spectator."

Fumio nodded. "All right, then. I won't call the owl."

CHAPTER TWENTY-NINE

FUMIO

In the evening, after supper at the Block 3 mess hall, Fumio walked beside his father.

"Father, do you remember the carpenter I told you about, the one whose hammer dropped on his toe? And on my letter, too?"

Mr. Miyota nodded.

"I saw him today."

Mr. Miyota's footsteps slowed as he looked toward his son. "He recognized you?

"He did, but it was okay. He is friendly." Fumio glanced up. "He is Paiute. But he'd rather not spread that around, because, because of . . ."

"Prejudice," Mr. Miyota supplied the word. "I can understand his difficulty."

"Anyway, we talked for a minute, and—"

"Fumio, was Joey there?"

"No, sir. Joey went off with Sam. I didn't want to go along."

Mr. Miyota nodded. "But this young man—"

"They are calling him *Dusty*, Father."

Mr. Miyota chuckled.

"He told me about an abandoned farm."

"Yes? What did he have to say about it?"

"When he found out we were farmers, he said I would probably like to spend a little time exploring the place. It is back over away from the highway, but it is inside the boundaries." Fumio pointed west, over his shoulder. "Father, can I go?"

Mr. Miyota frowned. "Fumio, I do not know how I would find time to take you."

"Father, can I please go alone? Just for a couple of hours? I will see the old barn—even part of the well. I will be careful." Fumio took a deep breath and waited.

"I suppose it would be all right if—and we have to ask her—if your mother approves."

Fumio's heart beat hard, hearing those words. *If! If* she approved. His father thought it was worthwhile to ask. *So, there must be hope.*

Back in their quarters, Fumio straightened the coverlet on his bed. He pushed his boots as far against the wall as they would go. He took the broom from its hook on the wall, went out, and swept the front steps.

"Fumio," his mother asked, "what is it you want?"

He pled his case and waited, breathless, while his mother considered her answer. Mrs. Miyota looked to her husband, saw in his eyes what *his* answer would be, and replied, "Yes, Fumio. I believe that will be fine." Then she turned her attention to making tea.

● ● ●

To avoid the heat of mid-day, Fumio planned his expedition for four o'clock. Likely to miss supper, from the noon meal he saved his serving of processed cheese. The stuff chewed like a mouthful of rubber and was hard to swallow, but it was easily at hand. He wrapped it in paper then again in a piece of cloth and, with an apple, he had provisions.

He let his mother know he was leaving and stepped out the door. Striding between tar-papered barracks, Fumio passed by people resting on steps, reading their hometown newspapers. He heard the chatter of young people trying to decide which mess hall to visit that evening. Two small boys and a young girl played catch on an area of bare ground known as a "firebreak." Fumio bird-dogged a missed ball then tossed it toward the nearest child.

As he felt the excitement of exploration and adventure build within him, he wished to drop his hand on Flyer's head, feel the warmth of Flyer's fur, know the answering nudge as Flyer pushed his head into his hand. An ache deep in his chest, he squeezed his eyes shut, opened them again and walked on, looking ahead toward the space and quiet of the farmstead.

As Dusty had said, it was a fifteen-minute walk. Cottonwood trees marked the site. He came to a stop under the branches of a big, rough-barked tree and reached for a low branch. Then he pulled himself up, threw a leg over, and sat in the camouflage of its branches.

• • • •

After a while, Fumio came down from the tree and walked slowly toward the well. Water. Water was everything. He understood this.

The presence of cottonwood trees told him water still flowed here, underground, pulsing beneath this well, and if his father applied himself to the task, the water would come. This farm's heart was still beating.

He skirted the barn, knowing beyond a doubt that snakes would have taken up residence. And why not? Every living thing needed a home.

Watchfully, step by step, he traversed a span of sparse vegetation bordered by scattered stones. Sensing sound more than hearing it, he stopped. Fumio found he was holding his breath. Then it happened. *Swoosh!* A flutter of wings and a small shape rose as if on springs, a little explosion of feathers. Just as quickly, it settled once more. Against the stones, it was nearly invisible, but a faint movement betrayed its hiding place. There it was, a *poor will*!

Again, *swoosh!* Although he could not see it, Fumio understood the *snap* was the purpose of that leap. Some poor insect meeting its demise. He felt a moment of regret for the tiny being.

So, this was the *poor will*, doing its job, finding its meal. Fumio stood on the periphery of its home, these bare stones, unyielding and offering nowhere to hide. Yet the bird found safety, solitude, in that sea of sameness.

Only with concentrated effort could Fumio distinguish the bird from the stones.

Retreating to the cottonwood where he had sat earlier, Fumio ate the apple and government cheese, as the sun continued to set and the air cooled. Silence.

Then, *Whoo-whoo-whoo! Whoo-whoo-whoo!* He knew that call. It was the great horned owl he had hoped to hear, but he wanted to see it, also. He jumped from the tree, landing softly.

One step, wait. Another step, wait again. Wings fluttered. The owl called, *Whoo-whoo-whoo!* Fumio moved toward the sound. Farther. Then farther.

He halted, knowing deep in his bones that he had crossed over the boundary. He turned his head, looking both ways and over his shoulder. No one. Fumio knew he could keep walking. No one was here to stop him. No one to even mark his passage. He could simply leave this place. Tonight. Now. Never return.

It was his choice to make.

CHAPTER THIRTY

FLYER

An important thing about being a dog is that *my* ears work better than people's ears. It's my job to take care of my family by *keeping my ears open*. I listen all the time.

This morning, lying on the Whitlock's porch, I hear footsteps in the kitchen. Cabinet doors open and close, and—*tk-clnk!*—a skillet is lifted onto the stove. Eggs crack, and soon I hear *sizzle-snap*. I know those sounds from my own family's kitchen.

My nose works better than people's noses, too, and while things happen in the kitchen, out here on the porch, my nose tickles. Someplace, not far away, something *odd* is happening.

• • •

Zachary comes out onto the porch wearing his best clothes and shiny shoes. "Flyer, I will be gone for an hour or so."

I try to tell him we should walk the fences. I look him straight in the eye. *Hphh-hphh!*

He pats me on the head. "Father and I are going to the bank for his usual review of the Miyota accounts. And, today, I will open my own savings account! Sorry you can't come along, but you know . . ."

Mr. Whitlock thinks I am a pretty good dog. But he does not want a dog in his car. That is fine. I do not want to ride in his car. I want to check the fields with Zachary.

Listen! An engine! Mr. Torres' truck! Here it comes! Mr. Torres is here to work today. He doesn't wave at dogs.

I walk along the fence toward the back of our farm. I will search for the *something* that is odd. I smell water, not *odd*. But I smell water mixed with dirt. It has not been raining. I stop, wait. Then I walk softly. My paws do not break blades of grass. My presence does not alarm birds. I hear a sound of water flowing in a way that is *not usual*.

The bank of an irrigation ditch has been damaged. Who's the culprit, I wonder? Pesky critters? But no. I see many wide, raw gashes, dug in deep.

I go to Mr. Torres. I lead him to the trouble. "Real strange," he says, "those gashes in the dirt. That break would've gotten bigger quick, wasted water. Could've ruined the field."

He gets a shovel and repairs the bank. "Good job, Flyer! We make a fine team."

CHAPTER THIRTY-ONE

FUMIO

Each July day is hotter than the last, Fumio thought, swatting at a fly. Generations of people had lived here and didn't complain about it, but he felt he would never get used to the hot, dry air.

Visits to this abandoned farm had made life more bearable. In the cottonwood tree on the branch he had come to think of as his, he leaned against the trunk with a pencil in his pocket and a tablet in his hand, waiting.

A gust of wind set the grass to whispering. Leaves to chattering.

Dry bark from an upper branch broke loose, tapping the back of Fumio's neck before sliding into his collar and down his shirt. "Get yourself a bandana, kid!" Dusty shouted to Fumio when he saw him walking through a cloud of sand. Fumio borrowed a faded blue handkerchief from his father and tied it around his neck. He adjusted it now and resumed waiting.

If he sat perfectly still—quieting even his breath—given time, small, wild things would behave as if he were not there.

He gazed past the well, the barn, the bare rocks, and beyond, where tumbleweeds traveled the desert. As common as they were, no effort was made to control tumbleweeds. Russian thistle, as it was otherwise called, was a crop planted by no man and harvested only by the wind.

Tumbleweeds, Fumio had learned, were not as harmless as they might appear. Once, he and Dusty had been engulfed by a wind-borne army of the prickly orbs. When the flurry had passed, Dusty commented, "Tumbleweeds can take a fence *down*. A bunch of 'em can get tangled in the wire 'til a whole section is thick as a mattress, and the wind shoves that fence to the ground. I've heard tell of the pesky things circling, round and round, twisting the wire 'til the nails pull clean out the posts. Cattle just step over the barbed wire and head for the hills."

He had laughed, then added, "And tumbleweeds, they don't make a good cook fire. Set a match to 'em, they flame up like sons-a-guns. They'll surprise you real bad."

Pulling his pencil from his pocket now, Fumio began to sketch the shape of the roots anchoring the tree in which he sat. He worked to show their strength, to give a sense of their depth. After a few minutes, he raised the tablet to study the effect.

With a flash of sun on silken fur, a kit fox slipped in and out of sight quickly. But for the twitch of a sagebrush bough, Fumio would have doubted he'd seen it.

Next, his ears caught the cry of a poor will. Then, another bird called, owl-like, but not familiar. Perhaps the bird's call would come again.

Instead, footsteps sounded. Twigs snapped.

Shifting on the branch, Fumio saw a slim man his father's age. The man's dark hair was nearly covered by a straw fedora that shaded his eyes, and he carried a large, shapeless black bag. He stopped, lowered the bag to the ground, worked the drawstrings to widen its opening, and reached inside.

Fumio debated his next move. He did not wish to spy, but he had not come here for conversation. How long would he have to wait for the man to go away?

Finally, Fumio made a noise in his throat, "*Hm-hmh*," then grasped a branch and shook it to make his presence known.

The man quickly pulled the drawstrings on the bag tight again, and its contents were hidden from view. He tipped back his hat and looked up, squinting. "Young one!" he called. "Come down, if you wish. My name is Toyo. My family and I live in an apartment not far from here. I heard about this farm, and I wanted to see it for myself."

Me, too, thought Fumio. He wondered what was in the black bag. There had been talk, recently, about dishonest people who were stealing food meant for residents and selling it illegally.

Who was this man? What was his business here? Fumio swung down from the tree. Feet on the ground, he said nothing, only peered at the bulky, black bag.

"My nephew will be along in a few minutes. We neglected to bring an important piece of equipment." The man paused. "That barn," he gestured, "appears as if it would collapse if a raven landed on its roof."

Fumio's gaze followed the man's outstretched hand.

"This was the Wilder family farm," the man continued. "But you probably know that."

Eyes still on the barn, Fumio shook his head.

"In 1908, Romeo Wilder *named* this area Manzanar. That is Spanish for *apple orchard.*"

"Uncle!" The call came from a short distance away.

Fumio turned. A boy who appeared to be just slightly older than himself approached carrying a three-legged contraption made from what looked like broom handles.

The man lifted his hand. "There you are," he said to the boy, then gestured toward Fumio. "And here *we* are! Why not introduce yourself?" he asked his nephew, whose face tightened in response.

As he was being studied himself, Fumio observed the boy. Narrow face, straight, dark brows, hair cut close to his head. The boy wore lightweight, gray pants and a short-sleeved shirt. Though now they were marred by dust, his shoes had been neatly polished.

Finally, the boy reached up to straighten a point of his collar and spoke in an uncertain voice. "Hello?"

The man nodded toward Fumio but spoke to his nephew. "This young man preceded us here. I believe his interest is in the wildlife," he paused, grinning, "and possibly the solitude, which, I fear, we have spoiled for him." He turned toward Fumio. "My apologies."

Hesitant, still, the man's nephew spoke. "My name is Hajime."

"My name is Fumio."

"It is against the rules, Fumio, for me to have a camera here at Manzanar. Regardless, I do. We are here to photograph this place," he swept an outstretched hand, "which is significant in the history of Owens Valley. The Wilder family called this valley home for many years. There were other farms, other families, too. Those families had no choice but to give up their farms when the City of Los Angeles got hold of the water rights for the whole valley."

"A *city* can take away water from people who farm right on top of it?" Fumio asked. "A city so far off you can't even see it from here?"

"The City of Los Angeles is, in fact, more than two hundred miles distant." He jerked his chin to the side. "But for someone to own land does not mean they also own its water rights."

Two hundred miles, Fumio thought. All of Bainbridge Island would be just a dot on the map in the space of two hundred miles. His stomach clenched.

This was another *surprise* that was *really bad.* Something Fumio had never worried about before. Waiting in the mess hall line, it was common to hear of Japanese Americans losing their homes, their farms. Payments had to be made. Taxes had to be paid. Their land was not being worked, so money was not coming in. Fumio knew his family was fortunate to own their land, free and clear. But, what about the water rights? Maybe that was just in California. That couldn't happen *at home,* on Bainbridge Island, could it?

The man lifted his hat and ran his fingers through his hair. "Some would say it was done fair and square. Right or wrong, it happened. Interesting, you might say that sort of thing happened twice in this valley. Before the orchards, before the cattle ranches—this land was home to the Paiute people."

Fumio nodded. *Like Dusty,* he thought.

"The Paiutes grew food on this land, built irrigation systems. But when others set their sights on this valley, the Paiutes were forced out, and the irrigation systems they built were then used by those who took their land."

"So, when the orchardists and ranchers got forced out, they got what they deserved," Hajime put in. "It served them right for taking the water and the land from the Paiutes, didn't it?"

The man put his hands in his pockets and sighed. "Seems like there should have been enough to go around, don't you think?"

Hajime shrugged, then asked Fumio, "Do you want to see the camera?"

Fumio did not particularly care if he did, but it seemed rude to say so. "Sure. Sure, I'd like to see the camera."

The man named Toyo reached into the black bag and pulled out a wooden box. Inside, he explained, was a lens. "You won't mind not spreading it around that you saw us here, will you? Tell your parents, of course. We do not exactly have permission to do this. But, I am not taking anything."

"Yes, you are, Uncle. You're taking pictures!"

The man laughed. "Okay, yes, I am taking photographs. I hope to gain permission to do so in the future."

"Why?" Fumio asked, then worried he was being impolite. "Sumimasen ga, Mr. Toyo-san, sir, if you could get in trouble, why take photographs? You can come here and look at the farm any time you want, can't you?"

Mr. Toyo didn't appear to mind the question. "I take pictures to preserve an image of this place as it is, now, Fumio, because in years to come, we will almost certainly forget. One day, we will look back, all of us who have bided time here, and some will remember dust storms, guard towers, fences, Military Police with rifles, bayonets, at the gate.

"Others, I believe, will remember games of marbles and baseball, socials, dances and music, the gardens we create," he lifted a hand, "and those incomparable mountains. Some of us will remember only free time and ease."

Fumio's brow creased. He wanted to argue that point, but he said nothing.

"Yes! You may doubt it, but I believe it is true. And so, I make photographs to preserve balance in our memories, balance in the way we tell our stories someday, years from now." He paused. "Also, I take pictures because I must. This is who I am. Young Fumio, who are you?"

The question puzzled him. "I am Fumio."

"Yes, certainly. But at the end of the day, when your work is done and your belly is full and you have an hour to spare, what would you most prefer to do with that hour?"

Fumio searched for an answer. "I make pictures, too. On paper, though, using a pencil."

"That is good. It helps you to make sense of it all. May I ask, do you have any of your drawings with you?"

"Only this sketch, sir, which I've just started."

The man reached out for Fumio's tablet. "I see you have drawn in the cottonwood's roots first. I like how you show the volume, their mass. You used the side of your pencil lead?"

"Yes, sir." Fumio took the pencil stub from his pocket. "It's a Number Two TrueLine."

"You value your tools." The man nodded. "That is good. It has been hard to get supplies with workers' paychecks often very late and the General Store experiencing shortages. And we are all being careful with our funds, not knowing what will happen next." He paused. "Do you wonder, young Fumio?"

"Sir?"

"Do you wonder what might happen next?"

"I wonder how long we will be here, sir. Some people said it would be three months, but that has gone by. Some say six."

"Some say they are going to round us all up and ship us to Japan!" Hajime burst out. "That's what I've heard!"

"Is that what you believe will happen, Nephew?"

Hajime shrugged again. "I don't know. I never thought *this* would happen," he said, pointing toward of the rows of barracks. "Why are we even here, Uncle?"

"Distrust," the man replied. "The word 'blindsided' has been used to describe the attack on Pearl Harbor. It was a shock, a tragedy, and, I think, an embarrassment. This," he said with a head-dip, "may well be retribution."

"But it's not fair!" The words escaped Fumio in a rush. "It wasn't us!" He inhaled then forced out his breath. "Sir, excuse me, but I wasn't there. My family wasn't there."

"You are absolutely right, young man, we were not there. And our sympathies were not, and are not, with the aggressors. Yet this," he touched his face, "is what others see. A visual image has much power. And so," he began working with the tripod, "I make photographs." He paused. "One more thing. Our *relocation* has cost the American people a certain amount of money, but it has given great wealth to many, by channeling government funds to contractors and provisioners. There is great power, also, in greed."

Silence was broken by calls from unseen birds as Fumio contemplated all he had heard.

"Fumio, it occurs to me to ask, do you have an extra sheet of paper I might use? I have come away without one."

Mentally, Fumio counted the cost of supplies: a pencil, five cents, a drawing tablet, ten cents, a composition book, eight cents. He thought of his coin jar and realized he could buy more with his own money. He did not have to ask his parents before sharing the paper.

The man continued, "I would like to make a trade. In my pocket I have a charcoal pencil, very good for shading. I do not know why I brought a charcoal pencil. I seldom use it. But paper, I could use a sheet of paper."

"Sir, I would be glad to *give* you *two* sheets of paper. You don't need to trade me for it. I have all that." He indicated his tablet, which the man still held. "I will tear off the sketch and you can take what you need."

His eyes crinkling at the corners, the man handed back Fumio's tablet. "Thank you. You are very generous, young man."

Fumio went down on one knee, propped his tablet on the other, and removed the sketch, slipping it next to the cardboard backing. He tore off two sheets of paper, stood, and handed them to the man. "My name is Fumio Miyota, sir."

The man dipped his head slightly. "I am pleased to make your acquaintance, Fumio Miyota. My name is Toyo Miyatake." He held the charcoal pencil toward Fumio. "This pencil is now yours, young man. I do not care, as I know you do not, to take without giving back."

The man waited, extending the pencil, until Fumio accepted it.

"Thank you. I will take care of it, sir."

"I know you will, Fumio."

Fumio dusted off his pants knees. "I should go, now. I don't want to worry my parents."

"Certainly! I hope you and I, and Hajime, too, will have the pleasure of meeting again. Please give our greetings to your parents."

Fumio began walking and, turning back once, saw Hajime wave. He waved in return then continued toward the barracks with his tablet tucked under his arm and his new charcoal pencil firmly in his fingers.

CHAPTER THIRTY-TWO

FLYER

The windows of *my house* where Jacob stays, and the Whitlock house, too, are covered with heavy cloth before the sun goes down. No light shows outside. It is because of the *war*.

Zachary talks to me sometimes, and he asks questions like, "What do you think about this war, Flyer?" I am pretty sure he doesn't know if I listen. He does not expect me to answer. I do listen, and I think about the questions.

What I know about this *war* is that it made Fumio go away. War is bad.

Fumio has not come back, yet. I waited and waited. Then, I understood. Everyone is waiting. What I do not know about war is *why*. Why did Fumio go away? Why have other people come to do his family's work?

War is why Reyna is living with her grandparents, instead of her own home. Because her father got hurt bad in the war and her mother is taking care of him.

Zachary says people, *nations*, fight over who owns land, even whole islands. I do not understand that. I do understand one thing about land: you must take care of it.

Jacob's car is in the driveway! He calls me, "Flyer! Wannacome?"

Wannacome? Yes!

Almost every night, Jacob visits places all over the island. He begins just before dark and does not come back until daylight is gone, long gone.

Tonight, Jacob wants my help. We'll do his *rounds* together. He will drive on old roads and look around *abandoned* buildings for *unauthorized activity*.

When we see small plank bridges, creek-crossings, no side railings, he will check that they are *undisturbed* and safe. I look for critters digging around foundations, tearing up creek banks, or chewing on *bridge pilings*. I look underneath, where it is wet and smelly. Jacob says I am an *expert*.

Jacob does not talk in those places. I do not bark.

The night is busier than people know. Animals hunt at night, some do, anyway. People read and think at night. Zachary does. And he writes.

CHAPTER THIRTY-THREE

FUMIO

Water flowing from the spigot into the pail splashed onto Fumio's pants legs. He stepped back and, leaning farther forward, allowed the pail to fill, then turned the water off. He was strong, certainly stronger than many who were required to do this chore.

Hurrying back to his family's apartment, he turned toward the now-familiar sound of a bus being downshifted, its brakes squealing in protest at the dust that had infiltrated the lining. This bus was filled with camp residents who were working temporarily outside the camp. As the length of incarceration wore on, Fumio often saw buses gathering or spilling out large numbers of Japanese Americans who had signed on to labor in fields or food-processing facilities, mostly in Montana or Wyoming. The work was hard. Living conditions were sometimes worse than in camp. And employers might send workers back at the end with less pay than had been promised.

"There is a call for men in Montana," he'd overheard his father say. "No one knows how long our money will have to last us. Perhaps I could find a job allowing our whole family to move out of here for a time."

"I suppose that is possible," his mother said. "I would like to be away from the crowds, someplace where our family could eat together, quietly, and wash the dishes in turns, as we used to do. But we have no information about how long we are to be kept from home. We left a great deal of work with the Whitlocks. Some room to breathe sounds appealing, but I think we must have no other commitments to keep us from going home immediately."

Fumio had not heard the matter discussed again.

CHAPTER THIRTY-FOUR

FLYER

I try hard to understand things that are important to Zachary. I help him with his work. Some jobs I am still learning.

Zachary says that, with so many lambs, it is important to spend time in the pen and the pasture with the sheep. He told me about a lamb getting its head stuck through a bucket handle. After he got the lamb free, he never used that bucket around sheep again. Zachary says he must stay *on top of things, even the small stuff.* He learned the hard way.

This morning *big trouble* came. A bunch of sheep trotted up the road to the strawberry field! How could that happen? I check their pen and the fences every day!

But it did happen. The sheep's hooves cut deep holes in the field. Leaves and vines dragged behind them. Their hooves pulled up strawberry plants by their roots.

I barked and barked and at last Zachary and two of our new hired helpers, Grandfather George and G, came and saw *what was happening*. At the edge of the field, they stopped. Grandfather George did not move. Zachary circled the flock. I was on the other side.

The man who is called Grandfather George *whistled* and raised his arm high in the air to get our attention. He pointed at G and, with his arm, motioned toward the fence. G moved to the fence, side-stepping, keeping an eye on the sheep.

Grandfather George *looked right at me*. He pointed *at me* and motioned, to show me how to help. I did not move *toward* the sheep. I went *around* them, but a little closer than they liked. The sheep did not move farther into the field, and some backed away from it.

Grandfather George signaled for me to do it again, in the other direction. Some of the sheep turned around. Grandfather George nodded at me. I kept following his signals.

Slowly, G began working the sheep out of the field, toward the road. From the other side, Zachary moved the sheep, bit by bit, toward Grandfather George.

Careful to not startle the sheep, Grandfather George crossed the road, then spread his arms wide. He whistled—low—pointed at me and waved for me to come.

Together, we got the sheep on the road and back into their pen. It took a long time. It was *discouraging*.

Zachary loves the sheep. I know he is not angry at them. They do not understand that they made trouble for Zachary.

But how did this happen?

CHAPTER THIRTY-FIVE

FUMIO

Fumio rode the ridge of the roof as if it were a horse, a winged horse soaring high over Owens Valley, far above Manzanar. No, not a horse. A dragon!

He had seen paintings of winged dragons on New Year's cards sent from Japan by relatives. The dragons were powerful, fierce, and free. Some breathed fire.

Sketching the picture in his mind, Fumio spread his arms wide, imagining himself taking in a deep breath and exhaling a blast of flames. Instead, his nose and throat burned from inhaling the sharp scent of sage and the stink of coal tar. Eyes watering and cheeks stinging, he adjusted his knit cap to ward off the wind. He'd had one earache already this fall, and one was enough. Sometimes his jaw still hurt.

The cap, a gift sent by Zachary's mother and made of handspun wool from the Whitlock flock, was soft. He pulled it down over the back of his neck. She had sent a cap for his father, too, and deeply textured tams for his mother and Kimiko.

On the ground below, Fumio's father spoke with a Block Manager. The man's position was obvious to Fumio by the clipboard he carried.

Fumio had begun carrying a small notebook in his pocket. He patted that pocket now. Yes, there it was in his shirt pocket, along with a short pencil. Since the administration had overhauled the payroll system and begun giving vouchers for back wages, his parents had given him a nickel every other week, most of which he spent on paper and pencils at the community-run store. Still, he was careful with supplies. If a pencil wore down to three inches, he set it aside to be a pocket pencil.

From the rooftop, he could see orchards and gnarled branches of trees that once, as he had learned from Hajime's Uncle Toyo, quenched their thirst with waters native to this valley. Then, when water rights were lost to the city of Los Angeles, farms and orchards were lost, too.

These trees, left untended for twenty years but cared for since April by internees, had in a single growing season produced thousands of dollars' worth of apples and pears. It was a strange turn of events, Fumio thought, that the water which allowed the trees to thrive was now flowing through canals to a city two-hundred miles away. It was, as Mr. Toyo had said, a matter of water rights, but Fumio couldn't understand. Why didn't people live where water naturally flowed?

His father's conversation with the Block Manager had ended. Walking away, the other man's step was brisk. As Mr. Miyota climbed the ladder, Fumio took the notebook from his pocket, glanced at the sun's position in the sky, and noted the start time for their morning's work.

Even in warm weather, Manzanar's winds could shriek and bluster like a hundred angry roosters. The camp's flimsy structures were under constant attack. Suspended on concrete blocks set ten feet apart, the weight of the buildings compacted the soil and caused the structures to sag. Open space below the flooring allowed sand to force its way through gaps, which residents covered with whatever they could scrounge. Lids from cans were preferred.

In late summer, when floor covering arrived, residents installed it themselves. Next came insulation, and they nailed gypsum board inside the flimsy wood panels, the only material serving as walls when they moved in. Now, the tar paper roofing on Manzanar's five hundred barracks was peeling off and blowing away.

Today, Fumio and his father were to work atop a barracks near the entrance of the camp, to begin the process of rescuing roofs. Most of the barracks were built after he and his family had come to Camp Manzanar.

One-by-eight still-green lumber was nailed over the barracks' rafters with edges rammed tight together to form sheeting, since plywood was in short supply. Heavy tar paper, fifteen-pound felt, went down next. Then, finally, thin wood slats, sometimes called battens, were nailed, grid-like, on the tar paper to secure it.

First, a full crew with crowbars removed whatever tattered tar paper remained, as well as the wood slats holding it in place. Salvageable material was saved for re-use.

Then, sheeting that had shrunk as the wood dried had to be loosened and re-nailed. This job, Mr. Miyota would do. Because the slope of the roof was not steep, he had judged it safe for Fumio to work by his side. This gave Fumio the chance to use his birthday gift, a tool belt made by a leather worker his father had come to know in the camp. He enjoyed the bump of the belt against his hip as he worked, the subtle twist of it when he climbed a ladder. The belt had only one pocket, plus a loop for a hammer. But it was just right for an eleven-year-old boy.

Fumio missed working in their own fields, but it was good to have a job to do, and he liked working with his father, even with the sun beating down on his head, and the wind—relentless—blowing sand in his face. If they were home now, strawberry harvest would be over, and he and his family would thin the plants to make room for next season's growth. They would prepare the strongest runners—the vines with most promise for bearing lots of big strawberries next year—to winter over.

He touched the knot of the faded blue square of cloth he wore around his throat, his neckerchief. Many residents wore something similar. In fact, many kept a pair of goggles on a strap around their necks, too, in readiness for dust storms. Recently, he'd received a bandana, signed by the boys who attended Zachary's birthday party. Too special to wear, he kept it stored in the trunk under his cot, but he liked to take it out to look at occasionally.

Fumio was glad for this chance to work on roofs. Besides sheer skill, roofing jobs called on a carpenter's constant awareness of incoming weather, attention to footing, and ability to shut out distractions. The last was a matter of safety and, on the ridge of a roof, the most difficult. To view the world like a bird, from such a height, was something Fumio had dreamed of. Here he satisfied his longing to see *without interruption*.

Across the 540-acre expanse of the central compound, he surveyed the roofs of hundreds of tar-paper-covered barracks. He gazed beyond administrative offices and white-painted staff housing units. A highway, US 395, ran alongside the camp. On it, Fumio saw the occasional vehicle, trailing dust as it motored on by or, occasionally, idling near the MP station where Military Police barred its way to ask for proof of identity and authorization to enter. Food and other supplies came by truck. New families came by bus, to be registered, assigned barracks, and given canvas sacks to fill with straw for use as mattresses.

Government vehicles brought administrators or other staff members. Private cars might bring visitors, some associated with the Friends Church, as were the Whitlocks, to help residents who needed legal or banking assistance.

Ministers sometimes delivered internees' important possessions. Gas was rationed, but doctors and ministers were allowed the use of more, because of services they provided to others.

Fumio shaded his eyes with his hand. On the opposite side of the highway was a pair of seldom-used landing strips. Shortly after the Miyotas arrived, a high-ranking administrator had come to speak to the residents. His plane landed on one of those airstrips. A person could leave the same way, Fumio thought. Just take off in a plane, with wings, like a bird. No, like a dragon.

CHAPTER THIRTY-SIX

FLYER

Today is Work Day! It was still dark when Zachary and his father loaded tools from the shed into their truck box and drove to my family's farmyard. Zachary rode up front. I rode in the box with the tools. Shovels, rakes, and pitchforks slid, bounced, and rattled. I kept an eye on them!

I have heard lots of talk about plans for Work Day through the screen door. Two *properties*, Mr. Whitlock said. Two farms, Zachary said. Too much work, Jacob said, and he laughed. We've fallen behind, our helper Mr. Torres said. He did not laugh.

Today we will catch up on *maintaining*—caring for—the Miyota farm.

If we do not make repairs on the chicken yard, Mr. Whitlock said, the chickens will be *in jeopardy*. Some of the chicken yard posts have *rotted*. The woven wire fencing and the covering have stretched, and they are sagging. A tall post is working loose.

Mr. Torres is here now! Do you hear that loud noise? Mr. Torres borrowed a post-hole digger and hooked it up to the Cleveland Crawler. The Crawler's motor gives power to the digger, and the digger makes deep holes for setting new posts.

Jacob is not back from being an air raid warden, but he will be here, soon. And, later, Mrs. Torres and Reyna will come to help.

Zachary's mother has walked from the Whitlock house, bringing hot coffee and a jar of water and a metal pan with a lid. Next, she will drive my family's truck, a *Chevy half-ton*, to go to Petric's for lumber and fencing nails.

• • •

The sun is halfway up in the sky. Zachary takes off his jacket. I see my family's truck. *Yipp*! *Mrs. Whitlock is coming back!* She drives slowly around bales of straw, stacks of lumber, and bundles of shakes for roofing. She turns off the truck's engine.

Zachary goes to the back of the truck, lowers the tailgate, and lets it rest, flat, on the chains. I see a crate with a picture of a chicken waterer on the side, a little wooden *nail barrel*, long pieces of wood which are called *two-by-fours*, and a gunny sack.

The gunny sack is wiggly, and the smell is *interesting*! *Yipp-ipp!* I tell Zachary, but his arms are full of two-by-fours and Mr. Whitlock is calling.

Yipp-ipp! I follow Zachary.

Mrs. Whitlock takes something from the floor of the cab and gets out. She smiles at me. She has my water dish!

A panel truck arrives. Mrs. Torres is driving, talking to Reyna who is slouching in the seat beside her. Mrs. Torres steps down from the truck and reaches behind the seat. Reyna shoves open the truck door and slides to the ground.

Mrs. Torres has a plate in her hand. I smell warm blueberries. Muffins! Mrs. Torres spreads a towel on a straw bale and lays the plate on top of it.

Zachary fills my water dish. The cool water is good! All the people talk and laugh—well, not Reyna, but everyone else. I wag my tail and *hupph-uph*. All the people smile at me—well, not Reyna, but everyone else.

The muffins are almost gone. The talking stops. I hear a sound so small, even I might not hear it if a breeze were blowing hard and leaves were rustling. I hear it again. Tiny cries come from the back of the Miyota truck.

I make tracks for the truck, jump up onto the tailgate, and nose around in the back. I cannot see the kittens, but I know them by the sounds they make: *mews*. I also know that kittens should not be in a gunny sack.

• • •

Work Day is almost over. Mr. Whitlock steps up onto a straw bale. "I cannot thank you enough! Regardless, I will try! Thank you, all of you! Let's drink the last of that cool water and congratulate each other!"

Everyone but Jacob fills a glass with fresh water.

Jacob grins, holding something behind his back. Then he throws his arms wide. "Ta-daa! Marshmallows!" And I see a small box.

"Marshmallows! Boy, oh, boy!" says Zachary.

Mr. Torres gets a match and starts a little *bonfire*. Are *marshmallows* for burning?

Jacob brings new branches with their leaves stripped off for *marshmallow sticks*. Everyone takes a marshmallow. Jacob asks Mr. Torres to please take marshmallows for Mrs. Torres and Reyna since they were *home* taking care of kittens.

I watch while Jacob pokes the end of a stick through the soft squishy thing and holds it near the fire. Part of the marshmallow goes dark. The smell is like breakfast toast but different.

Zachary comes to me. "This is for you, Flyer! It's sweet." He holds out a *marshmallow*.

Sweet? Like sugar. Fumio never gives me sugar. But marshmallows are special!

Whooph! Thank you! I take the marshmallow lightly in my mouth and hurry to the base of the willow tree. I bury it for Fumio. For when he comes home.

CHAPTER THIRTY-SEVEN

FUMIO

Fumio turned onto his side, trying to find a comfortable spot between the lumps in his cot. The straw in his mattress crackled, a stubborn stalk poked him in the shoulder. Finally, he made peace with the bedding and burrowed in.

Even in summer, nights were cold in the high desert. The pale sun disappeared behind the Sierras soon after supper. The Miyotas pulled their coats around them and hurried from the mess hall to their apartment where Mr. Miyota turned up the flame in the oil heater. The heater was a vast improvement over the early days in camp when they were burning twigs and scraps.

Fumio had known a soothing sameness in his family's routines for as long as he could remember. At the end of each day, his parents wove a loving cocoon around the small family: his mother's soft voice, his father's deeper one, the muted noise of chairs pushed back from the small table, the *clink* of pottery as mugs were cleared away, the *shuush* of papers gathered before bedtime. Like a period at the end of a sentence, or the last line in a book's chapter. A bit of blank space. In the morning, they would turn the page, and a new chapter would begin.

At Manzanar, the ritual played out against the change of military police duty officers and the security guard's knock at their door, ensuring that all internees were accounted for.

At their farm on Bainbridge Island, each night before his parents turned out the lights, Fumio's father opened the door, looked out into the darkness, listened for sounds of wind, weather, misdirected flows of water, restless animals in need of attention. If all was well, just before closing the door, he would say, "Goodnight, Flyer. It's your job, now."

In response would come a quiet "*Yipp*."

"Goodnight, Flyer." In his heart, Fumio spoke those words. In his mind, he sent them toward the island. With all his might, Fumio willed Flyer to hear him. "It's your job, now."

CHAPTER THIRTY-EIGHT

FLYER

This is an *interesting* time of year. Many things are *not quite*. Summer is *not quite* over. Plants still need water. And it is *not quite* harvest time, but the beans we planted are going to make a crop when autumn comes, Mr. Torres said.

I follow Zachary to the shed. He puts a rake and a pitchfork into a wheelbarrow. Going to the sheep pen, the wheelbarrow squeaks. Mr. Harvey sells oil. We need some.

Zachary works in the sheep pen, in the *loafing shelter*, where the sheep can rest out of the rain or sun. I stay outside the pen. After a while, Zachary comes out with a load of *very stinky straw. Puffuff.* The smell is so big, I can taste it. I want to know more about what he is doing. Sometimes Zachary talks while he works. "The sheep's old bedding, from last week," he says. "Pheww!" He makes a face.

He dumps the old bedding in a pile beside a tree and pushes the wheelbarrow back into the shed.

I hear an interesting sound coming from the lane. *Rrrr-bang-Vr-rrr-BaBang-bang.* A strange-looking truck pulls into the yard. It's bigger than a pickup truck, but not as big as my family's farm truck. The truck has a little house, a *real* house, where its box would be! I see a window and a door. Tools, ropes, and other things hang off the walls. I bark, *Whu-wuff!*

A woman gets out of the truck cab. "Hello, Pal!" She is talking to *me*.

I wag my tail. *Hello!*

Zachary comes from the shed, calls me to come, and asks the woman, "Can I help you?"

The woman says, "I need to talk to the boss! I'll wait here while you go get him." She walks off toward the sheep pen and begins looking over the sheep.

I think Zachary is going to tell her he is the boss, but the woman turns and says to him, "Time to trim their hooves."

I hear Zachary sigh. "Yes, ma'am."

The woman says, "I'm on the island today, lining up accounts. I need to speak to someone about taking on my uncle's customers. He's always sheared these sheep. But he is *getting on in years*, so I bought the business."

Zachary's head goes sideways. "You mean, Mr. Montero? He's your uncle?"

"Yes. My name is Anna Montero." She turns and points at her truck, "I'll be traveling throughout the islands, doing this work. That's my new home!" She sounds happy.

I like the little house, too, but it does not have a porch.

Miss Anna says to Zachary, "You have your hands full, young man. I'll bet you're glad you've got yourself a dog."

Quietly, Zachary tells her I am not his dog. I know he does not like to do that.

But Miss Anna says, "Is that so? Still, he must be a help to you." She asks, "Does the dog work to hand commands, or whistled signals?"

"Flyer is Fumio Miyota's dog," Zachary says. "The Miyotas didn't raise sheep."

"And yet they got themselves a border collie?" Her eyebrows go up.

Zachary whispers something that sounds like "a-band-a."

Miss Anna nods. "Lucky all around, wasn't it? Some poor sap, and it serves him right, dumped a real good dog. You are taking fine care of Flyer. He looks healthy."

Zachary smiles, finally.

She says, "Why don't you get started, now, teaching him to work with sheep? A dog likes to have a job."

"I wouldn't know how to do that, ma'am."

"Maybe I can help." Miss Anna shrugs. "I can spare a little time, next week. And maybe I'll be back in February, too. A little brush-up for Flyer, a few more pointers for you? When I shear the flock?" She laughs, just a little.

Zachary grins. "I think we can expect you will shear the flock. You're Mr. Montero's niece. And Flyer seems to like you."

Miss Anna nods. "You're Zachary, aren't you, Zachary Whitlock? My uncle told me about you. He said you're good to your flock." She follows Zachary into the house.

When she comes back out onto the porch, Miss Anna pats me on the head. I wag my tail. She climbs into the little house-truck and starts the engine. It growls, *Rrrr-bang-Vr-rrr-BaBang-bang*. The truck heads for the road. Tools rattle.

Miss Anna honks the truck's horn, and she waves. Leaning out the window, she shouts, "See you soon, Flyer!"

CHAPTER THIRTY-NINE

FUMIO

Fumio felt autumn's approach from his toes to his fingertips. Soon, school on Bainbridge Island would be in session. He dreamed of a three-ring binder filled with smooth-finished paper ruled in faint blue lines. Rectangular erasers, pink and perfect. Hexagonal pencils, shoulder to shoulder, six of them, in proud yellow coats.

At school, the floors would gleam, freshly waxed. The smell of new books would greet him at his classroom door. His teacher's name would be written in cursive on a blackboard that was glossier and darker than he would see it again for a year.

That would be sixth grade.

The first week of September at Manzanar, though, came and went with no school called to session. "Trouble recruiting teachers," murmured a woman waiting in line for the evening meal. A man speculated, "Low pay." "So far out of town, they'd probably have to live here." "You mean, they don't want to?" People in line laughed.

On Monday, the fourteenth of September, elementary classes finally began, and Fumio learned that a school day at Manzanar would be a test of endurance. The air inside the cavernous, uninsulated recreation hall where classes were held was frigid. Sweaters, jackets, coats in layers—hats, gloves, and boots, too—were needed. Fumio had experienced freezing temperatures before, but when working outdoors and generating his own warmth. He had never spent hours sitting directly on a cold wooden floor.

Nor had he ever been crammed into a learning space with so many other kids. He wasn't even sure he could count as high as the number of arms and legs in that open room where teachers in all grades spoke at once. No partitions, chairs, desks, school supplies, no textbooks.

That first day, one girl began sobbing, burying her fingers in her long, dark curls.

Charged with anger, her words came, "I have a school! I have a school, *at home* where I *really* live. My parents said they *paid taxes* for that school," she sobbed. Then, "*We had chairs!*"

The student next to her began to cry, too.

Fumio wasn't given to crying. When he was upset, his father said, "Go outside and work it off."

He was, however, tempted to throw in with the boy who snarled, "Well, if this don't beat all!" before storming out the door. *Stormed*, for a fact. As he stomped *out*, the tail end of a billy duster whipped *in* with a load of gritty dirt and pebbles.

• • •

Three days later, classes were suspended.

Fumio figured it was a good idea to let students stay home until the problems were ironed out. When the Miyotas learned that school was "temporarily closed for an unspecified period of time," they decided Fumio could practice his skills in language arts by reading aloud to Kimiko and writing letters to Zachary.

Mr. Miyota suggested Fumio could learn practical applications of math by working alongside him. This also could take the place of gym class. It would pretty much take care of recess, too, he said, and chuckled. For the next two weeks, Fumio helped his father.

School began again on Wednesday, the thirtieth of September. A week and a half later, on the ninth of October, Mr. Miller, the principal of the camp's elementary school, who was also an amateur pilot, died in the crash of a small plane. To honor Principal Miller's memory, the elementary school would be closed for three days. Fumio's father read aloud from an article in the *Manzanar Free Press*, under the heading, "In Memoriam": "The 10,000 people of Manzanar, both Japanese and Caucasian, have suffered a great loss."

Which am I? Fumio wondered. Not Caucasian, that was obvious. But also not Japanese. Had *he* suffered a great loss?

As he thought about it, he realized he was sorry for Mr. Miller's family—for his four-year-old daughter, who was the same age as Kimiko. *That must be terrible for the little girl and her mother.* Fumio's stomach twisted hard, so hard that he busied himself with other things to keep from feeling it.

CHAPTER FORTY

FUMIO

In the office of the Block Manager, surrounded by cascading stacks of past issues of magazines and old newspapers, Fumio sat on the floor. A request for reading materials for camp residents had gone out to the American public and this was the result. Mr. Chihara had given the children of Block 3 permission to come to his office to read them if they wished.

Fumio dug through the pile of back issues of the *Manzanar Free Press* until he found the very first, Volume 1, No. 1, distributed on April 11, 1942. Waiting in line at the mess hall, he had heard plenty of jokes about the newspaper's name: *Free Press*. Everything printed in the paper had to be approved by camp administrators, and some newsworthy happenings didn't make it in. For example, back in May, camp guards had shot an elderly man while he was gathering wood, and no story about that appeared in the *Manzanar Free Press*.

One long article in that first issue caught Fumio's attention: "We are the principals in an experiment unparalleled in the annals of American democracy. Much of our progress lies through uncharted ground. Democracy is being tested of its mettle right here. By our actions and by our attitudes we shall be responsible—responsible to this and future generations of free-men."

Fumio thought he did not like the idea of being *the principal* in this experiment, unparalleled or not. At home on Bainbridge Island, he had known where he stood. He preferred that state of being. He'd had a roof over his head and work to do. He had known where his next meal was coming from. His family *owned that garden.*

Fumio thought of one of Zachary's recent letters. The school year was underway on Bainbridge Island. The sixth-grade class had been in session for three weeks. Zachary especially liked that their new teacher, Miss Smith, was "big on science," as he had put it. They would do more than read about science. They were going to go out and find it, bring it back to school, and put it under a microscope. Exciting stuff. Fumio felt a pang. He was missing out.

What would they find if they put Manzanar under a microscope, he wondered? The image of an ant farm came to mind. Fumio elbowed aside the stack of newspapers, pulled his notebook from his pocket, and began sketching an ant farm, his father and mother, Kimiko and himself, trapped inside. When he was finished, he studied the picture, then penciled in a little packet in the hand of the sketched "Fumio" and labeled it "Magic Beans."

The door opened, and Dusty stepped in. "What's so funny, kid?"

Fumio looked up, grinning, and handed the notebook to the young carpenter. "Hello, Dusty! What are you doing here?" he asked as he levered himself from the floor.

"I'm checking on an oil tank my boss, Mr. Griffith, had me put up a while back. Hey, that sketch is flat-out funny! How'd you think of that?"

"I don't know. Stuff just comes into my head, I guess. Anyway, thanks."

Dusty nodded, returned the notebook. "Gotta make sure the platform is holding up and the tank's setups look right. Block Managers field calls for help when boilers go out. If the boilers fail, laundry rooms and mess hall kitchens run out of hot water.

"Another thing, it seems as how everyone's real worried about fire. There's a whole lotta wood in this place and not much water. Don't know why they put the fire house and trucks clear off to the edge of the camp, close to some buildings and far from others. I guess that's just the way the cookie crumbled." He shrugged.

"I'm s'posed to tell Mr. Chihara I'm following up," Dusty continued, "like the company promised. Do you know where he is?" He looked around, chuckled, "Or, maybe he's *here*, and I don't see him. What I do see is everything, from soup to nuts." He laughed. "Well, okay, not soup. But *soap*. Man, alive! *Will you look* at all that soap?"

Fumio *had* looked on earlier visits to this office with his father. He had seen the mops, brooms, buckets, floor cleaning oil, cartons of light bulbs, boxes of fuses, bales of toilet paper. It was the Block Manager's job to control the distribution of these supplies. The office doubled as a very small, tightly packed warehouse.

Pushed under a table backed tight into a corner was a jumble of rusted metal salvage.

"Is that a stack of brake drums? They keep old truck parts in here?"

"For the mess halls," Fumio answered.

"They cook in 'em? At the mess hall?" Dusty's cheeks went red, and he turned toward Fumio. "Sorry, pal. You've got no choice but the mess hall. I shouldn't've made a joke of it."

"That's all right. Besides, they don't cook in them." Fumio paused, then grinned. "I guess they do look like skillets without handles. They're for meal call bells. See, those are just the outside part of drum brakes, the cast iron covers. One hangs by a cord from a corner of every mess hall in camp. Hammer on it with an iron bar—or a wrench—and, *Soup's on. Come and get it*. I figure the racket can be heard all the way to Lone Pine."

Dusty shook his head and resumed surveying the space. Unpartitioned, the office occupied the same square footage as a single barracks apartment or, as Fumio thought of it, the Miyota chicken house.

Pushed against the wall was a table apparently built from scrap lumber and, in front of that, an upended wooden crate, most likely used as a chair. Stacked beside the table were boxes filled with sheets of paper in various sizes, some sandwiched with carbon paper. Many of the boxes were marked "Form" followed by a number.

Fumio knew that the Block Manager spent his days answering residents' questions, helping to solve problems, sometimes settling common disputes and calming resentments. The man translated letters into English for the older residents who spoke only Japanese, and into Japanese for the large percentage who spoke only English.

Perhaps the most difficult of all his responsibilities, the Block Manager was expected to interpret the administration's orders and see they were obeyed.

In the middle of the office, an industrial-sized sewing machine rested on a door laid across two sawhorses. In front of the door-table was a tall stool. A heavy electrical cord ran from the sewing machine across the floor to a wall outlet.

Dusty asked, "Do you think the man knows how to sew?"

Fumio shook his head. "Don't know. Maybe. He was here when I came in to read. He said he'd be back in a half-hour or so."

As hinges squeaked, Fumio and Dusty looked toward the door. Mrs. Miyota and Kimiko entered the office. Dusty removed his hat and held it at his side.

Fumio's mother wore a navy-blue coat with six large buttons placed in two rows. Her hair was covered by a yellow-bordered blue scarf tied neatly under her chin. Kimiko, wearing a light blue jacket and a headscarf with a pattern of pink flowers, held her mother's hand.

"Mother! Hello! This is ... this is ..." Fumio paused, frowned.

"It's all right, Fumio." Dusty stepped forward, brushed his hand on his shirt, and reached it toward Fumio's mother. "Everyone calls me Dusty, now."

Recovering his manners, Fumio stood straight. "Mother, this is Dusty." Then, "Dusty, this is my mother, Mrs. Yasuo Miyota."

Mrs. Miyota reached out to lightly grasp Dusty's large, work-roughened hand. The contact lasted but a moment.

Dusty inclined his head, "Ma'am."

"Mother, Dusty is the carpenter I told you about, the day, the day I—" Fumio swallowed.

"Yes, Fumio, I remember." His mother nodded and put her hand on Kimiko's shoulder. "Dusty, this is Fumio's sister, Kimiko."

Dusty dipped his head.

"Pleased meet you," came Kimiko's quiet reply.

"Kimiko, good job!" Fumio said.

Kimiko's face lit up, then she lowered her gaze and stared at the toes of her shoes, which, Fumio saw, were coated with a layer of dust.

"Fumio, will you please walk Kimiko home and look after her while I go to the post office? I will wait in line outdoors and," she touched her headscarf, "today is so windy."

"Yes, Mother, I will." Fumio reached out for Kimiko's hand.

The door opened again and, accompanied by a gust of wind, Captain Margaret Stone and the Block Manager, Mr. Chihara, entered the office.

"Why, this is my lucky day!" exclaimed Captain Stone, smiling at Fumio.

Mr. Chihara turned to her, his head cocked.

"I had planned to locate this young man, today!"

With a nearly imperceptible shake of his head, Mr. Chihara spoke. "Captain Margaret Stone, please meet Mrs. Yasuo Miyota, her son, Fumio, and . . ." The man faltered.

"And my sister, Kimiko!" Fumio finished the older man's sentence.

"Pleased meet you, Cap'n Marg'et," Kimiko piped, head lowered, gazing upward through her eyelashes.

A small, choked noise told Fumio that Captain Stone was suppressing a laugh. He felt a warming sense of gratitude in his heart.

"And I, you, little Miss Miyota," the captain replied. She looked toward Dusty.

"Captain Margaret Stone," Mr. Chihara spoke, "this young man is Dusty. He is a worker with Griffith and Company, out of Los Angeles."

"Ah, yes!" Captain Stone responded. "I have heard the Griffith men called 'magicians,' putting the camp up in a matter of weeks, all the while living in tents, themselves."

Dusty grimaced. "I believe that's the case, ma'am, but I came along a bit later than that. They've got me on the crew that deals with oil tanks and such."

"Why that's fine, young man! I am glad to make your acquaintance! It seems there is always something happening with oil tanks and boilers."

"That is true," Mr. Chihara burst out, "but it would help if someone could keep those fool boys away from them. They have been sneaking into the laundry boiler room almost every night to play cards. I have tried to be patient and explain it's not safe, but no—" Mr. Chihara froze, mouth open. "I beg your pardon, Captain Stone, ma'am. I shouldn't have—"

"No apology needed, Mr. Chihara. Block Managers have tremendous responsibility on their shoulders. I can only imagine what you deal with at all hours of the day."

As the adults talked, Kimiko moved near the sewing machine. One small hand reached out. "Kimiko," came her mother's quiet voice. The little girl drew back.

Captain Stone smiled. "Many Block Managers' offices hold sewing machines, I see. It appears your little girl is curious."

"Actually, Captain Stone, Kimiko is sad that we did not bring our sewing machine with us. I had promised to, someday, teach her to sew." Mrs. Miyota laughed.

"But that machine. *Phfft!*" Mr. Chihara pointed at it. "That machine is nothing but trouble. Always, young girls sew in here. Always, one of them says to me that machine is not working, and I should take care of it. I do not have that kind of time!"

"With so many people using the machine," Mrs. Miyota put in, "and some of them, perhaps, quite young, the tension may need frequent adjustment."

Mr. Chihara swung his head. "Yes. Something like that."

"Momma can fix it!" Kimiko offered.

Mrs. Miyota laid her hand on the child's head.

"Ah!" Captain Stone exclaimed. "I thought I would ask *Mr.* Miyota for help, but it seems I am *extremely* fortunate today. I have learned there is, shall we call it *tailoring*, to be done, and the machine allotted us is extremely cranky!"

Captain Stone moved a hand to her hip, frowning. "Mrs. Miyota, perhaps you know the Army has seen fit to send Manzanar hundreds of uniforms, very old, from World War One, by way of supplying warm clothing to the residents, here. The staff at the orphanage, Children's

Village, received a shipment a few days ago. I must say, the superintendents of the orphanage, Mr. and Mrs. Matsumoto, are baffled as to what use can be made of those uniforms."

"Sounds like some high mucky-muck messed up," Dusty murmured, brow wrinkled. At a burst of laughter, his eyes went wide, and he met the amused gaze of the captain. Any apology he might have made was dismissed by her upraised hand.

"It's all right, young man. You are welcome to say it. I can't."

"Army uniforms, huh?" Mr. Chihara ruminated. "Most of the children at the orphanage are very young, are they not?"

"Some are babes in arms," the captain replied. "A considerable number are in elementary school. Therein lies the difficulty. The Children's Village staff cannot afford to simply discard the clothing, but it is in no way wearable for their charges. They consulted me. I suggested altering the uniforms. Mrs. Matsumoto informed me that the sewing machine in their facility is out of order. Of course," she glanced at Fumio, "I thought of Fumio's father who, as we know, can fix anything." She smiled. "Now, I learn that Fumio's *mother* has a similar gift."

"I can fix a sewing machine," Mrs. Miyota replied. "But because we left my own at home, I did not bring tools to repair one."

"I can get tools for you and, Mrs. Miyota, I believe I have a project which may be of interest. May I explain?" She glanced toward Kimiko. "I will be brief."

Mr. Chihara excused himself, beckoning to Dusty, who waved farewell to Fumio before the two men went outside to talk.

Captain Stone continued. "The orphanage staff is hard-pressed for time to undertake altering those uniforms. And I am not sure they possess the experience. We may have an opportunity, here, to do something for the youngsters of Children's Village. If you agree, I believe I can put you in the position of earning a wage while working from your apartment."

"Me? You are thinking I should do this?"

"Only if you choose. I am quite certain I can requisition a heavy-duty sewing machine for your use, full time. One that works. Could you think about it? Doing the alterations for Children's Village, I mean?"

"I could consider it, yes, Captain Stone. I would like to look at the uniforms, get an idea of what would be required."

"Indeed. In fact, the uniforms were quite well-constructed, a quarter-century ago. The material is sturdy, the design is complex. A great deal of *un-sewing* will be necessary before the clothing can be cut down and re-sewn for the children." She lifted her hand and tapped her chin with a forefinger. "You might need an apprentice, Mrs. Miyota."

Mrs. Miyota nodded. "I prefer to talk with my husband about this. We should consider how it will affect our family. Is it acceptable to give you my answer within the next few days?"

"Yes, of course. I feel so fortunate to have met you, here, Mrs. Miyota!" She turned to Fumio. "I have to say, it seems young Fumio carries good luck with him."

CHAPTER FORTY-ONE

FUMIO

On a chilly Saturday morning in November, Fumio and Joey took turns forcing an empty wheelbarrow over uneven ground toward Children's Village. No matter how watchful Fumio tried to be, it seemed the implement's single wheel found every stone and dropped into every rut, jerking both the wheelbarrow and its driver sharply sideways, over and over.

Coated with grit and deeply gouged, the wheelbarrow had obviously been used to mix concrete in the past. The worst of its failings, though, was the split in its wooden left handle, which repeatedly pinched its driver's hand.

"Let me try again," Fumio said. He removed his bandana and wrapped it around the handle. Still, the going was rough.

Finally, he and Joey each took one of the handles and in tandem set off at a trot. It was very much like a three-legged race.

"Slow down!" Joey hollered.

"Keep up!" Fumio yelled back.

Joey put on the speed.

Near their destination and out of breath, the boys stopped to study Children's Village. The orphanage's three buildings were finished with white-painted wooden siding. Fumio had heard that each building had its own plumbing, plus three coal stoves, and the flooring kept dust and grass from coming in from below.

He took hold of both handles and pushed the wheelbarrow to the back of the middle building, where an older boy worked moving out crates piled high with clothing, all of it dull green. Olive drab. As they neared, he saw that the boy's eyes watered and his nose was red. In a moment, he and Joey knew why.

"Whath th' awful thmell?" Joey asked, covering his nose and backing away quickly.

Fumio took his bandana from the wheelbarrow's handle and tied it to cover the lower half of his face. "Moth ballth," he answered, "mildew, mold, and old wool."

"Ah, come on, you two!" the older boy exclaimed. "Are you telling me the smell bothers you?" He burst out laughing then started coughing.

"How'd you get stuck with *this* job?" Fumio asked. "Did you make somebody mad?"

"I could ask you the same question," the boy replied, and laughed again. "I'm part of the Salvation Army bunch, and I'm one of the oldest and strongest here. These are heavy." He pointed to the old wheelbarrow. "You brought your own wheels. That's good."

He gestured toward another wheelbarrow, shiny and probably new. "Use this one, too. You'll be making more than one trip. You're taking these to be resewn, right?"

"Yes," Fumio replied. "But first, we're taking them to the laundry."

"Think they need that?" The boy grinned. "Well, I'd better get back to work."

"See you later!" Fumio turned to Joey and spoke in a low tone, "You need to cover your nose and mouth."

"Yeah," Joey mumbled. "I know, but . . ."

"But what?"

Joey lowered his voice. "You *know* that bandana *looks* kinda *dumb*, right?"

"We would *be* dumb to not steer clear of these fumes. And we've got work to do!"

"Okay, let's get to work. But I'm not wearing *one of those*."

His arms loaded with uniforms, Fumio struggled to open the door to Block 3's laundry room. Joey followed, similarly burdened. Fumio's mother was adding detergent to a large wash tub, while her apprentice, Joey's older sister, Etsu, circled a wooden paddle through the contents.

Across the long, narrow space, other women toiled over other laundry tubs. "Back-breaking work," Fumio had heard Mrs. Kato call it. The smells of stress and sweat mingled with those of detergent and bleach and, now, the eye-stinging fumes of moth balls.

Clusters of small boys playing marbles wrinkled their noses. Exclamations of "Pssheeww!" "Yuck!" and, "What's that smell?" came from all around them.

"Come on, Joey!" Fumio spoke with quiet urgency. "Let's get this job done!" With two more relays, the uniforms were carried from the wheelbarrows into the laundry room and laid in piles near the washtubs.

"Boys, wait!" Mrs. Miyota pulled a clean handkerchief from her apron pocket, "Joey, you should use this. Tie it as you have seen others do when the air is bad."

Joey reached out for it. "Thank you, ma'am," he spoke in a low voice. When the laundry room door closed behind him, he stuffed the handkerchief in his back pocket.

Fumio bit down on a protest and, with a sigh, took charge of the old wheelbarrow. The boys did not talk on the return trip to Children's Village. Fumio looked over to see Joey gazing about, as if in search of something.

What Joey found was a deep rut. The front wheel of the wheelbarrow he pushed slammed into it. The impact threw him sideways, and he sat down hard.

"Are you all right, young man?" called a man's voice.

Turning, Fumio saw the man he referred to as Mr. Toyo-san and his nephew, Hajime, who carried a black bag.

Joey did not answer the question.

"I think he is, sir," Fumio replied.

Joey rolled onto his knees and rose.

Mr. Toyo nodded, asking, "Fumio, is your family well?"

"Yes, sir, we are. Mr. Toyo-san, this is my friend—" Fumio was interrupted by a shout.

"Joey! Hey, chump!"

Fumio turned again. This time, Joey's cousin, Sam, stood several feet away, his shirt untucked and his jacket hanging open. It appeared to have been a while since his last haircut.

Sam nailed Joey with a glare then glanced over his shoulder and jerked his chin.

Joey's face lost expression. He pulled the handkerchief from his pocket and handed it to Fumio. "Gotta go," he said and walked away.

When Fumio looked back at Mr. Toyo and his nephew, puzzlement flashed in Hajime's eyes. "Your friends?"

Fumio shrugged. "Joey lived not far away on Bainbridge Island. He is my classmate."

As their voices receded, Fumio heard Sam say, "Kato, you smell worse than a buzzard's last meal!" Joey responded, "Shuddup, Sam."

To Mr. Toyo and Hajime, Fumio said, "Sam is Joey's cousin. His family lived on Terminal Island." He turned his focus to the wheelbarrow's left handle, running a thumb across the split wood.

Mr. Toyo nodded. "Those from Terminal Island have much cause for anger. They had little warning. Perhaps the commercial fishers understood that their ownership of radio equipment *could* provoke suspicion in FBI agents, but reasonably assumed it was their *radios* that might be taken, rather than their actual selves."

"Sam's father is in Tuna Canyon detention camp. Joey's father, taken from Bainbridge Island, is at Fort Missoula."

Frowning, Mr. Toyo moved his hand to his chin.

"Joey's older sister, Etsu, is helping my mother alter Army uniforms to make winter clothing for children at the orphanage. Joey and I were taking uniforms to be laundered. This was our second trip." He sighed. "But Sam . . ."

"Yes," Mr. Toyo inclined his head. "Shikata ga nai?" he ventured.

But Hajime spoke up, "I'll help. You have two wheelbarrows. I'll help."

"Yes, Hajime," Mr. Toyo said. "I must go on with our errand. You can work with Fumio." He reached out and took the black bag from Hajime.

"After the uniforms are laundered, what comes next?" Mr. Toyo asked.

"My mother and Etsu will take out the seams, cut them to size, and reconstruct them. An industrial-sized machine has already been moved into a corner of our quarters, and my father is building shelves for the uniforms."

"It is fortunate we met here. This is a demanding job." He went on his way.

Fumio pointed to the shiny, new wheelbarrow. "Hajime, you can take that one. You don't know, yet, what you volunteered for, but I sure can use your help. And, that bandana you've got around your neck, you're going to need that."

He wrapped the split in the wheelbarrow's left handle with the handkerchief Joey had rejected and adjusted his grip, then he led the way toward Children's Village.

During the course of the day's work, Fumio introduced Hajime to his parents and Kimiko. They thanked his new friend for his kindness.

Evening approached when, after the last run, Fumio and Hajime left the Children's Village wheelbarrow with the boy "from the Salvation Army bunch," as he had described himself. Returning to the front of the white-painted building, Fumio saw his family coming toward them.

Hajime paused, bowed. "Mrs. Miyota-san, Mr. Miyota-san, Kimiko."

Kimiko giggled. "I getta ride in a wheelbarrow!" Fumio saw she had on a new pair of dungarees, rolled up at the ankles to *grow into*. She wore a heavy coat and a pair of gloves, too. The air was cool. "I ride in a wheelbarrow!"

"Fumio," his mother said, "she has been pleading with me since noon. She would have ridden on top of the damp uniforms if I had let her."

Fumio grinned, thinking, *I'd like to have been riding, too.*

"Hajime," Mr. Miyota said, "why not head to your quarters from here? You will make it in time to go to the mess hall with your family." Then he reached out his hand.

Hajime glanced toward Mr. Miyota and down, then reached forward and shook his hand. "Thank you, sir. And thank you for allowing me to help,

Mrs. Miyota-san." Slowly, Hajime bowed and continued to gaze down when he straightened.

"We thank you, Hajime," Mr. Miyota replied. "We hope to meet your family sometime soon. They seem to have raised a fine son."

Hajime bowed once more. "Fumio! See you around!" he said and took off running toward his family's apartment.

Fumio held the wheelbarrow steady while his mother laid a small rug inside it. His father lifted Kimiko and sat her down in the concave "barrow." Fumio took a deep breath and applied force evenly as he began pushing the wheelbarrow slowly toward the office of Block 3's manager. Kimiko sat still for a moment, but then began bouncing with excitement.

His father stepped beside Fumio and carefully took the handles of the wheelbarrow. Fumio walked along on one side of the wheelbarrow, while his mother walked on the other.

With only a whisper from a lifting breeze and an occasional complaint from the old wheelbarrow, the early evening became quiet.

Then, came a sound Fumio had heard once or twice before, but could not identify.

Boom . . . boom . . . boom . . . boom . . .

Fumio looked to his father and saw his father seek his mother's eyes. Fumio believed a thought passed between his parents, as though they heard more in those moments than he.

Boom . . . boom . . . boom . . . boom . . .
Boommm—Boommm
Boom . . . boom . . . boom . . . boom . . .

"*Taiko* drumming," Mr. Miyota answered Fumio's unspoken question.

CHAPTER FORTY-TWO

FUMIO

Fumio maneuvered a push-broom across the uneven floor of the recreation hall. His sixth-grade class used a corner of the space for lessons, and at the end of each school day, students took turns putting the classroom in order. Today—the calendar announced, Friday, the fourth of December—it was Fumio's turn, along with two other children. Fumio did not mind the extra time, knowing that Miss McCarren worked hard to teach her students in a difficult situation.

During classes, Fumio sat ten inches above the floor on a bench built by his father, a piece of two-by-four, twelve inches in length, with two shorter pieces attached perpendicularly on each end. He carried his bench to and from his classroom each day, as did all students lucky enough to have one.

Mr. Miyota made a smaller version for Kimiko, and managed, over the space of a week, to get enough scraps to make benches for the Kato children. He was working to find wood to build benches for whoever needed them, hoping desks and chairs would arrive soon.

The three students made quick work of sweeping the floor; cleaning the day's dust and grit from the windowsills; and doing whatever tasks the teacher might assign.

"Is there anything more we can do for you?" Fumio asked his teacher as he placed the broom back in its usual corner.

"Not today, thank you. You children have a good weekend!" Miss McCarren said, looking up from grading papers.

Fumio caught her smile and waved on his way out the door.

Outside, he paused, taking in the late afternoon's fading light. Against the insistent wind, he turned up the collar of his coat.

He had not gone far when he heard *Boom boom . . . Boom boom.*

Taiko! Knowing his mother would not yet be looking for him, he followed the sounds.

On the raised landing of the entry to Block 10's recreation hall, he stood near the open door. *Boom . . . boom-boom*, it resonated in his chest. *BOOM . . . BOOM*, and through the soles of his feet. He closed his eyes, focusing, *Boom . . . boom-boom*, until he heard a voice.

"Fumio?"

He jumped. "Hajime! Hello . . . I was just . . . ."

"Listening!" Hajime stepped outside and came down the stairs. "Sure! So many different tones. I often listen with my eyes closed, too!" He pointed to the door. "Come inside!"

"Thank you." Fumio glanced down. "I don't want to interrupt."

"The class will not have begun; come see the drums! The taiko dojo is a place for learning. We are all students. Except the sensei, of course."

Hajime climbed the stairs and, tentatively, Fumio followed.

On the landing, Hajime put his hand lightly on Fumio's arm and moved in front of him. As he crossed the threshold, Hajime paused, then bowed before moving into the room.

Fumio took a breath and stepped just inside the doorway. Eyes down, he lowered his head and his shoulders. He waited a moment, then moved inside. Looking to the right, he saw Hajime remove his shoes and stand with his back against the wall. Fumio did the same, and stood next to him. Hajime looked his way and pressed his lips tightly together. Nodding, Fumio conveyed his understanding.

In the dojo, Fumio saw, students stood near the wall or sat on the floor, cross-legged or kneeling, facing the center of the room. A few, their eyes closed, tapped out rhythms on their legs or forearms. No one spoke, but for a few students—high school-aged, he thought—who he could see were giving quiet instructions with the occasional sounding of a drum.

The drums were of many sizes and various shapes. He saw old tires stacked in the corner, too, but since every building in the camp served purposes of storage, it did not surprise him.

Hajime tapped him lightly on his wrist, and Fumio looked over to see that, from across the room, a gentleman dressed in a loose-fitting shirt and trousers walked their way. His gray-streaked hair was bound back from his face, and he wore a serious but friendly expression.

Hajime bowed.

Fumio bowed, keeping his gaze toward the man's shoulder as he straightened.

"Hajime." The man spoke the name with a nod. "Your friend?"

"Yes, Sensei Amabe-san. I would like to introduce my friend, Fumio Miyota." Hajime gestured, "Fumio Miyota, please meet Sensei Amabe-san, Master of our taiko dojo."

"Sensei, I hoped it would be acceptable for Fumio to see the drums. He is interested in woodworking. His father is a builder."

The sensei tilted his head sideways. "Certainly. One of our senpai, a senior student, will guide you, Fumio."

An older student came over. "Yes, Sensei?"

"Masato, please give young Fumio a few minutes of your time. Hajime tells us Fumio would be interested in the structure of drums. His father is a builder."

Fumio was sure he detected a faint smile on the sensei's face.

"I am pleased to meet you, Fumio," the senpai said. "Instruction begins in five minutes, so I must be brief. But we would be glad to have you visit us again." He turned. "Hajime, which drum first, do you think? Should it be the odaiko?"

Fumio was awed by the sight of the large odaiko, which, the senpai, Masato, said meant simply "the big drum." An odaiko, Masato explained, was shaped from a single block of wood and could be as large as six feet high and three feet across. Masato said that this less massive one was more practical to transport to Manzanar. He went on to tell Fumio that the drums used by the group he belonged to in Los Angeles were moved from a now-vacant Buddhist temple to a storage room in a Methodist Church, where the pastor had committed to safeguarding them.

As they passed the stack of tires, Masato asked, "What do you suppose those are?"

Hajime grinned.

"Well," Fumio frowned, "they look like old tires."

"Exactly!" Masato laughed. "Kohai, students of taiko, use old tires for practice sessions, to save the drums for performances. Taiko drums would be difficult to replace if damaged."

Fumio felt glad to see such familiar objects as old tires—grayed by long travels on rough highways and smelling of deteriorating rubber—sharing space with the drums formed of rare, costly woods, their heads composed of leather worn soft, their fittings ornate with brass and silk tassels. These drums were created to express taiko drumming's ancient and honored tradition.

Masato led the way to a wooden rack shrouded with canvas. He pulled the canvas back to reveal small drums. "Shime-daiko," he said, catching the eye of the sensei, who nodded. The senpai, with a glance toward the sensei, sounded a few beats on a drum.

Rather than return the shime-daiko to the wooden rack, Masato looked toward Fumio and slowly lowered it to the floor. Fumio followed the movement with his eyes and saw that the floor was darkly water stained. He looked up to the ceiling and saw a water stain there, too.

Ah. Fumio understood. *The roof is leaking.* Hajime's courtesy in mentioning Fumio's father had triggered the thought of aid. Fumio resolved to speak with his father.

The sensei had moved to the center of the room. Masato returned the drum to the rack.

The kohai walked to locations about the room and settled with their drums.

Fumio bid Hajime goodbye and went to the door, where he turned, awaited the sensei's notice, then bowed. The sensei nodded.

Stepping onto the landing, Fumio was struck by the sensation that he was leaving part of himself behind. He experienced it as a loss. Within the dojo, he had felt a connection with a greater force outside himself. As the drumming began, the feeling transferred to the inside of his body, a quaking that left him lightheaded. Internal movement, a shift, the drumbeats pulsing in his bones.

• • •

From the landing of the taiko dojo, he heard the low growl of an engine, a harsh grinding of gears. He saw a plume of dust rising above tar paper rooftops.

A truck careened around the corner of a building. From its flank waved a large black flag. Fumio had heard about this vehicle. The driver and his fist-pumping cohort were members of a gang known as the Black Dragons. They had evidently commandeered one of the camp's garbage trucks. The black flag the truck bore was emblazoned with crossbones.

In their fury toward the American government, members of the gang had declared loyalty to Japan. To increase their power, they harried Manzanar's residents with threats and violence.

It was the Black Dragons Fumio faced now. The driver accelerated straight toward the dojo's landing shouting, "Banzai! Banzai!" The truck was so close that Fumio could pick out individual dead bugs among the hundreds splattered on its grill. Finally, the driver pulled hard right, and the truck skidded sideways. Fumio threw his arm in front of his eyes as the truck's wheels threw rocks and sand.

Students erupted onto the landing. "What's happening?" "What in blazes was that?"

"Fumio! Are you all right?" Hajime pulled on Fumio's sleeve as he stood, stunned. Then, in a break from the clamor of those around him, he heard the roar of the engine as it approached once more.

A student moved to hurtle down the steps, but a senpai grabbed him and held on. "No! It's a truck, man! Think!"

Another student shook his fist and spoke a profanity. The sensei stepped to his side, shook his head, *no,* firmly, and pulled the boy's arm down.

The flag-flying garbage truck sped faster this time than before. Two senpai stepped in front of the sensei. At nearly the last moment, the truck veered. Stones pelted the students. Fumio could taste the bitter fumes of exhaust, could plainly see a wild grin on the driver's face as the Black Dragons sped off, leaving shock and anger in their wake.

The sensei pushed between the two senpai and moved to the landing's railing. "What is important?"

In silence, the students turned and walked back into the dojo.

CHAPTER FORTY-THREE

FUMIO

A beam of light slashed the darkness. Fumio knew what it meant. Eight o'clock.

Each night at eight o'clock, maroon-and-green-uniformed security guards, members of the internal police force, were deployed across the internment camp like an army to inventory residents. Wielding a flashlight, armed with a clipboard, each guard knocked, peered through partially opened doors, and surveyed the occupants.

Here! thought Fumio, mentally confirming his presence while standing in plain view.

And, while marking the chart, the man would still ask, "All here?"

How has it come to this? Fumio wondered. Almost a year had passed since Japan's military attacked US ships at Pearl Harbor and war was declared, yet his family and others were given no idea how much longer they were to be held.

Kimiko had been put to bed. Sitting in chairs built since the ban on the use of scrap lumber was lifted, Fumio's mother wrote a letter, and his father made a supply list for another job he had accepted. Fumio went to the cabinet and from a stack of old envelopes, chose one. Settling down at the table, he teased the envelope apart, laid it flat, and began to draw. He penciled a large square in its center.

We are fenced in, Fumio thought. *Boxed in*, too. Every night, at eight o'clock, an internal security guard makes sure of that. We can't turn off the light, our *only* light, without the guard's okay. But the searchlights in the towers? We can't turn them off, at all.

After studying the first square for a moment, Fumio drew another slightly smaller one inside of it. And then another, smaller again. *So much time has passed. We live in one room, share bathing facilities with strangers, carry a pail to a community spigot for water. Why?*

Because of the war, came the certain answer. A war the United States *had* to win. *But it's our war, too!* Fumio thought. The ships attacked at Pearl Harbor were part of *our* navy, and Japanese American sailors died that day.

Fumio held the paper at arm's length, returned it to the tabletop, and added four small squares in an upper corner, creating a larger square.

We must *wait it out* at Manzanar, he thought, *building a town where no one wants to live. But I see men clearing sagebrush, breaking ground to plant and harvest more crops, some to feed us, some to be sold for profit. I see men making the irrigation system better and bigger.*

With the edge of the pencil point, he broadened and darkened some of the lines. He studied the effect, then lowered the paper, his thoughts weighing heavy in his mind.

Curfews and searchlights hadn't kept someone from trying to burn down the internees' co-op store, he thought. *They hadn't stopped boys from sneaking into the boiler room at night to play poker. They hadn't overcome the gangs Hajime told me about, like the Dunbar gang from Los Angeles, or the Black Dragons, who were not actually Black Dragons, but had borrowed the name from a gang in Japan to sound tougher. And curfews and searchlights had not stopped angry people from making threats against the center's police force.*

Fumio turned over the envelope. Sent by the sixth graders from his school on Bainbridge Island, it was addressed to *Mr. Fumio Miyota, Block 3, Manzanar Relocation Camp, California.*

A knock at the door brought Mr. Miyota to his feet. Fumio let his hand go still. Mrs. Miyota rose, went to Kimiko's cot, and pulled the blue-patterned bedsheet they used as a curtain across, metal grommets rasping against the length of clothesline on which it hung. She stood there, where it would not quite close, blocking the gap.

Against his father's measured steps, the knock came again. Fumio saw his father place his foot near the bottom of the door as he pulled it a few inches toward himself then peered out.

Fumio felt the brush of a chill wind. His father reached for his coat and slipped it on as he stepped outside, pulling the door closed behind him.

"Go to sleep, dear one, Mama is here," his mother murmured, then came from behind the hanging bedsheet.

Some time passed before the door opened again then closed quietly. Stepping inside, his expression grim, Mr. Miyota looked toward Kimiko's cot.

"She is asleep," Mrs. Miyota said, walking quietly to the table.

Mr. Miyota gave a half-nod, went to the oil stove to adjust the flame, then took his place back at the table, and the three shared the enclosure of light within the darkened room.

Gazing from under his lashes, Fumio studied his parents. His father rested one forearm on the table while propping a hand on his leg. His mother sat straight, her face expressionless.

"We are fortunate," his father replied, "to have as our security guard a Bainbridge Island neighbor. Mr. Seiki-san does not, as a rule, bear tales, but he feels he must warn us. Most emphatically, he said, 'Stay alert!'"

"For weeks, now, I have heard rumors that trouble is brewing. Tonight, that trouble has come to a boil."

"What kind of trouble?" Fumio asked.

"People are angry about our lengthy confinement here, when Japanese Americans have made no attempt to undermine the war effort, have not been charged with any crime. Some people feel it is time to take a stand against injustice and insist that our grievances be heard."

"Would that be wrong?" Fumio asked.

"It is important to understand, Son, that many of us *are* standing up for our rights as citizens—writing letters to government officials, contributing editorials to newspapers, giving testimony to our beliefs, working hard, and living as good citizens do.

"But at Manzanar, there are groups—*factions*—of those confined here who argue that peaceful protest has accomplished nothing."

Factions, Fumio mouthed. The word sounded, to him, like *fractions,* and *fractured.*

"People in one group," Mr. Miyota began, and Fumio could almost *see* his father's points charted on a chalkboard, "believe the best choice is to cooperate with government instructions, whatever we are asked to do. Some are working to regain the right for Japanese Americans to join the military and fight, thinking it is the only way to be accepted as loyal Americans.

"Another group, a very loud and angry group, feels the time for cooperation and aiding the war effort has passed. They wish to be certain their resistance is *seen.* Others even wish to go to Japan and live there, where they feel they will have better treatment."

Fumio felt his stomach twist. "Would we do that, Father?"

"No, Fumio, we would not. Many of the mess hall workers, though, have held meetings and organized to ask for better pay and improved work conditions. Some are convinced that food intended for mess hall kitchens is being diverted, stolen from shipments and storehouses. They believe camp administrators ignore the theft, and the goods are sold on the black market."

"The black market?" Fumio frowned.

"If it is true, it means the food is being sold outside the camp at a lower price than it would be if it were obtained legally, or at a higher price, to people who can pay top dollar for goods that are scarce or rationed, such as meat and sugar." He shook his head. "Mr. Seiki told me there is much anger building here at Camp Manzanar."

Fumio did not care to be around angry people, although at Manzanar he could not always avoid it. *I am just a boy,* he thought, *who wants to sit at my own table in my own home, while Flyer rests on a scrap of blanket under the sink.* He turned the envelope over and read the address again, *Mr. Fumio Miyota, Block 3, Manzanar Relocation Camp, California.*

CHAPTER FORTY-FOUR

FUMIO

On Sunday morning, the sixth of December, 1942, according to the Feed and Seed Store calendar the Whitlocks had sent as a gift, Fumio came to consciousness before dawn, as usual, with his face turned toward the wall. He did not bother to open his eyes but tuned in to the sounds of the camp waking up. This morning, though, his nose tingled.

He opened his eyes, yelped, and fell backward. A spider hung on a strand of web that had been but an inch from his nose. *We were eye to eye*, he thought, although his eyes had been closed. Wide awake now, he lifted a hand, brushed at his nose, scooted sideways, and levered himself out of bed, staying as far away from the spider as he could manage.

He moved quickly and came back with a piece of paper and a cup. His father glanced his way as Fumio maneuvered the piece of paper behind the spider then placed the cup over the top of it, trapping the spider inside.

"Saving the spider's life?" his father asked.

"If I swatted it and missed, it'd get away and maybe go under my bed," Fumio replied.

"To join a hundred of its eight-legged friends," his father commented, and chuckled.

Fumio inched the door open, released the spider, and watched it skitter away, before pulling the door firmly shut again.

He returned to his sleeping area to dress for a trip to the latrine. *A rough way to start the day,* he thought, once outside and making his way across the semi-frozen ground. He had made use of outdoor toilets before—outhouses, they were called, or half-moon houses for the shape of the vent cut in the door—but never at such a distance, and never had he been forced to share the facilities alongside a dozen other men and boys with no partitions to separate them.

Other residents were on the same trek. Men were unshaven with undershirts only partially covered by coats hanging open. Women wore trousers and tattered sweaters under their husbands' overcoats, headscarves covering the pin curls still in their hair. In earlier days at the camp, people didn't leave their quarters unless they were neatly dressed and groomed. Now, there were no such niceties.

Wardrobe aside, this morning, something felt *off*.

Adults scanned the landscape from side to side while trying to appear disinterested. Attempting stealth, they watched each other from the corners of their eyes. While in the past there had been the occasional casual greeting, this morning there was only silence.

Fumio made use of the latrine and got back home as quickly as he could. As he re-entered their quarters, his father raised questioning eyes.

"Father, it's very quiet out there."

"Yes, it is. We must be cautious, Fumio. There has been talk of a kitchen workers' walk-off. It is said that, after breakfast, outside the Block 22 mess hall, there will be a meeting."

"Will you go the meeting?"

"No, Son. I do not see that I have any part in this fight. The theft of sugar may have affected us, but I do not think that is what this is about."

"What is it about, Father?"

"Injustices, insults. For months they have piled up like great mounds of tumbleweeds. Someone is about to strike a match."

• • •

Fumio and his family went to breakfast at the sounding of the bell. The mess hall was crowded, as usual. Many young diners were disorderly—sitting in groups, talking loudly, even throwing food from table to table—as had been increasingly the case over the months.

His mother kept Kimiko near while they went through the line, and Fumio followed his father. They were served toast and scrambled eggs.

The toast was unfailingly burnt, but when a whole loaf of bread was toasted at once, what could be expected? Scraping charcoal off the toast was a morning ritual at Manzanar.

The eggs? Fumio had seen cooks break four eggs in each hand over cavernous tin bowls, stir them through with a big fork, and dump two dozen at a time into a giant skillet. Great globs were flopped over once or twice, scraped into a serving pan—some portions solid enough to bounce, others translucent and gooey—then the whole mess was plopped in clumps onto plates. A constant cry was, "Pass the ketchup!"

The cookery was no different than usual, this morning; however, the servers scowled as they dumped eggs onto plates and tossed slices of toast onto trays. Diners who spoke their thanks, as Fumio had been taught to do, were granted not so much as a glance in return. And the words the kitchen staff mumbled were not fit for the ears of children.

Joey Kato arrived, along with his family. Since Joey had taken to spending the bulk of his free time with Sam, Fumio never knew what to expect of him. This morning, though, Joey wore a solemn, but not sullen, expression.

Mrs. Kato sat at one of the long tables. Etsu went through the line to receive her mother's meal, placed it in front of her, then went back for her own. Joey kept a hand on his four-year-old brother, Yushi, while they navigated the line together.

As the Miyotas gathered their empty dishes onto trays, preparing to leave the hall, Mrs. Miyota murmured, "I must ask after the Kato family's health before we leave."

Fumio waited with his father and sister as his mother greeted Joey's mother. Doing his best to avoid the appearance of intrusion on adult matters, still, Fumio saw that Mrs. Kato dipped her head, touched a hand to the base of her throat, and looked toward Yushi. Mrs. Miyota nodded, brow furrowed. She turned to Etsu, bowed slightly, and spoke quietly. Etsu smiled and bowed in return.

Walking back to their quarters, Fumio's mother shared that Mrs. Kato was tired because Yushi had been feeling ill the night before, and she was uncertain whether he was better this morning. "There might be sickness moving through the children of the nursery school," she said.

• • •

At lunchtime, Kimiko was fussy and did not want to leave the barracks. "She is flushed and warm," Mrs. Miyota said. "There's no question she is ill."

It was decided that Fumio would go with Mr. Miyota to the mess hall, and they would eat quickly and bring back something for Mrs. Miyota and Kimiko.

The hour was nearing one o'clock. As they walked, Fumio was surprised to see so many people who were strangers to him streaming past. They acted hurried. Those who spoke sounded angry. At this time of day, he would have expected people to be in the mess halls finishing their lunch, rather than striding around the compound.

Reaching Block 3's mess hall, he saw that there was no line outside the door. He and his father walked in, got their meals, and found a place to eat. An older gentleman sitting nearby lifted his head and nodded. The man chewed slowly, eyebrows raised. He looked as if he wanted to speak. The meat, today, Fumio thought, must be very tough.

Finally, the gentleman swallowed. "How come you two aren't at the big meeting? No matter who you believe—or don't believe—there's gonna be big speeches, and it should be quite a show." He looked toward Fumio. "You're missin' it, young man!" When he smiled, the gaps in the man's teeth told the tale of why it had taken him so long to chew the beef in the stew.

Fumio nodded, smiling.

"You're missing it, too, aren't you?" Mr. Miyota said.

"I'm old. I've heard it all. Doesn't matter what it's about, lotsa people are angry, and someone is gonna get strung up."

Fumio gasped.

His father put his hand on his shoulder. "He is using a figure of speech, Son. He means, some folks don't care who it might be, as long as someone appears to suffer for the wrong they feel has been done them."

Fumio was not sure he understood but didn't care to admit as much in the presence of a gentleman he did not know. He decided he would ask his father later.

•   •   •   •

In the late afternoon, Fumio's mother sat on the edge of Kimiko's cot, holding her daughter on her lap. The little girl's face was flushed, and she was fussy.

His father removed the lid from the family's water jar and used a long-handled dipper to fill a small cup and a shallow bowl, both of which Fumio took, along with a cloth, to his mother. She bathed Kimiko's face and persuaded her to swallow a little bit of the tepid water.

Mrs. Miyota's eyes were shadowed. Fumio could see that not only his sister felt ill.

When his mother was finished, he took the cloth and hung it over a nail to dry, placed the cup and bowl in the washbasin, and returned the dipper to its hook on the wall. Finally, he carefully tightened the lid on the water jar. Order and routine made life bearable at Manzanar.

Fumio saw that the water jar was nearly full, but the pail he used to carry water from the community spigot and that held his family's backup supply, was missing its lid and was empty. Water stored too long developed a dank taste, so one of Fumio's most important jobs was to renew the family's supply of fresh water each day.

Mrs. Miyota edged further onto the cot and, with her arms around Kimiko, leaned against the wall.

"Fumio," Mr. Miyota said, "please bring your mother's pillow."

His father lifted Kimiko and laid her on the straw-filled mattress, then urged his wife into a more comfortable position, moving her feet onto the mattress and placing her pillow between her back and the wall. She sighed and, her hand on Kimiko's head, closed her eyes.

At a quiet rap at the door, Kimiko stirred, but neither she nor her mother woke. Fumio closed the bedsheet drape. Mr. Miyota pulled the door ajar a few inches, then stepped back to open it fully. "Captain Stone," he said, with a slow nod, "please, come in."

As Captain Stone entered, a low-angled ray of sun glinted from the insignia on the lapel of her deep blue jacket and reflected off the brass hat pin securing her military cap. Her white gloves were marred by dust.

"Captain Stone, I apologize that my wife is not able to greet you. Our daughter, Kimiko, is not feeling well."

"I am sorry to hear that. I do believe . . . *something* . . . is going around in the center." She glanced toward Fumio and, with a trace of a smile, she nodded. "Fumio, good afternoon."

"Good afternoon, Captain Stone, ma'am."

The captain stood just inside the door. "I regret imposing on you, here in your quarters, but the situation is urgent."

Signaled by a movement of his father's eyes, Fumio went to the chair near the table and pulled it out, turning it toward the center of the room.

Gesturing, Mr. Miyota asked, "Captain Stone, won't you please be seated?"

"Thank you," she began, "but there's no time . . ." she paused. "Oh. Yes, thank you," she murmured, and sat down.

Fumio went to stand near his cot.

Mr. Miyota stood near the cabinet. "How can we help you, Captain Stone?"

"I know this is not a good time to ask, however, I desperately need help with one of the doors at the hospital. It is badly damaged. I couldn't say how it happened, but it must be repaired right away." Captain Stone took a deep breath. "There is really no one else I trust with this, at the moment. Could you please help?"

"Of course. Fumio will be here to help his mother, so I will come with you, now." Mr. Miyota got his tools and left with Captain Stone.

Fumio found a piece of paper and began sketching the huge odaiko drum he'd seen in the taiko dojo, reproducing the smooth curve of the wood, gleaming under its glossy lacquer. Recalling the taut skin covering the drum, he imagined how it might feel under his fingers.

He heard his mother's voice. "Fumio? I did not mean to sleep, only to rest my eyes." Mrs. Miyota came from behind the drape. "Your father?"

Fumio explained Mr. Miyota's errand.

"The door was damaged, and no one knows how it happened? Fumio, is the unrest in the center worsening, do you think?"

"I'm not sure, Mother. But nothing seems . . . as usual." He frowned.

Lines of worry creasing her brow, Mrs. Miyota pressed her arms to her sides. "Fumio, you must be hungry. I hope Kimiko will feel well enough to eat later. I do not believe it is wise, though, to go to the mess hall for the evening meal, especially since your father is not here." Fumio could hear fatigue in his mother's voice. "I have a small box of cream of rice. We can boil water in the tea kettle to add to the dry cereal and heat it over the oil burner. We have no milk, but we can add a pinch of sugar. Let me think . . . I put the cereal—"

"Mama!" Kimiko called, and Mrs. Miyota pivoted, knocking the water jar off the cabinet.

Bamm! Whoosh. The jar broke, shards of glass scattered, water spilled to the floor.

Fumio rushed to his mother's side. "Wait! I will clean it up! Mother, please. Sit down."

Mrs. Miyota inhaled a shaky breath.

Kimiko began to cry.

"Kimiko, please! Please, don't cry! It was just a loud noise, that's all!"

He put his hand on his mother's shoulder, guided her toward the chair. "I'll clean it up, Mother. Let *me* do it, please."

"Fumio! We have no water! We have never run out of water before!"

It was true. Each day, he carried the pail to the community spigot. When full, it held enough water to fill the jar twice. Today, though, routine had been disrupted. Never had there been a day when their water supply dwindled so low. Never had there been a day like today.

He had not wanted to leave his mother and little sister alone. "Mother, I am sorry. You were sleeping and Kimiko is ill . . ."

"No, Fumio! It is no one's fault." She bit her lip. "Perhaps when your father returns . . ."

Truth told, Fumio had begun to worry about his father. It shouldn't take so long to fix a door, should it? Had he run into trouble?

But, water—the family had to have water. "Mother, if you're feeling well enough, I'll go for water now, before dark." When his mother did not answer, he added, "I think it's best."

Fumio swept the broken glass onto an old issue of the *Manzanar Free Press*, which he then rolled up, enclosing the glass, and pushed far beneath his bed.

As he reached for his coat, he looked toward his mother. "You'll be all right?"

Kimiko began, once more, to cry.

Mrs. Miyota went to the chest at the foot of Fumio's bed, took out his knit cap, handed it to him, and watched while he pulled it on. Taking the pail, Fumio went out the door and into Manzanar's approaching night.

• • •

Fumio had not gone far when he heard unfamiliar noises, discordant sounds, raised voices. Turning a corner, he was shocked to see a crowd converging. Their destination . . . *where*?

It *was* Sunday evening, but people strolling toward services usually chatted in a friendly manner or sang religious songs. These people did not appear to be in a church frame of mind.

Perhaps a dance? With music—or a band? But, surely not. Tomorrow was a school day.

Curiosity pulled at Fumio. His family, though, was counting on him to come back soon, with water. His stomach growled, again, calling to mind the prospect of hot cereal.

The night was fully dark. Unseen until they were upon him, a small knot of men ran pell-mell into Fumio. He stumbled, regained his balance, then dropped the pail and inadvertently kicked it as he scrambled for it. The water pail was lost, and in a moment, so was he.

He was engulfed by hundreds, *perhaps thousands*, of people. Beefy shoulders boxed Fumio's ears. Careless elbows poked his chest. His heart seized, then began to pound.

Trying to escape the crush and get his bearings, Fumio took a step backward and came down on a large boot, nearly tripping again. Its owner growled, "Get outta here, kid! Go home!"

Among the crowd were carpenters Fumio had seen working on various buildings. He approached them, but they paid him no attention.

One foot in front of the other, Fumio focused on taking breaths and staying upright as he stumbled through the swarm, hoping to find a neighbor. He saw no one from Bainbridge Island. None of the uniformed, Internal Security Guards were anywhere to be found.

A man stood on the Block 22 mess hall landing. "I myself fought for this country in World War One!" he declared. "I have lived and worked here for many years. Yet, I cannot be a citizen! I cannot own land! I am not allowed to hold any official position. *I cannot be trusted*, they say, to represent my fellow workers!"

Cries of fury, near deafening, were silenced when the man raised his fist. "I tell you we have *spies* among us! Inu! Lying dogs, they make up stories to bring trouble to *their neighbors*, while they cover up the thievery of the government's men!"

The crowd roared. Fumio heard "traitors," and he shivered. He heard "stool pigeons" and felt pain between his eyes. He heard "disloyal," and his face burned for the person so labeled. He heard "inu" and wondered, *how does it make sense to insult people by calling them dogs*? He worked his way to the edge of the crowd, then out, and walked away, preferring the black of night to the darkness within the mob.

CHAPTER FORTY-FIVE

FUMIO

Fumio wandered blindly. *How far? How long?* He had no idea. Then he caught a familiar scent carried on a breeze, the fragrance of budding fruit trees.

In the first week of December? Surely not. A pear orchard in winter. *How could it be?*

Perhaps heightened by the desert air? Yes, *pears*. Golden globes of new life announced their intent to blossom as if it were spring. He walked toward that promise.

Soon, the ground softened. Fallow, now, still this soil was bursting with life ready to rush to the roots of the orchard's trees. For this *was* an orchard. Fumio laid his hand on the rough bark of an aged pear tree. He looked about, his eyesight adjusting to the dim glow of starlight working through the clouded darkness.

Perhaps a dozen trees were arrayed around him, their branches spread in welcome. Old trees, their trunks were sturdy. They had suffered the cold of thirty winters, thirsted through thirty seasons of drought. Each year, they had drawn what strength they could from this place. They had survived.

Choosing the nearest tree, Fumio began to climb, considering each foothold. About ten feet up, he settled into a y-shaped junction of branches.

He worried about his mother, ill and tired. He worried about Kimiko, so small and unwell. He worried about his father. Had he been caught in the unruly mob? Fumio worried about his family, without food and water, all because he had lost his way.

But his father would not fail to find him. His mother would not let him wander for long. Even little Kimiko would look for her big brother until she had him by the hand.

From his perch in the pear tree, he heard cries of fear and outrage. He heard the blaring of a truck's horn. He heard a volley of gun fire. A few moments later, from nearby, he heard racing footsteps. He heard despair. He heard fear.

The turmoil persisted, hour after long hour, finally quieting when the moon came from behind the clouds.

Fumio surveyed his surroundings and saw no one. He had no idea where he was, still, he thought it best to come down from the tree and try to find out. Stretching cramped muscles, he looked toward the ground—and groaned.

Near the base of the tree lay a large rattlesnake. It was obviously very much awake and not happy. A stone had been turned. The snake had been disturbed from its place of hibernation.

No mistaking it—the beige and brown-patterned scales of the snake, the flat head at one end and rattler at the other, all marked it as, so Dusty had warned, *venomous*. Fumio also learned from Dusty that, although rattlesnakes did not hear well, they were sensitive to vibrations. Nor was their vision sharp, but their sense of smell *was*. Very.

Why here? Fumio wondered. *Of all the places that snake could have high-tailed it to, why here?* Could rattlesnakes climb trees? Had Dusty mentioned that?

"Leave them alone!" Dusty had said, and, certainly, Fumio would. How long, though, might he have to wait? Calling out wouldn't bring help. Weren't all known friends behind closed doors, sheltering from danger?

An eerie sound split the air. Not human, but the sound of a hunter. Fumio saw it circling, high above. An owl, following its natural rhythms, had sighted *dinner* and targeted its prey.

Dusty had said, "If you call the owl, it will come."

Fumio hadn't called the owl, had he? He understood hunger, but, peering up through the darkness, Fumio hoped *he* was not the answer to the owl's prayer, that he was not its *prey*.

He could not help but be fascinated by the skill with which the owl wielded the power of its wings. It swooped, soared, and dived directly toward the rattlesnake.

The snake reared back to strike.

Fumio gasped.

The owl shrieked and back-pedaled, its wings working the air five feet above the snake, almost hovering, before it wheeled and lifted again into the air. Another circle and the owl began the same dance, finally plummeting toward the ground.

The snake slithered away to find an opening in the earth and disappear. The owl screamed once more before turning in its flight and heading for the open desert.

Fumio began shivering hard. He feared he would lose his grip on the tree. He closed his eyes, trying to control his breathing.

When he opened his eyes, he saw a light coming toward him through the darkness.

"Fumio? Where are you, Son?"

"Here, Father! I'm here!" Fumio heard his own voice and it sounded strange to his ears. He called again, "Father, I'm here!"

The lantern approached more quickly. His father's face became clear.

"Fumio!" His father's voice was thick with emotion. "Fumio! Are you all right?"

"Yes, Father! I will come down soon. My hands are numb, and my arms have gone to sleep. And there was a rattlesnake. But it's gone now."

Fumio willed himself to climb down, his father stretching up to take hold as soon as was possible. Fumio nearly fell into his father's arms but caught himself against the pear tree. He looked toward the place where the snake had waited and said a word of thanks to the owl.

• • •

"An owl attacked the snake?" Mr. Miyota asked as they walked. "What kind of owl?"

"I don't know, sir. I'll have to describe it to Dusty, see what he says." After a moment of silence, "Father, how did you find me? It was so dark."

"The owl. I heard its scream. That sound nearly stopped my heart." He put his hand on Fumio's head. "But it brought me to you." After a few more steps, "What, though, do you think brought the owl?"

Fumio pondered the question. "Dinner." He glanced at his father. "The owl was hunting."

"For snakes or for eleven-year-old boys?"

"Neither, I think. But I'm not sure. Next time I see him, I'll ask."

Mr. Miyota laughed.

"Father, I lost the water pail."

"It is all right. At our quarters, we will pick up the kettle and go for water, together."

At the barracks, the single light bulb still burned. Mrs. Miyota rose quickly from the chair when they entered.

"How is Kimiko?" his father asked.

"She seems better. I think the fever has broken."

Fumio sighed. "Mother, I lost the water pail. I'm sorry. Father said we can—"

"It is all right. We have water."

"We do?"

"How did we come by it?" Mr. Miyota asked.

"Mr. Seiki knocked on the door. I looked out the window before I opened it. He was not in his Internal Security Guard uniform, but I recognized him. He said he was checking on our neighbors. Not with authorization, but as our friend."

She went on, "He asked where you were. I told him about the spilled water, about Fumio going out and not returning. I told you you had gone to search for our son. Mr. Seiki left." She paused. "He came back twenty minutes later, with water. He took his family's rice pot and went to get water for us." She gestured toward the cabinet. "I will make us something to eat. Fumio, you must be so hungry!"

Mrs. Miyota, bewilderment on her face, went to her son and picked a twig from his knit cap. "*Hmmh*, do you smell pears?"

Fumio smiled. "Yes, as a matter of fact, I do." He took the twig and put it on the cabinet. Tomorrow, he thought, he would put it in water.

CHAPTER FORTY-SIX

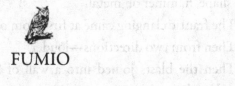

FUMIO

At eleven o'clock, in the dark of night, Fumio welcomed the meal of cream of rice sweetened with the pinch of sugar that Mrs. Miyota so carefully meted out. Once they had finished and the bowls were cleaned and placed in the cabinet, his father used the remaining hot water to make tea. For Mrs. Miyota, the chair was brought near the oil burner. Mr. Miyota settled on an upended crate and Fumio sat on the edge of his cot. All leaned toward the oil burner.

Swallowing the last of his tea, Fumio studied the bottom of his cup. Was it true the future could be read in tea leaves?

Mr. Miyota sighed deeply. "Kimiko is on the mend. And you?" he asked Mrs. Miyota.

"Better. Perhaps I have some immunity."

Seeing Fumio's frown of puzzlement, she said, "I am older than Kimiko, Fumio. I've weathered sickness, fought it off."

Fought it off. It was as if his mother were saying she had rehearsed it, had *prepared* for an invisible attack.

He thought of Mr. Harvey back home and heard his words: "Keep your guard up! Stay on your toes, boy!"

Right now, Fumio's toes were tired. They ached. He had spent hours in the pear tree. He surrendered to an enveloping yawn.

Then, *Bamm! Crash! Bamm!*

And again, *Bamm! Crash! Bamm!*

The racket startled Fumio and his parents into alertness. The clash continued, followed by reverberations, increasing in volume. The window glass began to buzz.

Fumio covered his ears with his hands. The hair on the back of his neck stood up. Images of Flyer on alert came to his mind.

Bang-Clang! Bang-bang! Clang-Bang! Not quite rhythmic, not quite random, he compared it to the sound of his father in his shop pounding iron into shape, hammer on metal.

The frantic clanging came at first from one direction—loud.

Then from two directions—louder.

Then the blasts joined into a wall of sound. *Bang-clang-bang-bang-bang-clang-bang!*

A sense of pressure arose in Fumio's nose and throat. At last, he recognized the source of the noise: the mess halls' brake drum bells.

Now the brake drum bells of possibly all thirty-five Manzanar mess halls clanged at once, on and on, without end, until Fumio thought his eyes would explode. He pressed his hands over his ears. His body shuddered with the sound.

The clamor escalated to a roar, the barracks shaking and rumbling like a train.

Kimiko cried out. Her mother rushed to her. Mr. Miyota sprang up, hurried to the door, threw his shoulder against the thin wood as if to bar it, then leaned to peer out the window.

"What is it?" Fumio began to rise but his father waved him back.

Mr. Miyota went to the cabinet and from a nook beside it pulled out a length of two-by-four. Back at the door, he slid the piece of lumber up under the latch then hit it with his fist and finally kicked it into place, wedged between the floor and the latch.

Occasionally the clanging stumbled, only to begin again. At times it sounded distant, then as if it were right outside the door. Fumio watched his parents' facial muscles tighten.

If only, Fumio thought, *if only I knew what this meant.* He was glad Flyer was not with him. What this might do to Flyer's ears, he could not bear to consider.

He went to the wooden chest at the foot of his bed, took out his knit cap, and pulled it on. His mother went to a chest she shared with Mr. Miyota, located her husband's cap, and took it to him. She removed the tams from the tissue paper in which they had been stored, donned her own, then did the same for Kimiko, who was already in her nightclothes, before arranging the little girl's blanket high over her ears.

Fumio and his parents, still fully clothed, moved to their cots. Fumio pulled his blanket high over his head then tucked it tight around his ears. Still, the brake drum bells clanged, their assault relentless.

His little sister whimpered. Soon, Fumio heard his father's footsteps moving toward Kimiko, heard the rustle of straw as he picked her up and carried her to lie beside her mother.

His father approached him, leaned close. "Son, will you be all right?"

Fumio nodded, pressing his lips tight.

Mr. Miyota removed his own knit cap and pulled it over the cap Fumio wore, carefully arranging it over his son's ears. Laying his hand on Fumio's head, he nodded.

Fumio slept fitfully. He suffered loud dreams: his parents held captive on iron tracks in the headlight's glare of a freight train bearing down. The engine roar of an airplane, flying low, propellers spinning dust into Kimiko's eyes. The blast of a ferryboat's horn, the vessel pulling away from Eagledale dock, spiriting his family into the unknown.

CHAPTER FORTY-SEVEN

FUMIO

The cacophony of brake drum bells continued. Fumio tried to shut it all out, the incessant noise, the early light of this Monday morning, the troubling events of the past few days. Still, a faint *tap-tap-tapping* slipped past the hubbub of the cast iron bells, slipped under the blanket tucked tight around his head. A quiet *tap-tap-tap* slid under the pillow, wove through the thickness of his two wool caps, and came as a tiptoe of sound to his ears. Fumio lowered the blanket, lifted his head, and peered toward the door.

Bam-Bam-Bam-Bam-Bam!

His father stepped to the window. He looked toward the stoop, then moved over and opened the door. "Joey, hello!" he said, as Joey slipped under his arm and into the room.

Mr. Miyota's eyes followed the boy, amusement in his expression. "Well, then—won't you come in?" Before closing the door, Fumio's father scanned the area outside, then turned. "We haven't seen much of you, lately, Joey."

"I guess you'll be seeing a lot more of me, now, Mr. Miyota!" Joey caught sight of Fumio. "Oh, Fumio! There you are! Jiichan Ryono-sama said I can't eat with Sam at the Terminal Island mess hall, anymore! Jiichan Ryono-sama said, 'Families eat meals together.' He said, 'You belong with your family, with people who care about you!' Then he looked right at Sam," Joey added, wide-eyed, "and Jiichan said, 'Even *knuckleheads* like you!'"

Fumio had heard of Jiichan Ryono-sama, an esteemed elder of the Terminal Island community. The Japanese Americans on Terminal Island were so abruptly evicted from their homes that they were forced to sell their fishing boats and other businesses at steep losses. Jiichan Ryono-sama was said to have taken charge of that community's young men and boys, those who had gained unsavory reputations due to their boisterous behavior and rough exteriors, calling on them to respect their traditions and mend their ways. Apparently, Sam and Joey had come under the influence of this man.

Fumio recalled Joey's boast, months earlier, of working with Sam and other boys from Terminal Island to create a cave under one of the barracks. Joey was so covered in Manzanar dust that he appeared to be *wearing* some of that cave this morning.

Joey moved farther into the Miyota quarters. "My mother will allow me to spend only an hour a day with Sam. Besides, I think Sam's not so keen on having me around anymore."

"Joey," Mrs. Miyota cut in, "your mother, is she feeling better?"

"Yes, she is, thank you."

"And, Joey," Mrs. Miyota said, "you spoke of Jiichan Ryono-sama. Have you found your jiichan—your grandfather—here, at Manzanar?"

Joey shook his head. "No, ma'am. He's not really *my* grandfather, Mrs. Miyota. Father's father lived in Japan. He died before I was born. And Mother's father died when I was a baby. But *everyone* who speaks of Ryono-sama-san calls him Jiichan!

"Jiichan Ryono-sama said all the Terminal Islanders, everyone in Blocks 9 and 10, had to come to a meeting, and he gave them a talking to! *Everyone* does what Jiichan says to do!"

That must have been quite a talking-to, Fumio thought.

"Even the Internal Security Guards do what Jiichan tells them to do!" Joey said, referring to the Japanese American men and women hired for the nightly patrol inside the center's fences.

Mrs. Miyota moved to the cabinet to take out cups and a container of tea. "Joey," she asked, looking over her shoulder at the boy, "what brings you here, this morning, so early and after the—*What brings you here so early?*"

"Oh!" Joey looked toward Fumio. "There's no school today!"

"How do you know that?" Mr. Miyota asked.

"The Terminal Islanders know a lot of stuff, because the Chief of Internal Security moved into one of their apartments a couple of days ago, before all hell—" Joey glanced at Mrs. Miyota. "Excuse me, ma'am. We're not allowed to swear in front of a lady."

"Yes, Joey. Please go on." She went to Kimiko, who was awake now, and pulled the drape partially closed.

"Anyway, the Chief of Internal Security has been living in one of their apartments since a couple of days ago. He moved his wife and children in with his parents, and he went to bunk with some Terminal Islanders."

"Why did he do that?" Mr. Miyota frowned.

"He'd heard rumblings. He was in danger. He needed help. Terminal Islanders are strong and determined. Since Jiichan Ryono-sama laid down the law, Terminal Islanders stand together. And we, *they*, stand with the chief. The Chief of Internal Security is not *for* the administration, and he is not for the gangs. He has *our* best interests in mind, and he deserves our help. That's what Jiichan Ryono-sama says." Joey paused then, touched his hands to his ears, and squeezed his eyes tight.

Fumio's ears and jaw hurt. "It's awful, isn't it?" he said, and Joey nodded.

The teakettle whistled. Mr. Miyota poured water into the teapot. "Why does the noise go on and on? Has it been said?"

Joey shook his head. "They say at first it was because the bells signaled a meeting was called, and meetings were held all over the center, all night long. Some people, lots of people, wanted to take over the center." He drew in a deep breath, then exhaled. "So, at first the bells were for meetings. After a while, I guess, they were just a way for people to blow off steam."

"So, this is about a bunch of people blowing off steam?" Fumio asked.

"It's about anger, Fumio," Mr. Miyota said. "Frustrated plans. No way out." He shrugged. "It's an explosion in a bottle with the cap screwed on tight."

"When will it stop?" Fumio asked.

"The anger? I wouldn't hold my breath," Mr. Miyota answered.

Fumio nodded. "The brake drum bells, when will they stop?" He looked toward Joey.

"Soon as we—" Joey stopped, studied his shoes. "Soon as it gets figured out, I guess."

"So, no school. And, I suppose, no meals." Fumio shook his head. "All those mess hall bells and no breakfast."

"Ironic, isn't it?" Mrs. Miyota said, and Mr. Miyota chuckled.

Fumio didn't get the joke. His stomach growled.

"There will be breakfast!" Joey said. "The kitchen crews for Blocks 9 and 10—"

"Well, I suppose *Sam* will see to it your family gets fed."

"No!" Joey put in. "The Terminal Island kitchen crews promised! If it's needed, they will feed the whole camp!"

"Do they mean it?" Fumio asked.

"Yes! They mean it. They will."

The sound of a fist pounding on the door sent Mr. Miyota to look out the window again. Once he saw who was there, he stepped over to open the door to Mr. Seiki.

Mr. Seiki, a Bainbridge Island neighbor, came up onto the step, his hat pulled down around his ears. Not wearing his Internal Security Guard uniform, he appeared not to be on duty.

"Mr. Seiki-san," Mr. Miyota greeted the man, "will you come in?"

"I can't, just now," Mr. Seiki replied, "but may I help you in some way?"

"Do you have news?"

Frowning, Mr. Seiki, nodded. "The center was patrolled throughout the night by Military Police and the National Guard."

The National Guard? Fumio realized he had never seen National Guard uniforms. Thinking about it, he felt curious at first, then guilty, then ashamed. The camp was swarming with soldiers, this place the government said he should call home. It would be in the news, broadcast on the radio. Newspaper reporters would write about it. There would probably be an article in the *Bainbridge Island Review*. Zachary would read it.

Fumio heard Mr. Seiki say, "I believe they think they have more important things to do than quiet those infernal mess hall bells." At a sound from inside the apartment, he straightened. "I beg your pardon, ma'am," he said to Mrs. Miyota. "I hope the little girl is better today?"

"She is. Thank you!"

"I must be on my way, but I wanted to be sure you knew there's no school today. The mess hall, though, will serve meals."

"A moment, please, Mr. Seiki-san?" Mr. Miyota extended his hand. "Thank you for your consideration of my family last night, for the water."

Mr. Seiki gripped Mr. Miyota's hand. Each man gave a small nod.

Mr. Miyota closed the door as Mr. Seiki hurried off to notify his other neighbors, the two hundred residents of the Bainbridge Island block.

Fumio and Joey watched as Mr. Miyota filled a cup with tea for his wife then poured a small amount into a mug, adding a pinch of sugar, for Kimiko. He placed a tray holding both the cup and mug on a stand near Kimiko's cot.

Fumio's father looked toward Joey. "Is it time for you to head home, Joey? To see if your mother needs you?"

Joey nodded, "Yes, sir."

"You can walk along with us, then split off and head for home. Fumio and I will go to breakfast, although that will take us close to one of those brake drums that cannot seem to stop."

Mrs. Miyota laughed.

Fumio was puzzled by her laughter, but also glad. It was likely a sign that his mother was feeling stronger this morning. He opened the blue trunk and took from it a green bandana.

"We will bring back meals for Mrs. Miyota and Kimiko. Joey, if you find yourself doing so for your family, at the mess hall, we hope you'll sit with us."

"Thank you, sir. Fumio," he said, glancing aside, "do you have an extra neckerchief?"

Fumio returned to the trunk, pulled out a gray bandana, and handed it to Joey. He tied his green bandana over his head pirate-fashion, covering his ears, dulling the noise somewhat. Joey did the same. Fumio took his coat from a hook and pulled it on as they stepped outside.

They had walked ten feet or so when Mr. Miyota called, "Go on, boys. I need my coat!"

Fumio and Joey walked on.

Joey crossed his arms over his chest. "Fumio . . ."

Fumio looked toward Joey, straining to hear his words.

"Fumio, Jiichan Ryono-sama says we boys have made mistakes. He said, because our fathers are gone, since they've been taken away, we have not behaved respectfully. Jiichan said we must . . . We must say, 'Sorry.'"

Fumio watched as Joey drew in a deep breath.

"Fumio, I'm sorry."

"It's all right. You and Sam, you are cousins, and cousins are family. I get that. But you and me, we're pals."

Fumio stopped, turned toward Joey and reached out his hand. Joey unwrapped his arms from across his chest and gripped Fumio's hand. Each boy nodded once.

Mr. Miyota was beside them, then, and the three walked together as the bells rang on.

• • •

At noon, Monday, the bells stopped ringing, the uproar's ending as startling as its onset.

At three o'clock, Fumio peered out the barracks window at massive dark clouds rushing in from over the Sierras. In minutes, rain began thundering—with a sound like drums!

"Mother! I have to go to the dojo—the taiko dojo! The drums!" He grabbed his coat, thrust his arms in the sleeves.

Fumio saw her moment of hesitation. Then she nodded. "All right." From the cabinet, she took their wash basin. "Set this outside our door, please."

Fumio took the basin and did as his mother asked. Then he was off, running toward the dojo. On the landing outside Block 10's recreation hall, he found the senior student he had met before, Senpai Masato-san, drenched, inserting his key into the lock of the door. Hajime came running across the muddy ground, his steps creating small geysers of dirty water.

The door to the dojo opened, hinges protesting. Other students came onto the landing and Senpai Masato-san held them back as he stepped inside, paused, and bowed toward the center of the room. Moving aside, he removed his shoes and left them against the wall. One by one, students of the dojo followed, each pausing to bow and remove shoes before hurrying to the drums. As was the tradition for the newest student, Fumio entered last.

The roof was indeed leaking, especially along the room's edges. Masato began moving drums away from the walls. Other students joined in. Watching Hajime, Fumio helped as best he could before kneeling against the wall.

Beneath his knees the floor was wet. The dojo bore the smell of encroaching mildew. In his mind's eye, Fumio could see the rain pounding on the roof, worming its way under shingles, and swarming down the slope to gather over the eaves. With his physical eyes, he could see it cascading down the walls to join in the puddles that spread across the floor.

Along with odors of sodden wood, crumbling tar paper, and soggy canvas tarpaulins, Fumio detected a faint note of old rubber. He looked to the worn tires stacked in the corner.

Hinges sounded as the dojo's door opened. Wind whooshed in with a splatter of rainfall. Sensei Amabe entered. A young senpai hurried to close the door, then bowed.

Pausing, the sensei bowed, too. He removed his shoes. He looked about and saw that the drums had been moved to safety. He nodded and walked to the center of the room.

The sensei raised his arms; the drummers came near. "Masato," the sensei said, and gestured toward the great odaiko drum. Masato moved to the odaiko. Others went to stand near various drums. Some students, Hajime among them, took old tires from the corner of the room. With a motion from the sensei, the rhythm began . . . *Boom . . . boom-boom . . . Boom.*

The drumming continued for several minutes, until, during a pause, Masato went to the stack of old tires. He looked toward the sensei. The sensei nodded. Masato placed a tire near Hajime and beckoned to Fumio.

Fumio rose and, head bowed, approached Masato. The young man smiled, nodded, and addressed him, "Little brother?"

CHAPTER FORTY-EIGHT

FUMIO

On her cot, Kimiko lay asleep. Today had been her best day since the onset of her illness eight days earlier, but she remained tired, or "wrung out," as Mrs. Kato had described the condition of her youngest son, Yushi, who also weathered the worrisome sickness.

"Camp Manzanar is quiet today," Fumio's mother said. "Too quiet. Yet, I welcome it."

She tiptoed to Kimiko, laid a hand on her forehead, then snugged the blanket under her chin. Kimiko's eyes drifted closed. Mrs. Miyota returned to her chair, sighing heavily.

Fumio's father motioned toward the extra blanket draped at the foot of Kimiko's bed. Fumio passed it to him, and his father then laid it across Mrs. Miyota's shoulders and tucked it lightly around her. "Sachiko," he said, "Fumio and I will go to the mess hall and bring back Kimiko's meal and yours. Is there anything you would especially like?"

"Our kitchen table? The yellow-checked curtains?"

Fumio saw his mother's weary smile and a familiar scene played in his mind: the Miyota kitchen in the morning, early chores done, he and his father coming through the door with Flyer trotting in behind them, circling, lying down. Father stirring the coals to build up the fire, Mother tending a skillet. Kimiko, in her own chair, quietly singing.

He went for his coat and pulled it on.

Walking with his father across Manzanar's confines, Fumio considered the tension felt in the center during the past two-and-a-half months. Mess hall kitchens still served, but schools remained closed. The camp newspaper had made no mention of "The Protests of December 6." Frustration and anger roiled, relentless as the desert wind. Day after day he made his way to the taiko dojo, pausing after entering and putting his thoughts in order with a respectful bow. Then, with guidance from the sensei, the drumming began, *Bmm-bm—Boom . . . Bmm-bm—Boom*, and Fumio released his worries to the rhythm.

Lifting his eyes, Fumio's vista became the Alabama Hills, the Sierra Nevada mountain range, and the sky—a frigid blue on this morning, poised between late winter and early spring. Fumio blinked against the hard-edged sun. He felt miniscule in comparison.

Inside the mess hall, Mr. Miyota, balancing his tray, swung one leg, then the other, over the bench and under the table. Fumio slid in from the side. Conversations were muted, yet the undertones of anxiety filled the large, relatively empty space like a roar.

Etsu entered the mess hall alone. With her tray, she came to sit across the table from Fumio. Clambering over the mess hall benches could be difficult, yet she managed to sit, swivel, and pull her feet over the bench in one graceful motion. After placing her tray on the table, she rose slightly and smoothed her dark green skirt.

"Etsu," Mr. Miyota said, with a nod. Gaze lowered, Etsu smiled, then turned a quick smile toward Fumio.

"Etsu, hello," Fumio said. "Joey's not here this morning? He isn't sick, is he?"

Joey was on an errand for Mrs. Kato, Etsu said, then she took a small bite from a piece of burned toast thinly spread with the mess hall's "mystery jelly," rumored to be concocted from withered apples—seeds, peels, and all. An acquaintance of the Kato family had offered a portion of takuwan, which had been a gift from a friend. A treasure.

Recalling that Grandfather Miyota had relished the powerful aroma and strong, salty flavor of the preserved daikon radish, Fumio was surprised by a sudden desire for even the smallest taste.

"What d'ya know, Fumio?" Joey had crept up behind them. He slid onto the bench beside Fumio and, grinning, placed a small, glass container on the table. "Ta-da!" When he twisted the lid and opened the jar, a pungent aroma wafted. Heads turned, and Fumio could see the deep inhalations of other diners. Joey replaced the lid and went to get his meal.

When he returned to the table with his tray, in addition to his plate and cutlery, he brought a small bowl and table knife. He removed three of the white, semi-translucent slices of takuwan from the jar and cut them into quarter-inch pieces. He put two pieces on Mr. Miyota's plate, then two on his sister's, Fumio's, and his own.

Joey stood and progressed around the dining room, sharing bits of takuwan. He carried the remaining thirteen cubes to the head cook, who nodded, smiled, took two tiny pieces, and gave the rest to the kitchen staff to share.

Silence fell as neighbors closed their eyes, nibbling fermented radish. The mood lifted. Conversation began again and quiet laughter was heard.

Fumio and Mr. Miyota thanked Joey and went to get food for Mrs. Miyota and Kimiko.

In their apartment, Mr. Miyota pulled his handkerchief from his pocket and spread it open on the table. Fumio did the same. Mrs. Miyota's face lit up at the sight of four small portions of takuwan. Just enough.

CHAPTER FORTY-NINE

FUMIO

In a letter from Mrs. Whitlock, Fumio and his family learned that, during the winter holiday, a group of Bainbridge Island residents had drafted a letter expressing concern for the well-being of their Japanese American neighbors. Following this, the *Bainbridge Island Review*'s editors had requested the relocation of Island internees to bring them close enough in miles that people from home might visit and offer support. Then, word came that Camp Manzanar's Director Merritt was "taking it under review."

Soon came whispers that Bainbridge Island internees might be transferred to Camp Minidoka in the state of Idaho. Fumio knew about Idaho only what he had learned in school. It had no seacoast. On its west side, it shared a border with the state of Washington and on the north, Canada. Its chief crops were potatoes and sugar beets. Ten thousand Japanese Americans lived there, under armed guard.

"My cousin, Sam, nearly blew a gasket!" Joey told Fumio. "He was fuming. 'Why move from a California desert to an Idaho wasteland? You think they have fancier tar paper there? Better barbed wire? I hear the weather's even worse in Idaho than it is here! Don't go, Joe!'"

Joey said his mother might decide the Katos would stay at Manzanar, near her cousin's family. Another long journey to yet another unfamiliar place, she thought, offered little chance of bettering their situation.

Since August, Joey said, when Mr. Kato was transferred to Heart Mountain Internment Camp in Wyoming instead of Manzanar, the family had stopped hoping it would be only a matter of days until they were together again.

Fumio knew Mr. Whitlock was consulting a lawyer, a member of the American Friends Service Committee, to put right the bureaucratic tangle ensnaring Mr. Kato, to show he was a good manager, a good farmer, a good person whose family needed him. And not a threat to national security.

Fumio pondered the fact that, with the stroke of a president's pen, people's homes and families, entire communities, could be ripped apart.

Zachary had sent news. Flyer was eating well, making his rounds of the fields, checking fences, seeing to the stream and pond. Even learning to help with the sheep.

Fumio didn't love Manzanar, didn't *like it*, even. But he had made a few friends: Hajime, Mr. Miyatake. Even Sam wasn't as bad as he had first thought.

Captain Margaret Stone had done the family a few good turns. Those kindnesses had been repaid, Fumio knew. Even so, she held rank, and she didn't *have* to be nice.

Dusty. Fumio had learned much from Dusty about dealing with the climate. Dusty, of course, had benefitted from Mr. Miyota's advice on construction challenges.

Fumio had become a student of taiko drumming. He had Hajime to thank for his introduction to the dojo. He would regret the loss of it.

What about school? How much more could he miss without being thrown back a grade? Manzanar wasn't an easy place, but he had found a certain balance.

Would the Miyotas leave now, start over, set up elsewhere? Pack their possessions again and not go *home*? Just *go*? To another *camp*? Another barracks *apartment*? Again?

Mr. Miyota had heard from Zachary's brother, Jacob, who had thanked him for the generosity of their house. He was "sitting lightly," he said, ready to move out the moment they were on their way home. Meanwhile, a feed storage shed had been built using two of the metal grain bins from the stable area, and the shop was carefully maintained. Fumio felt gratitude for neighbors who looked after the farm and their home, and for Zachary who cared for Flyer.

CHAPTER FIFTY

FUMIO

It was happening. Camp Manzanar administrators had said that anyone from Bainbridge Island who wished to transfer to Camp Minidoka—which was all but five or six families—were to complete the paperwork and begin packing.

First, Fumio went to the taiko dojo to let the sensei know that his family was leaving.

Then, on an errand for his father, he brought Captain Margaret Stone a final summary of supplies for improvements to the medical clinic.

"I heard the news," she said. "You are leaving." She turned to her desk. "This is for your father." She handed Fumio a large white envelope. "A letter of recommendation. I hope it may bring Mr. Miyota benefit. I will miss you, Fumio. You and your family, I will miss you."

Fumio bowed and left the captain's office.

Then a week of more paperwork, farewells, letters from Bainbridge Island, packing. Neighbors advised each other on what to take, what to leave behind.

Soon, a scant three days stood between Fumio and "transfer day." Even though they didn't know who would move into the apartment they were leaving behind, his mother was determined that it be left spotless.

"I have nearly worn the bristles off the broom," Fumio grumbled to his father.

"You might as well wear them off all the way, Son. We are not taking it with us."

On the Tuesday before they left, as he swept the barracks steps for what he was sure was the tenth time that day, Joey approached at a run.

"Fumio! Hey, guess what?" Joey yelled.

Fumio put the broom down and went to meet him, wiping dust from his face. "What?"

"We are going! We're transferring! Father sent a letter. The Quaker lawyer persuaded them he's okay! He said for us to go to Minidoka, and he'll be there soon!"

• • •

By Friday morning, the floor of the barracks apartment was crowded with their belongings. Fumio sat on an upended box, cleaning shoes, when Joey knocked at the door. "Fumio, the worst news ever! Yushi woke up early, and he's *sick*! Captain Stone told my mother to watch out for a—a—relapse. Mother thinks it's a relapse!"

Mrs. Miyota said, "Joey, go to your quarters. Tell your mother I will be there soon."

The noise of Joey's sigh blew across the apartment. He turned and went out the door.

Fumio thought back to last April, shortly after his family entered Manzanar. He had been in line at the clinic, waiting for inoculations, when it was discovered that a child whose family lived in the next block showed symptoms of chicken pox. The child's father had argued loudly against it, but the nurse took the girl away to place her in quarantine. The child's mother dropped to her knees in the dust, crying, as the two-year-old wailed.

He had overheard his mother, later, telling his father that, in the woman's fear for her child, she had sobbed uncontrollably and would not eat or drink even a sip of water. At length, her husband had gone for help to an *Auntie*, a woman near the age of his wife's mother, but nothing could be done to restore the mother until her child was returned.

Mrs. Miyota asked her husband to take from their high shelf a tiny bottle of willow bark powder. "As much for the mother as the child," she said. She asked Fumio to retrieve a freshly washed blanket from a carton, then took a small amount of tea from a jar and went out the door.

Fumio looked toward his father. "They won't let Yushi travel if he's sick."

"They will not."

When Mrs. Miyota returned, she wore a frown. "Everything the Katos own is packed. The child is ill, no question. A nurse visited before I left. She cannot approve their travel." She looked toward her husband. "A nurse from Children's Village is there, now, talking with Mrs. Kato, so I felt I could leave."

His mother looked at him. "I am sorry, Fumio. I know you and Joey had planned that we'd travel in the same train car."

And go to school together that first day, eat school lunch at the same table, Fumio thought. He said, "Yes, after the bus, on the train, we were going to play the Roy Rogers game Joey got for New Year's."

He caught his parents' glance toward Kimiko, playing with her dolls. She had not understood, but soon, when they left for Minidoka, she would know that her best friend Yushi and his family would be beyond her reach. Left behind.

CHAPTER FIFTY-ONE

FLYER

It is cold tonight and I am allowed to sleep in the kitchen by the door. Zachary put some old towels on the floor for me. I turn and turn until they are just right.

The storm door rattles when the wind blows. I know that noise, so it is all right. Last night, I heard a loud bird sound. I know that sound, too. Even in winter the owl hunts. Our chickens are safe. Their yard is covered with wire. The sheep are safe. I help with them now. I know the important words—the *commands*. I do not scare them. I think they like me.

The Whitlocks try to help me feel *comfortable*. Zachary talks to me. His mother talks to me, too. His father talks, but not much to me. He writes books, textbooks for college classes, Zachary said. He works at night. He comes down to his *study*, turns on the light, and closes the door. I can hear him read out loud, maybe so he can hear himself think.

Also at night, Jacob goes by in his car, on his way to be an air raid warden. New people have moved to Bainbridge Island, he says, meaning more people are here for him to help.

Other people have left the island. Dirk left. Zachary told me. Dirk's father was *not doing well*, Mrs. Whitlock said. *There were issues*. She said she wished she had seen it earlier. Now Dirk lives with his aunt in Seattle and that is good because his father did not like him very much. Zachary said, "It must have been rough on Dirk. I hope his life gets better."

CHAPTER FIFTY-TWO

FUMIO

Wednesday, February 24, 1943. The day had come. His family's belongings were packed and gathered near the door, awaiting a truck for transport to the camp gate. There, they would be loaded into the belly of a bus, to be handed over yet again to a railway worker who would stack them high and pack them tight in a train car along with other families' bundles, crates, and pasteboard boxes for the trip to Minidoka.

He carried a sketchbook. Pocket pencils were stowed in his jacket. His laid his hand on the box of belongings for which he was responsible. He thought of the Katos, staying behind because of illness. He thought of Dusty, glad for the chance to run into him on Monday at the Block Manager's office. He and his father had gone there to help with paperwork so that the Katos could stay in their apartment until Yushi's illness had passed. His father gave Dusty their Bainbridge Island address, asked him to please come visit "when this is all over."

"Fumio," Mr. Miyota said, "the truck is here."

Fumio buttoned his jacket and began pushing the carton forward.

At the open door, smells of diesel and dust greeted him, along with the thrum of an idling engine. Families sat in the truck box, high atop their belongings. Fumio was taken aback. He'd readily clamber into a truck box, but what of his mother and Kimiko? As did most, the Miyotas wore many layers of clothing, as well as their winter coats, to save space in their baggage. The climb would be awkward, even dangerous.

Mr. Miyota oversaw lifting the family's possessions into the truck. Fumio stayed close by his mother's side, holding Kimiko's hand. He was glad to see a worker put in place a ladder with a gentle slope. A Bainbridge Island neighbor, a woman of the family's acquaintance, came to the rear of the truck box and reached down while Mrs. Miyota guided Kimiko up the ladder, Fumio staying nearby to steady her.

When it was Mrs. Miyota's turn to go up the ladder, Mr. Miyota came quickly and handed her up to the helpful neighbor. He stood by as Fumio climbed, then went back to secure their belongings before scrambling aboard himself. The engine's roar sounded, and in a whirl of grit and fumes, they were on their way.

Fumio recalled his family's arrival by bus on the day of their induction into Camp Manzanar. He remembered his first look at the many hundreds of tar-papered barracks huddled together in heat-seared, water-starved Owens Valley, flanked by the strange masses of the Alabama Hills, and encircled by the looming Sierras—mountains that were, in their aspect, both beautiful and forbidding. He remembered the stunned expressions on the faces of his neighbors. Today, he saw fatigue, resignation, a measure of calm.

With a grinding of gears and the squeal of brakes, the truck stopped near one of the waiting buses where, Fumio saw, a small number of the Islanders' new acquaintances milled about, waiting to say their goodbyes. He hurried with other men and boys to unload possessions.

Becoming aware of traces of a melody, nearly inaudible amid the general clamor, Fumio glanced left, right, then looked up. Perched on the nearest oil tank platform, Dusty strummed a guitar.

Fumio reached toward his father, tapped him on the shoulder, pointed. Mr. Miyota turned, saw their friend, and lifted a hand. Dusty smiled and strummed more boldly.

"Mother!" Fumio called quietly, directing her attention.

Seeing Dusty, Mrs. Miyota offered a small wave, whispering to Kimiko.

After that first day, Fumio had thought Manzanar might be nothing but dust storms and jackrabbits. He'd seen too many dust storms, but he hadn't seen even one jackrabbit. Too bad, he thought. Maybe at Minidoka.

And while Minidoka was not home, it was nearer to home than Manzanar. Manzanar was nearly a thousand miles from Bainbridge Island. Minidoka was a little over six hundred. Fumio almost laughed at the thought: *only six-hundred miles*.

•   •   •

True to his word, the stone-faced bus driver who'd brought the Islanders to this place almost a year earlier had not returned to take them away. Today's driver showed a friendly manner toward his passengers, lending a hand as mothers climbed the steps with young children, sharing small jokes with school-aged youngsters, offering a handshake to adults who were open to it.

The bus's horn bleated twice. A voice called, "Gotta skee-daddle, folks! We're leaving early, but everyone's accounted for. Let's hit the road!"

They were leaving early? Fumio's gaze swept the area near the bus. He had thought maybe . . . but, no. Sure, this was a big thing to him, but to others? People had their own concerns. They couldn't just drop everything to watch a bus leave.

Hajime would be at the dojo drumming with other students, all of whom had bid Fumio farewell at the last practice he had attended. Life goes forward, despite our small dramas. It was a wonder Dusty had come to see them off.

Fumio waved once more to Dusty and turned toward the bus's double-hinged door.

From the oil tank platform a series of chords. Dusty began to sing "Happy Trails to You."

Folks laughed, called out their thanks for the music, and began boarding. The Miyotas found seats. Fumio peered out the window at the faces of well-wishers, pleasant, but unknown to him. Amid a tumble of mixed emotions, he felt a touch of disappointment. He had thought he would at least see Joey, and maybe—

Suddenly, Joey appeared, as always at a run, crossing the compound. He skidded to a stop a stone's throw from the bus and began waving wildly. Fumio grinned and waved back. Etsu arrived moments later, halting near Joey. They waved farewell together, Etsu mouthing, "See you soon," to Mrs. Miyota.

Then Hajime came jogging into view as well. He stood off to the side of Joey and Etsu, pantomimed beating the odaiko, the big drum, then waved with both arms.

From his station on top the oil tank platform, Dusty raised the guitar in a salute.

CHAPTER FIFTY-THREE

FUMIO

The rumble of the engine and a cloud of dust dulled everything outside the bus. Fumio straightened his shoulders and looked ahead.

Passengers spoke of what was to come. He heard remarks of hope, although many carried the worries concerning the realities of Camp Minidoka. The Island neighbors had been warned about the great distances to be traversed when walking between buildings and informed of the camp's severe weather. They'd also heard that Minidoka's barracks were much the same as those the Islanders had encountered when they had first arrived at Manzanar.

The improvements they had labored over would now be relinquished for others to enjoy, if "enjoy" was the correct word for simply having floors without gaps big enough to let in insects and even snakes; walls without holes through which one could be viewed by strangers; basic shelving, and inside locks on their doors.

The bus ride passed quickly. In just a few hours, the passengers were gathered near a depot. Fumio was not surprised to find the train was old, dirty, and smelly.

The window shades had gone gray in the sun and bore a permanent film of dust. As was the case on the trip *to* Manzanar, soldiers bearing rifles demanded the shades be closed upon departure and for the entirety of the first day.

On the second day, that requirement was relaxed, which puzzled Fumio. If a reason for secrecy existed on day one, what was different on day two? After a breakfast of bread, nuts, and canned beans, a soldier reached past Fumio to raise the shade. "Better, kid?" he asked.

Squinting against the sudden brightness, Fumio nodded. His mother used a blanket to shield Kimiko, who was sleeping, from the glare.

His sister had slumbered much of the first day. When Fumio had offered to draw pictures to entertain her, Mrs. Miyota had replied, "Let her rest. Soon enough she will be *all slept out*, and you can entertain her to the limits of your patience." Then she had smiled and reached out to ruffle his hair. He would have let her, with no complaint, but she pulled back, apparently remembering that he was nearing the completion of his sixth-grade year.

By the end of the second day, Fumio was tired, his muscles ached, and boredom pressed in upon him as if it had actual substance. Like wet cement. Then Kimiko awoke and suddenly began climbing on his knees and shoulders as if he were a set of monkey bars. He heaved a sigh, knowing that, if he were her age, he would be doing the same thing.

• • •

Fumio came awake to a call of "Eden, folks! Eden, Idaho! You transfer to a bus, here!" Passengers began the by-now routine process of gathering their few possessions and moving on. Five buses waited near the train station. After being cramped in a train car for two and a half days, even the short walk to board a bus was a relief, an opportunity to stretch out and breathe air that, while it tasted of diesel fumes, was free of the smell of crowding and inactivity.

A dozen or so spectators leaned against automobiles watching, blatantly curious. The military guards traveling with the Bainbridge Islanders made themselves more than usually evident—their posture stiff, their voices sharp and loud.

Fumio kept hold of Kimiko's hand and followed as his mother went into the bus to find their places. His father saw to the securing of the family's possessions.

With all passengers seated, the driver shouted to the guards, "Let these folks open the windows, boys. I'll take responsibility if anyone tries to wiggle out." A youngish man in the row ahead of Fumio snorted. Others cleared their throats. But the soldiers made no argument, and soon the *thunk* of windows being lowered sounded from both sides of the aisle.

This bus, Fumio saw, was clean and, with the windows lowered, the air was not stale. Some travelers played cards, some slept, a few snored. One man played a harmonica, and Fumio recognized songs he had learned on Fridays, at school on Bainbridge Island.

Through the window, Fumio saw flat grassland wearing winter's brown coat, the sun reflecting in places on patches of dirty snow. The bus driver waved to farmers in their trucks.

Across a landscape of frozen fields, houses were few. Small outbuildings huddled close around them as if to offer protection from the cold.

Fumio saw a man, who wore a cap but no coat, take his mail from a box by the side of the road and push the red flag downward. Then he turned toward the bus, nodded, and gave a wave. A few passengers gasped, then came a murmur of laughter.

Two hours after leaving the train station, the bus left State Highway 25 to follow Hunt Road. From atop a rise, a guard tower loomed against a pale blue sky. Stone pillars bolstered an entry gate bracketed by soldiers bearing dull metal rifles with fixed bayonets.

CAMP MINIDOKA, HUNT, IDAHO, FEBRUARY 26, 1943

CHAPTER FIFTY-FOUR

FUMIO

Waiting for a barracks assignment, his mother held Kimiko's mittened hand while the Island neighbors spoke of what had been heard and what they had read of their new location in past editions of the camp's newspaper, *The Minidoka Irrigator*, which were handed around before leaving Manzanar. His coat buttoned from top to bottom, Fumio listened.

Construction of the Hunt Internment Center, also known as Camp Minidoka, had begun with the blades of giant bulldozers scraping off the natural face of the earth. A few of those bulldozers loomed, still, at the edges of the compound. From science lessons at school on Bainbridge Island, Fumio knew what followed: erosion, dust storms, and displaced wildlife.

Camp Minidoka's residents, once arrived, had begun improvement of the grounds at once, planting gardens and placing stones to please the eye and calm the mind. The people of the nearby towns of Twin Falls and Jerome acknowledged the residents with a gift of trees, which were planted, watered, and tended, so that the land *between* the barracks soon took on a more agreeable character. Beyond the barracks, though, Fumio saw barren land—rolling acres of nothing after nothing.

The landscape was so drab, so brown, he could almost believe he had taken a tumble and come up with his head in a gunny sack, drawing breath through musty burlap.

He shook away the notion. He had a choice. It was up to him to open his eyes, adjust his senses, throw off the gunny sack. He inhaled a gusty breath. What did he smell? Sagebrush. And water. He'd been told of an irrigation canal at the edge of the compound that ran swift as a river.

A field was being plowed for early planting. The freshly turned soil was damp and scented with the composting roots of prairie grasses. He heard the growl and clatter of the tractor, a sharp *clank* as the plow was hauled upward to allow for turning at the end of the row.

Fumio heard the cries of gulls, startling so far from the Pacific Ocean. They had made the transition from picking tiny creatures from the sea to plucking earthworms from broad furrows, and they thrived. Did the gulls long for the ocean? Perhaps.

At Camp Manzanar, the surroundings chafed like ill-fitting clothes. At Minidoka, the same. He wondered if *expectations* contributed to his current discomfort. He'd heard about the weather, the vastness, the need to cover great distances on foot. He would not be alone, though. He straightened his shoulders and vowed he would dig deep into his personal resources, work hard, and make his family proud.

• • •

Well ahead of eight o'clock on his first day at his new school, Fumio went out the door of the Miyota's Minidoka apartment, his shoes polished, and hair combed.

He had a mile-and-a-half walk ahead of him and did not want to be tardy. Grasping his notebook, and with pencils in his pocket, he strode along the open ground next to the curving row of barracks that stood between his own Block 44 and Stafford Elementary. When the school building was in sight, he slowed his pace, trying to appear nonchalant, but—too late.

"Where's the fire?"

Looking ahead and off to his right, Fumio saw two boys facing each other, kneeling, one eyeing the ground. *Marbles.*

"Hey, what's your hurry, new kid?" came the question, from a blue-shirted boy whose hair looked freshly cut, but uncombed. The second boy's shirt was striped, black and white. He wore a gray baseball cap.

"I want to be on time for school," Fumio said as he moved closer. From the looks of their pants knees, the boys had been playing a while.

"I'm Peter and he's Okes," blue shirt said. "You could shoot marbles with us. We won't be late. We do this all the time."

The boys looked friendly enough. Fumio moved nearer.

"It's not so bad here. You can't beat the food." Peter patted his stomach. "I can hardly wait for lunch."

"So," Okes said, "Bainbridge Island? Block 44?"

"Yes," Fumio replied. "That's right,

"Sixth grader?"

"Yes," Fumio answered.

"Do you know a *Fumio*?"

"Umm, yes. I *am* Fumio."

"Gee! That's swell!" The boy pulled a folded sheet of paper from his pocket. "I've been keeping an eye out for you. Sensei told me that, without fail, you must receive this *today*."

"Sensei?" Fumio unfolded the smudged paper. He noticed the handwriting was tidy, in perfectly straight lines. He had a hard time not letting his lines run off the page at an angle.

Fumio Miyota,

The Sensei of Manzanar's Taiko Dojo notified us of your transfer. We have been waiting for you. Once your parents give permission, come to the dojo. Kohai Okamoto-san will inform you of the place and hours. Peace.

• • •

On his first day as a student of Minidoka's taiko dojo, Fumio arrived early. Inside the door, he bowed before moving to stand at the perimeter, as he had learned to do at the Manzanar dojo. After a few moments, a senpai came to speak to him.

"So, you are Fumio Miyota. I am Oshiro, assistant to Sensei Wakatsami-san, master of our dojo. Today, Fumio, you will play the chu-daiko." He placed in Fumio's hands one of the medium-sized drums.

Fumio bowed, and the assistant walked away. "Chu-daiko," Fumio repeated the name of the drum in a whisper.

The dojo door opened and a man, whom Fumio assumed to be Sensei Wakatsami-san, entered. A senior student hurried forward, closed the door, and took the gentleman's jacket. The man paused, bowed deeply, and straightened. He went to a chair placed against a wall, sat down, and slipped the shoes from his feet. Fumio saw that the man wore tabi, the traditional Japanese split-toed socks.

Fumio glanced about. All the dojo's students wore tabi. *Right down to my toes,* Fumio thought, *I am the new kid.* Then someone sneezed. He turned toward the sound. No one else did. Every student's eyes stayed focused forward. No one, he realized, was interested in his feet.

At the signal, Fumio went to his assigned drum, inched it back, and stood slightly behind other students—as he had been taught a new student should do—to show a humble attitude.

He again experienced the familiar feeling of being *the new one,* but he relied on the rules, the traditions. Eyes always forward, he spoke not one word unless addressed by the sensei or a senpai. He watched, he listened. He lost himself and found himself in the drumming.

After half the length of time usually spent in a session, the master drew himself up and swept the learners with a gaze. "Students of Dojo Minidoka—be conscious of the honor in hard work. The more arduous the work, the more estimable is the honor." He changed his shoes and accepted his jacket from a senior senpai, then exited the hall, accompanied by the senior senpai.

A student went to the front of the group. Looking toward Fumio, he smiled and said, "I am Haruo Sawada, a junior senpai. Fumio Miyota, we welcome you to our dojo!"

Fumio responded with a bow and a deep nod.

Okes, the boy Fumio had met his first day at Stafford Elementary, looked in his direction, nodded, and smiled.

The junior senpai announced, "Students of Dojo Minidoka, the floor must be cleaned. We will undertake the task now."

Drums were returned to racks and for nearly an hour, young kohai, directed by junior senpai, scrubbed floor tiles on hands and knees. No one spoke, except for the occasional, "You missed a spot!"

When the job was done, along with other students, Fumio tiptoed around the edges of the still-damp floor, put on his shoes and jacket, and made his way onto the dojo's front landing. The last one out was Okes. He closed the door firmly, then looked toward Fumio, grinning. "That was some welcome, huh?"

CHAPTER FIFTY-FIVE

FUMIO

"May I please be excused?" Fumio asked one evening in late April. His father nodded. Balancing a metal tray, plate, and utensils, Fumio swung one leg, then the other, over a wooden plank that served as seating in the Block 44 mess hall.

That evening, the mess hall smelled of hot dogs and sauerkraut—again. The bottomless supply of sauerkraut was due, people said, to a bumper cabbage crop in Minnesota. Fumio's plate retained a smear of ketchup and most, but not all, of the sauerkraut. According to the Miyota family rules, all types of food must be given at least a trial taste.

Fumio handed his tray to a dishwashing crewmember who dropped it in a large tub atop a tottering stack. After a quick glance at the yellowed strings of uneaten sauerkraut that hung from the stack of trays, Fumio hurried back to his family. "Father, Mother, I will see you at the dojo," he glanced up at the wall clock, "in an hour." He added, to Kimiko, "You, too, squirt."

"See you later, alligator," his little sister replied.

Flashing a smile, Fumio pivoted toward the double doors at the end of the hall.

"Fumio," Kimiko called after him, "say it! Say it, Fumio!"

"Afterrr a whiiile, Crrrocodiiile," he growled, and exited the hall's double doors.

• • •

Glad for the coat he had tied around his waist, Fumio pulled it on and zipped it up. He scanned the dusky landscape for the source of the crack of a baseball bat he'd just heard smacking a hard ball. Even at this hour, players were out jumping the gun on the beginning of baseball season. He had heard that baseball season never ended at Camp Minidoka—that camp kids played the game when blowing snow hid the base lines and below-zero temperatures compressed the ball into a bat-breaking missile.

Apparently, many Minidoka youngsters took advantage of those cold days to skate, too, on ice formed by water channeled from the North Side Canal into a depression near Block 44. Fumio was told ice skating stretched through February and into March. All the cold-weather talk made him wonder about the effect such cold temperatures might have on the dojo's drums.

At Manzanar, Fumio had learned to drum accompaniment for traditional dances, such as those occurring during a Bon Odori Festival. And he had been asked to fill in for one or another of the drummers who provided rhythm for Manzanar's judo dojo. Tonight's performance would be a public introduction of the taiko dojo.

The word "dojo" meant "The Place of the Way." A dojo was a place of instruction and practice, where traditions and skills were shared from person to person. Tonight, they would share taiko with their families and friends.

Striding toward the dojo, Fumio tried to get a better sense of Camp Minidoka's crescent-shaped arrangement. With rows of barracks at his right, he knew the North Side Canal was a half-mile distant, on his left.

Outside the curve lay high-desert prairie, with tall grasses, sagebrush, and cactus. Inside the curve, close to the entrance gate, sat the white-painted office buildings of the War Relocation Authority. In the next block were twelve tar-papered buildings, bordered by narrow dirt avenues. There, community service offices were located.

Walking briskly now, Fumio was glad Stafford Elementary School, the taiko dojo, and Kimiko's nursery school were only a little over a mile from the Miyota apartment and that he hadn't stayed longer at the mess hall before beginning his walk.

A thwack on the toe of his shoe pulled his attention to a patch of loose rock, and his focus back to his surroundings. Ahead were four ungainly legs—wooden beams, twenty-feet long—supporting a guard tower. Near one beam lay a ragged coil of barbed wire, debris from the fence that had been removed from behind the back perimeter. Nothing beyond that fence to run to, it had been taken down.

Angling his gaze upward, Fumio imagined meeting the eyes of a gun-carrying, uniformed man, watching from the guard tower. But, no soldier. And no searchlight. The eight perimeter towers were not fully functional because electrical components were in short supply. The towers might be useful in spotting fires, though.

How quickly could he climb that tower, Fumio wondered? To be twenty feet up in the diamond-studded darkness, far above the ragged sagebrush. To look across the Snake River Plain toward the Sawtooth Mountains.

Boom, boom, boom. Fumio had responsibilities.

At the dojo, Fumio hurried to mount the steps. He paused before the senior students on the landing to perform the traditional bow. The young men smiled. One bowed, and the other, Senpai Oshiro, extended his hand. Fumio shook the senpai's hand, then, all three bowed.

Entering the dojo, he paused, bowed, and found a place to remove his shoes, taking a moment to admire his first pair of tabi, a gift from his mother who had reworked a pair of slightly over-sized socks to fashion the split toe covers.

Assigned their instruments in advance, students quickly moved them from the storage racks to the front of the hall, placing them on stands or resting them on the floor. Then the kohai retrieved their preferred bachi and, with one stick grasped vertically in each hand and held tight to their collarbones, found a place to wait, standing at attention along a wall.

A few at a time, then in groups, the visiting audience entered the room, bowed toward the senpai, and found seats. People shifted positions, chairs creaked, small children were *shuushed*. Finally, silence settled over the hall.

Fumio glanced at the floor. It was scrupulously clean.

With a subtle movement, the senior senpai signaled the students: *go to your drums.*

Fumio stepped to his place. Shoulders straight, eyes ahead, still he could see his sister, father, and mother. On Kimiko's face he saw curiosity. On his father's, expectation. On his mother's, affection. He breathed deeply to quell a grin.

Senpai Oshiro stepped in front of the audience, bowed and said, "We are honored by your attendance. We hope to repay you for the gift of your time by sharing with you the art of taiko drumming. To begin, we ask your forbearance as we introduce you to our instruments, for it is only with *their* permission that we may play them."

A murmur of assent and a chuckle or two rippled across the audience.

The senpai smiled, continued, "I will tell you about the largest drum, the odaiko, but I cannot show it to you. We do not have one here. We did not wish to risk moving it to this place because the odaiko is *so very* large. In fact, its name means, 'big, fat, drum.'" More laughter. "An odaiko entrusted to Sensei Wakatsami-san is in storage in Seattle, where a kind-hearted minister watches over it. I think the odaiko misses us tonight, don't you?" He joined the audience in good-natured laughter.

Advanced students showed five types of drums from the dojo's collection—the nagado-daiko with its ring-shaped handles, the deep-toned hira-daiko, the rope-tensioned okedo-daiko, and the chu-daiko sitting on its slanted stand. The tone of each drum was demonstrated.

Another senpai spoke about the construction of taiko drums and their costly nature. Their expense, he said, was the reason for the pile of old tires in the corner of the room. The tires were used during practices. This sparked a smattering of surprised exclamations.

Senpai Oshiro thanked the students who had helped with the introductions. Then he and each of the junior senpai moved to a drum. Sensei Wakatsami-san appeared and was introduced by Senpai Oshiro. The sensei was greeted with respectful, subdued applause, which he acknowledged with a deep nod. He turned to face the drummers.

Fumio felt the audience lean in.

The sensei raised his arm and cried, "Ahaiii!" Then, "Haiyii!" The sensei took command of a hira-daiko. Pausing for a moment with a long, tapered naga-bachi held high over his head, he plunged it rapidly downward to draw forth the drum's deep tone—once, twice, three times— *Boom . . . Boom . . . Boom.* On the fourth strike—*Boom*—the beat became measured, even.

Fumio applied discipline to focus on his own drumming. Never had he expected to see the master join the uchite, the ranks of drummers.

Momentum built as the music climbed, quickened, slowed. The drums told a story to be understood in the mind and heart of each listener.

Fumio's gaze went momentarily to his parents. He saw concentration in their expressions, and happiness, too. Kimiko's hands were clasped. She had laid them over her heart. Within the perfect oval of her face, her eyes shone. Kimiko had fallen in love with the music of the drums.

When the resonance of the last beat had faded, the master nodded to the drummers and walked to the side of the hall. The senior senpai bowed to the audience, "We would be glad if you lingered, as we would like to greet each of you. Thank you for joining us this evening."

Fumio waited his turn as the drummers racked the drums and shelved the bachi. The vibrations of drum strikes still echoed through his arms from his fingertips to his shoulders. The same thing had happened after each practice session. The buzzing sensation would ease up as he walked back to the barracks. A satisfying discomfort, it was a measure of his effort.

The chu-daiko safely stored, Fumio looked to the senior senpai and bowed. The senpai extended a hand, "Fumio!"

Fumio approached, bowed again. "Yes, Oshiro-san?"

The senpai said, "Fumio, I wish to greet your parents. Will you introduce me, please?"

Fumio nodded and led the senpai to where his family waited.

Mr. Miyota wore a dark cardigan over a white shirt. His tie was carefully knotted. Mrs. Miyota wore a sky-blue suit, her jacket neatly tailored in a loose cut. Her dark blue gloves and small hat matched impeccably. Holding her mother's hand, Kimiko stood on tiptoe, wearing a yellow dress embroidered in designs of tulips and birds. Fumio's chest warmed.

"Senpai Oshiro-san," Fumio began, making introductions, ending with the youngest, Kimiko.

The senior senpai and Mr. Miyota shook hands. "Thank you for coming, Mr. and Mrs. Miyota, and you, little miss. We are glad Fumio has joined the dojo. Although he is young, he has had excellent teaching. Sensei Wakatsami-san sent a letter to Manzanar's dojo saying that your son represents well the quality of the dojo master's instruction."

Mr. Miyota responded with a deep nod. Mrs. Miyota also nodded and smiled politely.

"And you," Senpai Oshiro addressed Kimiko, "did you like the drumming?"

Kimiko raised her eyes and spoke directly to the senpai. "It was *beautiful!*"

Fumio's mother laid her hand on Kimiko's shoulder.

"I am glad you enjoyed it."

"I did! And I want to drum, too! Can I come here to learn to drum?"

The senpai ducked his chin, shook his head. "I'm sorry, little miss, but the drums are very big, and you are very small and, you see, women do not *do* this sort of drumming."

Kimiko's cheeks reddened. She nodded before lowering her eyes.

Mr. Miyota nodded. "She is young. We thank you for your work on behalf of our son."

The senpai bowed, then nodded to Fumio and Kimiko one after the other, before going to talk with another family.

After a moment or two, the master, Sensei Wakatsami, joined the Miyotas. Fumio, again, introduced his family. The master spoke to Mr. and Mrs. Miyota. He smiled at Kimiko. "We are glad you could be here to watch your big brother drum, young lady."

Eyes down, Kimiko nodded. Sensei Wakatsami moved on.

Fumio said his farewells to his friends—waving at some, speaking briefly to others.

The Miyotas walked into the night. Passing a new ornamental garden, Mr. Miyota commented, "A lot of work is being done here, but none of this can be eaten, not one whit!"

"Yasuo, life isn't only about filling our stomachs," Mrs. Miyota chided.

"I know. There is enjoyment to be found in planting a garden like this, but I found enjoyment in raising strawberries. Chickens, they were a daily challenge, but they were *ours*, our challenging chickens. We looked after them, we fed them right, we had eggs. It was that simple. Here, everything is an *issue*—an argument. I just want to raise food and, yes, *eat it*!"

Mrs. Miyota looked up at her husband. "But we are lucky, don't you think?"

"Lucky? How do you figure that?"

"We are together." She placed her hand on her midsection. "All of us, we are together."

Once inside their apartment, Mr. Miyota adjusted the oil burner. Mrs. Miyota put the kettle atop it. Soon, a plume of steam ascended from the kettle's spout. Mrs. Miyota opened the drawer of a cabinet Mr. Miyota had built against the wall. She took out a metal mesh tea strainer.

Kimiko followed her, pulled two big spoons from the drawer, and began beating against the cabinet. "*Boom! Boom! Boom! Boom!*"

"Kimiko, dear, our neighbors are very near!"

Kimiko nodded and transferred her attention to drumming on the chair, which was, by virtue of the size and thickness of its "drum top," somewhat quieter. "I want to be a drummer, too. Why can't girls be drummers if boys can be drummers? Mothers are girls, and boys have mothers. So, girls can drum!"

Stepping side to side, Kimiko began to pound out a rhythm with the spoons. "I can do it, see?" She did not wait for an answer but continued to beat on the chair seat.

Later, after Kimiko was in bed, Fumio sat on his cot as the last of the vibrations running along his arms subsided. The excitement of the performance, however, still fluttered in his stomach. His father sat near the stove, rubbing grease into his work boots, preserving them. His mother sat mending and talking with Fumio about the evening.

Fumio said, "Kimiko took a liking to taiko drumming."

"She did," his mother answered.

"She was disappointed when the senior senpai said she could not be taught to drum at the dojo."

"Perhaps she was even more disappointed when he said she could not because she is a girl."

"Do you think that should matter?" Fumio asked.

"What do you think?" his mother said.

Fumio frowned, pulled his knees against his chest, and encircled them with his arms. "I think Kimiko is right. It makes no sense at all."

CHAPTER FIFTY-SIX

FUMIO

Sitting at the table in the square of light from their single window, Fumio made drawings and discarded them, while his mother and little Kimiko visited the library. Fumio sketched drums, considering the dimensions and materials needed to make one. Many plans looked workable until he listed the steps involved. Design flaws became obvious, or a need for some material unavailable at Minidoka.

Fumio was determined to give his sister a drum on the twenty-first of May, the day she became five years old—an important birthday. Kimiko would begin kindergarten in September. She was growing up. Her world was changing, and she was giving signs of being capable. Taiko drumming had ignited a spark inside her. She had not stopped talking about the drums. She drew pictures of drums. She asked questions about what Fumio learned at the dojo. He did his best to explain. But Kimiko needed a drum of her own.

Grasping a folder of flawed plans, he asked his father if they could discuss the project. Mr. Miyota listened as Fumio reported what he now knew would *not* work.

"A good beginning," his father said. "A smart builder creates detailed plans. Projects always run half-again as long as expected and cost twice as much. You need to know that in advance, Son. Still, careful planning saves headaches down the road." Mr. Miyota took a broad, flat-sided builder's pencil from his shirt pocket.

Fumio sharpened his TrueLine and laid out his drawings. Three complications plagued his search for the best way to build the drum. A wood-staved barrel emptied of roofing nails might be perfect for the body, but it would be far too big for Kimiko to manage. To buy leather for the drumhead was beyond his means. Fancy nail heads would be an impressive way to attach the drumhead, but were expensive, and driving them required specific tools and advanced skill.

After talking with his father, Fumio adjusted his sights. What sort of thing was cylindrical and hollow, not overly large, and available at Minidoka? Glancing up to the shelf on the wall, he saw the tiny green tin of coffee his mother had bought for guests who did not drink tea. The tins stored on the mess hall shelves were larger, yet not too big for Kimiko. He would ask at the mess hall if he might have a coffee tin. No, he would ask how he could *earn* a coffee tin.

Material for the drumhead must be something he could cut and shape himself, something *malleable*. He recalled the stacks of ruined tires near the garage at Manzanar. "Victims of road-wear and heat," his father had explained. The rubber gave way—occasionally exploded—leaving the tires in tatters. That rubber was much too thick for his purposes, but an inner tube would be perfect. He would go to a garage and ask the supervisor how he might earn an innertube.

He would attach a piece of innertube to the body of the drum with some type of lacing. He looked from object to object around the apartment, landing finally on the place under his parents' bed where his father's work boots usually sat—except, of course, when his father was wearing them, as he was now. He knew his father did not have a spare pair of boots or laces. Someone, though, must have a used pair of extra-long work-boot laces he might earn.

As for the bachi, he would search the perimeter of the camp for suitable wood from which to carve them.

CHAPTER FIFTY-SEVEN

FLYER

I am wagging and wagging my tail! I am happy! Mail came today from both Fumio's mother *and* Fumio. Supper is over. Mrs. Whitlock gave me an apple! And Zachary is reading Fumio's letter *aloud* to his family and me.

Fumio says almost everyone in his school plays baseball. And he drew a picture of *prairie dogs* that live beyond the ball fields, in towns of little dugouts with tunnels in between. The prairie dogs stand on their hind legs on top of piles of dug-up dirt to *communicate* with other dogs. I think they talk about where there is food and tell each other if there is trouble!

Mrs. Whitlock reads the letter Mrs. Miyota wrote. Kimiko is learning her ABCs and numbers. I know some numbers, now, because I help Zachary with the sheep. He points: *one, two, three,* next, *four, five,* and *flock.*

At Minidoka people build water gardens. With ponds! That must make Fumio happy!

Mrs. Whitlock smiles and says, "Zachary, you can help me with this. Mrs. Miyota sent a money order for postage and asks if we could please send their kitchen curtains. You remember, don't you? Yellow-checkered, edged with embroidered baby chicks? She knows Jacob took them down to keep them clean. They're in our attic. First thing tomorrow, we will hang them on the line to air out."

I thump my tail. When my family lived in our house, the curtains hung at the window *above the sink*. They were in front of the place where I laid *under the sink*, too. Mrs. Miyota pushed them to the side, so I could see my family.

Zachary will help with the curtains in the morning. He asks if Mrs. Miyota will hang them at their barracks window.

"No, she is planning a project. The fabric will be perfect for a *layette*."

Zachary asks, "*Layette?*"

I don't know that word, either.

Mrs. Whitlock tells us a *layette* is a set of matching clothes for a new baby and, maybe, a coverlet for the crib. She holds the letter closer. "*Residents* can use a sewing machine in the Block Manager's office, but Mrs. Miyota plans to do much of the work by hand."

"A friend is expecting a baby, I suppose," Mr. Whitlock says.

Mrs. Whitlock smiles. "*Hmmm . . .* maybe. But to sew a layette by hand will take a great amount of time. What do you think? Could we send her sewing machine to her at Minidoka? Crate and ship it by train? It would have to travel the last of the distance by truck, of course."

"Or," Zachary says, "we could load it up and *take it to her*, in *our own* truck!"

"I like that idea," Mrs. Whitlock says. "It is a six-hundred-mile trip, though."

"Three days of travel." Mr. Whitlock taps his chin with his finger. "A household sewing machine might not have been allowed in camp a year ago, but restrictions have eased. And fuel for the truck is allowed with our clergy classification. Let's do it!"

"Yes!" Mrs. Whitlock nods. "We'll take Mrs. Miyota's rocking chair, too."

I *thump, thump, thump* my tail. Three times.

CHAPTER FIFTY-EIGHT

FUMIO

Saturday morning, Fumio lingered in the mess hall, sipping a glass of orange juice, making it last until the other diners left. Taking his tray to the long metal counter, he carefully placed his dishes and utensils in the bus tubs where they belonged.

He spotted an older man scrubbing trays that had held the morning's scrambled eggs.

"Excuse me, sir," Fumio said. "Can you tell me how I might earn an empty coffee can?"

Grasping a wood-handled brush, the man cast a glance over his shoulder.

Following the man's gaze, Fumio saw a woman with a long, dark braid, cleaning an oversized cake and pastry mixer. He moved to face her and waited until she looked toward him.

When she did, she did not exactly smile, but asked, "Yes?"

"I hope to earn a coffee can."

"Ah. You will have to see the man in charge." She gestured vaguely to her right.

Tracking her gesture, Fumio saw a middle-aged man with thick, wavy hair and bushy eyebrows pulled down in a fixed scowl. The twin lines between his eyes were deep as culverts.

Fumio glanced back at the woman in the flour-dusted apron.

"Yes, that is him. Mind you, wait until you are given permission to speak. Then get right to the point. He does not like children, much. Keep it brief, and maybe he won't eat you."

Fumio trudged across the kitchen toward huge tubs in which water boiled, sanitizing cutlery. Steam spewed from the pans. The heat burned Fumio's face from several feet away as he stood waiting to gain attention and permission to speak to *the man in charge*.

He waited a full ten minutes before the man barked, "How long you gonna stand there? Make yourself useful," and threw him a clean towel.

Fumio caught the towel and began using it to dry a pan big enough to bathe in. When finished with that pan, he picked up another. And then another.

As Fumio dried the last of the monstrous pots, the man watched, then barked "Hai! Why are you not playing baseball, danshi?"

Sweat made a swamp of Fumio's shirt. He dashed his sleeve across his face. As advised by the woman in the floury apron, and relying on his family's teaching, he said, "Ojamashimasu, I hope to work to earn a coffee can."

"What do you want with coffee? Too young to like coffee. Do you not like baseball?"

"Sumimasen, I do like baseball. I *do not* like coffee. I wish to work, so I might earn an *empty* coffee can." He hurriedly added, "I need one for the gift I am making."

"A coffee can?" The man shrugged. "Hai! Everyone wants one of those."

"Everyone wants a coffee can?"

"Hai! I got a waiting list. The new poultry set-up, they use 'em for chicken feed."

Despite the heat in the kitchen, a shudder ran down Fumio's spine. Was he going to have to tend *chickens* to earn a coffee can?

"Also, people fill 'em with water and use 'em on top the coal burners because the air is so dry," he waved his hands through the kitchen's moist air, grimacing. "Especially older or sickly folks. Gardeners treat coffee cans like porcelain. Yup! Everyone wants coffee cans." He shrugged. "Maybe you can find a tender-hearted gardener. Hai! Green thumb with a soft heart."

The man turned, laughing. "Danshi, you are a fine kid. Hai! Ganbatte!" He followed the words with a deep nod.

CHAPTER FIFTY-NINE

FUMIO

Baseball *ruled* at Camp Minidoka. Several games were in full swing as Fumio walked out of the Block 44 mess hall. Joey would have loved this, he thought. The Katos, however, were not transferring until later in the summer. At Heart Mountain Relocation Center, Mr. Kato was teaching an adult education class on business practices. He thought it best to complete that assignment before the family reunited in Idaho.

Fumio himself might have gotten caught up in the commotion of baseball. Emphatic calls of "Strike one! Strike two!" The crack of the bat. The roar of the crowd. The verdict of the ump: "Yerrrrrr out!" Shouts of disagreement: "He's safe, I tell ya! Safe!" or "Nahhh, he's out!"

He liked the chatter, the rhythm of it. He liked the energy of the game. But his energy must be directed at finding a gardener with a spare coffee can. It could take some persistence, but gardens could be found across Camp Minidoka. Vegetables plots were planted between barracks and beside front steps to supply familiar, fresh foods.

An ornamental garden was being built near the dojo. Perhaps he would have luck there. He had seen men using pry bars to adjust the placement of stones, and shears to shape the collection of shrubs, twig by twig. In large buckets, they brought water for thirsty plants, and in shallow baskets they carried soil to cover tender roots exposed by wind and rain. A group of a dozen or more men of the community labored there now.

Fumio slowed, pondering who he should approach when he heard a sound—*Sswaaash—Plunk!*—and a cry of "Hon-n-nto nano!" from his right.

Walking toward the distress call, he saw a patch of tilled earth and a puddle of spreading water. In its midst was a bent figure topped by a gentleman's wide-brimmed hat. One heavy canvas glove lay in the muck beside an overturned bucket. "Come ahead, then!" the figure said.

Fumio stepped to the edge of a good-sized garden. Rows of tiny green sprouts peeked above the uneven soil.

"They are peas, if you would like to know, danshi—green peas. Some call them *sweet peas*. But sweet peas belong in vases." Laughter arose from the figure. "These peas are good eating, if you have a chance to taste them."

He came nearer.

The woman—for a woman she was, he saw now—wore two pairs of bulky socks, one pair blue, the other brown, that peeked out above shoes with thick soles. Gray trousers, visible up to her knees, disappeared into a purple skirt. A man's button-down shirt hung past her hips, and layered over it was a heavy lavender sweater, frayed at the cuffs. A purple ribbon circled the crown of her tattered hat, knotted at the side where a wilting sprig of green was tucked beneath it. She gave the appearance, Fumio thought, of a character from a book of folk tales.

She wiped her shirt sleeve across her forehead. "Do I know your family?"

"Sumimasen ga, ma'am, I am not sure. My name is Fumio Miyota." He bowed. "My family lives in Block 44."

She nodded. "Bainbridge Island people."

"Yes, ma'am."

"I am happy to meet you, Fumio Miyota. I am Mrs. Takujo Otani. My husband—he was known as *Tak*—passed on two years ago." She blinked, looked away, then asked, "So then, danshi, do you need something?"

"No, ma'am. Yes, ma'am," Fumio replied, keeping his eyes down. "I am here to ask if you have work I can do so I may earn from you a coffee can, if you have one you will part with."

"A coffee can?" She shook her head. "Everybody wants those."

Fumio sighed and, with his shoe, traced a line in the loose soil.

A boy, towing by rope a cart with wooden runners, came into sight. His dark hair on one side fell over his eyes. He was, at most, a few years older than Fumio, and near the same height.

The youth addressed the woman, "Mrs. Otani-san, good morning."

"And to you, young man. Your father, and your brother?"

"In good health, thank you." The boy bowed, then nodded toward Fumio, "I'm Paul."

Fumio gave a brisk nod in return. "I'm Fumio."

In the silence that followed, Mrs. Otani, Paul, and Fumio turned their attention to the cart and the small boulder resting upon it.

Paul said, "Basalt."

Recognition stirred. An image formed of Paul wearing a judogi. Fumio had filled in for an absent drummer at the judo dojo. That was where he had seen the boy. He smiled.

At the same moment, Paul spoke. "Ahh!" he said, as a smile lit his eyes. "Taiko."

"Judo," Fumio replied.

Once more, Paul bowed to Mrs. Otani. "Sumimasen ga, my father asks, can you please find a place for this stone? In our hunt for boulders and plants, we chose more than we can use. We do not wish to return the stone to its former place, which is at least three miles from here."

Fumio was taken aback by the immensity of the task described. The chunk of basalt was roughly the size of a hay bale. "How did you move a boulder as big as that?"

Mrs. Otani spoke up. "Paul and his brother go into the desert behind the camp with their father. It is okayed. They use a tool—such as that one." She pointed to the crowbar lying in the cart beside the stone. "Inch by inch, the stone is shifted onto the cart. Then it is towed to the garden being built by Block 5."

"You could help, if you like," Paul said, looking toward Fumio.

Among Japanese American neighbors, it was usual to consider the building of ornamental gardens a man's job and the tending of a family's vegetable garden a woman's. But, glancing about, he saw many ways in which he could be of use here.

"Thank you," Fumio replied, with a quick nod, still meeting Paul's gaze. "But I hope to work out a trade for labor, here, in this garden."

"Sure," Paul answered, returning the nod. He inclined his head, then, and asked, "Mrs. Otani-san, may I place this stone for you?"

She pointed, and he tugged the cart to a corner of the garden, where he maneuvered the crowbar beneath the boulder. As gravity overtook the stone, the cart tipped on its runners. The boulder hit the ground with a thud, and the cart righted itself again.

The woman went to the steps of her apartment, reached underneath and returned with a container that had once held tinned meat. Lowering herself to her knees, she worked her hands beneath a six-inch square patch of pea sprouts, loosening the roots, then gently transferred the patch of sprouts to the tin. She gazed intently at Fumio, and he stepped up to offer his arm.

Once Mrs. Otani had been raised from the ground, she brushed dirt from the sides of the tin and extended it to Paul.

Paul bowed deeply, took the container, and carefully placed it on the cart bed beside the crowbar. "My father thanks you." He towed the cart onto packed earth and toward Block 5.

"That boy is spare of speech," Mrs. Otani said. "You know him. He is in your class at school?"

"No, ma'am. He is older than I am, but I have seen him at judo practice."

"You are a student of judo, young man?"

"No, ma'am. I am a student of drumming—taiko drumming." Fumio paused. "It is to make a drum that I need a coffee can. My little sister, Kimiko, wants to learn to drum. But she was told she cannot because she is a girl. I want to teach her what I know about taiko. I want to give her a drum for her birthday."

"Ahhh," the woman breathed. "I see."

"I am a good worker, ma'am. I could come after school, unless I must attend the dojo, Mrs. Otani-san, ma'am." Fumio held his breath.

"If we work together in the garden, danshi, you might think of me as Auntie, or Oba-san. Oba-san would be my choice."

Fumio bowed, taking a sharp breath in and out, before lifting his head. "Thank you, ma'am—Thank you, Oba-san."

She smiled. "As I said, many people have asked to be given coffee cans. At first, small cans. For the lids, you know."

Fumio nodded. He had seen the round pieces of tin nailed over holes in the floor of their barracks room. The same as Manzanar.

The woman went on, "There was big noise in Camp when snakes started coming in from . . . *out there*," she motioned toward the expanse of brushy desert, "to spend the winter under the barracks. Rattlesnakes."

The backs of Fumio's legs prickled. He glanced over his shoulder to scan the ground. At Manzanar, it was known that insects—tarantulas, even—could enter through holes in a floor. Nobody at Minidoka had mentioned rattlesnakes.

"Yet people make dug-outs beneath floors. Got to have the space!" She clicked her tongue. "You need a coffee can. I have three. I have two from my home in Tacoma. One holds a jade plant, the other a bonsai. The third was filled to the top with coffee grounds when my name came up on the head cook's list. Coffee grounds are good for soil.

"Vegetable plots we call Victory Gardens now. I had a garden at Puyallup's Fairgrounds, too. Things grew good! Those cubbies we stayed in smelled like horses. But, do you know, the soil outside our doors was *rich*!" She laughed.

"I tell you every garden is a Victory Garden. If one green thing comes up, that is a victory. In this camp, I can help, use my green thumb, grow needed food. So, here I am, with gloves made by my neighbor as she begins to sew." She waved her hand and the glove she held flew loose, joining its mate in the puddle. She stooped to pick up both gloves and tossed the pair toward the steps. "These boots, I have owned them for twenty years. No time for 'style' as the young folks speak of it." She shook her head. "Wabi-sabi!" she added and laughed.

Fumio could only shake his head.

"Wabi-sabi," the woman repeated. "It means, 'What it is, let it be.'"

"Wabi-sabi. Yes, ma'am, Mrs. Otani—Oba-san."

"Before you set your mind to this job, you should see the tin to be earned in return for your work. It is not much." Mrs. Otani went inside and came back carrying a coffee tin, green, with spots of rust. A dent marred the surface where the brand, "Kitchen Pride," was printed.

Fumio tightened his face to hide his disappointment. Beggars can't be choosers, he thought. But he wasn't a beggar. Maybe he should back out now. Nothing lost. If he found one gardener willing to part with a coffee tin, surely there would be another. But, no, this woman needed his help. So the coffee can was in bad shape. He knew how to remove a dent from metal. Maybe he could find a job to pay for paint to cover the rust. He could make this work.

The woman's voice cut through his thoughts. "I am waiting for another coffee tin. But it could be weeks, months, before it becomes my turn. A neighbor with a small child, she tries to help with the garden." The woman smiled. "But with the tot hanging onto her skirt, she does her best. This need for constant watering should pass in a week—less than two. I can find someone to hook up the hose from the washroom's rinse tub soon."

She pressed her lips together, nodded. "Then things are fixed good for this garden. For now . . ." She walked to her apartment where she had lined up three large commercial-sized metal containers, the sort that food-service supplies came in. The label of one declared it had formerly held lard. Two containers had handles. One did not.

Fumio made a note to himself to bring work gloves. Those handles would bite hard into his hands. "It would be well if you had a cart, Oba-san. Like the one Paul and his family use."

"Maybe someday. For now, it is shank's mare. The strength of our own backs, danshi."

Fumio risked his opinion. "Sumimasen ga—excuse me, ma'am. This is heavy work. The fields around us are filled with men cultivating acres and acres of vegetables, irrigating from a canal. They have tractors, trucks."

"Vegetables in this garden are spoken to! They are weeded by hand and hear our hopes for them to become a living part of the human race. Is this true for field vegetables?"

Maybe, Fumio thought, but he said, "No, ma'am, not as it is for *these* vegetables." Bowing, he sealed the deal.

Immediately, he began hauling water from an irrigation ditch half-a-mile north, a fifteen-minute walk to the ditch with two empty buckets, and twenty minutes or more back after they were filled. This Fumio did, repeatedly, until the thirst of every garden row was slaked.

Stopping only for a dipperful of lukewarm water from a jar, Fumio worked until an hour before mealtime, thanked Mrs. Otani, and went home to clean up. After supper, he fell across his bed, intending to read. He woke later, in a haze, his father pulling the shoes from his feet and his mother covering him with an afghan.

CHAPTER SIXTY

FLYER

The porch is piled high with *possessions* to take to Camp Minidoka. I helped my family pack before. I thought they would take me with them. Later, Zachary told me dogs weren't allowed there. Are they allowed now? My insides feel strange. I don't want to drink the water Zachary puts out, and I don't even want the bone Mrs. Whitlock brought home.

Zachary told me about the trip. In the evening, after supper, the Whitlocks talked about the best *route* to take to Camp Minidoka. I heard the names of towns: Gooding, Greenleaf, Echo, Wilder, Fruitland, Eden. Places I don't know.

Mr. Petric's truck comes into the yard. He brought something wrapped in an old quilt. "Do you think there's room for this? We want our neighbors to know we look forward to seeing them back in their own homes. Until then—" Mr. Petric pulls back the covering. He says it is an island cedar tree carved from cedar! *It will withstand the weather*. He looks at his shoes.

Mrs. Whitlock smiles. "It is wonderful!" She touches the carved tree. "You made this."

Mr. Petric nods. Then, he says to me, "I guess you will pack up your old blanket real soon, won't you, Flyer, for the trip to Minidoka?" He hands me something shaped like a bone, but not a bone—a *biscuit*. I like Mr. Petric. I like the treat, too.

The late afternoon sky is dark. Hard winds blow, in *gusts*, from the east. I know *east*. *East* is toward town for a doughnut, on mornings when Mr. Harvey takes me on his sales route. But this wind does not smell like warm sugar, it smells like *weather*.

Zachary frowns. "I hope that storm takes a *detour* and misses us."

Mr. Whitlock asks, "Should we get the truck and its cargo under cover?"

Jacob says, "Yes, better safe than sorry. The Miyota shop is big enough. If it held horses once, it will hold a truck. You can back it in there."

CHAPTER SIXTY-ONE

FUMIO

Across ten days, Fumio hauled water to Mrs. Otani's garden. It was demanding, sweaty work. Smelly, too, as waves of stench rolled in on gusts from the camp's garbage dump. The route took him into open terrain, far enough to hear the commotion of earth-moving. Canal drop construction was underway.

His father had been interested in working on the canal project. However, he had accepted a position as facilities engineer at Camp Minidoka's medical clinic. Communication from Captain Margaret Stone made it clear to the camp administrator that Mr. Miyota was the man for the job if he would accept it, and he had.

In Fumio's work, he used a shovel and a hoe, when necessary—and it often was—to repair furrows damaged by erosion. When no one was nearby, he talked to the plants.

On the tenth day, as suppertime drew near, Fumio shoveled the last scoop of earth into place, shoring up the bank at the end of a furrow.

The door of Mrs. Otani's barracks opened, and Fumio heard her voice. "That is good, danshi. I will go get the coffee tin." He turned to see her smiling as she added, "It is not the one you expect."

Fumio's stomach tightened. Something had gone wrong. *It was not the tin he had been promised.* Mrs. Otani had not understood how important this was to him. He took a deep breath, squared his shoulders, and, as the woman came slowly down the steps, assured himself that if he had done what was necessary to earn a coffee tin once, he could do it again.

Mrs. Otani extended the coffee tin, tilted so that the metal of its interior was visible, shiny, with no rust.

"Thank you." He bowed, accepted it and pulled the tin to his chest.

She explained, "My name came up today. I have just returned from the mess hall. The head cook apologized that the tin did not contain used coffee grounds for the garden, but, because I had told him of our need, he gave me this."

Fumio looked down, shifted his hands, and saw the coffee tin, gleaming, bright red. Two grooves, defined by purple enamel, were pressed into the can near the top and close to the bottom. The coffee's brand name stood out in yellow-gold—*Excelsior*—and below that was a graphic of a golden eagle. The tin was beautiful.

"Oba-san, ma'am, this is a wonderful tin. It should be yours. I was promised an old one."

"Both tins are mine to do with as I please, danshi. I see that this tin will make a fitting gift for your sister, Kimiko. Someday, with joy, I will hear her drum. I anticipate that."

CHAPTER SIXTY-TWO

FLYER

Zachary and his parents eat supper and go to bed early. On the porch, I lie on my blanket, my head on Fumio's baseball mitt.

In the night, I wake. *Rap—rap—rap*—the wind rattles the screen door against its wooden frame. I don't worry. The truck and the cargo are in the shop, under cover.

I wake again when footsteps sound on bedroom floors. Soon, boots pound down the stairs. Zachary comes onto the porch beside me and looks out. Tree branches whip in the wind.

Mr. Whitlock stirs the fire. I hear water coming from the faucet. Mrs. Whitlock calls, "Good morning, Flyer!" and, metal against metal—*clnnk!*—she puts the kettle on to heat. "Zachary! Come inside! Bring Flyer with you, if you like."

Mrs. Whitlock scoops oatmeal cereal into bowls. She sets the little bottle of cream right on the table! Zachary adds two spoons of sugar to his oatmeal.

His mother says, "Zachary . . ."

Zachary says, "It's going to be a big day!"

His book, his *Farm Log*, lays open beside his bowl.

His mother asks, "Is every item checked off?"

He grins and nods.

Once breakfast is cleaned up, Mr. Whitlock and Zachary put on their coats. Zachary's mother hands him a small basket that smells like chicken and pickles. She hands him something wrapped in paper. It smells like ham. "For Flyer, since chicken bones are dangerous for him."

I wonder if I can have pickles. *Do I want pickles?*

"Ready, Zachary?" Mr. Whitlock asks.

Zachary puts his hand on my head. "Ready, Flyer?"

Yipp-ipp! Ready! I pick up Fumio's mitt by the wrist strap.

At my family's driveway, Jacob meets us, his coat not buttoned. "It happened a few seconds ago! I heard a groan, a crash—*BOOM!* The old willow tree's come down—smashed through a corner of the shop! The big lift door is blocked. No way can we get that truck out!"

Running ahead, I see the giant willow has fallen in front of the big shop door. The smell of the mud clutched in its roots is so strong it hurts my nose. I remember when I buried the marshmallow, to save it for Fumio, but I cannot see a marshmallow now.

Mr. Harvey pulls into the driveway. He wants to help. He says, maybe the truck can be ready to go on the ferry this afternoon.

Mr. Whitlock shakes his head. "That's a big tree, planted thirty years ago! A corner of that roof is ruined. Before we can leave, we must repair the shop's big door so we can close and lock it."

I know Zachary's father *doesn't care for* the smell of a dog. But I lean against his leg.

He doesn't notice. He says, "I'm afraid we'll have to make the trip later."

Bundled in a coat and scarf, Zachary's mother walks up the lane. I wait while Mr. and Mrs. Whitlock, Jacob, and Zachary talk together near the roots of the willow tree.

Then Zachary comes to me. "Flyer, that's a *massive old tree*. Moving it will take some time. I'm sorry, pal, we can't start our trip today. We will have to wait."

Mr. Torres is there, and he and Mr. Whitlock talk about buying lumber and shingles and hiring helpers to saw the tree. Zachary is looking after the chickens.

The baseball mitt held firm in my teeth, I head for the lane. I will not wait. I am going to Fumio.

* * *

The sun was not up when I *hit the road*, but the morning is brighter, now. Birds say *good morning* from their nests. It is almost breakfast time. A breeze brings the smell of toast. I am hungry, but I must keep going.

The delivery truck has a picture on its side of a cow with spots. The driver of the truck is called a *milkman*. He wears a cap that is flat on top. He brings milk to our door and the Whitlock's door. Not every day, though, and not this morning. Zachary is the only Whitlock who must drink his milk.

The milkman smiles at me. "Howdy, there! You're the Miyota dog, aren't you? Well, you can sure enough ride along with me! I'd be obliged for your company. Quite a windstorm last night, wasn't it? Toting a parcel, aren't you? How far you taking it?"

I don't know the milkman's name. But he is friendly. Zachary's mother would say the milkman *has a cheerful heart*.

We stop near the harbor and the ferry dock. There's a smell of fish and engine oil in water. I hear, *WHOAAHHAAAAWWW—WOOF!— WOOF!* It is the blast of the ferryboat's horn!

Yipp?

The milkman opens the door and reaches out his hand. "Shake?"

I shake.

He grins and waits while I make sure of my hold on Fumio's mitt and jump down.

CHAPTER SIXTY-THREE

FLYER

A ferryboat sits, rocking on the water, near Eagledale Dock. Little birds with sharp bills hurry on shore. Other birds fly overhead, more than I could ever chase at once.

A crowd of *vehicles* waits, drivers standing near them, frowning. Beside a little shed with an open window, people complain, "Do I look like I got all day? When is this ferry going to get moving?" A man snarls, "I could've swum to Seattle in the time I been waiting for this boat to load. Can I get my money back?"

From inside the little shed, I hear, "No, sir, you cannot get your money back. Is it our fault if a car's tire goes flat on the deck ramp?"

A man stands facing the flat-tire car. He holds a box to his eyes and pushes something with his finger—*czzick!*—a light flashes. *Czzick!* It flashes again. I see, the man is taking pictures with a camera like Jacob's.

Nearby, another man standing close to a truck raises a hand and shouts, "Hi-yah, bud! I see you're on the trail of a big story!" He laughs.

The man with the camera calls back, "Hi-yah, Link! Yeah, I caught a story on the island." He waves.

I stand to the side and watch as people start crossing the walkway toward a gate. A man with shiny shoes stands there. He looks at small pieces of paper in people's hands and says, "Black Ball Line, boarding for Seattle." He says the words over and over.

I go to the man and raise my muzzle, holding the baseball mitt to show him I am carrying something important, too. But he lifts his hand and says, "No. Go away, dog."

Fumio went on the ferry! I must go on the ferry! The man with the camera is walking toward the gate. I am next. I walk ahead. The man wearing shiny shoes throws his arms wide. "Go away, dog!"

Czzick! Pop! A bright light flashes in my eyes! I can't see! But I hear the shiny-shoed man shouting, "Knock it off, you! I got enough problems, here! Some guy driving on bald tires gets a flat tire smack in the middle of the ramp, passengers are bustin' my chops like it's my fault. And a newspaper reporter with a camera shows up, just when all hell is breaking loose on the ferry dock. You work for the *Review*? I've got half a mind to complain to your editors!"

The man hollers back, "Oh, yeah? My paper is in Seattle and my editors are going to get a hoot out of this. You. Standing there arguing with a dog!"

The too-bright spot is gone from my eyes, so now I can see. The shiny-shoed man and the man with the camera argue nose to nose. They do not pay attention to me, at all.

A little girl with a big bow in her hair calls, "Come here, dog. Come! You can have part of my sandwich. That man will not let you get on the ferryboat."

She is right. And I am hungry. I move closer, but not too close. She holds a sandwich. It smells *delicious*. "Here!" She tears off a chunk, puts it down on the walkway and steps back.

With the mitt between my paws, I thank her, *Yipp-ipp!* Then I down the sandwich in one gulp, pick up the mitt, and walk toward the gate again.

Someone begins to whistle. It's a quiet sound, but easy for *me* to hear. It works its way through the noises of other people and machines. I look around, and there he is, near the back of a middle-sized truck, the whistling man who called to the *reporter* with a camera. This man wears sturdy clothes. Gloves poke out of his back pocket.

The whistling sound grows a little louder as I go closer. Standing at the back of the truck, he is still whistling. The truck's box has a canvas cover, folded back.

He shoves aside a stack of folded newspapers and looks right at me. "You have some place you gotta get to, dog? What the hay? I admire your gumption. If you want, you can ride in back, with the newspapers that didn't get sold."

I check my hold on the mitt, jump in, and move forward while the man pushes the stack of papers back where it was. The whistling man goes to sit behind the steering wheel. On the ramp, a ferry dock worker holds up both hands and beckons. The truck moves ahead into the deep shadows of the ferryboat.

The truck's engine stops. The ferry's engine growls, *Grroarr-roarr-roar-roar*. Stacks of folded newspapers fill most of the space. I smell ink. I know the scent from Mr. Whitlock's hands and Fumio and Zachary's schoolwork.

A while later, *Sshhwh! Bump*. The window at the back of the truck cab opens! I am surprised! The man says, "Hello, dog. How are you doing back there?"

I thump my tail. *Yipp!*

"Are you thirsty? I saw you eat that chunk of sandwich. Pretty nice, huh? Lotta folks are nice. Some not so much. That Black Ball steward, though, he was just doing his job."

I don't know *steward*. I don't know what a steward's *job* is.

On the ferryboat, the truck is moving up and down, up and down, like a duck! I am moving up and down, too, but I am not a duck. I don't like it. My head feels strange. When I stand, turn and try to get comfortable, my feet are mixed up.

The man gets out of the cab and comes to sit in the box, near the back. He carries a Thermos bottle in his hand. I know Thermos. Mr. Torres has a Thermos bottle with a special cover, so it won't get *dinged*, he says. *This* man unscrews the wide top and pours something into it. He places it near me. Steam rises. "Here, dog, have some tea."

I twist so Fumio's mitt is far back and lay it down. I turn. The whistling man doesn't move toward the mitt. I lower my head to drink, but the cup scoots away. He moves the toe of his boot against the cup to steady it and I lap the tea. It is not like Mrs. Miyota's tea, but it is good, strong and bitter.

"That was some long wait, right? Car with a flat tire on the ramp. Poor luck. Now I'm off schedule. As you can maybe see, I transport newspapers, wholesale, for the *PI*—the *Post-Intelligencer*. Don't suppose that concerns you, does it?" He laughs.

He thinks I don't know what he means, but Zachary's father reads the *PI*. Not every day. He buys it when he goes into town.

Whoop-ooph!

The man drinks from the Thermos. "Name's Lincoln. Friends call me Link. Rhymes with ink," he holds up his hands, "the stuff I'm covered with by the end of the day." He smiles. "What's your story, dog? You leaving home or going home?"

His name is *Link?* Like part of a chain!

Link takes off his hat, runs a hand over his head. "Good to see the sun. Better have another swig of tea. We got a long drive ahead of us—few stops for the *PI* and, this afternoon, my second job." He puts a finger to his lips. "Strictly on the QT. Mornings, I work for the *PI*. But, afternoons, I transport the *Seattle Times*. So, I'm heading east, as far as Cle Elum. Come along, if you're up for it, dog." He grins.

Seattle. Cle Elum. I don't know *Seattle. Cle Elum.*

The ferryboat's horn sounds: *WHOAAHHAAAAWWW—WOOF!— WOOF!*

"Know what that means, fella?" Link asks. "That sound is called *a warp and two woofs*. It means, *heading for port*." He climbs out of the box and goes back to the driver's seat.

• • • •

A shrill sound, like Fumio's *whistle that can be heard on the moon*, comes from behind us, and the *reporter*, the man with the camera, hurries to the truck, "Link!" He sounds out of breath. "Hey, Link! Can I get a ride with you? Yeah, to *The Times'* office. Don't worry! I'm not going to spill the beans. Work's work, right? Anyway, I'm on foot today. I sure would appreciate a ride."

Link turns to look through the rear window, at *me*. "What do you think, pal? Should we give him a ride?"

Yipp-ipp! I answer, and the reporter gets in front. He turns, smiling. "Well, then, fellow, that baseball mitt. What's the story?"

Phwuphh! I let him know I'm listening.

"No comment? Okay. Anyway, you made my day!"

A corner of the canvas covering is left folded back for me. *Seattle* is noisy. Tall buildings crowd against the walkway. We stop. Link takes a few newspapers, *the ones that didn't sell*, from the back of truck and walks with the reporter into the building.

Soon, he comes out, whistling. At the back of the truck, he lowers the metal gate and points to a patch of grass, Quick, I hop out, go to a tree, and return to the truck.

"Do you like apples, pal?" Link asks me. He uses his thumbnail to cut the apple's peel and then twists it, hard. The apple breaks in half! It tastes good, and I was thirsty.

With Link behind the steering wheel, we drive through *Seattle* again, then park and Link goes through a very wide door. Some men come out with him. He tells them, "Take it easy with those papers. I've got company. A real fine dog."

The men put stacks of newspapers, different newspapers than before, in the truck. "What's with the baseball mitt?" one of them asks.

Link answers, "I couldn't say."

• • •

The truck is what Mr. Harvey calls *a good runner*. We drive east. To *Cle Elum*, Link tells me. The sun tells me we are on the downside of the day, afternoon. When Link parks behind a building, he tells me he must find *a person to take delivery* of the papers. I put my paws on the side rail of the truck box to look out.

When he returns, Link brings a man and a boy who unload stacks of papers while he marks on a clipboard. When they are done, he points toward a big, noisy machine spewing steam, bigger than my family's *Cleveland Crawler*. He asks, "Where's that one heading?"

"Northern Pacific Locomotive, Engine Four-Zero-Zero-Three. This train is heading east in *five seconds, four, three, two, one—*"

Mmm-Wwaaaahhhhh-Ahhhhh! Mmm-Wwaaaahhhhh-Ahhhhh!

The *locomotive* wails, a sound that rattles the truck's windows. *Engine Four-Zero-Zero-Three.* A big arm pumps the wheels forward and back, forward and back, turning them all at the same time with an awful racket. The ground beneath me shakes.

I howl a warning, *Whooo-Oooo-Oooo-Whooo-Oooo! Look out! Look out! Look out! The angry machine is on the move!*

Link is on his knees beside me. "Friend, it's all right," he says. "It's okay. That blast must hurt your ears something awful. I'm sorry, dog."

The bad noise stops, but Link keeps talking, in a quiet voice. "You gotta understand, that's an everyday train noise. You'll hear it again, and I don't want you to be confused. A man called an engineer, it's his job to run the train. He signals when the train's about to move, to keep people safe."

Link stands. He meets my eyes. "So, dog, what's next? Come with me, if you want. I like your company, and I wouldn't mind having a dog. Got to drive home, though, get back to my jobs, both of them. I think back-tracking is not your desire. Am I right?"

I thump my tail once and answer, *Whoooph-Ooph-Ooph.* I grasp the mitt and jump down from the truck. I bump Link's knee with my nose before I leave, to tell him I am on my way to see Fumio.

CHAPTER SIXTY-FOUR

FUMIO

Fumio crossed the compound, heading in a southerly direction toward Warehouse Building No. 5, also known as the Motor Repair and Tire Shop. He felt pressed to *get this over with*, having no idea what to expect. Would he be allowed to talk with the person in charge? Would his request for an innertube be met with courtesy, impatience, or, much worse, laughter?

Within ten minutes, the bulk of Building No. 5 loomed ahead. Resting on a concrete pad, the shop was enormous—as wide as it was deep, tar-papered, and imposing. Fumio estimated the building to be about twenty feet tall. Large windows spanned the upper third of its walls to allow in, Fumio understood, as much natural light as possible.

The building's doors were broad. They could be accordioned back, like those on the Fire Station, to accommodate large, heavy-hauler trucks. A sign read "Caution! Workers."

One door panel stood ajar. From the bright sunlight of midday, Fumio stepped inside to total blindness. Deafening metallic clangor rang out repeatedly. Then came a sudden, hollow *Bang!* followed by an off-color remark.

A man called, "Watch your mouth, Ralph! Don't you see a kid's standing by the door?"

Fumio's gaze adjusted to the gloom. He faced a cavernous expanse, a blur of charcoal gray, then, as his eyes adjusted, a few streaks of color. Finally, with his head angled sharply back, a bare wood ceiling more than fifteen feet above his head came into focus. In places, steel chains secured winches to iron plates on the exposed rafters.

Bang! The noise echoed throughout the shop, followed by more cursing.

"Ralph, I swear—" A man balanced atop a short ladder leaning against the fender of a big truck, pulled his upper body from under the truck's hood. "Have a care, man! A danshi is in the garage!" The man, apparently the shop supervisor, descended the ladder, swinging his head. He walked toward Fumio. "Don't mind Ralph, kid. He's easily riled. Nearest we can figure, he's got a chip on his shoulder."

"You bet I do!" called Ralph. "The chip is *iron,* and it could've put my eye out, Zuko—I mean, Mr. Shizuko-san, sir. Dang tie rod busted all to smithereens."

"That's what safety glasses are for, Ralph. They don't do you any good in your pocket."

Mr. Shizuko-san wore grease-stained coveralls over a grease-stained shirt. Covering his head was a grease-stained cap. On his feet, steel-toed boots. Walking toward Fumio, he wiped his hands on a faded-red shop rag.

Fumio dipped his head, bowed. Straightening, he felt surprise at seeing the shop supervisor reaching out to shake his hand. With a deep nod, Fumio took the man's hand. When his fingers closed around a thumb and fewer than four fingers, he was careful to not react, but the man opened his palm and said, "A mechanic's job is dangerous. Even if he keeps his ducks in a row, there's always some turkey on hand to trip him up—or something waiting to fall."

Fumio's eyes went to the ceiling where a winch hung. He stepped sideways.

Mr. Shizuko-san laughed quietly, shrugged, "The place is enormous, isn't it?"

"Yes, sir. It's like—like a gigantic cave!"

"You like caves, kid?" Ralph ambled across the floor, pulling off his cap and wiping his hands on it. "Over that way," he tipped his head west, "you should go see the big root cellar they're building. Y' know, just drop in." He laughed.

"You understand," Mr. Shizuko spoke in a low tone, "he's making a joke of it because he, himself, is afraid of tight spaces." The shop supervisor grinned, winked. "We let him be. He's kind of entertaining, and we wouldn't want that spoiled. What you say is true, though. This shop is like a gigantic cave. It takes some getting used to."

"Yes, sir. I helped my father in his shop on the island, Mr. Shizuko-san, sir, but it was nowhere near this big.

"On the island? Have you recently been transferred here, then?"

"Yes, sir, from Bainbridge Island, in Washington State. My parents are Mr. and Mrs. Yasuo Miyota. I am Fumio Miyota. First, we went to Manzanar in California. Now we are here."

"Welcome, Fumio Miyota! We're glad to have you here—since you can't be home. Shikata ga nai. Anyway, it's almost time for the noon meal. And you probably aren't here to match wits with Ralph. What can I do for you?"

Fumio took a deep breath. "I hope to have the privilege of working to earn an innertube, Mr. Shizuko-san, sir."

The supervisor frowned. "An innertube? Sorry, kid. Everybody wants those."

Fumio's shoulders sagged. "They do? What do they want them for?"

"For swimming! Or for *not swimming*, really. For splashing around in the pool."

"And for sliding," Ralph said, "belly down when it snows. Isn't that why *you* want it?"

"No, sir—*uhmm*, Ralph-san," Fumio nodded toward the man and returned his attention to the shop supervisor. "Mr. Shizuko-san, I wish to use a piece of the innertube to form the head of a drum I am making for my sister's birthday."

"A drum? Well, that's not your ordinary gift, is it?"

"No, sir. My little sister, Kimiko, went to a performance at the taiko dojo, and now she wants very much to learn to drum. Taiko drums cost thousands of dollars. I want to make a practice drum for her to learn on."

"*Hmmh*, I didn't know there was a taiko dojo." The supervisor swung his head to the side. "Son, that's good of you, *real good*, but, I'm sorry, I have a waiting list for innertubes—"

"But Zuko," Ralph cut in, "do you have a waiting list for a *piece* of an innertube? The kid don't need the whole thing." He walked to a corner where old tires were piled, plunged his hand into a crate beside it, and drew out a fistful of ragged strips of rubber.

Fumio held his breath.

Mr. Shizuko-san strode to the crate, dug into the contents, and came up with part of what had been a very large innertube. He showed it to Fumio. "We use small pieces of rubber from time to time. This came off a heavy-hauler. It exploded."

"The truck exploded?"

"No, the tire. Tires can explode on a hot day, even a cold day. Heat builds up from road friction. A tire gets . . . *tired*." Mr. Shizuko-san chuckled. "It's called *material exhaustion*—wear and tear. The rubber becomes brittle, it cracks, sometimes there's a puncture."

"Then, *Ka-boom! Bang!*" Ralph slammed his hands together. "A good beginning for a percussion instrument, don't you think?"

The shop supervisor shook his head. "Ralph, if you don't watch it, the fellows are going to figure you out." To Fumio, he said, "Don't tell anyone. The man likes to play the buffoon, but he has a degree in engineering. So, then, Fumio Miyota, would a *piece* of an innertube work for your project? If it would, I think we could find a job you can complete in one afternoon, during which *Ralph* will watch his language.

"Come back with measurements for the size you need. If the piece of innertube is acceptable, and you are agreeable to the work, you should begin as soon as possible. If I lay down this scrap of innertube where it can be seen, someone will pick it up and cut a rubber washer from it. And, now, I am breaking for lunch!"

Fumio hurried to ask, "Mr. Shizuko-san, sir, would it be all right if I returned right after lunch, in work clothes? I will bring the template for the drumhead."

Mr. Shizuko-san nodded. "Here's the deal. This shop floor is just shy of twenty-five-hundred square feet, it's concrete, and it's rough in places. Every workday, it is coated with a new layer of oil and fine dust, bits of steel from lathes, clippings of canvas, and trails of thread from the sewing machine Riko uses to repair upholstery. We sweep the floor daily, of course, for the sake of safety. But it could use a careful going-over with special attention to corners. I would not trust the job to just anyone. This person must have experience in a mechanics' shop. He must understand the value of tools and equipment. He must give evidence of respect for all workers."

"Yes, sir! That's me, Mr. Shizuko-san. I can do that!"

The shop supervisor went to a nearby tool bench, beneath which rested a trunk marked *Zuko*. With a key from his pocket, he unlocked the trunk, shoved the piece of rubber inside, and relocked the trunk. "Nobody's going to mess with that, now, kid," he said and strode toward the door. Then, standing on the border between the shop's dim interior and the glare of high noon, he looked back. "See you later, Fumio Miyota," he said, and went out into the bright sunlight.

● ● ●

Fumio worked through the afternoon and into early evening, sweeping the floor of the immense Motor Repair and Tire Shop. When others stopped for a break, he drank from a ladle kept near the water bucket and went back to sweeping. He used a coarse-bristled push broom when it was right for the job, but he had been told to give special attention to corners and hard-to-reach places. For that, a slant-head, corn broom was best. When necessary, Fumio got down on his hands and knees to use a whisk broom.

In the cleaning closet, Fumio found a long-handled dustpan. He emptied sweepings from the dustpan into a no-handled coal scuttle. Wrapping his arms around the scuttle, he carried it to a blowout behind a sandhill fifteen paces from the building and dumped it there. The blowout, Fumio was told, would someday be covered with a layer of soil, and "no one would ever know the trash was there."

By four-thirty, men were putting tools away, taking their coats from hooks, picking up Thermos bottles, and preparing to go to their quarters to clean up for supper.

The supervisor, Mr. Shizuko, retrieved the piece of rubber from his trunk and asked, "How will you cut the circle? This stuff's tough. We use tin snips—metal shears."

Ralph, returning a welder's helmet and gauntlets to a nearby cabinet, called to Fumio, "Don't you go using sewing scissors, kid. That'd chew 'em up real bad. The next time your mother cut your hair, you'd end up half-bald."

Fumio grinned, rubbing the top of his head. Ralph laughed and slapped the gloves against his knee.

"Come over here, Fumio," Mr. Shizuko beckoned, walking toward a work bench. "You can use these tin snips to cut the circle and the drumhead will be ready to go."

"Oh, no. Excuse me, sir, Mr. Shizuko-san. My father told me I must never borrow tools."

"Your father is correct," Mr. Shizuko replied, "but you have the template. You can make an accurate cut. I will be standing only a few feet away, so it will not be borrowing. After all, I am the supervisor of this shop, am I not?"

"He is," Ralph said, "and none of us is likely to forget it." He took a pack of gum from his pocket and gave a stick to the supervisor. Removing another, he handed it to Fumio. As he strolled away, he folded an unwrapped stick of gum in half and tossed it into his mouth.

Fumio held the gum in his outstretched palm, neatly wrapped in precisely folded paper. Glancing up, he saw Mr. Shizuko, laughter in his eyes, tuck the gum into his shirt pocket. Fumio did the same.

The shop supervisor showed Fumio where to return the tin snips when he was done and, as promised, went to work on a task nearby.

The work bench was tall. Standing on tiptoe, Fumio concentrated on his project.

Thump. An overturned wooden box materialized near his feet. He turned to say thank you, but no one was there. Fumio stepped up, took a deep breath, and guided the tin snips into the scrap of inner tube.

CHAPTER SIXTY-FIVE

FLYER

I need to get away from Engine Four-Zero-Zero-Three. The machine is *distracting*. Under a tree is fresh, moist grass. I lay the mitt down to nibble a few blades, but then I smell a new smell and hear footsteps.

"Gettin' some greens, fella?" a man asks. "In the past, I've enjoyed collard greens, with a touch of bacon grease. Of course, we have none of that now, do we?"

The man sits several feet away, leaning against the trunk of a fallen tree.

"*Poplars*, such as this tree, grow fast. They decline quickly, though, and the old ones fall." He points to the downed tree. "As here we have *evidence*.

"Don't let me disturb you, my canine friend. I have come to this grove for a nap." He pulls a cap low over his eyes, and soon he is snoring.

All that has happened presses down on me.

I dream about the old weeping willow tree, lying on the ground, branches spread across the farmyard. In my dream, a bird nest has tumbled from the branches and lays broken on the hard earth. Zachary stands nearby, his face sad, his freckles seeming to stand away from his skin. "The train is waiting, Flyer," he says.

I come awake to the sound of a *locomotive, huphh-puphh . . . huphh-puphh . . . huphh-puphh*. My head is crowded with questions. The *locomotive* is big like the ferry. Does it know where Fumio is?

The snoring man awakens and says, very quietly, "There you are, friend. The fellows and I will be heading for the depot."

The snoring man and three other *fellows* head toward the train's house, the *depot*. Careful footsteps, no talking. I walk nearby, with a firm hold on Fumio's baseball mitt.

Beams of light shine down from tall poles at the back of the depot. No people wait in line for tickets. No one carries cases or bundles.

The men walk to the edge of the tree nearest the locomotive. The snoring man leans down, close to my ear. "We must be quick, my friend. Railroad guards mean to see that we do not ride without tickets. Follow me to the tracks. We will board that freight car there." He points to a metal shed with wheels—a *train car*—sitting on long, narrow pieces of metal—*tracks*.

The men look from side to side, *watching for guards*. I don't think *dogs* need tickets to ride the train, but I search the darkness, too. Gravel cuts into my paw pads. We reach the wooden side of the *freight car*. Its door is partly open.

A man jumps and is inside in one bound. Others scramble up. The snoring man swings in by holding onto a metal bar. He reaches down to me. "The mitt, friend," he speaks in almost a whisper. "I will hold it while you jump."

I raise my muzzle and lift the mitt to him. He holds it and stands aside while I leap into the freight car. Then I take it back again.

The train follows tracks around curves. It goes up hills, and the engine works harder. On the downhills, I brace to keep from slipping forward. The brakes squeal. And always, *clickety-clack, clickety-clack, clickety . . .*

The snoring man tells the others his name is Bevington. We are lucky to be riding on a *livestock hauler*, he says, because *the ventilation is superior*. The car is divided into stalls made of smooth-sanded wood. It is swept clean, but it still smells of farm stock.

During the night, the locomotive wails, long and loud. The train begins to slow. From ahead comes metallic clanging, like an anvil being beaten. *Ga-Biing Ga-Biing Ga-Biing Ga—*

I wake often but go back to sleep easily, until the train slows again, this time with the scream of a wounded animal. My muscles tense, and I am ready to spring, when, *Sshhsshh-Sshhsshh-Www-Phhh*, the noise and motion of the train stop.

Men drag packs near and pull on boots. Mr. Bevington whispers, "Dog, come here." Gripping the baseball mitt, I belly-crawl toward the sound of his voice.

Footsteps crunch on gravel. No one in the car moves as it is swept with light that shines through narrow cracks between planks. In the silence and darkness that come afterward, I hear, "That railroad guard doesn't *want* to know we're in here." Another says, "Yeah, I reckon he understands a man has to get to his next job, somehow."

Mr. Bevington leans close to me. "Friend, take a break, hop out, stretch your legs—all four of them. Bushes for our convenience are but a short way hence."

I thump my tail, once.

He nods.

A man, he is called Charlie, eases the door back, looks out, leaps. Each man does the same until it is just Mr. Bevington and me. He opens the door wider. We jump at the same time.

The men know when to return to the train. All are in place when it begins *whupph-whupph-whuffing*, and the door is carefully closed.

I shut my eyes, my muzzle on Fumio's baseball mitt, until my nose wakes me.

Old boots smell of every place they have ever been, every tire they have kicked, every pigeon pile they have squashed, every pair of unwashed socks stuffed into them, *right there*, for a dog to smell.

The odor is strong and getting stronger. Maneuvering the mitt behind me, I rise and am eye to eye with Charlie reaching for the mitt!

GGRRrrr-UURR-Rrrr! Yii-eep! Yii-eep! Yii-eep!

"Holy smoke!" yells Charlie.

"Back away, Charlie!" Mr. Bevington says. "Don't you know better than to disturb a sleeping dog? Use your head, man!"

Charlie complains that he wanted to see the writing on the baseball mitt.

"Well," a man named Rex says, "you saw it, Charlie. What's it say?"

Charlie *scowls*. "Best I can make out, it'd be, Fu-mi-o Mi-yo-ta, Bainbridge Izzle Elem."

"Huh?"

"Like I said, Fumio Miyota, Bainbridge Izzle Elem."

Rex asks, "What's an Izzle Elem?"

Charlie says he reckons it is a kind of tree.

Mr. Bevington laughs. "Sit down, Charlie. Some of us need to sleep."

Charlie crosses the car and lays his head on his pack, but his eyes stay open and he is looking my way. The other men go back to snoring.

I lie on top of the mitt and wonder, *what is an Izzle Elem*?

• • • •

The movement of the train stops. One of the men listens near the door of the car, for footsteps, I think. "All clear," he says, and slowly opens the train car's door. Cool night air rushes in. Carrying the mitt, I leave the car and make my way alone. I have not gone far when I hear water flowing around boulders, rippling over rocks, lapping at a grassy edge. The moon is only a sliver.

Zzwoo-Slpp, I hear, and a quiet, "Yesss!" *Splash!* A muffled laugh. *Splash!* "Gotcha!"

Closer, I see a figure in the river, holding a fish, lowering it into the water, then hands coming up empty. It is a woman, in to her knees. She uses a long stick to swing a line over the water, it drops, she waits. I watch. Then, *Splash!* "Yesss!" And she laughs. She has another fish!

I move even closer. A twig snaps. She turns and sees me before I can dart behind a tree.

"Are you a dog or coyote? Not a wolf, surely." She turns and swings out the line again. "I hope you're not hungry. I catch them—I don't keep them." *Splash.* "It's something, isn't it? To communicate with another living thing like this—a quiver and a tug, through a fly line?"

I do know *coyote*. I don't know *wolf*. It is time for me to go back to the train.

Mr. Bevington is already there. I wait beside him. One by one, the men gather, out of sight of the railroad guards *who do not really want to know we are here*. When it is time, Slim goes first, then Rex and Louie. Train noises tell us time is getting short. Charlie, Mr. Bevington, and I make a run for it. Holding the mitt for me, Mr. Bevington grabs an iron bar to swing up, I leap, and Charlie scrambles. As my rear paws grasp the edge of the boxcar floor, *Bbuummpp!* Charlie knocks against me. I fall back. The train is starting to roll.

"No!" Mr. Bevington shouts. "Wait!"

The whistle blows, loud in my ears, and the train picks up speed. I know I cannot run fast enough to reach the door and jump again.

"Dog! Dog!" Mr. Bevington calls.

Yipp-Ipp!

Mr. Bevington throws the mitt. I make a dash for it, take it in my mouth, and watch as the *train* moves on without me.

At a *junction* somewhere up the track, a bell clangs. The train's whistle blares. Livestock cars race by in a blur and cattle bawl. I drop to my haunches, until a little car with a box on top speeds past. The end.

When I am sure the train is not coming back for me, I walk to the water.

I hear, *Zzwoo-Slpp. Splash!* The woman is still here. I sit, several feet distant, and listen. I like her voice, and the way she talks to the fish as she catches them and sends them back into the river, like Reyna talks to the kittens—and even the chickens.

The woman standing in the water says I may come nearer, that if I were going to attack and eat her, I would have done it by now. She laughs. This woman is *cheerful*. She must be brave, too, to walk into the water—she is in to her waist, now—wave a stick and throw a string, in the middle of the night.

Yipp! I let her know I am listening, and I am friendly. I move out into the open. She turns, one sideways-step at a time, to face me. I see she has a shorter stick, thicker than the other, floating at her side. She grasps it at the top and shoves it down into the water with each step. But she does not act afraid. At the water's edge, she lays down the long, thin stick with the string, and reaches out with one hand to steady herself as she climbs the bank.

She says, "I see you are a fan of the great game of baseball. Who's your team? Cards or Yanks? Well, they will have to do without Johnny and Jimmy, Joe and Red this year, right?"

I don't understand. While she talks, she watches me, as others have, waiting, I guess, while deciding what sort of dog I am.

Yipp! I sit down.

She walks toward me, and I brace myself.

I won't let go of the mitt, even if she offers a sandwich. I must not wander too far from the depot. I know the train would have taken me *east*. I can follow the *tracks*.

The woman gathers the sticks, rolls up the string on a metal spool with a little handle. She picks up a basket from where it sits on a tuft of grass and walks away from the riverbank. She tells me she works at a *twenty-four-hour café* and does her fly fishing when she can. She says her home is close by the depot. I follow along, a few steps behind. "I can tell you're not a wild one. If you want to, you can bunk at my house tonight, under the porch."

I walk behind the woman, not too close. One small light burns in her home. No dark curtains cover her windows. She goes up the steps, opens the screen door. I go under the steps where the dirt is soft. Fumio's mitt on my paws, my muzzle on the mitt, I sleep.

• • •

Soon the sun is up, and the woman gives me an egg. The egg is still warm, and it is good. I drink leftover rainwater from a hollowed-out stone at the corner of the house. In a few minutes, she comes back outside with a purse over her arm.

I feel *anxious*, walking along the packed dirt path, following the woman. A voice comes from behind us, "Good morning, Miss Cora. Who's your friend?"

The woman, *Miss Cora,* turns, smiles, and tells the man that she doesn't know my name or where I *hail* from. She tells him I appeared last night, shortly after the Northern Pacific pulled in, when she was *on the river.*

The man steps toward me, and I am ready to run. But he leans forward and the corners of his eyes fold into wrinkles. "What's it say? Oh! Bainbridge Island. Huh! Where do you suppose he intends to go?"

"I haven't a clue, but he's a charming fellow, isn't he?"

The man shrugs, and Miss Cora says, "Help the dog out, Wes." He frowns.

She says, "He was clearly headed east. You always head east this time of day. Let him ride in the back of your truck. It'll get him closer to *wherever* he's going."

"All right, all right, I'll take him as far as Roza." He sounds *cranky,* but he smiles.

Mrs. Whitlock raises roses! We are going to a garden!

Wes walks with Miss Cora into the café.

Waiting outside, I yawn so big my eyes close. When I open them, I hear *Czkk!* and, "Man, what a great picture! I'll bet that makes page one!"

Soon, Wes comes out of the café eating a doughnut and carrying something wrapped in paper. At the rear of his big truck, he whistles. Holding Fumio's mitt in my mouth, I jump in and move toward a screened opening near the cab. Wes tosses a piece of bacon in after me. "Miss Cora sent that."

Yipp! I put the mitt down, fetch the bacon, and return to a place at the front of the truck box that Mr. Bevington from the train would like: *The ventilation is superior.*

The big door at the back is pulled down and closed, the truck's engine roars, and we are on the road, *headed east.* To Fumio.

CHAPTER SIXTY-SIX

FLYER

Roza is not a garden. It is a town. It *was* a town. No one lives in Roza anymore. Wes stops and waits while I jump out of the truck. *Yipp-ipp!* I thank him. The road is busy, so I find a quiet, smooth-dirt lane, and I follow it, heading east.

Water. The smell of it flowing over dirt and the sound of it working around reeds growing along banks tell me a small ditch is nearby. An animal is very close. I crouch and *sort* the odors—*concentrate*—to learn what kind of animal this is.

Oh! A frog! Frogs live near our pond! They are quiet during the day, but loud when the light fades. I want to know for sure where the frog is. There! A dark, open place in the dirt beside a big pipe where the irrigation ditch goes under the road. I lay the mitt in soft dirt, stand over the open place, and lower my nose.

Rrrriiihhggggettttt!—Rriiihhggettt!

Rriiihhggettt!—Rrawwrhhhhggettt!—Rriiihhggettt!

A crowd of frogs! Even though the sun is bright, they set to making a racket!

I tell them, *Rrruuppphhhh-yip-yip! Hush, frogs!*

But, *Rriiihhggettt!* They grow louder!

Carrying the mitt, I cross the culvert—*Goodbye, frogs!*—walk into the stand of trees, and out the other side. The trees are tall and skinny, planted in a line around a pasture.

In the pasture is a small flock of sheep with a few lambs. I move quietly and find a place in the shade. If the sheep know I am here, they don't care.

A man sits on a low tree stump, in a place well-lit by the sun, working with a piece of rope. His hat is worn, has lost its shape. Beside the man's feet, I see a sturdy stick and a flat-shaped bag with a long, thin strap. The bag is *fancy*, like Mrs. Whitlock's weaving. A design is in the weaving. A design of frogs!

The man looks up and sees me, then he is busy again. The rope must be *frayed*. He watches his hands and says, "A rope, it busts, sure, I can fix it. But I would sooner fix it before it busts." He reaches into the bag and pulls out something that he spins with his fingers until it looks like twine. Then he works until he makes it part of the rope.

I know about rope. When my family had to leave, I went to the Eagledale dock to go with them. Zachary followed me and stopped me. He said I had to stay behind. But Zachary is not Fumio, and I was *going to go* with Fumio. Mr. Harvey brought a piece of rope. He looped it around my neck. It did not hurt, but Zachary held the rope firm. It has been a long time since I have seen my family. I remember the smell of that rope. I remember that day, and the day after. I waited for my family to come back for me. I waited and waited.

But look! A big, dark shape hovers at the far side of the pasture. It shifts and streaks toward a target I cannot see.

The sheep *baa-aah* warnings and run. One lags. A lamb is in jeopardy!

The man grasps the stick, pulls himself up. "Hawk!" he cries. I see the bird's eyes, beak, the spikes of its feet. The bird sees me. It touches ground, takes off, and climbs into the sky.

GGRRrrr-URR-Rrrr! Wrawruff-Uff! I call after the bird. *Now, scram! Do not come back!*

Fast, with the mitt in my mouth, I go after the sheep that are scattered in the trees. I remember everything Miss Anna taught me, everything

Zachary and I practiced, and I turn them before they reach the lane. The man goes toward the sheep nearest him.

Inside the circle of trees, the grass smells sweet. The hawk is nowhere to be seen. The sheep return to the pasture. I watch in case they break again. The man returns to mending rope.

From the lane, an engine growls, voices call, dogs bark. I hear the sounds a horse makes—a *whinny*, Zachary says—almost like laughter. And the *clip-clop* of horseshoes. A stock truck backs in at the edge of the pasture. Dogs pile out, but most stay near the truck.

The man stands, leaning on the stick. One dog goes to him, and he reaches down to touch its muzzle.

Boys jump down from the truck box. They lower the rear gate and set up a long ramp off the truck bed.

A young boy riding a horse comes to the pasture. The horse is dark and shiny at its front, but at its back, down to its tail, it is light with dark spots.

The boy says, "Whoa, whoa," then slides down from the back of the horse—there is no *riding saddle*—and walks the horse over to the man, still standing near the tree stump.

"Shall I hold the cornhusk bag, Uncle?" the boy asks.

The man shakes his head. "No. It is a gift. I will carry it myself." He places a bag over his shoulder. He uses the stick and, with one hand on the boy's shoulder, works his way on top of the stump. The boy reaches for the stick.

Leaning across the horse's back, *Uncle* holds the mane with one hand and, *quick*, he is on the horse. He fits the stick behind his back through a loop of his clothing.

The spotted horse twists his head to the side and nods.

"Good to see you, Apple," the man replies. "Ready to work?"

The man and the horse, three boys on foot, and four dogs herd the flock toward the truck. One sheep is forced up the ramp, then another. *Uncle* finds me with his eyes. "Heya, dog! We're burning daylight! Aren't you going to help us here?"

A boy who is tall comes from the truck's cab. He shouts, "I'm sorry, Uncle. I never thought the truck would blow a ring today, of all days."

"Well it did blow a ring today! And what if it had been on the highway?" the man answers. "We gotta get these sheep *home*, into their own pasture!"

Home. I come out into the sunlight.

The other dogs are not much interested in who I am. We work together and get the flock up the ramp with little trouble, once the sheep understand they are going home.

The flock waits, talking to each other, while the boys put the ramp back in the truck box, and I walk toward the lane, ready to head east.

"Heya, dog!" Uncle calls from atop the horse. "Aren't you comin' with us? It's getting late, close to supper. A good meal is waiting if you care to eat. I owe you, dog, I sure do!"

A boy asks, "Uncle, why's he carrying a baseball mitt?"

"I got no idea. You want to ask him?"

The boy shrugs.

I do not climb into the truck with the other dogs. I go alongside *Uncle* on the horse, *Apple*, carrying Fumio's mitt. The truck moves on ahead of us.

We pass through a land of open space, scrubby bushes, and fences, some wood, some wire. I see more sheep than I have ever seen, more than I could imagine there are in the world. Zachary's flock would disappear among all these sheep.

Ahead is a very tall gate. A mailbox stands beside it. "Here is our place," *Uncle* says. He looks at me. "You can stay here with us if you want to. I got a lot of dogs. One more won't be any trouble. Fact is, I can see you are a dog who knows his business around sheep."

I watch his face and listen to his voice. He is nice. But he has four dogs. He does not need me. And I have to go to Fumio.

Apple stops. The man reaches into the cornhusk bag and pulls out something wrapped in thin paper. He tosses it carefully to the side of the road, on a patch of soft grass. "Roasted meat and fresh greens, t' boot." He taps his hat brim. "Good luck to you, dog. You get back this way, stop by, hear?" He nudges *Apple* and rides through the tall gate.

CHAPTER SIXTY-SEVEN

FUMIO

The Miyotas returned from their evening meal to a room that was chilly. Mr. Miyota scooped coal into the pot-bellied stove. Mrs. Miyota, with Fumio's shirt draped over her arm, brought her sewing basket from beneath her cot and, after moving the chair, sat within the circle of light under the single bulb. She opened her small tin of spare buttons. Fumio remembered that, when he was very young, he'd sometimes played with the button tin, fascinated by the shifting shapes and colors, like those in a kaleidoscope.

Kimiko pulled a small quilt to a place near her mother's feet. "Mama?" she asked, reaching up.

Smiling, her mother handed her the tin.

Kimiko, her eyes closed, shook it, listening to the buttons rattle. After a few moments, she handed it back, curled up with knees to chin, and began drumming on the toes of her shoes.

Once the coals glowed in the stove, Mr. Miyota removed his boots and laid them beside Kimiko.

She grinned. "Thank you, Papa!" Then she went to the drawer for wooden spoons.

Facing the corner to avoid Kimiko's notice, Fumio sat cross-legged on his cot, holding the sketch he had made, studying the drum's dimensions. From under his blanket, he pulled the circle he had cut from the innertube and tugged on the rubber, feeling it give, stretch. The diameter was right for covering the coffee can's opening with a three-quarter-inch overhang.

"Whatya doing, Fumio?" he heard his sister ask.

"I am doing some work, Kimiko."

"What kinda work are you doing, Fumio?"

"Kimiko, dear," Mrs. Miyota said, "Fumio is thinking *hard* about something *complicated*. Let's give him some quiet time."

"Okay." Kimiko went back to drumming.

Fumio turned to his mother, nodded his thanks, and continued studying the sketch. He had so far searched without success. *Where could he find a pair of leather boot laces?*

Mr. Miyota came to stand by the bed. "Fumio," he spoke quietly,

"Yes, Father?"

"Today, at the post office, I recognized a man your grandfather worked with, years ago. Your ojiisan referred to him only as *Kats*. He was a friend. I went to him, to introduce myself as Kito Miyota-san's son, even though I did not know his full name. Still, he, Mr. Kats-san, spoke of deeply missing those days of working alongside your grandfather, 'logging the great trees.' When the man's wife became ill, they moved to Seattle. Then Order 9066 came down, and they were confined at the fairgrounds in Puyallup. There, his wife's heart gave out and she died. Mr. Kats-san came here. Alone."

Fumio was puzzled, "Is there more, Father?"

Mr. Miyota gazed toward the floor. "I found myself at a loss for words when Mr. Kats-san said, 'I miss the great trees,' and gestured toward the shoes he wore. He said, 'I miss the tall boots. It has come to this, shuffling along in two-bit slip-ons, when once I strode in tall, leather boots.' I had no reply. He said, 'Working for the city, in park maintenance, I wore them, anyway. Why should I not wear a good pair of tall, leather boots?'"

"And you think he might no longer have use for the boot laces, Father?"

"Maybe?"

"Father, do you know where Mr. Kats-san, lives?"

"As it happened, we walked most of the way from the post office together, and parted company near Block 40."

Picturing that section of the compound, Fumio nodded. "Thank you, Father."

Mr. Miyota laid a hand on Fumio's head, then walked away.

Fumio pondered. The tallest boots he had ever seen were logger's boots. A pair had stood, side-by-side, near their home's back door, the entrance to Grandfather's private living area. Logging such as Fumio's ojiisan had done was no longer practiced on Bainbridge Island. The giant trees were gone.

Grandfather Miyota, in his later years, had worked at the lumber mill. Still, from time to time, Fumio had seen him rubbing mink oil into those boots, preserving the leather. A good pair of boots is the most valuable thing a worker might own, Ojiisan had said. Now, the boots were in a box in the Whitlock attic. Fumio wondered if, someday, he would grow into them.

• • • • • •

The sun was halfway down the western sky when Fumio walked along the row of barracks, returning home from school. Progressing more slowly than usual, he glanced at people working in vegetable gardens—weeding, watering. A woman held a small tin basin, harvesting. The lettuce was up early. A faint, green sweetness drifted toward Fumio.

The bright day brought a chance to dry laundry outside the cramped barracks. Freshly washed work shirts hung from a clothesline. Farther along, Fumio saw toddlers' dresses with ruffled hems, pinafores and rompers, children's clothing in crayon-box colors. On a second line, strung behind the first, he glimpsed diapers waving like flags in the breeze.

The crack of a bat told Fumio that after-school ball games had begun. His pulse quickened. *Later. There would be time for that, later.*

Barracks doors stood open. People leaned against handrails, sitting on the wooden steps, atop small cushions sewn from fabric scraps. They talked, laughed, and sipped tea. Fumio's eyes were drawn to their shoes: oxfords, sandals, loafers, wooden geta. There! A pair of slip-ons!

Elbows on knees, hands held loose, a man sat slumped forward, cap pulled low to shade his eyes. Over white socks the man wore slip-on shoes, very new, very stiff, slip-on shoes that looked wrong on his feet. Fumio ventured a glance at the man's face, a glance that was not returned. The man sat alone and without a cup of tea.

These barracks were very near Block 44. Fumio hurried to his family's quarters, asked to use the kettle, and made tea. With one finger through the handle of a mug and carrying the jar of brewed tea wrapped in a furoshiki, Fumio returned to the barracks steps where, still, the man sat.

Fumio approached, paused, bowed. "Sumimasen, sir."

The man did not look his way.

Fumio came nearer. "Ojamashimasu. I am fear I am disturbing you." He bowed, again. "But I brought tea, sir."

The man looked up. "You are speaking to me? I did not expect that. You brought tea?"

Fumio held out the furoshiki. "Yes, sir, sencha."

The man's face brightened with a smile. "Won't you please share these steps with me?" He squinted. "You have only one cup." He rose, with some difficulty. "Wait here, danshi, and I will get us another cup."

Fumio watched the man turn and go up the stairs, holding tight to a railing. It wobbled. Looking closely at the structure, Fumio saw that both its railings had worked loose and leaned outward. Thin pieces of wood were needed for shimming. The treads were warped. One had split. They should be re-nailed to the risers. The cracked tread would have to be splinted from beneath or replaced. Though the heads showed some rust, the nails might be all right for re-use. He would need a level and a plumb bob. At home, Fumio decided, he would draw up a list of what was needed to repair the steps.

The man came through the door smiling, carrying a cup. "I found one. It is cracked. My Mari-san would be embarrassed. Kichōmen, she was. But it is thoroughly clean." Holding the handrail, he lowered himself to the step. The railing shook, the step groaned, but the man sat safely, and sought Fumio's eyes.

Fumio met his glance for a fraction of a second before dropping his gaze to the jar of tea. "Sumimasen, sir, I brought a cup, but perhaps you prefer to use your own?"

"I *will* use my own, and you may use the cup you brought, as I imagine it is not cracked." He extended his hand. "Will you take a seat? You are young. Do you drink tea?"

"Sometimes, with my family. It's nice to share." Fumio poured tea from the jar.

"It is *very* nice to share, yes." The man sipped.

Fumio heard a faint slurping and smiled, thinking of his grandfather.

"I admit, I am at a loss. Do I know your family?"

"Sir, I believe you knew my ojiisan, Mr. Kito Miyota-san."

"Kito Miyota-san! My old friend! You are his grandchild?"

"Yes, sir, the oldest." Fumio stood, descended the steps and bowed. "My father is Yasuo Miyota, my mother is Sachiko Miyota. I am Fumio Miyota. My younger sister is Kimiko."

"And I am Katsuya Katsumoto." The man spread his hand on his chest and nodded deeply. "First grandchild of my friend, thank you for sharing tea with me. I am honored." He tapped the step beside him, and Fumio resumed his seat. "Are you on an errand, danshi?"

"Ojamashimasu, my hope is to meet someone who, like my ojiisan, has done logging, or some other very heavy work, and that this person would have a pair of long boot laces which I might earn. Perhaps it would seem unnecessary to keep a spare pair of boot laces, since no one here at Minidoka is cutting down giant trees."

The man smiled. "That is true. There are no giant trees, here. Still, I brought the tall boots because I had heard this was rough terrain. And it is." He shook his head, lowered his voice. "But years of labor take their toll. I have a bad back and knees that do not care to bend. I can no longer get those boots on. I cannot lace them." He sipped his tea. "You need a pair of logging boot laces, and I do, in fact, have them. I am curious. Why do you want them?"

Fumio's heart beat faster. He straightened his shoulders. "My little sister, Kimiko, heard taiko drumming at the dojo, where I am a student. She wants to learn, but cannot be taught at the dojo, because she is a girl. I will teach her all I can, but she needs a drum. I am building one as a gift for her fifth birthday, which is soon. I have a coffee can for the ko, and a scrap of an innertube for the kawa, the drumhead. I need the laces to attach the drumhead to the body. Sumimasen ga, Mr. Katsumoto-san, sir, I hoped I might be allowed to work for you in trade for the boot laces." Fumio held his breath.

"So, you need a pair of old boot laces," and he laughed.

Fumio sighed and his shoulders sagged. "Yes, sir, but you don't have to say it. I know. Everybody wants those."

The man's gaze swiveled toward Fumio. "My old bootlaces? You think everybody wants my old boot laces? No, no, danshi. No. The truth is, I have come to feel that, at my age, *I have nothing anyone wants.*"

Fumio picked up the tea jar and refilled the man's cup.

Mr. Katsumoto told Fumio he had saved at least three pair of old boot laces, although one or two of the laces might have broken and been re-knotted. "My Mari-san used to say I was a bit of a packrat. But you never know when you might need to attach something to something," he chuckled, "and what could be better than leather laces? I do not need to tell you that, do I, young Fumio?" He paused. "I can think of nothing more pleasant than a visit from an old friend or from the grandson of an old friend." The man began to rise. "Well, let me get you those boot laces!"

"Please, sir, wait. What work may I do to earn the laces?"

"I would not require anything of you, but I think you will not be content unless you feel you have earned them. What I would like most is for you to bring the drum, to show it to me when it is done. Could you do that? Could you slip it out of the house without your sister seeing it?" He smiled.

"I don't know!" Fumio blurted. "Maybe I could hide it in a pillowcase. I can't even figure out where I am going to build it without Kimiko seeing it. She hardly ever takes a nap now." Fumio ducked his head, mortified that he had spoken disrespectfully. "Sumimasen, Mr. Katsumoto-san."

"You can build it here." He gestured to the open door. "I have nothing but space. My Mari-san passed away," he paused, grimacing, "at 'Camp Harmony.' And other than companionship, what does an old man need? There is a cot in there and that is all, except I pounded together a table. I will find a chair somewhere." He nodded and said again, "You can build the drum here. Please ask your father to talk with me. We will make it so."

Fumio stood and picked up the tea jar and cup he had brought, then straightened and inclined his head, preparing to leave.

"Danshi, wait." Mr. Katsumoto raised his hand, his index finger pointing skyward. "There is one thing I would ask of you."

"Yes, sir, of course. What can I do for you, Mr. Katsumoto-san?"

"You have excellent manners. Your parents have taught you well. But there is this. It seems we are to see each other from time to time. I would be most honored if you would call me as your ojiishan did—Kats."

Fumio felt his mouth drop open. What would his parents have him do? "Yes, sir. If that pleases you, Mr. Kats-san. I think my ojiishan would like that."

"Indeed, that is very good, Fumio. I look forward to seeing you again, soon."

CHAPTER SIXTY-EIGHT

FLYER

I have been on the road for a while, walking and walking, heading east. It was good to help tend to sheep and keep them safe. I would have liked to get to know Apple better. She seemed like a nice horse. But I couldn't stay. I am going to Fumio.

Now, from behind a clump of tall weeds, I see a truck turn in at a driveway and stop near a barn. The driver climbs out, the truck still running. I hope he set the hand brake so the truck will stay put.

The driver is a *young man*, like Jacob. But not like Jacob, because his clothes are dirty. Mrs. Whitlock would say, "Time for a haircut!" He drops the truck's tailgate and unloads *salt blocks*. Zachary buys salt blocks for the sheep. He buys them at Petric's Feed and Seed.

The driver carries the blocks into the barn.

I run fast and jump into the truck box among bags and other farm supplies. The bags have pictures of animals eating. The corner of one is torn and feed is spilled out. I can help clean up the mess! But first, I move behind a crate and listen while the tailgate is lifted.

A voice shouts, "Earl! Earl, wait! You forgot your keys, man!" It's the customer.

"Oh, yeah. Guess I wouldn'ta got far." The truck door slams, and then I hear *Click!... click!...* Nothing. Mr. Harvey would say the engine needs a *tune up*. But the man keeps trying until, finally, the truck starts.

I begin cleaning dried bits from the truck box floor with my tongue. The bits taste *odd*. When my stomach is not empty anymore, I step away from the bag and see, on the side of it, a picture of rabbits.

The driver parks under a building's overhang. We are at the back door near a loading dock. The driver walks inside. When I see him again, a small piece of paper is in his hand.

Before the building door slams behind him, I hear a woman's voice from inside call out, "See you tomorrow, Earl! Try to be on time!"

Earl looks back toward the door, raises a hand, throws a leg over what looks like a big bicycle, and kicks *down* on something. I hear a motor roar, and he rides away.

A thin man steps out the door carrying a piece of paper. A woman pulls up in a car. Two children are in the backseat. The man opens the car door and the children shout, "Papa!"

"Ice cream, tonight!" he answers as he gets into the car. The family leaves.

A woman whose hair is tucked high on her head walks out of the building, slipping something into her pocket. She locks the door and goes to a car that looks old but starts fine.

I will stay near this feed and seed store for the night. My nose tells me I am not near houses—there are no supper smells. Out of the truck, I look around. Nothing to eat is left outside but the rabbit food. There is a spigot. It has been left dripping, probably by *Earl*. The water is cool and good. On a pile of gunny sacks, with my head on the mitt, I sleep.

• • •

Noisy birds tell me the sun is rising. I find clean water in a shallow dish that was left out in the weather. Dog food has spilled onto the driveway near the loading dock. It's good to find food, but Mr. Petric's dog biscuits taste much better.

After a quick walk, I am careful to be in the truck box looking through the sideboards before the workers come to the store. The man with the loose coat arrives, and the woman whose hair is piled high on her head, too.

Earl rides into the parking lot on the roaring machine that is like a big bicycle. He goes into the building, then comes out.

He is coming toward his truck.

I hear a woman's voice again. "Earl, wait! You must take this check to the feed mill to pay for our order!"

"Oh, yeah. Thanks. I'd forget my head."

The driver, *Earl,* climbs into the truck without even walking around and kicking the tires. I stay low while the engine grinds. Finally the truck starts.

The truck goes and goes a long time before it downshifts. I slip to the side of the box away from the driver to look out. In the distance, I see a very tall post holding a big sign, a picture of a horse with wings.

Real horses do not have wings—they do not fly. Mr. Harvey told me the sign means *Buy gasoline here!* Under the sign of the horse, there are tall metal barrels called *pumps* to put gasoline into *vehicles.*

When we are closer, I see a packed dirt yard filled with trucks, more trucks than I have ever seen in one place. It looks like a farm where trucks grow, side by side, in rows.

Many are as big as the *two-ton* truck that brought the Cleveland Crawler to our farm. Giant wheels hold their cabs and boxes high off the ground. Some trucks are smaller, like the truck I am in.

Earl passes the *gasoline pumps*, maybe to find a place to park. With the mitt gripped firm in my mouth, I am ready. When the truck stops, I leap and run to a spot where I am out of sight, on the other side of a tall truck. I listen hard to be sure the cab is empty and then sit by a giant wheel, looking up past the running board and a door so shiny I can see a reflection of the dark clouds growing bigger and bigger in the sky.

Some truck engines are running, *idling*. Most trucks are not. A man's feet stick out from under the hood of one truck. I hear *clank-clank-bang!* And I hear words Mr. Harvey says when he is working on a motor that won't *cooperate.*

Watching and listening, I run through rows of trucks, fast but careful. I jump over a small ditch and into a field. The soil is dry, so I put down the baseball mitt and watch people going in and out of a small building. When its door opens, cooking smells come out.

The driver of a truck pulls up to the pumps, fills the gas tank, parks at the edge of the truck yard and goes into the building. The truck is old, beat-up, and dirty. It has no tailgate!

Looking both ways—*All clear!*—I run straight for the truck. In back is a couch, a rolled-up rug, and some old blankets. I crawl behind the couch and rest my head on Fumio's mitt.

In a little while, a *cough*, someone spits. A squashed paper bag lands in front of my nose. The pickup door opens, *squeeeak,* closes, *thunk!* The engine starts and the pickup truck moves.

I snatch the bag, push it open, and find a piece of hamburger, some bread, and strips of fried potatoes. The food smells *good.* It *is* good.

CHAPTER SIXTY-NINE

FUMIO

"Applesauce cake, still warm, *from a pot-bellied coal stove*!" Fumio grinned. "It worked, Mother!"

Her answer was a bright smile.

The smells of warm sugar, cinnamon, and raisins filled the Miyota quarters on the afternoon of Kimiko's birthday. Never sure of success until it emerged from the oven, Fumio's parents had whispered plans for making the cake during Kimiko's infrequent naps.

Sugar was costly, but was purchased, as well as a small amount of lard, at the co-op store.

Their one baking pan was square, but it would fit neatly on the rack designed by Fumio's father to be slipped into the stove, once the fire had burnt low. At Mrs. Otani's suggestion, the carefully rinsed tin wash basin was placed over the top of the cake as it baked, to prevent over-browning.

Mrs. Otani had also devised a way for Kimiko to be out of the house while the cake was made. She escorted her to the library where the two sat side-by-side, Kimiko turning pages while Mrs. Otani talked about the pictures. Mrs. Otani reported to Fumio's mother that both she and Kimiko hoped to do it again.

A square cake, it was felt, did not fit Kimiko's image of a "pretty cake," so the corners were carved away. Mr. Miyota liked the idea, knowing the leftover corners would be in his lunch box in days ahead. Mrs. Miyota smoothed the cake's cut edges with the back of a spoon, then the finished cake was put away, out of sight, to be tucked into a basket later. The aroma, though, was unmistakable. And mouthwatering. Not usually fond of sweets, Fumio was surprised to find he was looking forward to this special dessert.

A few days earlier, hurrying from taiko practice toward the mess hall, he had seen Mrs. Otani in her garden, beckoning to him.

"Mrs. Otani-san!" Fumio bowed deeply. "What may I do to help you?"

"How goes the work on the drum, danshi?"

"It goes well, thank you, ma'am, Oba-san. The drum is finished, and I am whittling the drumsticks from two pieces of desert wood."

"That is good."

"Yes, Oba-san, this is an important birthday. Kimiko is excited that, in September, she will attend what she calls 'real school.'"

"Ah, yes. Will she have a party?"

"Yes, ma'am, on Friday. She insists we must sing *Happy Birthday* to her."

"And she wants nothing more?"

"She imagines having 'a pretty cake,' because she will be a big girl." Fumio had shrugged. "A cake with white frosting and colorful decorations."

"Not easy to make that kind of cake, here." Mrs. Otani swept an upturned palm to indicate their surroundings. "Hmmm, I have an idea. I can speak with your mother."

• • •

Kimiko was given a pair of gleaming, black patent leather shoes, ordered from a catalog, the style all young girls were wearing for special occasions. In the box, also, a pair of white, lace-edged anklets. Kimiko was excited. "Look! I can see myself in the toes! May I wear them, please?" she asked and received permission because this was a special day.

"Fumio," his mother said, "after supper, when you come here to get— *umm*—will you please also pick up the food basket? Do you think you can manage it?"

"Yes, Mother. I will do that."

The Miyotas made their way to the mess hall, which was noisy and crowded, but as Fumio ate, his mind returned repeatedly to the taiko drum under his bed, carefully wrapped in newspaper and camouflaged by an outgrown shirt on the floor in front of it. He ignored the tapioca pudding lying in a puddle on his tray.

"You gonna eat that?" he heard from over his shoulder. A lanky older boy stood there, looking hopeful.

"It's all yours," Fumio replied, and lifted his tray so the boy could spoon off the pudding.

"The stuff tastes bad, but whaddya gonna do?" The boy shrugged. "My mother says, being thirteen, I got a hollow leg."

Fumio grinned.

Soon, the Miyotas were returning their trays to the kitchen. "Hey, kid!" Fumio looked up to see the kitchen supervisor. "Did it work out okay? Did you get the—?"

Fumio moved his head, *yes,* but indicated *no* by slashing his hand in front of his chest.

"Oh, I see." The man chuckled. "That is good, then."

Fumio *whooshed* a deep breath. Secrets could be traps, he thought, easily set and hidden, ready to be sprung when least expected. Thank goodness today was Kimiko's birthday!

Walking toward the garden, Kimiko skipped along, linked with her parents, hand in hand. When Fumio veered off to their quarters, she turned. "Fumio, it's time for my party!"

"Don't worry, Kimiko," he called, "I will be right there!"

In the apartment, Fumio patted his shirt pocket. Yes, the small tin he had been given by Mr. Kats-san was still there. He took his large, cold-weather coat from a hook on the wall and spread it open on his cot. From far under the bed he withdrew the drum and bachi. The bachi, he slipped into a pocket of the coat, buttoning the flap. He lay the drum—now wrapped, by his mother, in white tissue—on the coat's lining and tucked the coat around it, enveloping it securely. Then, he knotted the sleeves together tightly and, slipping his arm through them, wore the bundle like a shoulder-pack.

He carefully picked up the food basket, which held the applesauce cake, went out, stopped to close the door behind him, and hurried across the compound.

He found his family near the edge of the garden on a mat spread in a gentle hollow near a miniature stream. A length of desert wood rested on its side, just right for sitting. The sun peered over barracks roofs as the evening began to cool. Birds called.

"Meadowlarks," Fumio said. "They have nests on the ground, not far away."

"Yes?" Mr. Miyota said. "How do you know that?"

"Paul told me," Fumio answered, settling onto the twisted length of log. "The birds are common in these parts, but we don't often hear their calls. Camp noise drowns them out."

Kimiko began to bounce. "Now, Mama?" she asked. "Now, Papa?"

"Yes, dear, now!" His mother lifted from the basket the ceramic plate that held the careful circle of fragrant applesauce cake. Fumio felt a twist of worry, seeing his mother watch Kimiko's expression as she revealed the brown, raisin-studded cake.

"Smells good, Mama!" Kimiko said, her face bright with happiness.

"It does smell good, Mother." Fumio felt his tension ease.

From the basket, Mrs. Miyota took a jar with a blue label and twisted open the lid.

"Oh! What is it?" Kimiko asked.

"Marshmallow crème! Your father bought it at the co-op store, after work."

Fumio had seen advertisements for marshmallow crème in grocery store ads before the war, but never scooped from a jar in swirls of white fluff. *The stuff is beautiful*, he thought.

"Thank you, Papa!" Kimiko went to her father, squeezed his hand, and turned back to watch her mother spread mounds of marshmallow crème atop the applesauce cake.

Reaching again into the basket, Mrs. Miyota took out a small bouquet of flowers arranged in a blue tin decorated with a picture of a winged insect and labeled, "Mrs. Harper's Moth Balls."

"Pretty flowers!" Kimiko exclaimed. "And look! A butterfly!"

Mrs. Miyota withdrew a loosely knotted pink handkerchief and gently tugged it open, revealing a handful of short-stemmed pansy blossoms, purple, lavender and white. One at a time, she placed them atop the marshmallow mounds. "Kimiko," she said, "Mrs. Otani gave me these pansies especially for your birthday. They are *edible*. We can eat them. Not all flowers! But these are safe to eat."

Quick as a flash, Kimiko plucked a pansy from the bouquet in the blue tin, put it in her mouth and bit down.

Fumio gasped, then laughed. "How does it taste?"

"Oh!" The little girl squeezed her eyes shut. "It tastes like . . . like . . ."

"Like a pansy?" her mother asked.

Kimiko swallowed. "It's good!" she said and licked her lips. Her tongue was green.

"I am glad, Daughter," Mr. Miyota said, chuckling.

"Father, Mr. Kats-san asked me to give this to you." Fumio held out a small red and white box.

"Matches? Well, you never know when you will need a match."

"That is exactly what Mr. Kats-san said," Fumio replied. "But I think there is something besides matches in there."

Mr. Miyota pushed against one end of the box. It slid open, and he took from it a pink birthday cake candle, then a blue, a yellow, a purple, and a green candle. Each tiny candle was a different length, the wick of each was charred.

"Birthday candles!" Kimiko cried, clapping her hands together. "All different colors! Just like I wanted! Can we put them on the cake, *please*?"

Mrs. Miyota pushed the little candles into the cake. "We will tell Mr. Katsumoto-san how much you like his gift."

Mr. Miyota took a match from the box and struck it against the sole of his boot. He quickly lit all five candles, using a hand to shelter the flames from the rising breeze.

"Ooohh, pretty," Kimiko whispered.

On the day the drum was finished, Mr. Katsumoto had held it in both hands, turning it this way and that, watching the light reflect from its shiny red body. "Exactly as it is written, Fumio! Excelsior! The drum turned out well!" He traced the word with a fingertip.

"Thank you for bringing coal." Mr. Katsumoto-san had gestured toward the full scuttle. "I appreciated your company as you worked on the drum."

"Thank you, sir. But you know I will be back."

"The drum is finished."

"Yes, sir, Mr. Kats-san! But that coal will last only a few days. Nights are still cold. And then there will be . . ." Fumio paused, spread his hands. "I will be back."

Mr. Katsumoto's face had brightened. "I will be glad to see you, Fumio Miyota."

"*Happy birthday to you,*" Mrs. Miyota began singing, now, and Fumio and his father picked up the tune.

"*Have-a birthday, to me,*" Kimiko joined in, too.

"Happy birthday, Kimiko! Happy birthday!"

Kimiko pursed her lips and blew. The candles snuffed out, the family cheered.

Mrs. Miyota removed the candles and put them in a basket to be cleaned and offered back to Mr. Katsumoto. She brought out flowered cloth napkins and made much of placing a piece of cake on each one. Forks were not needed. Dropped crumbs did not matter. Crows would be the cleanup crew, later.

Fumio saw the pleasure in the eyes of his parents. The cake was a triumph, both *pretty* and delicious. Kimiko licked her lips. She licked her fingers. Very grown-up, she wiped her hands on a cloth napkin. For many minutes the silence was unbroken, then . . .

Boom, boom . . . Boom, boom . . . Boom, boom . . . Boom!

From the taiko dojo came the sound of a single drum. As Fumio had asked, Senpai Oshiro-san had adjusted his usual schedule to rehearse a traditional rhythm pattern now.

Boom, boom . . . Boom, boom . . . Boom, boom . . . Boom!

Kimiko came to her feet, leaning toward the sound. She turned to her brother. "Fumio! Drumming!"

.He placed the gift atop the log. Kimiko hurried to him and stared, unmoving. Fumio reached for her hand and, together, they nudged aside a loose edge of the wrapping. It crackled and a small tear revealed a glimpse of red, the gleaming curve of the ko. Kimiko pulled away the paper. "A drum!" she cried. "Fumio! It's a taiko drum!"

"Yes, Kimiko. *Your* taiko drum!" He handed her the bachi.

Resting the drum on the log, Kimiko grasped the drumsticks and gently tapped the drumhead, once, twice, testing its tension. "Fumio, it is beautiful! I can learn, now! Thank you, Fumio!" Once, twice, again, Kimiko increased the pressure of her strikes, then fell into the rhythm being drummed in the dojo.

CHAPTER SEVENTY

FLYER

The wind is cold. The air smells odd and tastes strange. Clouds at the edge of the sky are dark.

No birds are in sight. They do not call or sing. I walk on, along a strange road.

I hear voices and crouch behind the brush. On the other side of the road, people use long-handled hoes to weed rows of plants. Workers, some are children, bend low to slide the blades of the hoes just under the top of the earth. That means the weeds are small, their roots shallow.

With strangers so near, I worry they will see me. I watch. I wait.

A man takes off his hat and studies the sky. "Storm comin'," he says.

The wind blows colder. One boy wears overalls like Mr. Harvey's, except the knees are patched. He looks at the sky, closes the top of his shirt and works faster.

Tree leaves rattle. A flash lights the sky. Rumbling sounds roll toward me, growling—*GrrRrrr-GrrRrrr! B-BOOM! B-BOOM! B-BOOM!*

"Aahhh!" The workers slap their hands over their ears. Hoes fall like pick-up-sticks.

People crouch or go down on one knee. Children cry. A baby wails. I flatten against the dirt, covering Fumio's mitt with my belly.

GrrrRrrr . . . Boom! Boom! BOOM! BOOM! The noise comes again. On our farm, the Crawler is very loud, but you can see the Crawler. This giant noise has no tractor.

The rumble grows louder, louder. *Bammmm! Bammmm! Bammmm!*

Raindrops fall fast and hard. They hurt. I forget to stay hidden and, *Yipp-yipp!*

Then I hear, "We are going back to the cabins, dog," and the boy with the patched knees stands right in front of me. "You better go on in with me. It's not safe out here."

The boy's hands are jammed in his pockets. Rain runs from the top of his head and drips from the end of his nose. Up close, I see his freckles, like Zachary's. I wait for him to go away.

He says, "Dog, *please!* You'd be better off inside with me."

I am getting very wet; the mitt is getting very wet. *Inside* sounds like a good place to be. But the boy is a stranger. I watch.

He frowns, not like he is angry, more like he is *curious.* He leans forward, his head tilted. "*Perro? Ven aqui, perro!*"

Perro? I don't know *perro.*

The boy pulls one hand from his pocket. "All right." He lifts his arm and calls, "Come."

I know *Come,* and I know water is running into my ears. Maybe I *could* go with him. I thump my tail, once. I wait.

The boy bends down, his hands on his knees, until we are eye to eye. "I just want to get you in out of this storm, dog."

• • •

We run to a panel wagon parked at the side of the field and the boy opens the door.

"Get in!" someone yells.

"The dog, too?" the boy asks. "'Cause, if not, he and I'll take off for the cabin on foot."

"In this storm? Come on! Both of you, get in!"

The boy gets into the paneled wagon and scoots his legs aside. With Fumio's mitt in my mouth, I climb onto the running board and fit myself inside next to the door.

We ride for a while, then the boy opens the door, and we are in front of buildings like the little houses at the Boy Scout camp on the island. They are called *summer cabins*.

When the boy goes into a cabin, I think I will sleep under its eaves, and *not* out in the field where the angry storm growls.

But he turns around and calls, "Come on in, then, dog."

The house is warm. I see a round metal stove. The stove pipe goes straight out of the wall, like the one in Mr. Miyota's shop. The heat tickles my nose.

It is good to be out of the rain. But it is bad to feel water dripping off me, and *I cannot shake*!

Across the room—there is only one room—the boy uses a towel to wipe his head and face. I am surprised when he brings another towel to *me*. I can smell the good scent of wash-day soap on the towel.

The boy comes close enough to lay the towel over me. He steps back. Very carefully, I shake myself.

The boy laughs. "Now, that's better, isn't it? I'm Bo. Beauregard, really, but nobody can get their mouth around that, so Bo is what I go by."

I lie down with the towel on my back, my muzzle on the mitt.

The boy, *Bo*, steps forward. He asks, "All right by you if I dry this spot behind your ears?" He rubs my neck and my back with the towel.

Pwuph-whuph.

"You are welcome, dog," *Bo* says and goes back near the stove.

I hear a woman's voice. "Beauregard, son, you might ask the dog if he'd like to come closer to the heat."

The woman speaks, friendly, slower than what I'm used to. It sounds a little like *music*.

Bo asks, "You want to come over here where it's warmer, dog?" I hear *the difference* in Bo's voice, too. It is *interesting*.

I move near the stove.

"Where do you think the dog came from?" the woman asks.

"'Don't know. But he would've froze if he'd stayed out there. Or gotten hit by lightning. Those lightning strikes were coming real close. I counted to only two-Mississippi."

The woman laughs, "I surely do wish your Aunt Florence had not taught you that trick. Lightning is scary enough without keeping track as it comes closer."

A coat hangs over the back of a chair in the corner of the cabin. It is dripping. Water runs across the floor. Bo wipes it up and hangs the towel from a nail by the stove.

The door opens. A man comes in. His coat is dark with rain. Water drips off the brim of his hat. I remember that hat from when I saw the man hoeing, in the field. He drove the panel wagon, too. He shrugs. "Mr. James says this storm was expected, but predicting the weather is never better than fifty-fifty."

"You surely did get drenched, husband," Bo's mother says.

"I did. But Mr. James thanked me for helping him get the outbuildings shut. I ventured to say a *Nebraskan* knows how to deal with a storm." He hangs his coat near the stove. "There's the possibility of a job here. A house comes with that."

Bo's mother replies, "So I heard, and Mr. and Mrs. James seem like good people. But I try to not think about it overmuch."

"We have a house guest," Bo's father says, looking at me.

Bo grins. "He's new around here, Father, so I'll make the introductions. Mr. Beauregard McCallum, Senior, meet—" The boy shrugs. "Meet, I guess, *Dog*. I don't know his name or anything about him, except he does not come when you call him in English or Spanish. He doesn't come when you call him, period, unless he wants to. That's all right. I don't, either."

Mrs. McCallum smiles. "The dog has good manners. Someone is grieving his absence."

"What do you reckon is the story behind the baseball mitt?" *Mr. McCallum* asks.

I hear *baseball mitt* and I shift until it is underneath me.

"A name, an address. Looks like the dog has somewhere to be," Bo says. "I wish we did."

"Maybe we will, soon," *Mr. McCallum* replies.

Mrs. McCallum looks away.

At suppertime, Bo puts water in a bowl for me. He gives me a little piece of stew meat and a bit of potato from his bowl. There is some talking and a lot of yawning. Bo's father says, "It'll be an early morning."

I wait for Bo to send me outside. But his mother says, "I can't allow as I like the aroma of a wet dog drying, but the wind coming in around that door ought to clear it out fast enough."

"This night is not fit for man nor dog," says Bo's father. "Let the dog stay inside."

Soon the lights are out, and Bo's family is wrapped in blankets.

It is dark outside. Then lightning flashes.

From Bo's cot I hear, "One, Mississippi. Two, Mississippi." Thunder rumbles, then rumbles again. It sounds nearer.

Another flash. *Banggg—BAAMM!*

Yipp-ipp! So close! The strange smell, the smell of the storm, is all around me. I want to scoot under the sink. There is no sink.

Banggg—Banggg—BBAAMMM! I close my eyes. I smell smoke. I bark. FIRE!

"Let the dog out!" Bo's father says.

Bo comes to me. "You really want to go out there, dog?"

Do I want to go out there? *No.* But I've got to. I bark again.

Bo opens the door. Wind *swoosh*-es in. I run out.

A fiery glow shows me where to go. The rain comes slower than before, but the ground is wet. My paws sink into mud so deep I must pull them free with each step. As fast as I can, I find my way.

The smell of smoke is coming from a tree. It is too dark to see much about the tree, except that it is big. Its trunk is split, and fire comes from the broken place. The tree leans against a small building. Flames come from the roof's shingles. From the building comes a shrill cry. Fear! Stamping, whinnying. A horse! A horse is inside! I bark! I bark and bark!

A light comes on in the biggest house, the porch light flares. "What in the hey is going—Fire! Fire! Rosemarie! Call the R.F.D.! Fire!" A man's boots tromp down steps, splash through puddles. "Fire! Fire!"

From the small building, the flames burn brighter, leap higher, they have spread. Bo is here, and his father and mother. They brought towels. They soak them in puddles and slap them against the building's door.

The man in boots comes off the porch, running toward the fire. Bo's father calls, "We're here, Mr. James!"

"Thanks, Beauregard! Mrs. McCallum, young Bo, move back! I can get at that door, now!" *Mr. James* pulls open the door. A big horse runs out and into the muddy yard. "Goldie! The man waits until the horse calms then goes to her. "Goldie! You're safe, girl." He leads the horse away.

Field workers come out of the cabins and help. Trucks roar into the lane and pull up near the fire. Men hook up hoses to a truck with a big tank on the back. The rain stops.

When the fire is out, a man who came in a truck says, "Sure glad it wasn't worse, Mr. James, and Goldie got out safe. That's one fine horse. We'll be back tomorrow to get this tree out of the way and chop it up for firewood."

Mr. James says his thanks. The men get in the trucks and leave. The field workers return to their cabins.

In the McCallum's cabin, I sit just inside the door while Bo's family warms their hands near the stove. The smell of their clothes is strong with smoke! At a knock, Bo's father opens the door. He greets Mr. James and invites him inside. Mr. James steps in and takes his hat off. "You saved her!" he says. "You and your family saved old Goldie!"

"We're glad we could help, Mr. James," Bo's father says, "but we have that dog to thank!" He points at *me*. "He smelled smoke and sounded the alarm."

The man asks, "Is that your dog, young Bo?"

"No, sir, he is not. I had a dog back in Nebraska. We had to leave him with friends."

"Hmmh. We could use a dog around here. Mr. McCallum, please come see me in the morning. I'd like to talk to you about a full-time job here, at Double J Farms." He shakes Mr. McCallum's hand and goes out.

• • •

For breakfast, Bo gives me fresh water and half his fried egg. *Yipp!* Thank you! *Whuphh!* I paw at the door. *May I please go out?* I pick up the mitt.

Bo opens the cabin door. He looks sad. But I will not leave without saying goodbye. I am looking for a private place.

When I head back to the cabin, I see the volunteers gathering near the burnt barn. A shiny car is parked near the biggest house. A man with a camera stands on the porch, talking with Mr. James. They go to Bo's father, and Mr. James says, "Pete, this is my new foreman, Beauregard McCallum, *Senior.* Beauregard, this is Pete Finn, editor of the paper." The men shake hands.

Mr. James says, "We'd have been in a heap of trouble last night, if young Bo hadn't brought a stray in, out of the storm. Middle of the night, dog sniffed out trouble, sounded the alarm. Saved the life of our ol' draft horse, Goldie."

"Goldie!" *Mr. Finn* says. "Saved by a hero dog! I know you set a great store by that horse." He looks around. "Where is Goldie, now?"

"I put her in the back outbuilding until I can fix up something better. Why?"

"Why, I've got to get a picture of Goldie and—where is this hero dog?"

Everyone is looking at me. Bo has come out of the cabin, and he sees there is some new excitement happening. He comes to stand near me. I suppose that draws the attention of the men. I have Fumio's mitt in my mouth, and I do not like the way they are looking at me.

Mr. Finn holds a box up to his eye. *Czzick-ck!* "Got it!" he says, and his smile is big. "Wait right here, dog!" He walks fast. "Let's go get Goldie. The two of them in front of the charred barn, the dog carrying a mitt. This is going to be great!" I hear him ask, "What's up with the baseball mitt, anyway?" but I do not hear the answer.

I turn toward the cabin, Bo at my side.

"Being on the road is hard," he says, "I know. Leaving one place and then another. Always leaving. Just when you think things are gonna get better. But I kinda think things are going to get better here, on this farm. And you helped with that, dog.

"I wish I knew your name, but, oh, well, I know *you*. And I know you are on a mission. I can see you are important to someone, someone you care about, a lot." He looks hard at the mitt, but he doesn't reach for it. "Fumio Miyota," he says, "Bainbridge ... Island Elementary. That Fumio, he's a lucky kid."

Bo walks with me toward the road. Goldie is safe. Mr. McCallum has a job. Soon, Bo will have a home. *Yipp!* I look into his eyes. He raises a hand, *Goodbye*. I take to the road, look back, once, then head east.

• • • •

The grass along the fence line is very wet. In some places the barrow pits that line the road are filled with water from the storm. Not far from the cabin at Double J Farms, I have no choice but to walk on the edge of the road. I am careful to listen for cars or trucks on the road behind me, but if one comes along, I will have to swim. That would be hard to do, carrying the baseball mitt.

Ahead, a truck is stopped with its engine running. A man is there, moving fallen branches. I am near enough to hear that he sings while he works, like Zachary's mother does. The man is very busy, and I go still, hoping he will not see me. But not even looking my way, he says, "Hello, there! It's a good day for ducks, isn't it?"

Ducks? I look around. I don't see ducks.

"Oh, you aren't a duck?" the man asks.

He is talking to *me*. Maybe he is *telling a joke*. He comes to the rear of the truck and says, "You are in for a rough time if you're going far in this weather." He points. I see clouds, dark, like yesterday.

"So!" he grins. "You're a ball player! Shortstop? Pitcher? Nah, don't tell me. You're a catcher, am I right?"

The man tells jokes, like Mr. Harvey. He sings while he works, like Mrs. Whitlock. He wears a straw hat, like Mr. Torres. His eyes are kind, like Fumio's father.

I move nearer. The smells of the farm truck come to me, diesel, grease. *Sugar beets*! Like the smell of the truck that brought the Cleveland Crawler to our farm.

The man says, "My name is Theodore Nikomura. You can call me Ted." He grins. "All my friends do."

I walk to *Mr. Nikomura*, just out of arm's reach. His eyes go to the mitt. "What you are carrying must be important to you, boy." He leans closer. "Ah, wakari masu. I understand." He nods once, slowly. "You are delivering something." He twists his head. "And the name is—Miyota."

He smiles. "Well, I don't have any *longtime* neighbors by the name of Miyota. But I have about ten-thousand *new* neighbors, most of whose names I don't know. You are heading in the right direction. But the way could get complicated from here. And the weather, another storm is coming. Hop in, if you like, and we will see if I can help."

CHAPTER SEVENTY-ONE

FLYER

Mr. Nikomura is friendly, but I do not get in his truck. He tells me his farm is up this road, not far. I will see his truck in the yard, and if I want to, I can get under cover from the rain in his barn or, he says, *in the breezeway*. I don't know *breezeway*.

The road is gravel, the edges are muddy. Water runs in the barrow pits, rushing through stalks of grass and weeds with a whispering sound.

I pass by farms—houses, barns, pastures. Goats are in their pens. Cows crowd near the barns. Chickens are in their coops. Farm equipment is parked in the yard. The fields are too wet to be worked.

Crops come up in fields so big that the rows go over hills and disappear. None of the plants are strawberries, but a sweet smell is carried on the wind. It's a rough wind, though. It pushes at my ears.

When I see Mr. Nikomura's farm truck parked near his house, raindrops are hitting me on the nose. Beside the long driveway, an irrigation ditch overflows and water laps at the lane. Maybe I will get *under cover* in the barn—or the *breezeway*. For now, I walk toward the truck.

Mr. Nikomura comes out from a building close to the house, the garage. A pickup truck is parked inside. "Hello, boy! I hoped I'd see you here. Just in time, too, right?" He motions toward the clouds. "Come along, boy!"

I follow him to a place between the house and the garage, where packed dirt is under my feet and a roof is overhead.

"Wait here in the breezeway," Mr. Nikomura says, and goes into his house. I am glad for the roof, but I know why it's called a *breezeway*. On two sides it has no walls. The wind blows through, and it brings the scent of sheep! In this weather, they would be in their pen.

"Woof!" A dog! Not big, not little, the dog is the same size as I am, with ears that stand up and a furry tail—a tail that is not wagging. She leans her head to the side, like I do when I'm thinking hard. She is watching me.

Whooph-ooff! I say, *Hello!*

She turns and walks toward the barn that must hold sheep. A lot of sheep, I think.

Mr. Nikomura brings me a bowl of water.

Yipp-ipp! Thank you!

He sets down a plate with a piece of bread, toasted, but not hot, and an egg, cooked hard, cold. "You ever eaten fried duck eggs? Maybe not. They will taste different from what you're used to. They're *healthy*. Not much of a market for duck eggs. I fried more than I needed this morning, and more than Beatrice needed, I guess. Beatrice is probably with the sheep."

Mr. Nikomura returns to the house, then comes out wearing a heavier coat, a rain hat, and gloves. From the *breezeway's* edge I watch as he unloads bags of feed from under a tarp in the truck box. He takes the ones with sheep pictures to the barn and the others to the shed.

Beatrice sounds a *Come here, now!* bark. Mr. Nikomura hurries to the low-roofed shed.

"Shoo, cat! Out!" he yells. "Scat! Shoo! Shame on you!"

He shouts, "Come, boy! Come!"

Mr. Nikomura needs help.

The shed is open on the side. Mr. Nikomura is just inside. "Boy," he calls to me, "help us out! That ornery cat scared the *ducklings*, and they've scattered.

"Beatrice," he calls, "go!" and she takes off, out into the heavy rain.

"You, boy! Here!" He taps the wall. I go to him. There are hooks on the wall of the shed where a few sheep harnesses are hung. He reaches out slowly, takes the mitt from my mouth, and hangs it on a low hook, near my nose. Then, he points, and he and I both go out.

Ducklings are baby birds, bigger than baby chickens. Still, when it rains, they should be near their mothers, who are *ducks*. Ducklings' feathers are soft—they look fuzzy. Their feet are flat, and they run rocking side to side.

Herding ducklings is easier than herding chickens. Their beaks aren't sharp, so they can't peck dogs. It's easier than herding sheep because ducklings don't butt dogs with their big heads. But herding ducklings can be *confusing*. They run in circles, *quack-quack-quack*, then dive into a bunch of grass or a pile of straw—*lickety-split!* Zachary would say.

As we gather the ducklings, Mr. Nikomura, Beatrice, and I get very wet. Finally, though, the ducklings are under cover and safe. I go into the shed for the mitt, then catch up to Mr. Nikomura and Beatrice walking to the house. The sound of a storm rolls toward me.

I step under the breezeway's roof and—*pPp-ppP-Ppp-Ppp-pPp*—a different kind of rain comes down in hard little pieces that rattle on the hood of the farm truck, the roof of the house, the roof of the garage, and my head.

"Hail!" Mr. Nikomura says.

The hard raindrops, *hail*, fall into puddles left from yesterday's rain, and muddy water splashes up on my underside.

Back under the breezeway roof, the bread and egg wait. Mr. Nikomura goes to the house.

Whooph! I tell Beatrice. *I will share the food.* No answer. This weather, *hail*, must not be new to Beatrice. She goes to her rug, a *rag rug*, like the one at my family's house, the rug Kimiko sits on when she plays with her dolls. Beatrice circles, settles, and closes her eyes. I finish my meal, lie by the step with my nose on the mitt, and watch hail fall like stones from the sky. When it stops, all over the farmyard, hail lies in piles like gravel.

CHAPTER SEVENTY-TWO

FUMIO

Rain had fallen off and on—mostly *on*—for the past few days. When the sun came from behind the clouds, Fumio made a dash for the post office to pick up his family's mail. The hoped-for letter from Zachary did not arrive. Fumio sighed. He would have to make do a while longer with *supposing* how Flyer was getting along with the season's new lambs. Were the chickens laying? And what about that bean crop? Would it be worth the trouble? With a sales circular and a copy of *The Minidoka Irrigator* in his inside pocket, Fumio was zipping his jacket when he heard his name called.

"Fumio Miyota? Wait, please!" Fumio turned to see one of the Japanese American staff members, holding an envelope. "This came for your parents. Will you take it with you, please?"

Fumio turned and walked back to the counter. Eyes lowered, he bowed. "Yes, sir, I will."

The man nodded, slowly, and handed an envelope through the bars of the service counter.

A chill snaked down Fumio's backbone at the sight of the rumpled yellow envelope boldly marked WESTERN UNION. A telegram. He had seen the yellow envelopes crushed in the hands of people who had answered the door to receive them.

What could have happened? A neighbor's death? Mr. Whitlock? Mr. Torres? No one to run the farm, keep up taxes? An angry Islander? Vandalism, a fire, destruction of the house? Trouble with their bank account? Foreclosure, loss of the farm and the equipment?

Telegrams brought only bad news. Fumio forced himself to breathe. He saw that people were looking at him, at the envelope in his hand, with, he thought, pity in their eyes. Maybe fear. Fumio had to get home, now.

A few steps beyond the post office door came the rumble of thunder. Ominous, it echoed in his mind. He picked up his pace, despite the uneven, muddy ground.

Midway across the compound he heard, "Fumio! Fumio! Wait!"

He forced himself to stop, to turn. Paul.

"Fumio," Paul began, but, looking toward the yellow envelope, he shook his head. "No. Go on home, Fumio. I'll visit you another time."

Fumio ran. Near Block 40, he felt the hairs on the back of his neck rise. The sky went white with a flash of lightning, leaving behind an odd smell, like bleach on laundry day, and the sharp odor of scorched sagebrush. Thunder roared from the near distance, then a furious rattling pounded on the roofs of barracks. Hail. The faster he ran, the more it stung.

On the barracks steps, he grabbed the railing, breathing hard. He had a bad feeling. Fumio did not want to give the yellow envelope to his mother. Whatever news this envelope brought was something he could never undo.

Crraaash! Another bolt of lightning.

The door opened. "Son! Come in! I heard the lightening, the hail. I was wor—" His mother put a hand on his shoulder, drew him through the door. "Fumio! What has happened?"

Kimiko played at reading a story to her dolls as Fumio's mother took the envelope from his hand. She brought a towel and helped him dry his hair, put the damp towel away, then sat beside him on the edge of his cot. He watched as his mother, her hands shaking, opened the yellow envelope printed with their family's name and mailing address. She pulled out the telegram and read it, drew in a deep breath, then held it so he could see the sender, "R. Whitlock," Zachary's father, and the words:

SO SORRY, CAN NO LONGER DELAY TELLING YOU. FLYER IS MISSING AND MAY BE TRAVELING TO IDAHO. WE ARE FOLLOWING AND SEARCHING. SO SORRY.

Fumio could not breathe. He had found peace in knowing Flyer was with Zachary. Now Flyer was not with Zachary. The Whitlocks had no idea where Flyer was. And Fumio knew he would not be allowed to take part in the search.

His mother put her arm around his shoulders. "Fumio, Flyer is a smart dog, very smart. I'm sure he is not lost. The Whitlocks will find him."

Grateful for her attempt to comfort him, nevertheless, Fumio felt he might suffocate in despair. The high desert was vast and offered no signposts, none that Flyer could read.

Six hundred miles! Nothing would be familiar to Flyer. The dry desert air sucked the water out of most types of plant life, plants with tough exteriors and thorns to thwart a dog's need for moisture and deny him cover from the big storms that filled the broad sky, edge to edge. Storms like the one pelting Camp Minidoka now.

Where would Flyer find drinking water, shelter, and safety, and then the freedom to go on his way? Fumio himself daily felt the pinch of strangeness here, even with his family nearby. Flyer had foregone every manner of comfort and safety.

CHAPTER SEVENTY-THREE

FLYER

The sun has sunk to the roof of the barn when Mr. Nikomura brings out supper. The meat scraps smell good, and there is a little rice.

Beatrice eats her food then goes to the sheep barn. She does not ask me to help. When she returns, her fur sparkles with water drops. She shakes, the droplets scatter.

The night is noisy with rain pounding on roofs. Thunder shakes the house. Lightning is quick but bright. I think of Bo at the cabin, *one Mississippi.*

Rainfall eases, picks up again. Small streams flow across the breezeway. I move to higher ground.

Morning comes. Rain splashes into big puddles that spread across the ground. The door opens, and Mr. Nikomura stands holding a steaming cup. Tea. He pulls a small rug onto the step and sits down. Beatrice comes from a place in the garage to lie on her rug.

"Oh!" Mr. Nikomura says, then he sets the teacup on the step and goes into the garage. He brings a scrap of blanket. "There you go, boy. That concrete must be cold." He lays the blanket down beside the step and I move onto it.

Finally, the rain stops, the sun comes out, and after the noon meal of fried duck eggs, Mr. Nikomura asks me, "Boy, are you ready to go find Fumio?"

Whoop! Whoop! I am ready! I go to the water dish, which Mr. Nikomura keeps filled, for one more drink. Beatrice stands, watching. *Yipp-ipp-ipp*, I tell her. *It looks like I am leaving.*

She dips her head, turns, and walks away.

I take the mitt in my mouth and jump into the cab of the pickup truck. Mr. Nikomura and I drive slowly along the road, slick in places, watching for holes hidden by puddles. "I wish you could've seen this place in good weather," Mr. Nikomura says.

Ahead, a car comes toward us, slows to a stop, and someone waves. Mr. Nikomura brakes the truck. "Afternoon!"

"Good afternoon, Mr. Nikomura!" a woman calls. "And how is your mother? Have you heard from her recently?"

"Yes, just last week. She is doing well at my sister's home in Twin Falls, even done a little gardening."

"That's wonderful improvement! Please give her my best when you write her next. We have a problem, though, Mr. Nikomura." The woman frowns. "The bridge is down. Vehicles can't cross!"

"Can't cross? For how long? Do you know?"

"I asked, but they're not sure. A couple days, anyway. Looks like you have a new dog! A fine dog, too!"

"He is a good dog. Not mine, but a nice visitor. So, a couple days, huh? I'll be taking this dog back home with me, then. Thank you!"

"You're very welcome, Mr. Nikomura. You take care, now!"

Mr. Nikomura turns the truck around. "Boy, I hope you'll wait."

Wait? I don't want to wait after so much waiting already.

"You don't want to wait, I understand. This is important to you. But..." He sighs. "The guards. Their rifles. And you, carrying that mitt. You have a better chance of getting into the camp safely in a vehicle. I will see you get to Camp Minidoka, boy. I promise."

I know what it means when *the bridge is out*. Trucks cannot drive over water. They must have a *bridge*. Or a ferry. Now, I must decide. The fields are too wet for running or even walking fast. This place is strange to me. Traveling in the dark is not a good plan. I do *not* want to wait, but I will.

•   •   •

I keep a firm grip on Fumio's mitt while I check fences with Beatrice. We circle the sheep pen. Every post must stand straight, every wire must hold strong.

An engine's rumble tells me a truck is pulling into the yard. I walk toward the garage. Beatrice walks alongside me. A truck door slams. Stopping at the building's corner, I listen.

"'Morning, Mr. Nikomura!" A man's voice.

Mr. Nikomura replies, "Hello to you, Driz! What brings you here this morning?"

I step forward and watch. Beatrice edges forward, too.

The visitor, *Mr. Driz,* says, "I'm covering every inch of my territory, never mind this infernal rationing. I'm talking with any customer who ever bought so much as a pack of shop rags from me. How's the truck holding up, Ted? I know you keep an eye on the oil, seeing's how it sips a little."

Mr. Nikomura nods. "Yes. I'll need another case of oil next time you come around."

"And how are you getting along, Ted? All things considered."

"Do you mean, considering I am a Japanese American who lives far enough inland to remain free, and so many aren't? It feels rotten. Thanks for asking, though. Anyway, Driz, would you like to sit down? Can I get you a glass of water?"

"I'm sure sorry about . . . well, I'm sure sorry. And I appreciate the offer, Ted, but, *no*, to the water. I won't stay a minute. A cousin—lives in Washington State—called me on the telephone—rang up long distance, can you imagine? Seems as how a dog left in the care of his friends has gone missing. Then, couple days ago, a picture of the dog showed up in the newspaper. Now they figure he's likely coming this way. My cousin asked me to be on the lookout for the dog, maybe ask around."

"What kind of dog?" Mr. Nikomura asks. "What's he look like?"

"A border collie. With herding skills, my cousin says, and that's a great thing—we keep a few sheep on our farm. Anyway, the missus and I, we hauled a tractor over there a few years back. I saw him, then." He squints. "In fact, Ted, he looks like *that*."

He points *at me*.

"Wha-da-ya know!" *Mr. Driz* says. "Hello, there, Flyer! I surely am relieved to see you! Your folks are worried, Flyer!"

Flyer. I have not heard my name called in a long time. A few steps closer, I see his eyes, his smile, his overalls.

"Flyer, remember me? I'm cousin to your friend, Mr. Harvey. I'm Driz, remember?"

I do remember. Mr. and Mrs. Driz brought the Cleveland Crawler to our farm! The wheels of their truck smelled like sugar. The Crawler's tracks smelled like sugar, too! I did not know that smell then, but I know it now!

Mr. Nikomura says, "Driz, I take it your cousin lives on Bainbridge Island."

"Sure enough. How'd you know?"

"Look at the baseball mitt Flyer carries. Don't touch it, though. He's particular about it."

Mr. Driz steps close to see Fumio's mitt. I know he is a friend, so I don't need to tell him to keep distant. He nods. "Well, then . . ."

"I've been planning to take Flyer to his destination," Mr. Nikomura says, "to Camp Minidoka. From the address on the mitt, I'd guessed his friend Fumio and his family were part of that first group forced out. They'd have gone to Manzanar, been there during all that trouble, and then they'd have probably come up here. With everything those folks have been through, the least I can do is get the boy's mitt *and his dog* back to him. But this weather . . ."

"Right. Weather's been bad. Bridge out, and all. That's fixed as of this morning. I have business at that camp, today, Ted. No shipments have gotten through, and the Motor Repair and Tire Shop ran short on solvent."

Mr. Nikomura frowns. "Might be a good thing if you take him. You've made deliveries there, often. They're more likely to let him through the gate if he's with you."

"Oh, there are a few dogs there. Strays, I guess."

"I can see how that would be. But Flyer's carrying valuable cargo, and I have heard the guards can be uncooperative."

"Can be. Some are, some aren't. A fella's gotta take potluck."

"Sending him with you is the better plan." Mr. Nikomura sighs. "Although I gotta tell you, I wish I could keep him. Beatrice acts uppity around him, but I know she likes the company. They would make good pups. When will you take him?"

"Today, I suppose. Good a time as any."

Mr. Nikomura says, "I'll be waiting to hear how it went, then." He reaches out, slowly, puts his palm under my muzzle. His hand is warm. He touches the top of my head, strokes the soft place down to my ears. He says, "Go along, then, boy. *Flyer.*"

Standing next to me, Beatrice makes a soft noise. I feel her muzzle against my ear. She steps back. I will miss Beatrice. It is good to be understood.

• • •

Mr. Driz lets me ride up front. The engine is noisy, but, like Mr. Harvey would say, *the truck's a good runner.* I sit up to watch. The roads are still wet with the last few days' rain, but the sun is bright. A bridge is being repaired, and one lane is closed. As we wait our turn to cross, Mr. Driz rolls his window halfway down then reaches over in front of me and lowers mine a little.

Finally, Mr. Driz is waved ahead. Going by a worker, he calls, "Thanks, Calvin!"

Calvin waves.

"Tell you what, Flyer," Mr. Driz says, "I have a couple of deliveries I usually make before lunch, but I reckon we should get you where you're headed. You must be raring to go."

Raring to go. If that means my chest hurts with waiting, then I am *raring to go.* I lean forward feeling that, if I try hard, I can make the truck move faster. Water runs across the road in one place, and I am afraid Mr. Driz will say we have to turn around. But he doesn't.

Mr. Driz takes off his cap, drops it behind the seat and reaches for a felt hat with a brim. It's hanging from a hook fastened to the truck cab. He puts on the hat. "Look professional, now, do I, Flyer?" he asks me.

Professional? I make a noise, *phwuphh,* to say I am listening.

We come to a road with *barbed wire* on both sides. I know barbed wire. I have seen it at Petric's. Ahead is a small building on poles as tall as trees. I tip back my head to look up. In the building are men with *guns* with long barrels, like the guns at the ferry dock when my family went away.

Our truck turns in at a wide driveway and stops at a little hut made of big stones. In front of the hut is a man who is young, like Jacob, but the man carries a rifle with a long knife on it. Jacob would not. Mr. Driz reaches across in front of me to the glove box and pulls out pieces of paper. "Sit very still. Be very quiet," he says. "The entrance guard must okay us, Flyer. Welcome to Camp Minidoka."

· · ·

Past the windshield and the hood of our truck are many buildings. Long, low and dark, they all look alike.

Yipp-ipp! Is Fumio here?

Our truck's side windows are rolled down a little and a warm breeze blows in, telling me about this place. Outdoor smells, fields plowed, and water for irrigation. Work smells, oil, gasoline, and grease. New wood, coal tar, and people sweating. Yard smells, cut lawn grass, like at the Whitlocks' home, fruit trees, and gardens. House smells, soap for dishes, and clothes. Cooking smells, mixed together like company is coming. Soy sauce— Grandfather Miyota called it *shoyu.*

Everywhere there are people. *Is my family here?* People big and small, old and young are walking, running. A toddling baby, trying to walk, holds a woman's hand. A girl sits in a chair with wheels that is pushed by another girl—they are talking and laughing. Little boys crouch on the ground, maybe playing marbles, like Fumio and Zachary sometimes did.

Fumio is here, I know he is! I cannot wait to jump down from the truck!

"Papers, please." The guard has a rifle. His voice is not friendly.

Mr. Driz hands sheets of paper through the window.

"I see. Uh-huh. Mr. Driscoll. Uh-huh. And the dog? Where are *his* papers? And what's that he's carrying? I'll have to take that."

"Begging your pardon, sir, it wouldn't be a good idea to try to take that from the dog. He's come a long way and gone to a lot of trouble—"

"*Trouble?* There'll be a lot *more* trouble," the guard says, "unless I get whatever it is the dog is carrying. *Contraband.* You know the rules."

"Contraband? It's a mitt. A baseball mitt."

"Don't care. Doesn't matter. Dog can't come into camp, regardless. And I *will* have whatever that dog is trying to smuggle in."

The guard steps up onto the driver's side running board and reaches through the window toward me, bumping Mr. Driz's nose. Gripping the mitt tight, I growl, *Stay away!* He jerks back and steps down.

"That's enough!" Mr. Driz shouts. "He is a dog. He doesn't have papers."

Mr. Driz looks at me with only his eyes and speaks from the side of his mouth, "Flyer, sit!" He raises his voice and tells the guard, "He isn't trying to smuggle anything in! And you know me! I deliver products to your Motor Repair and Tire Shop a couple times a month!"

The guard shakes his head and says in a loud voice, "Nope. You cannot enter—"

A man in greasy coveralls watches us. He turns and runs into a building with big doors.

The guard is still talking—"Unless you can produce the dog's authorization!"

I lean toward my side window and lift my head, thinking of the best way to go through the small space high up and still hold on to Fumio's mitt.

"Flyer, stay!" Mr. Driz speaks, quietly.

Though I lower my head, my tail—*thump-thump thump-thump*—beats against the seat. We are so close! *Yipp-ipp! Whoo-whooph* I scramble toward the window. I must get out, now!

"Flyer!" Mr. Driz says, "That'll do."

Those words I know. Miss Anna taught me how to work with sheep, and Zachary said *those words mean business.* But I must get out of the truck! Fumio is near, I know it! My insides shake. My whiskers quiver. I sit, but I sit tall, and I watch out the window.

The man in greasy coveralls comes from the building with big doors, shouting, "Hey! Driz! I brought the boss!" He and another man in greasy coveralls hurry to the truck.

"Good idea, Ralph!" Mr. Driz lifts his hand. "Mr. Shizuko, am I ever glad to see *you*!"

More men with grease on their clothes walk toward the truck, wiping their hands on rags.

Mr. Shizuko, the boss, asks, "What's going on here, Driz? Ralph says they won't let you make your delivery."

He walks to the driver's side of the truck and says to the guard, "The mechanics are four days behind on truck repairs on account of this weather and that bridge being out. We've gotta have Mr. Driscoll's product delivery! What's the holdup?"

"The dog has no papers!" the guard says. "And he's carrying contraband!"

"It's a baseball mitt!" Mr. Driz's voice is loud. "Fumio Miyota's baseball mitt!"

"It's Fumio's mitt?" *Ralph* asks. "Hey, Zuko! It's Fumio's mitt! He's a good kid," the man says, "and that is one very loyal dog."

"This is Flyer," Mr. Driz says. "He is Fumio Miyota's dog, and—"

Mr. Shizuko breaks in. "This sure is too bad for *someone*," he says in a loud voice, "because every mechanic in the shop is behind on his work since we ran out of Mr. Driscoll's products. We don't have the supplies we need to repair the Jeep that *someone* requisitioned for tomorrow night." He stares straight at the guard. "Looks like *someone* is out of luck."

A tall thin man in a dark uniform comes from the stone hut and walks to the truck. "You say, the dog is carrying Fumio Miyota's baseball mitt?" He frowns as he asks the young guard, "Soldier, don't you read the newspaper?"

"Sir! No, sir! The paper doesn't come to our barracks, sir!"

"Be that as it may, this dog is famous!"

There are words, and more words. I lean toward the side window to sniff, stretching up as tall as I can to see out. Finally, I hear, "Let this truck pass."

"Yes, sir! Right away, sir!"

The tall man looks toward the mechanic's *boss*. "If you wish to, Mr. Shizuko, you might help Mr. Driscoll complete his errand." He raises a hand. "Oh, yes, please tell the dog's family there will be no problem with his presence. Strays come and go. No one objects. His family will keep the dog close." He turns and walks toward the hut.

Pulling the truck forward, Mr. Driz stops just past the gates. "Wait, Flyer," he says before getting out to talk to Mr. Shizuko.

"Driz, Fumio Miyota has done some work with us, at the shop. I am acquainted with his father and know the location of their barracks. Shall we go there?"

Yipp-ipp! I answer. *Yipp-ipp-ipp! Whooph!*

"I think that's your answer," Mr. Driz says.

Mr. Shizuko nods. "If you would drive on over to the Motor Repair and Tire Shop." He turns. "Ralph, could you see to it the truck gets unloaded?"

Ralph hurries to the shop.

Mr. Driz reaches out his window, slaps his hand on the truck door, and asks Mr. Shizuko, "Hitch a lift?"

A foot on the running board, a hand on the side mirror bracket, Mr. Shizuko rides along. In front of a very big building with large doors across the front, the truck stops and we get out.

"Flyer," Mr. Driz says, "please walk beside me."

A sound I don't know comes from a distance. I see buildings and more people, all around us, walking and pulling their feet from the mud with each step. Many people look our way. I stay beside Mr. Driz, carrying the mitt, until . . .

Boom—boom! . . . boom-boom-boom-boom! . . . *Boom—boom!* The sound rolls toward me like thunder. But the sky is clear now. The air is calm.

CHAPTER SEVENTY-FOUR

FUMIO

His back to a window, Fumio stood in a square of bright sunshine, surveying the floor of Camp Minidoka's taiko dojo. Satisfied that he had swept it clean of the most recent wind- and shoe-born coating of volcanic ash ground to dust, he looked to Senpai Oshiro-san. Receiving an acknowledging glance, Fumio bowed, turned, and pulled on his shoes.

He was not eager to leave. Here he could hold at bay the flood of sorrow that constantly threatened, since learning that Flyer was missing. On the landing, he waited as his eyesight adjusted. It was nearly noon. He would go to his quarters before walking to the mess hall with his family.

The smell of diesel fuel was strong today. Fumio looked toward the Motor Repair and Tire Shop where a delivery truck pulled up to the broad doors. Mr. Shizuko rode on its running board. The truck stopped near the Repair Shop, and he stepped to the ground. Climbing out, the driver left the door slightly ajar, and walked toward the back of the truck with Mr. Shizuko.

Fumio heard a faint "*Yipp,*" then, "*Yipp-ipp! Whooph! Whooph-ooph! Whoophh-ooph-ooph!*" The truck door was jolted once, twice, three times. Out tumbled a dog. With something gripped in his mouth, the dog leaped in circles, but abruptly went still, ears erect, pointing, then began walking slowly, as though finding his way.

Fumio felt himself stopped by invisible forces, unable to move, between the dojo behind him, the sound of the drums—

Boom—boom!... boom-boom-boom-boom!... Boom—boom!

Boom—boom!... boom-boom-boom-boom!... Boom—boom!

—and the sight before him: a medium-sized, black-and-white border collie.

In Fumio's heart a tumult broke loose.

Flyer.

CHAPTER SEVENTY-FIVE

FUMIO

He had imagined this moment over and over, awake and in his dreams. Pressing his face against Flyer's neck, inhaling the scent of his fur, experiencing the roughness of Flyer's warm, wet doggy tongue on his chin.

This was not a dream. This was real. Fumio laughed. He laughed and laughed. He felt the press of paws on his shoulder, his ears boxed by a wagging tail as Flyer leapt and circled and leapt again. Then, without warning, wave after wave of emotion overtook him, and he felt his knees would not hold him. His sobs came in gallops as he knelt on the ground, and Flyer licked and leapt and curved his body more, trying to calm Fumio by touching every part of himself to every part of Fumio. But how did Flyer get his baseball mitt? He must have nabbed it before the boxes of keepsakes made it to the Whitlock attic. It occurred to him that Flyer was much smarter than anyone had realized, which started another round of convulsive tears. Fumio cried more in these few moments than in his entire life before today.

"I expect you'd be Fumio."

Wiping his eyes, He glanced up to see the delivery truck driver and Mr. Shizuko.

"Forgive me, Sir." Fumio sucked air in heaves. "I—"

"Son, don't you apologize one bit. I'm choked up myself. Likely you don't remember me," the driver spoke. "I am Ed Driscoll, Harold Harvey's Idaho cousin. You were just a tyke when I hauled the Cleveland Crawler to your farm on Bainbridge Island. Your dog got himself to a farm north of Eden belonging to Mr. Ted Nikomura, a customer of mine. By the information on that baseball mitt, we figured Flyer would find you here." He smiled.

"Thank you, sir. Thank you very much."

"At the gate," Mr. Driscoll said, "we ran into some trouble. The sentry wanted to see Flyer's authorization papers. Mr. Shizuko came to our aid."

"As did an Army officer. And Flyer, himself, by acts of courage. You can be proud of your dog, Fumio. The officer called Flyer a hero dog!" Mr. Shizuko touched his hat brim, saying, "I'll take off now. Come visit us at the shop soon, Fumio—and Flyer!"

"May I walk with you to your barracks, Fumio?" Mr. Driscoll asked. "The Army officer wanted me to let your parents know this has been *authorized*."

• • •

At the door of his family's apartment, warmed by the weight of Flyer leaning against him, Fumio rapped lightly, giving notice of a visitor, Mr. Driscoll, waiting a few paces behind. Fumio heard the approach of quick footsteps, the working of the latch.

"Fumio! Why ever did you knock?" his mother asked, then looked past his shoulder. "Oh. A visitor. How may I—"

"*Yipp!*"

Her gaze dropped. "Flyer!" she cried. Her hand went to her mouth. Her eyes, Fumio saw, filled with tears.

Kimiko dashed past her mother's knees to Flyer's side.

"When—" Mrs. Miyota began, but hurried down the steps and laid her hand on Flyer's back.

"Hello?" It was Mr. Miyota's voice. "May I help you?" Fumio heard his note of concern and in a moment, his father's arm was around his shoulders. "Fumio, is everything all right?"

Fumio knew the instant his father saw Flyer, felt the tension ease in his father's arm, heard his strong exhalation.

"Flyer!" Mr. Miyota's hand went to Flyer's head, but he sought Fumio's eyes.

"It's all right, Father," Fumio said. "Flyer found his way here, and he is okay."

"Mr. Miyota." Mr. Driscoll came closer, smiling.

Turning toward the voice, Mr. Miyota blinked, then smiled in return. "I don't understand. How are you here? You are Harold Harvey's cousin, former owner of the Cleveland Crawler."

"That I am, sir. And I'm eager to hear how that old powerhouse performs for you. But that's not your chief interest right now. First, the earlier nonsense notwithstanding, we gained entry at the gate with the okay of an Army officer. No problem with Flyer being here. Keep the dog close, it goes without saying. But here's something else I think you'll want to know—"

"Please," Mrs. Miyota prompted, going to the door. "Come inside, Mr. Driscoll."

"Thank you kindly, ma'am. I can't stay long."

Fumio felt the brush of his family and Mr. Driscoll edging by. His arms around Flyer, Fumio whispered, "Come on in, pal. It isn't home. But it's our family."

In the apartment, Fumio took a towel from a hook near the basin and looked to his mother. She smiled, and he put it on the floor. Flyer laid down.

"Shall I make tea, Mr. Driscoll?" Mrs. Miyota asked.

"Not for me, thanks. But a drop of water would be appreciated before I get on the road again."

Mr. Miyota twisted the lid from the water jar and filled a glass for Mr. Driscoll, one for himself, and another for Mrs. Miyota. Fumio shook his head, and Kimiko, on the floor beside Flyer, showed no interest in water.

"Please, Mr. Driscoll, you were saying?" Mr. Miyota asked.

"I have it on solid authority," Mr. Driscoll said, "that Flyer is now famous. Across the Northwest, in newspaper articles he is called a 'hero dog.'"

Fumio, sitting on the floor now, scratched Flyer behind the ears. He struggled to squelch the hiccups left by his convulsive crying. He felt his mother's eyes upon him, but could not bring himself to meet them.

"The officer at the gate," Mr. Driscoll went on, "said that Flyer's picture was in the Twin Falls paper, *The Times-News*, along with the story.

"Evidently, the first picture of Flyer carrying that baseball mitt was taken on the Bainbridge Island ferry dock, but by a photographer from *The Seattle Times*. From the *Times*, it was picked up by the national press. Other photos were taken here and there on Flyer's journey.

"Near Echo," he looked toward Fumio, "that's a small town in Idaho, during a bad storm, Flyer found shelter on Double J Farms, the property of a retired army colonel. Lightning strike caused a fire and Flyer sounded the alarm. He saved the colonel's favorite horse." He paused. "I surely wish you could talk, Flyer. No doubt, you have tales to tell."

Mr. Driscoll drank deeply from his glass of water. "I heard a few days back that the Whitlocks are coming this way. They'd been planning a visit to bring a few of your things, thought you could use them. But a tree went down, blocked their truck. Later that day, they saw Flyer missed supper, but him being a dog, they thought, *well, he'll be back tomorrow*. It hurt my heart to hear how that boy, Zachary, grieved. Not just the dog's absence, but how he'd let his friend, Fumio here, down.

"They searched, made inquiries. Then they got a call from the *Bainbridge Island Review*. The editor said a photo of Flyer on the ferry dock had showed up. That set them to thinking the dog was coming this way. So, soon as they could get things squared on those two farms, the Whitlocks set out in this direction. Harold called me. So, here we are."

He took a small card from his pocket. "This is us, Verna Fay and me. We're Driscoll Mechanics Supply. That's our phone number. Call me. Or I'll be in touch. Or you'll see the Whitlocks. Soon." He rose. "Thank you for the water. You have a good dog there, Fumio. I'm privileged to meet you all again." He extended his arm as if taking in a view. "I'm sorry about all of this.

We all are. It's wrong. Inhuman. I would change it if I could, but meantime, you need anything, anything at all, please call me, and I'll check in on you as best I can."

• • •

No one spoke. Both his parents leaned on each other momentarily. Fumio had never seen either his mother or his father fully in tears before. But now, today, he had seen both take a handkerchief to their eyes and noses. He had never considered the possibility that either of them had reason to cry. Did they cry together at night in their room before the trip away from Bainbridge Island? He himself, today, had cried only as he'd seen his sister Kimiko do, in great upheavals that left him gasping for air. Calm came over the room. Fumio felt a sensation of deep relief and of groundedness, of capability, of his feet resting on the earth. He saw a glimpse of himself in the future, as an old man, remembering every detail of this moment.

• • •

Flyer rested on a small rug with Kimiko sitting beside him. Fumio knelt, his eyes scanning Flyer from his nose to the tip of his tail. He saw no sign of injury. Gently, he teased a few burrs from Flyer's glossy coat.

He pulled on the baseball mitt and, making a fist with his other hand, Fumio punch-punch-punched into the pocket of it. "Thank you, Flyer."

"Yipp!"

• • •

He paused by a small boulder at the entrance to Block 5's ornamental garden and ran his hand down the warm fur at the back of Flyer's neck. "This garden is a special place where people—and dogs, too—can sit and think. I need to tell you something, you must understand." Fumio sat on a low stone. Flyer pressed against him.

The setting sun glanced at a low angle off wind-burnished boulders, the warmth deepening the scent of evergreens. "Pal, I wish you could stay with me, but then you'd have to stay *here*. And, Flyer, a relocation camp is no place for you to live. You need your job on the farm. You need freedom. When the time comes, remember, I'm not sending you away for keeps. We have to *wait*. I don't know for how long. But I promise, we'll be together again."

That evening, on the apartment door, Fumio found a handwritten note:

Miyota Family—Received phone call from Mr. Driscoll. Whitlocks stayed at his home last night. Arriving camp mid-morning—Best regards, Ralph

Fumio, Flyer, and Zachary watched as Mr. Whitlock backed the truck near the double doors of Block 44's mess hall. Mr. Miyota directed, tracing circles in the air and signaling *Back it up, try again*. Finally, Mr. Whitlock cut the engine and climbed from the cab. A uniformed officer waiting there accepted from him several sheets of paper which he slipped onto a clipboard.

Bainbridge Island neighbors helped to unload, the officer checking off items as they came into view. When the truck box was empty, the officer went to the cab, opened and peered into the glove box, and looked behind the seat. "All right, then," he shouted toward Mr. Whitlock, and walked away, toward the administration building. Some neighbors lingered, thanking the Whitlocks and exchanging pleasantries.

Fumio felt as if he had so much to say to Zachary he didn't know where to begin. Then, Flyer yipped and pranced in a circle around the boys, tail wagging. They laughed. Fumio lowered his shoulder and fake-bumped Zachary's. Zachary returned the gesture.

"How long can you stay, Zachary?" Fumio asked.

"A few days. We're at the Driscoll house. Mr. Harvey suggested it." Zachary bit his lip. "I am relieved to see Flyer. I don't blame you if you are angry."

"Why would I be angry?"

"Flyer was my responsibility. You trusted me, and I failed. I'm sorry, Fumio."

"It's not your fault. Flyer's got a mind of his own. I wish we knew what he's been up to. Flyer's had one of the best adventures of his life."

Fumio was struck with an idea. "We should have an adventure. Tomorrow, let's go exploring. Bring a flashlight, okay?"

• • • • •

His baseball mitt on one hand, Fumio held a dingy gray baseball, threads tattered, in the other. "Think fast!" He lobbed the ball to Zachary, who caught it barehanded and threw it back.

Flyer leaped and pivoted, following the path of the ball.

Progressing across the compound, each throw longer than the last, they were approaching the Motor Repair and Tire Shop when a little boy dashed in front of them. Fumio pulled the pitch at the last moment.

The ball hit an electrical pole and dropped in front of a man coming through the shop's big doors. "For Pete's sake!" the man hollered, and nabbed the ball.

Fumio hurried forward. "Sorry, sir! Moushi wakenai! Oh! Mr. Ralph-san! I apologize!"

Ralph lowered his brows and frowned—then he laughed. "No harm done," he said as he handed the ball to Fumio. Looking toward Zachary, he added, "You have guests!"

"Yes, sir, Mr. Ralph-san, my next-door neighbor from home, Zachary. And this is—"

"No need to introduce us. We've met. This is Flyer, the hero dog!" Ralph grinned. "So, what are you up to, today?"

"Exploring, sir. Zachary will be here only a few days. I want to show him some of the most interesting things about this place."

Ralph frowned, seemingly in thought. "I'm taking a truck and some tools out to one of the canal drops, about a mile from here. Something's going on with one of the diggers. Would you like to go with me? Flyer, too."

"Really? That would be great!"

"I'll get a couple of gunny sacks to cover the seat. It's greasy. And I'll bring the truck to the front of the shop." Ralph handed the ball to Fumio.

Fumio passed the baseball to Zachary, "Thanks for bringing that along!"

Zachary dropped the ball in his pack, watching Ralph walk away. "Fumio, should we be doing this? Who is that guy?"

Fumio looped the mitt through his belt. "He works at the Motor Repair and Tire Shop. Father knows him. It's okay."

An engine rumbled. Ralph in the driver's seat, a truck pulled up.

Zachary's face brightened. "Man, look at the huge tires on that truck!"

"The terrain must be rough where we're going," Fumio replied. The truck's brakes groaned. *Dust*, he thought as Ralph rolled down the window.

"Should Flyer get in back?" Fumio asked, tilting his head toward the truck's box.

"Nah, the three of you can jump in front here."

On the passenger side, Zachary stopped and stared; the running board met him at his knees. He reached for the grab bar alongside the door and hoisted himself into the cab. Fumio helped Flyer, then clambered in himself.

The truck jounced over a rutted dirt track, churning up a rolling dust storm. Ralph talked over the engine's roar. "This is all part of an irrigation project run by the Bureau of Reclamation. There've been attempts to develop this land for farming over the past forty years. Now, seven miles of a channel about fifteen feet wide have been dug, extending the Milner-Gooding canal to bring water to fields near the camp." Ralph dipped his head. "It's us, removed from our homes, who've done the digging of that canal."

Bang! The truck lurched, its wheel falling into a deep hole, throwing Flyer and Zachary against Fumio. Fumio's teeth slammed together.

"Seein' stars, danshi?" Ralph glanced toward Fumio. "Hang on! We're driving to an engineered canal fall, or, a *canal drop*. At least nine of them will have been built by October."

"You're an engineer, Mr. Ralph-san," Fumio put in. "You could do this work."

"Maybe, Fumio, but see, I worked in an office, at a desk—calculations, design—"

"Calculations?" Zachary asked. "You mean, mathematics?"

"Right. Geometry, algebra. These workers, they use math, too. Plus, gumption and grit. Weather gets hot as—it gets real hot out here. And look at the boulders they're moving into place." At the work site, Ralph stopped the truck, set the hand brake, and turned off the engine. He slid from behind the steering wheel, then looked back. "Sorry you can't leave the truck, but you can sit in the cab or the box. You can sit on the hood. Heck, you can sit on the roof. It's heavy-duty. Here!" Ralph took an empty gunny sack from behind the truck seat. "Use this to protect the paint." He picked up his toolkit and set off toward the canal drop.

Fumio paused, staring at the distance between the ground and the truck seat. Then holding the gunny sack, he dropped down, reaching the ground standing, and kept his balance. Zachary, a look of doubt on his face, followed and was also successful. He grinned.

Fumio laid the gunny sack on the truck's hood before taking hold of the front bumper and going down on one knee. "Zachary, give Flyer a boost onto my shoulders and up to the hood."

"Flyer, here, pal!" Flyer scrambled onto the hood and, with a little help, reached a resting place on the gunny sack. Finding a solid foothold, Zachary went up next, then Fumio. In front of them were the rushing waters of the broad Milner-Gooding Canal.

A sturdily built man stood, scratching his head, beside a mammoth yellow earth mover that was currently moving no earth. Fumio assumed, from the man's expression of dismay, that he was responsible for the wounded beast, and he was sure of it when Ralph, carrying his toolkit, approached him.

Scattered across the job site were at least twenty workers. Most used picks and shovels, reshaping the rock-riddled soil, others peered at clipboards. Fumio knew from working with his father that those men were consulting the "specs"—the specifications, for each stage of this job.

Ralph materialized near the driver's-side door. "You-all comfortable up there?" he called. "What's going on here is," he looked toward Zachary, "this project will bring water to the fields already planted and about a thousand acres more in the months ahead." After selecting a few more tools, Ralph headed back to repair the digger.

"Fumio," Zachary spoke quietly, "Mr. Ralph said as many as *nine* canal drops, more than a *thousand* acres of crops. *Why?* How long are you going to be here?"

"I don't know, Zachary. No one knows, at least, none of the residents. The administrators say, 'for the duration.'"

Yipp! Flyer's ears went erect. He leaned toward open ground. *Yipp-ipp!*

"He's spotted something," Fumio said. "Probably a prairie dog. You ought to see those critters, Zachary."

"Wait! I got a spyglass as a present from my parents." He pulled a small telescope from his pack. "Here, try it."

Fumio grasped the wooden handle and raised the device to his eye. Zachary explained how to adjust the focus.

"This is great! I could tell you the color of the men's hatbands. But that heavy digger is much more interesting." Fumio peered at the enormous machine.

Zachary rose to his knees. "Let's move to the truck's roof. Sorry, Flyer, not you. But you have extra-sharp vision, anyway."

Zachary pulled a canteen from his pack, took a sip, and handed it to Fumio.

"What all do you have in that pack?"

"Our lunches, a small piece of ham for Flyer. Other stuff."

Fumio returned the spyglass. "That's a good gift. Do you carry it with you all the time?"

"No. But, coming here, we were searching for Flyer, and..." Zachary sighed. "It's useful. I can see great distances. And bring small things close. I've been wanting to tell you about something I saw a couple of months ago, toward the back of the property. Fumio, you know when you and your father saved the owl, freed its talons from the chicken wire? And it tore your sleeve when it flew away?"

"Sure. Mother mended the shirt. She wasn't happy about how close I was to that owl."

"Well, the strip of blue and white fabric from your sleeve, the owl worked it off, and it became part of its nest. It's in one of the Douglas fir trees near your pond."

"What? How do you—? Oh!"

"Yes! I saw it with the spyglass. And Fumio, there were owlets in the nest."

• • •

"Thank you, Ralph-san!" Fumio called.

"Any time, son. Good meeting you, Zachary, and seeing you again, Flyer!"

Zachary waved as Flyer jumped from the truck.

"Now," Fumio announced, "we are going to go see *another* gigantic hole in the ground."

"Is this one engineered, too?"

"Yes. Wait 'til you see it! You'll be glad for a flashlight. Oh. There may be bats."

Zachary groaned. "So, then, Fumio, where is *your* flashlight?"

"Just kidding. We're going to see a root cellar. But it is *huge*."

Sounds of splashing and the happy shouts of children came over a rise. "Swimming holes," Fumio pointed south, "two of them."

"More holes? Why not just swim in the canal?"

"It's dangerous. The current is strong, it never slows, and the water is deep, the edges go straight down. It's hard to get out of a canal once you're in, not like a river." Fumio drew a deep breath. "Zachary, what is it like on the island now? We read news in the *Bainbridge Island Review*, but how is it—for you?"

Zachary looked away. "At school, the day after you left . . . empty desks. I was asked to help move them toward the back of the classroom . . . It was . . ."

"So Jacob is an air raid warden. Do you get to go with him?"

"No." Zachary shook his head. "Flyer does, though. Jacob says he's a real help."

Flyer's tail wagged. Zachary stroked the top of his head.

"Fumio, hundreds of soldiers live in tents on the island, now. Two-hundred WAACs—that means Women of the Army Air Corps—come and go. Rich Passage is rigged underwater with submarine nets, from shore to shore. And, to guard the harbor, barrage balloons hover on steel cables to snag low-flying enemy aircraft and stop them from dropping bombs."

Fumio's footsteps slowed to a stop. He turned toward Zachary.

"And, of course," Zachary shrugged, "the usual—air raid sirens and blackouts."

Fumio's stomach lurched, understanding: his family home had changed. Once again, he felt the press of tears. An ammonia smell rose in his nostrils as he struggled to hold back.

Beyond the swimming holes, they came to a gigantic mound of bare earth. White painted double doors flanked the opening on one side, an open maw into what looked to be a dim-lighted space. A truck backed toward it. Men hurried in and out of the structure.

Fumio chose an out-of-the-way place to watch. "The workers who made this cellar," he said, "started by digging a trench over a hundred feet long, two feet deep and fifty feet wide. They built a frame inside, thirteen feet high, and covered it with roofing boards, then hay bales, tar paper, and, on top, dirt." He nodded. "That keeps the contents cool."

"What *are* the contents?"

"Root vegetables—like carrots, turnips, onions—*onions*! You know, onions are an interesting crop. They might grow well on the island. I've been thinking you might look into it."

"Then we could build a giant root cellar when you get back?"

"Then we could build a giant root cellar when I get back."

Zachary laughed. "In that case, it's a deal."

"Mostly, this cellar holds potatoes. Idaho is famous for potatoes. This cellar can hold fifty boxcar loads of them."

A yellow truck pulled up near the big doors. Workers hustled about, loading a truck with un-bagged potatoes.

Flyer rose to his full height. "*Yipp!*"

Fumio smiled. The cellar would be heaven for a dog, he thought, with its slew of smells: cool, dark earth and last year's potatoes, some sprouting.

"*Yipp-ipp Yipp!*"

"Flyer, better not bark." Fumio said. "They might make us leave."

"*Yipp-ipp-ipp!*" Flyer shifted from paw to paw.

"He has his eye on something, doesn't he?"

"*Why-yi-yyie!*" Flyer surged forward and came, face on, to two mice. One mouse scurried away, the other seemed frozen.

"Flyer is working out a plan for herding mice," Zachary whispered.

"Sure. Goof."

Zachary burst out laughing. "It's been a long time since anyone called me that."

"*Yipp-ipp-yipp!*"

The mouse took off. Flyer gave chase, skidding to a stop when the mouse was well away.

A dozen workers cheered. "We've been battling mice for months!"

"Flyer!" Fumio called. "Here, pal! Flyer!"

"Hey!" a worker called. "It's the traveling hero dog, Flyer! Hold the presses! Ken, you got that camera the newspaper editor loaned you?"

"Right here!" A man shouted back, raising it into view.

Fumio stepped toward him. "Sumimasen ga, sir. Flyer is trained to roust vermin."

"Looked to me like the dog was doing his job! Would you and your friend and your dog, Flyer, join us for a picture?"

Fumio nodded. "Yes, sir. We can do that."

The man snapped a few shots. "Thanks, boys," he said. "You, too, Flyer! Look for one of those photographs to show up in *The Minidoka Irrigator*."

"Hello, there!" A man approached with his hand extended. Fumio glanced downward, then reached out. The man shook his hand, then Zachary's. "I'm Gilbert Yohei, the foreman here. I rarely do this, but would you three like to see the root cellar?"

"Boy, would we!" Zachary replied.

As Fumio had imagined, the cellar's interior was dim, and it smelled like potatoes. But vents kept the air circulating, and bulbs dangling on electrical cords gave light for work. A massive machine dominated the center of the space.

"That's a sorting machine," the foreman said. "Eighteen-foot. Noisy. Saves a lot of time over sorting potatoes by hand."

"Sorting for what, sir?" Zachary asked.

"Size, quality, conformation."

"We should go," Fumio said. "Thank you for showing us the root cellar, Mr. Yohei-san."

"Sure thing, kid. Always proud to show it off."

Back in the sunlight, workers smiled and waved.

Zachary pulled a small camera from his pack. "Excuse me, sir, Ken . . . Ken-san? Would you mind taking a picture for me, a picture of the three of us?"

"Glad to do it! How about in front of the cellar doors?"

Zachary, a thumb hooked through the strap of his backpack, dropped an arm on Fumio's shoulder, and Fumio, the baseball mitt looped through his belt, laid his hand on Flyer's head.

• • • •

Walking west, Fumio and Zachary faced the sound of rushing water. The North Side Canal, marking the camp's southern border, ran near the highway and the railroad spur, upon which the train carrying the Miyotas had arrived four months earlier. As Ralph-san had said, the canal's purpose was to further the development of the Snake River Plain. Here, barbed wire fencing remained in place. Unlike the stream on the Miyota farm on Bainbridge Island, which chose its own path, the canal was carved by human hands through Idaho's tough, rocky soil.

Flyer lifted his nose, appearing to sample the early evening breeze.

Against a sky edged in sunset colors, men and women stood on the bank eyeing bobbers on their fishing lines for telltale tugs. Zachary's pace slowed as a woman cast her line. "Let's wait and watch her reel one in!"

"We'd miss supper. And probably breakfast. We have a long walk back."

"But I read about it! The fishing is good in Idaho. She might catch a bigmouth bass!"

Fumio shook his head. "Not here. Fish don't naturally live in waters like this. Here, any fish—let's say, a *largemouth* bass—would have been forcibly transplanted, grabbed from a river by an eagle or osprey. The fish struggles, frees itself, and falls . . ." Fumio gestured toward the canal, "in there, where there's no quiet water, no place to rest and feed."

Zachary frowned. "And the eagle goes without dinner."

"Fumio!" Kimiko called, "Flyer! Zachary! We came to meet you! Come to our picnic!"

Near a bend in the channel, faded green packing blankets were spread and baskets were opened. Fumio saw Mrs. Whitlock take hold of his mother's hands. "You'll let me know, won't you? I'll be waiting to hear."

"I like what you've told me about raising onions," Fumio's father said to Mr. Whitlock. "It's a good plan." He gripped Mr. Whitlock's hand. "Yes."

Fumio sat on a corner of the blanket, cross-legged, Flyer's head on his knee. Zachary stretched out his legs, leaning back on straightened arms.

While plates were filled with fried chicken, sliced tomatoes, and fresh rolls, Mrs. Whitlock told them that Mrs. Driscoll had prepared their picnic supper as a gift.

"Look!" Kimiko's face glowed. "Pretty food like home!"

When all were nearly finished with their meal, Mrs. Whitlock removed the lid of a tin. "The oatmeal crisps are sweetened with honey."

Zachary took a cookie and, creating a tiny explosion of crumbs, broke it in two, giving half to Fumio. Fumio broke that half in half and gave one part back.

Grinning, Zachary popped it into his mouth.

Just then a voice rang out. "Hai!" A fisherman rose from a low stool beside the canal, grasping a deeply bent rod that had, Fumio saw, no reel.

"A tenkara rod," Fumio's father observed, "in the tradition of old Japan."

The rod, Fumio judged, was at least fifteen feet long.

Pulling line, hand over hand, the man brought in a writhing fish. "See? Hai!" he cried.

Fumio turned to Zachary. "*That* is some sort of trout!"

Onlookers cheered, "Yaaattaa! Yaaattaa!"

"Yaattaa!" Fumio's father called.

Zachary looked at Fumio with raised brows.

"'Yatta!' means 'Hurrah! Good job!'" Fumio explained as he stood to walk toward the canal bank. Zachary and Flyer followed.

"Yatta! Yatta!" Fumio and Zachary both called.

Flyer joined in, "*Yip-ipp!*"

One hand under the fish's belly, the fisherman carefully lifted it out of the water just far enough for all to see the sun's rays glance from its silver scales and the ivory silk of its fins.

"Aaahhhh . . ." came murmurs from those gathered along the canal, and then, voices slightly raised, "He's letting it go! He's letting the fish go!"

Fumio, Flyer, and Zachary reached the bank just as the fish slapped its tail, a spray of rainbowed droplets arcing from the water's surface. *Splashhh!* It slipped away.

"Flyer!" Fumio went down on one knee. "Flyer, did you see that?"

With a quick movement, Flyer licked Fumio's face.

Fumio remembered his father's words: *We do what we can with what we have. We work, we watch, and if we must, we wait.*

Wait. *But for how long?*

AFTERWORD
by Jimmy Kamada

Since childhood I have had great respect for the surname Kamada. My parents, Isao and Yuriko, exemplified good citizenship. Hardworking, scrupulously honest, loving parents, they supported me and my two siblings with much patience, often reminding us to uphold our family's good name. My birth in an internment camp in Idaho was, to me, merely a footnote to my personal history. My parents never talked about "camp," nor did friends who were there with them.

My marriage to Shirley changed the footnote to a question. *I was born in an internment camp?* How did that affect my young parents and their life afterward? What were their losses, isolated from general society while establishing a home and family? Shirley wanted to know. She began to dig through history websites. She took notes. She created charts, timelines, maps, and now we have an extensive library focused on the topic, vintage references as well as the new books continually being added.

We traveled twice to Idaho's Camp Minidoka National Park Site, and toured Camp Manzanar. We've repeatedly visited Bainbridge Island and walked along the Eagledale Ferry Dock, even battled the mosquitos during a guided tour of the Yama Village archaeological dig.

No longer a footnote: I was born at Camp Minidoka.

Released in 1945, my father found work on a nearby farm. We waited two years to go home to Seattle, prevented by rules intended to force Japanese Americans from returning to their former locales—to scatter them widely.

When we did return to Seattle, on my first day of first grade, the principal asked me my name. My name? *Fumio*. To the principal, I said, "Jimmy."

Our hope is that all who read this story will be moved by the humanness of those who endured the injustice of internment, by their self-discipline, their creativity, their determination to build homes, communities, and, regardless of all obstacles, to thrive.

As Shirley says, "Diversity is beautiful." To that I would add, "Diversified thought makes the world a better place."

Jimmy Fumio Kamada
U.S. Army Veteran
Retired Officer of the Federal Reserve Bank of San Francisco

ACKNOWLEDGEMENTS

I did not know that Japanese Americans were uprooted from their homes and interned in remote, quickly constructed camps after the bombing of Pearl Harbor until two years after I married Jimmy. In a social situation, a friend casually asked, "So, where are you from?" Jimmy later in the car said to me, quietly, "I wasn't really born in Jerome, Idaho. I was born at Camp Minidoka, an internment camp."

What did he mean, an internment camp? Jimmy's older brother, born at Camp Harmony, had no firsthand memories of it. Jimmy's father and mother, both born in Seattle, had not spoken of it—at least not in front of me.

The World War II internment—incarceration—of Japanese and Japanese American citizens living within the West Coast Exclusion Zone was one of the most grievous violations of civil rights in United States history. What caused our government to imprison 120,000 legal residents, two-thirds of whom were citizens, one-third of whom were children?

Later, from an oral history video his sister Janet had created, Jimmy transcribed for me his mother's answers to these questions. In the film, their mother Yuriko shared memories of her childhood, her wedding, the camps. Not only her words but her facial expression—eyes turned aside—and the clenching and unclenching of her hands, told a story long held in silence.

Memories fade and are buried, but the pain remains. Hard facts do not soothe sorrow, still I dug for truth. The result is *No Quiet Water*, a work of historical fiction. I filled in the gaps using history websites, academic papers, and the ever-growing library now filling our home. Yoshiko Uchida, in her prologue to *Journey to Topaz* writes that the world "was totally different from the one we know today . . . there had been no freedom marches or demonstrations of protest. Most Americans might well have considered it treasonous" had Japanese Americans resisted.

Jimmy, once the door was opened, became deeply interested in his own history, and in understanding its lasting, profound effect on families, his and thousands of others. We wonder, what has been learned from this tragic occurrence?

Through the nearly ten years of writing this book, what I might in the beginning have called "facts" were constantly updated by my study of government records—even new archaeological digs at internment sites. I was forced to constantly update, revise, and correct the story to align with new findings, becoming further convinced of the story's importance.

On one topic I have taken some small liberty. Taiko drumming was not widely considered an ensemble performance art in 1942. It was, though, an integral part of camp observances of the Obon Festival, during which the dead are honored and remembered. I believe taiko's metamorphosis was building even then. Taiko drumming is the perfect vehicle to convey the spirit of the story and Fumio's coming of age.

Perhaps the question then arises, why fiction? Fiction allowed me to create a multi-dimensional picture of World War II in a way that non-fiction could not. And, while there are many worthy non-fiction books on the subject, I couldn't find any that included a really good dog. I have enjoyed meeting Flyer and his buddies Fumio and Zachary, and I hope you find *No Quiet Water* to be valuable to your understanding of this terrible time in history.

Always in the writing of a book, many people must be thanked. Firstly, to Isao and Yuriko Kamada: Your family honors you and your example of living with the long view. When obstacles loomed high, you overcame them with integrity and resilience. You have our deepest gratitude.

To the extended Kamada family who graciously shared memories, photograph albums and mementos, I appreciate your trust. To family in Japan, your hospitality is incomparable. We cherish our time with you.

To my husband, Jimmy. While I wrote this book, your patience, assistance, and sometimes your amusement at my dogged determination sustained me. As did your amazing culinary skills, which are, evidently, common among your family.

Many thanks to my brother, Larry Miller, also a writer, who shared his thorough grasp of farming and construction. Knowledge gained from first-hand experience is priceless. And to my cousins who refrained from asking, "Have you finished that book, yet?" Bless you.

To editor Julie Molinari for her valuable insights, my great appreciation.

For encouragement along the way and the completion of this book's journey, I am indebted to Paula Coomer and her unfailing support.

I have drawn heavily from the curated historical documentation offered by Densho's Digital Repository. Special thanks to Tom Ikeda, Founding Executive Director, to Brian Niiya, Content Director and Editor of the Densho Online Encyclopedia, and to Natasha Varner, Communications and Public Engagement Director, each of whom graciously responded to my questions personally.

My gratitude to Rachel Thomas, George Fox University Archivist, who was uncommonly generous with her time in introducing me to on-site primary sources and who arranged a private lunch with Dr. Ralph Beebe, a Quaker historian, George Fox professor, emeritus, and a prolific author (since deceased). Dr. Beebe, who was known as a strong Pacifist, spoke with Jimmy and me about the meaning of living by the tenets of the Peace Testimony.

Rod and Debbie Goodwin, owners of Rockin' Bar Border Collies, in Moses Lake, WA, invited us to view their kennels and talked with us about border collie personalities and strategies for partnering with them in their work as stock dogs. (http://rockinbarbordercollies.com)

Lastly, I have been inspired daily by Bambi Miller, owner of Parke Creek Farm, Ellensburg, WA, who creates a photo journal through the seasons, sharing her life as a farmer, gardener, shepherd and fiber arts specialist. (www.cngfarming.org/parke_creek_wa)

I have met with such kindness, it is impossible to list everyone. With that in mind, further mention of people who have helped me is included on my website at www.shirleymillerkamada.com.

RESOURCES FOR ADDITIONAL INFORMATION

- Burton, Jeffrey F., Farrell, Mary M., Lord, Florence B., & Lord, Richard W. (1999) *Confinement and Ethnicity: An Overview of World War II Japanese American Relocation Sites*. Western Archeological And Conservation Center. National Park Service. U.S. Department of the Interior.
- Niiya, Brian (Ed.). (1993) *Japanese American History: An A-to-Z Reference from 1868 to the Present*. The Japanese American National Museum.
- Densho.org – a digital archive of videotaped interviews, photographs, documents, and other materials relating to the Japanese American experience. Additional information on the project is available at www.densho.org.
- Densho Digital Repository. *Bainbridge Island Review*. ddr-densho-68.
- Densho Digital Repository. *Manzanar Free Press*. ddr-densho-204.
- Densho Digital Repository. *Minidoka Irrigator*. ddr-densho-173.
- Japanese American Internment | National Archives – www.archives.gov/news/topics/japanese-american-internment
- U.S. National Park Service – https://www.nps.gov/index.htm
- Website: Bainbridge Island Japanese American Exclusion Memorialwww.nps.gov/miin/learn/historyculture/bainbridge-island-japanese-american-exclusion-memorial.htm
- Website: Manzanar National Historic Site www.nps.gov/manz/index.htm
- Website: Minidoka National Historic Site www.nps.gov/miin/index.htm

ABOUT THE AUTHOR

Shirley Miller Kamada is a former educator, education director, and bookstore owner. She lives in Moses Lake, Washington, with her husband Jimmy and their two adopted dog children Priscilla and Phoenix. *No Quiet Water* is her first novel.

NOTE FROM THE AUTHOR

Word-of-mouth is crucial for any author to succeed. If you enjoyed *No Quiet Water*, please leave a review online—anywhere you are able. Even if it's just a sentence or two. It would make all the difference and would be very much appreciated.

Thanks!
Shirley Miller Kamada

We hope you enjoyed reading this title from:

www.blackrosewriting.com

Subscribe to our mailing list – *The Rosevine* – and receive **FREE** books, daily deals, and stay current with news about upcoming releases and our hottest authors.
Scan the QR code below to sign up.

Already a subscriber? Please accept a sincere thank you for being a fan of Black Rose Writing authors.

View other Black Rose Writing titles at www.blackrosewriting.com/books and use promo code **PRINT** to receive a **20% discount** when purchasing.

CPSIA information can be obtained
at www.ICGtesting.com
Printed in the USA
BVHW080928161022
649420BV00005B/24